THE COMPLETE CASES OF VEE BROWN, VOLUME 2

Carroll John Daly

CARROLL JOHN DALY

THE COMPLETE CASES OF

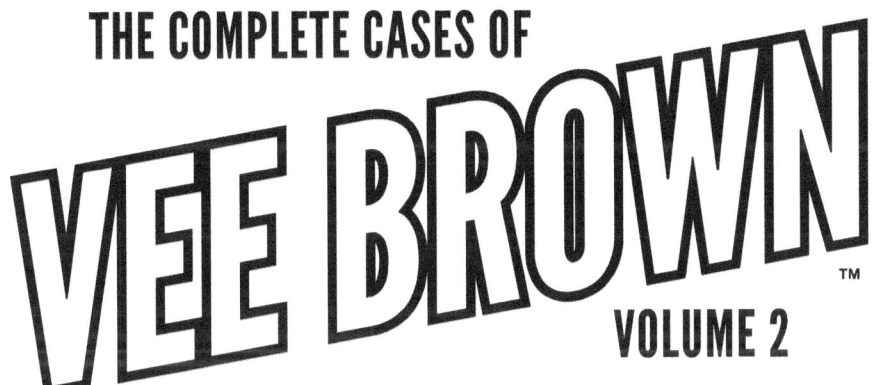

VEE BROWN™

VOLUME 2

CARROLL
JOHN DALY

ILLUSTRATIONS BY
JOHN FLEMING GOULD

STEEGER BOOKS • 2019

TABLE OF CONTENTS

THE BLACK WARNING 1

THE DEATH MASK 63

THE SWINGING CORPSE 163

MAKE YOUR OWN CORPSE! 257

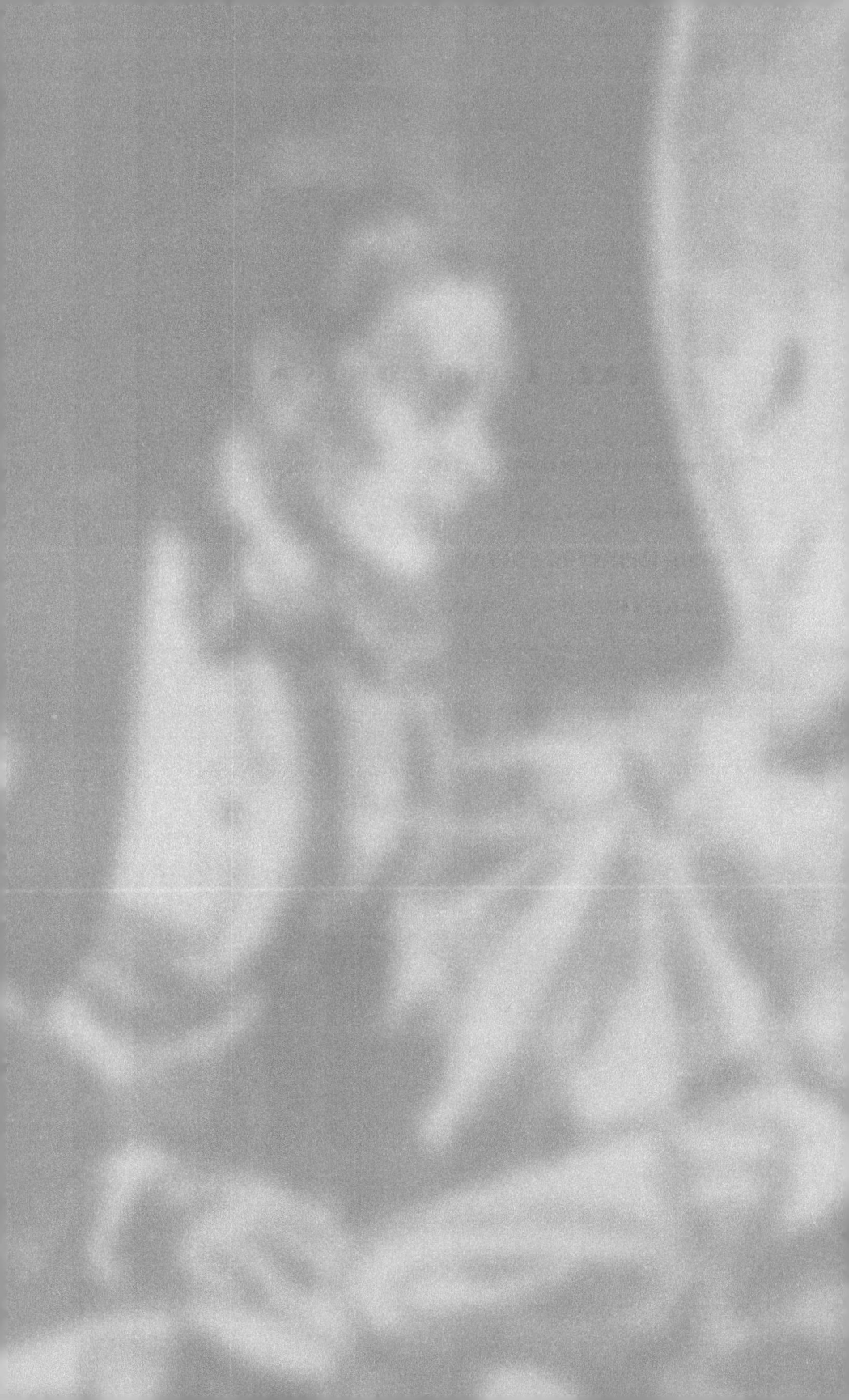

THE BLACK WARNING

OVER THE WHOLE CITY HUNG
A GHASTLY MURDER PALL—THE
DREAD SHADOW OF THE BLACK
DEATH. AND ONLY DETECTIVE VEE
BROWN—THE CRIME MACHINE—
KNEW ITS SOURCE. KNEW THAT
THE KILLER WAS WHETTING HIS
BLADE TO CARVE AT A BLOOD
FEAST.

CHAPTER ONE
THE CAT MAN

DETECTIVE VEE BROWN leaned far back against the high dining booth, held up his bottle of beer, looked at it a long moment, then poured it into a glass, raising the bottle as he did so. A thick foamy head appeared filling almost one third of the glass.

"And they call me The Crime Machine," he said, with that little twisted smile. "I work for years to eliminate crime and along comes a small bottle of amber fluid that does more to wipe out crime in the country than the entire police system of the nation all put together. I wonder someone didn't think of it before." He took a long drink and puffed on his cigarette. "Three-two caliber," he said. "What a deadly weapon against the racketeer!"

As a rule I didn't like Vee when he was in a facetious mood, and I didn't like him now. I said: "How does it effect this master blackmailer that you're the only one who believes in?"

"Now, now." He wagged a finger at me. "You're talking like Inspector Ramsey. But it may have a lot to do with it. We come here after the show because the food is good. Perhaps this blackmailer will find us out and spill his hand, or—" He set down the glass suddenly and smiled. "I'm getting psychic, Dean, for there's the Cat Man now."

I turned my head and saw Vincent Van Houton. He was tall, distinguished-looking; his wavy blond hair gave him almost a boyish appearance. It was hard to believe that this man was the city's most dangerous criminal, as Vee Brown classed him. Blackmailer and murderer! The Cat Man, Brown called him because of his interest in, and evident study of, cats.

But I had seen Van Houton before, and now looked at the woman with him. She was proud, erect, with an outward tilt to her chin that was almost a defiance. I could not see her over-well in the dimly lit room, yet there seemed something familiar about her. I turned to Vee.

"Gertrude la Palatin." He answered my unspoken question. "Stars in Goodman's Review. Played a bit in Europe and now is presented as a foreigner, though I understand she actually was born in this country; Cleveland or New York. Made quite a reputation abroad as a mimic and does some very remarkable work in the review. Her impersonation of Marie Dressier is almost a miracle, when you take into account her small stature, her slimness and—"

"Take it!" the man lipped.

"A friend of Van Houton's?" I cut in.

"If a man like Van Houton can have any friends." He nodded. "It's hard to tell, Dean, if she's an agent or a victim of his; or perhaps both. Her list of acquaintances would be a great help in his work. He—" Brown paused, and then, "He's going to pay us a visit, Dean, and I'm fortunate in having finished my lobster. The man nauseates me."

VAN HOUTON was on his feet, leaning over the table, talking to the woman. Then he turned and came directly to our table. His blue eyes sparkled, his lips parted; he extended a hand toward Brown and spoke.

"Detective Brown." His voice was affable and I did not recognize the derision in it that Brown claimed afterward was there. His face may have changed for the fraction of a second when Brown ignored that hand, but if it did it was smiling pleasantly again as quickly as his hand moved and gripped mine. He was talking, too.

"Thought I recognized you, and— May I sit down? I am sure it will be to your advantage."

"Sure." Brown moved toward the outer edge of the booth, barring Van Houton from sitting beside him. "Sit next to Dean. He's got an exceptionally strong stomach."

Van Houton dropped easily into the seat beside me and looked across at Vee Brown.

"We all," he said slowly, "like to have people think well of us. That, I imagine, is a natural failing of the human race. But you don't think I would join you here like this, knowing your unfounded suspicion of me, just for the purpose of having the good opinion of a detective; even such a brilliant detective."

"That's right," said Brown. "You are going to make a threat."

Van Houton grinned. "If I were the man you think me, with all the diabolical characteristics with which you invest me, perhaps I would make threats. Instead, Mr. Brown, I have come to your table to warn you that your activities at present, regarding a certain young society matron, must cease." And with a sudden sneer that he could not control, "This talk of yours, of blackmail—well, you should know all about that. You're blackmailing this young woman."

"A remarkable system." Brown nodded. "Just how much do you know?"

"I know this," said Van Houton. "That Mrs. Clarence Moore is being annoyed by you; that you threaten to expose her for some past misdeed, unless—well, unless she does as you suggest."

"That," said Brown, "is quite correct. Mrs. Moore is being blackmailed. Unless she discloses to me the name of the blackmailer I will expose the very thing she has been paying well to hide. You are well informed, Mr. Van Houton."

Van Houton sat up and said, somewhat stiffly: "Mr. and Mrs. Moore are my friends. To a certain extent she has confided in me. You are the law; the law that should protect her. Yet you threaten her. And she does not know who is blackmailing her."

"That's quite right," said Brown. "But she knows who is carrying on the negotiations for this blackmailer, and he knows who the blackmailer is. And, maybe, Mr. Van Houton, he will talk; and you may be—shall we say, embarrassed? For it is embarrassing to sit down in the electric chair and have the juice turned on."

I think Van Houton paled for a moment, but only for a moment. Then he smiled.

"At least, Brown; when you are wrong, you are one hundred percent wrong. I can't for the life of me see how you first connected me up with this thing. Neither Commissioner Doran or Inspector Ramsey take any stock in your queer ideas. But suppose you are right; suppose, as you say, there is a master blackmailer known as the—"

"The Black Death," Brown cut in, and I remembered the card that was found on the body of the murdered Mrs. Townsend and the horrible suggestion that Brown attached to it. Remembered that it was the method this blackmailer used to inspire fear in other victims who were reluctant to pay.

VAN HOUTON showed even white teeth. "Well—well. Now, if you did find out the name of this agent, you could hardly prove he was more than a go-between, if that. You would, in proving this, ruin the name of a woman, my friend, and learn nothing of the identity of this real black-mailer."

"Yet," said Brown, "you are greatly interested. And this man might talk."

"Certainly. As you know, I was blackmailed myself for a while. In a small way I am trying to discover the identity of this man; and will, of course, bring any information I may obtain directly to the law; to Inspector Ramsey."

"Well," said Brown, "come to the point."

"I will." Van Houton nodded grimly. "I have received information that this woman will die if you molest her further; persecute her with your threats, which are nothing less than blackmail."

"That's a threat, eh?" Brown nodded.

"That's a warning. A warning that you'll be directly responsible for this woman's death."

"The woman will not die," Brown said emphatically, "and this man will talk. Since you have been kind enough to give me a warning, let me give you one. I'm going to get you, Mr. Van Houton. Tomorrow, the day after, a month from now—what does it matter? Since you haven't got the stom-ach for killing personally, you must hire someone to do that. And those you hire, those close to you, are the ones I'm going after. This blackmailer of Mrs. Moore's, for instance! Do you think I'll prosecute him when I find him? No, I'll get him to talk."

"You are very well informed about—about this blackmailer and his activities lately. There must be a leak in his establishment." And now Van Houton's soft blue eyes grew hard and shrewd as they studied Brown.

Vee's black eyes smiled. "Even a detective must learn something in time, if he sticks long enough," he said. "Give me credit for that."

"A leak!" Van Houton's eyes sought the ceiling. "You can perhaps, knowing as much as you do, imagine just what will happen to the one who supplies that leak when that one is discovered."

Brown shrugged his shoulders expressively. "I am sure," he said, "that such a wonderful organization would not permit leaks. About Mrs. Moore! She will be interested in this warning of yours. Death, wasn't it? I will advise her of that and feel sure that she will talk to me first. You find that interesting?"

"Interesting?" said Van Houton. "Well—perhaps if she *could* talk to you first. Oh, I'm not pronouncing her sudden demise, you understand, but I have a strange premonition of death." He came to his feet. "And I feel, now, that you will not be alive for her to talk to."

"Really!" said Brown as Van Houton turned. And then, "Very interesting, Dean." For Van Houton had only stopped at his own table long enough for him to speak to Gertrude la Palatin, who came quickly to her feet and left the restaurant on his arm.

"Van Houton certainly is coming more or less out in the open," I said to Brown when the couple had left the room. "That was almost a direct threat to kill."

"Almost." Brown laughed. "I tell you, Dean, I'm getting under the man's very superior skin. First, it was good-natured indifference; then a sort of contempt; maybe, when Stokes died, a hatred. But now, Dean, I think it's fear—yes, fear and pride."

"How pride?"

"Well, for him to tell me about it. Somehow he wanted me to know before I died. That's the conceit of the man. It's to happen suddenly, and for a split second I'm to realize the truth. The great master; the mind of minds; the hand of hands has struck."

"And the fear?"

BROWN LEANED over the table. Both his hands were on it. One toyed with a napkin as he talked to me but he looked out into the room; at the table near our booth, with the square-jawed, broad-shouldered man eating at it; the service door with its red thick curtains, beyond him; and the many tables, a dozen or more of which were occupied.

"I'm getting close to him. He's right about the leak, Dean. You remember the girl who visited you that night with the dead woman's note, and whom later we saved from both Pete Stokes and the police. She hated Van Houton, you said. I can't be sure, but I think she's the leak. At least it was a woman's voice on the phone, that told me about Mrs. Moore."

Vee had unfolded his napkin as he talked and was toying with it, his right hand close to the wall and near the water carafe.

Generally he was never nervous; at least, in the face of death; a threat of death. But then, this was something big; something bigger than he had ever tackled. A menace that would strike through others; an unknown menace to all but Vee Brown. Yet, unmistakably Van Houton had made a threat of death.

"A leak, Dean! The greatest fear of the criminal, the greatest enemy of the criminal. The one he trusts betrays him. Hate or fear, or greed! Van Houton realizes it now. He doesn't know who it is. He doesn't know why. He— Don't move, Dean."

And the thing happened.

The man sitting at that table so close to the little door just swung out of his seat, moved a step toward us, and leaning into our booth shoved a heavy automatic smack toward Brown's head. It was the quickest and most surprising attack I had ever seen.

"Take it!" the man lipped.

I did move. I stretched out my hand toward that wrist as the shot came and I saw Brown pitch forward on the table. Stunned? Yes, I was stunned. For a full second I guess my eyes closed, then my hand shot out again toward the gunman's arm.

And I saw him; saw him as my eyes bulged. Saw him topple upon the table, the upper part of his body sprawled there. Then he slid slowly back, half knelt upon the floor and suddenly sank against the table in a grotesque heap.

Brown! What of Brown? And Brown was on his feet. I saw the napkin drop to the table, saw the tiny hole in it and the blackened edges about that hole. Saw, too, the gun in Brown's hand as he slid from the booth and toward that little servant's entrance.

So quickly had things happened that Brown had jerked those curtains aside, ducked his head in and out again and was calling in a loud voice before the hysteria really got under way.

"No cause for excitement, people. I'm a police officer. There, there! Leave if you wish to, but no—" And with a sigh of relief as a uniformed policeman burst in from the main entrance, "Take charge of things, Flarrity. A man has been hurt."

Excitement after that. Other officers; Inspector Shannon. And Brown, saying with a grin to Shannon's question, "Was he badly hurt?"

"Bad enough to bury him, I think. No, no. He never even pressed the trigger. Do you think I'm a fool?"

IN THE taxi on our way to see Mrs. Moore, Brown explained. "No, Dean, I won't say that I actually expected it. But I will say that when it came it wasn't entirely unexpected—if you understand me. Van Houton talked too much, for I know that Mrs. Moore is going to tell me the name of her blackmailer tonight. And I guess Van Houton knew it too; and he said I wouldn't be alive. There was the nearness to the servant's entrance, of course, and a man or two there to cover the killer's retreat. But I didn't expect it like that. The man who tried for the kill played his part well, just one slip—or rather two."

"And the slips?" I asked.

"Feet." Brown nodded. "Feet behind those curtains. I saw them plainly just before I put the gun under the napkin. Like the rats they were, they scurried to safety the moment their friend took the lead."

"The second mistake?"

"The drama. The drama that the would-be killer put into death. After all, Dean, death is very simple. Just two words; hardly a second to utter them. 'Take it,' was all he said. But in that split second I had jerked up the napkin and fired." Then Brown started to whistle a tune.

"Brown," I laid a hand upon his knee, "many men have tried to kill you. But never like that, in a public dining room. The daring of it! The man must have been desperate, and—"

"Desperate?" Brown laughed. "Why, he's a stranger to these parts, or I would have known him. Nothing desperate, Dean. Rather, clever. On a side street; from a heavily curtained motor; in a lonely house! All that is expected and watched for, and guarded against. No, Dean. We must give the man credit for being clever." He chuckled. "Did you see what Inspector Shannon took from the dead man's hand and gave me before we left?"

Brown opened his hand and I looked down. In the flashing street lights I saw the oblong bit of card; and also, with more difficulty, made out the words upon it.

THE BLACK DEATH
No. 4

"Well, well." Brown seemed in a particularly good humor. "The blackmailer's notice of death. Imagine it! The man presents himself with a one way ticket to hell. Just a hired assassin. I'll bet you a good dinner that personally he didn't even know the meaning of it."

So we drove in silence but for Vee's occasional humming. But I was thinking of the dead man on the floor; the peculiar position of the body; the grotesque curve of those hands; the right one, which held the gun.

And Brown said: "The leak. The girl of the night; cruel, sinister and beautiful, Dean. Gad! I wonder if she's got a voice. I've got a tune for her—damn it! And a name for the piece. A simple name. It's a wonder I never thought of it before. But it needs a girl like that to put it over. It's— But here we are, Dean, at Mrs. Moore's. And you never asked me the name of the piece!"

"What is it?" I said without much interest.

"The devil, Dean!" He put an arm on my shoulder. "You'll never take it right. It isn't as if it were the first man I ever killed, you know. I can't go home and mope about it. Besides," and there was a little glint in his eyes, "it wasn't bad shooting; and certainly no man ever asked for it more, or was more deserving of it after he got it. Cheer up! The name of the song will be *Girl of the Night*. It goes like this— But, hell! Back to business." This as the taxi drew up before the Moore residence.

CHAPTER TWO
BLACK WARNING

THE BUTLER who opened the door was not my idea of the well-trained butler. His face was tanned and hard, and he grinned at Brown in no servile manner.

Brown nodded and said: "Anything happen, Johnson?"

"Well—no," said Johnson. "There was a telephone call for Mrs. Moore. I listened in downstairs. The voice—a man's voice—said: 'Don't listen to this Detective Brown. He won't make good his threat. But,' and the lad got a deal of feeling into his voice then, 'these others will.'" Johnson consulted a little book, and then, "A boy brought a letter about eleven o'clock this morning. It sort of threw Mrs. Moore—and her husband comes back from his trip the day after tomorrow. I tell you, outside of the coat and collar I got to wear, this is the deadest job I was ever on."

Brown looked at the man and spoke very seriously. "Deadest! Watch out, Johnson, that it doesn't turn out just that way. I picked you above all the dicks on the force, and this may turn out your biggest case. Certainly, be sure it is your most dangerous one."

"Yeah?" The big man seemed unconvinced. He half turned and looked over his shoulder. "There's Rhoden. And, damn it, he looks almost natural in that monkey suit."

And the man did. I knew of course that this was another detective, dressed in a neat-fitting chauffeur's uniform—leggings and all.

"He should," said Brown. "Used to be a motor cop." He waved the chauffeur back into the servant's quarters. "Other servants take you all right?"

"In a sneering sort of way." Johnson nodded. "They believe that Mr. Moore sent for both butler and chauffeur, and have the idea that we're depression servants and that the Moores are doing things cheap."

Brown grinned and patted Johnson on the back. "If I were picking two men for just amateur theatricals I could have done better. But I didn't want good actors, Johnson. I wanted bad actors. Don't be lured into a sense of security by the inactivity." And very seriously, "Murder hangs over this house. One of you must always be on the job. And Mrs. Moore?"

"Oh, she feels the atmosphere you've created, if Rhoden and I don't. If you're waiting for her to break, now's the time, I think. She keeps the shades down in her room, though the people across the street have lived there for years."

"Well," said Brown, "I'll have a talk with her. Do your butlering."

And Johnson did. He bowed stiffly, put on what we Americans consider an English accent and led us up the stairs.

"Mrs. Moore will see you now, sir. Directly, sir. Will you go above, sir?"

MRS. CLARENCE MOORE proved a surprise. She was a timid-looking little blonde, with great blue eyes that looked appealingly up at Brown. Brown introduced me and said in his best professional manner: "A witness, Mrs. Moore. Now, the name of the man you've been handing money to."

"I can't. I won't." She came to her feet. "I want to see my lawyer."

"My dear Mrs. Moore," Brown was very patient, "you've had several days in which to see your lawyer. You have been glad to let me place two detectives in this house, so you understand your danger. You are, in your refusal to give me this name, endangering others; a great many others."

"I'm not being blackmailed." She started in to cry. "And I don't believe you know; I don't believe you could know." And suddenly, "There is nothing for you to know."

"Vincent Van Houton called you on the phone and advised you not to talk—to anyone."

"He's my friend," she said.

"He's your worst enemy," Brown told her.

"He can't be. He can't be. He lent me money."

"Yes," said Brown, "probably lent you a thousand, to make five when you could raise only four; since it all came back to—" He paused and looked at the woman, and suddenly, "The indiscretion happened at Atlantic City. The man's name was Robert Carse." And when she jerked erect, with a little startled cry, Brown crossed the room and took her hand. "I'm not going to expose you, Mrs. Moore, whether you talk or not. I wish to save you from being exposed, and by your telling me this man's name I can save you."

"How?" She was on the edge of her chair now, dabbing at her eyes, watching Brown closely, suspiciously. "You said yourself that they'd—someone would kill me, like Mrs. Charles Townsend was killed. The Black Death!" And suddenly bursting into tears and tearing something from her handkerchief, "I've had the third warning—the last warning."

Brown took the card and looked at it.

THE BLACK DEATH
No. 3

He nodded very grimly. "The last warning!" he said. "Now listen to me, Mrs. Moore. You can't raise any more money, so they would expose you. Maybe through a letter to your husband; maybe a simple note to an unscrupulous columnist."

"But they'll kill me if I tell. I don't want to die. My husband and I have been so happy since—so happy. It was all a bad dream. And then the letter; later, threats; and newspaper clippings of others who had been exposed, others who have died. Now—why should they harm me? I have no more money. I am useless to them."

"Anything but useless to them." Brown shook his head. "Exposing you now has a great commercial value. It will convince reluctant victims, and I believe there are many of them, that this Black Death means business. Exposing others; driving others to self-inflicted death convinced you, didn't it?"

"But I don't want to die," the woman cut in and began to cry again.

Brown patted her on the shoulder. Where his voice might have been meant to be comforting, his words struck me as anything but.

"Mrs. Moore," he spoke very slowly and distinctly, "these people—this man, who calls himself the Black Death, knows that I know you are being blackmailed by him. Perhaps he doesn't know that you will tell me the name of the man, but he fears you might. The only way he can be sure you won't talk is by making it impossible for you to talk. Now—if you give me this man's name there will be no use to try and keep you silent The thing he most fears will have happened."

"You think so. You think so!" She looked up eagerly, her big blue eyes shining through her tears. And then a new thought. "But he will expose me. He will break up my home; ruin my life, and—"

Brown shook his head. "I think not," he said. "He will have little time for you. His own affairs and the danger to his associate will keep him rather busy." Brown grinned evilly. "Let me assure you, Mrs. Moore, that things will happen so quickly after your information, that Mr. Boss Blackmailer will have plenty to occupy his mind. I don't think he will further aggravate the cause of his trouble."

SHE HESITATED a long moment, and then, "I don't see how it will help you. I have known the man for some years. He has been in our set. Wealthy at one time, but now his fortune is gone. He is—Tony Straus."

Brown was surprised and he showed it.

"Who—" And remembering that the woman had told him, "Where does Tony Straus live?"

She told him, and then produced a folded sheet of note paper. "This came with the card," she said. "But I can't go. I won't go. I'm afraid."

Brown read the note and showed it to me. It was a simple typewritten sheet.

> Meet me the same place—same time—tonight. There is no danger if you won't talk.

"And the time and place?" Brown asked.

"Twelve thirty. Central Park, just in from the Seventy-second Street entrance. Of course I won't go."

Brown hesitated. "But you will go." And after a long moment, "No, I guess you won't. You have done very well, Mrs. Moore; you won't regret it. I'm sure, as far as you are concerned, things will smooth themselves out. I feel that this Black Death will not want this thing dragged into the open. Let us hope he will have sense enough—and fear enough, to write it down as one of his failures; at the end." And as he reached the door, "You will be well protected tonight. If you are telephoned and asked, say you'll be there at the Park entrance on time. Good night!"

As we left, Brown spoke to Johnson. "Guard Mrs. Moore carefully tonight, Johnson; especially after twelve thirty."

We walked east, entered a drugstore, and Brown traced down the S's in the phone book until he found the name of Tony Straus.

"How can he help you?" I asked Vee. "I know him slightly. A good-for-nothing, harmless sort of fellow. Certainly not one of the big lieutenant's connected with Vincent Van Houton. A bachelor, and quite a man with the ladies. Money and all that!"

"Had money," Brown corrected me. "Van Houton is getting more careful. I have long since given up the idea of striking directly at Van Houton. His associates; the few big ones who take his orders and know him, are the ones I want to get. One of them may talk, and if not"—he shrugged his shoulders—"Van Houton's is a big organization that must go on. If we eliminate his trusted men, he must come out in the open himself, or— I think Tony will help us. You see the idea, of course. Mrs. Moore was to be murdered in the park tonight, if the plan to kill me failed—maybe murdered anyway."

Vee sat at the soda fountain and sipped mineral water.

"Twelve thirty," he said at length. "Ten minutes more, and we'll give Mr. Tony Straus a ring."

And ten minutes later he did, squeezing me into the booth with him.

"I want you to hear his voice, Dean," he told me. "You've got a good ear for that."

Tony Straus answered the phone himself. Brown said, deep down in his chest as he held the receiver between our heads: "Well, it's over. Went through without a hitch."

"And she won't talk?" A nervous voice came over the wire.

"No," said Brown, "she won't talk. Won't ever talk."

"Good!" And suddenly, the voice rising to high pitch, "What do you mean—won't—"

Brown laughed into the mouthpiece and hung up. But he frowned when we left the booth.

"I don't have to ask you, Dean. He didn't know she was to be murdered. Now for a taxi and a quick visit to Mr. Tony Straus, while he puzzles over that laugh."

TONY STRAUS opened the door to us. Dissipation had aged him considerably, but he was still a fine-looking man. He nodded at me in a puzzled way, as if my face were familiar but he couldn't quite place it. Brown he did not know.

"I am Detective Vee Brown," Brown said as he dropped easily into a chair in the living room. "Nice outfit you've got here for a man who's broke. There, there! Don't put on any dignity. I've come to see you about the blackmailing of Mrs. Moore."

"I know nothing of it. I've tried to help her. She asked me to."

"That's right," said Vee. "I simply want to know to whom you turned over the money."

Tony Straus opened his mouth, closed it with a snap, opened it again and said: "She never gave me any money. I deny that." And in rather a high-pitched voice, "My word will be as good as hers."

"Better," said Vee Brown. "Far better, Mr. Straus. The dead can't speak, you know. Mrs. Moore was murdered tonight. Shot to death at the entrance to Central Park— Seventy-second Street entrance."

Tony Straus clutched at his chest, then raised a hand to his throat. His face went white; he sank into a chair.

Brown came slowly to his feet. His steps were heavy as he crossed the floor and laid a hand on Tony's shoulder.

"I want you for the murder of Mrs. Clarence Moore," he said.

"No, no." Straus' head jerked erect, there was fear in his face—abject terror. "I didn't do it. I couldn't do it. I was here all evening. I—"

Brown smiled down at him. It was a mean smile; a hopeless sort of smile. "You sent the note that brought her to her death," he said. "It wasn't the first one you sent her. It won't be hard to prove that you sent it. You're just as guilty of the murder as the man who fired the shots. I must warn you that—"

"No, no." The man was on his knees now, clinging to Vee's coat. "I tell you I didn't know. I just thought someone was going to talk to her. I never would—I couldn't. My God! they'll burn me for this."

And Brown was at him. Both hands on the kneeling man's shoulders. He talked fast. "No one knows but me," he said. "I don't want you. I want the man behind these crimes. I want the one you took orders from. Tell me that, and you can go."

"They'd kill me. They'd kill me!" the groveling man shrieked.

"They won't. They can't." Brown shook him now. "You can leave the city. You can—"

The man's head turned and he looked toward the curtains of the door behind him.

"I'll tell, I'll tell. But first, him. He was there when you came. He may be there yet. It was—"

And I shrieked my warning. I was looking directly at those curtains. I saw the whiteness of the hand, the blackness of the gun, and heard, too, the shot.

Tony Straus didn't talk. He raised his hand and gripped Brown by the wrist. His head hung sideways on his shoulder. I saw Brown jerk his hand free, saw his gun flash in that single quick movement, and heard the shot. Then I thought that I heard a door slam, but could not be sure. My own gun was out, of course, but the hand and arm were gone long before I could fire.

Tony Straus half knelt, half lay upon the floor.

"Stay with him, Dean," Brown called out, hopped over the body and dashed between those curtains; passing from light into darkness. I waited, listened. Was he going to his death? But no other shot broke the stillness. I gave my attention to Tony Straus, turned him over on his back, put a pillow under his head.

I'M NOT a detective and didn't think to try and make the man talk. Tony was still breathing, though there was a hole in the back of his head, far down by the base of the skull. Blood was coming out of his mouth, trickling over his lower lip.

He muttered something that sounded like "water." I held his shoulders as he forced himself to one elbow.

"I didn't do it." He fairly cried out the words. "The man— My God! They bled me clean of everything, then made me bleed others. Mrs. Moore—the man—he worked for the Black Death. I took orders from him. He knows— he knows—knows the Black Death."

I came to then and cut in on him. "His name, Tony—the man's name?"

He turned wide, staring eyes at me; sightless eyes. He wasn't going to talk. He couldn't talk. But he did talk! He said very loudly and very clearly: "The man who black-mailed Mrs. Moore, and for whom I worked, was Johnny Casserelie. He just shot me. Johnny Casserelie. C-A-S-S-E—"

And that was all. I was holding a dead man in my arms. Very gently I put his head back on the pillow. Voices were calling now, somewhere a police whistle blew, and Brown was back in the room.

"I was a fool," he said. "But I never thought of another entrance to the apartment. I tried the fire-escape first, then it was too late. When I found the door the hall was full of people. I don't know if he went up or down." He shrugged his shoulders. "A bad failure that. I should have searched the place when we first came in." He looked down at the body. "And detective-story writers make quite a thing out of it." He sighed. "After all, murder and the escape of the murderer is very simple. I went to a window instead of a door."

"But I heard the door slam," I said.

"Thanks, Dean." His grin was sarcastic. "That helps a lot. Dead, eh? And with the name on his lips."

And I told Vee. Told him all that Tony had said.

"Johnny Casserelie." Brown rubbed his hands together. "Of course I know him. The assurance of repeal is certainly driving the big boys out of the booze racket. He's class, Dean; real class, of his kind. Van Houton must be making a fortune out of his Black Death."

"But can you put the screws into a man like Casserelie?"

"Can I?" Brown smiled like a school boy as he stepped indifferently over the body. "Before, it was extortion and blackmail that might be hard to prove. Now, it's murder." He looked for a long time at the body of Tony Straus. "Just weak and foolish and trapped into crime. But that's life, Dean. Crime is the strength of the few controlling the weakness of the many. Write down just what Tony said, as an *ante-mortem* statement. I'll swear to it, of course."

"But you didn't hear it," I objected as I pulled out my notebook and pencil.

"Even you can't be sure of that." He smiled at me. "But here are the police. We surprise them again, Dean. Our story, of course, is that he died without talking; at least that is our story until we see how Casserelie likes the other one."

My hand on the door knob; the door rattling under the pounding fist, I turned to Vee. "You won't—wouldn't let him go after a brutal murder like that?"

"If he gives me evidence to convict Van Houton, I will."
Brown nodded emphatically. "If not, we'll let him burn."

"I wonder," I told him, "why you don't strike directly at
Van Houton."

Brown grinned. "He's not like any other criminal, Dean.
He's like a general of an army. Far behind the lines. This is
war, and in war you wipe out the army first, and then— But
there! Open the door before that flat-foot beats it down."

CHAPTER THREE
THE GIRL WITH
THE GREEN EYES

ON THE way to our penthouse atop one of Park
Avenue's most pretentious apartments Brown
hummed softly. As for me, I tried to study him in the flashing street lights. Strange, queer little man, though I never
dared mention the "little" aloud, for Brown was quite
conscious of his slender but wiry frame. Indeed, it was his
size, and absence of strength, which made him study for
years to obtain his great proficiency with a gun. Now—I
wondered. Here was a man who earned some three thousand, five hundred dollars a year as a first-grade detective
assigned to the district attorney's office, and made twenty
times that figure writing popular and sentimental songs
under the name of Vivian. The identity of Brown was not
known even to his publishers.

"You're not going to see this Johnny Casserelie tonight?"
I asked Brown.

"No." He shook his head. "It's too late, and he'll be laying
low. If I inquire for him it will warn him."

"And Mrs. Moore?"

"She should be safe now. No point in eliminating her but vengeance. She has told all she can, and Tony is dead. You see, Dean, we—or rather I, am not responsible for Tony's death. I'll hazard the guess that Casserelie got there only a few minutes before we did. He was waiting for a report on Mrs. Moore's death. When it didn't come in, well—" he spread his hands far apart. "It would serve the same purpose if Tony died. So his death was inevitable."

"Will Johnny Casserelie talk to save his life? He's pretty big and pretty well known, isn't he?"

"Sure. But men only rise in the racket by tramping on others. We'll be able to talk to Casserelie. He's a killer, of course, but he's a sensible man. He'll weigh the possibilities of beating the Tony rap. Then he'll figure what information he can give on Van Houton that will leave him in the clear. Oh, he's tricky and shrewd, but he won't burn through any sense of loyalty. He'll think of Johnny Casserelie and no one else."

Wong, Brown's Chinese servant, let us into the penthouse. He grinned, and throwing back his head jerked a thumb over his shoulder.

"The little missy," he said. "The one you said always to admit. She sits now in the living room; music-room door locked. I did not go about her person for deadly weapons."

"No, no. We couldn't expect that, Wong." Brown grinned, and very low, "Just what is your opinion of the little missey?"

Wong's eyes slanted, his mouth opened, yellow teeth showed. "She goes about with the face that slits men's throats. But her inside tell her outside to play at being bad and cruel."

"By God!" said Brown. "I think Wong's right. And you, Dean?"

"She did us a good turn; and saved my life that night she hid in the music room and impersonated you. Beautiful? Yes. But I wouldn't trust her, Vee. It's a sinister, cruel sort of beauty."

"Like the inside telling the outside to be bad," Brown mused as he walked down the long hall and into the living room.

ONLY FOR a moment did I get a look at the girl in the light of the lamp. The black hair under the small hat; the full lips and the heavy shadows beneath her brilliant green eyes. She was made up heavily, I thought. Still— Then her hand shot up and snapped out the light of the lamp above her head.

"Why do you fear the light?" Brown asked her.

"Because," she said, "I'm a woman of the night. And I don't like the scrutiny you give me. Bad people don't like light."

"The worst man I know can look me straight in the eyes under an arc light," he told her.

"That will be Vincent Van Houton," she said, curling her feet up under her and looking very small in the shadows.

"Yes, it could be. You must hate him a great deal."

"A great deal." She repeated his words. "But why do you think I come to you?"

"Vengeance. Hate. Van Houton, of course."

"Part of it, to be sure. But why not pick the D.A.; Inspector Ramsey; a hundred or more coppers?"

"Because I'm irregular."

"It might be because—I like you, or—"

"Or because you know that I hate Van Houton. And tonight?" The last abruptly.

"I want to know about Mrs. Moore."

And Brown told her. When he came to the part about wanting Tony for murder, she nodded and muttered, "Clever." But he didn't tell her the name of the man who killed Tony.

She peered at Brown shrewdly out of the darkness, her green eyes gleaming like a cat's.

"And the man who killed Tony Straus. You know who that is?"

Brown hesitated, and then, "Yes, I know."

She watched him. "I want to know, too. There! Don't shake your head. I need you and you need me, but you need me most. Some day I will deliver Van Houton to you. But I must know the truth. Who killed Tony?"

Brown studied her a long time. "And if I don't tell you?"

She shrugged her shoulders. "Then I am through with you. If I must be in the dark, I will go back and live in the night."

"The man," said Brown, "was Johnny Casserelie."

"I thought so. I thought so." Her head bobbed up and down.

"You know him?"

"Yes, I know him. But I was never sure he was in it. He's a very careful man. I know him," her eyes knitted to thin green slits of fire, "and sometimes I am afraid that he knows me."

"He is a danger to you?"

"A great danger. He suspects me; maybe more than suspects me. The other day at—but no matter where, he held my hand a moment. 'You are a woman,' he said, 'who does much as she pleases. You fear only one man. Yet, whenever I wish I can make you do whatever I ask.' I was afraid then."

"You won't have to worry about him long, Miss—" and Brown's whimsical smile. "Should I too say I must know the truth?"

And the girl smiled; white teeth flashed in the shadows—yes, heavy shadows. But it seemed that for those few seconds the cruelty went out of her face and she was just a young girl. Nothing sinister about that beauty either; nothing— And the smile was gone and the face was cold, impassive; the eyes hard and penetrating again.

"I'll give you a laugh," she said almost harshly. "My first name is Maria, and that's the truth. Funny name for such a person, isn't it?"

"I don't know." Brown shook his head. "Condon, over there! They labeled him, Dean. As for me!" He paused, for his real name was not Vee, but Vivian—the name under which he wrote his music.

"Vivian." The girl nodded quickly. "Life is funny. What a name for a killer, and what an occupation!"

Brown's black eyes flashed dangerously. He looked at me, then at the girl as he walked over to her. "What do you mean?" he said. He had guarded that secret well.

She shrugged her shoulders and looked up at him; for a moment her teeth showed again. The anger went out of Vee's face. He was trying to study her there in the dimness.

"It doesn't matter," she said. "It's safe with me. I think I've known for a long time, but when I was in the music room a few weeks back I was sure."

"But how? There was nothing there to tell; nothing but a half-finished composition. You—"

"No one but Vivian could have written that melody, those words. *Sun-kissed Sands*, was the name of it, I think," and she began to sing softly. Then as Brown stood and watched her she stopped. "There's one other thing I came for. I can't always get you on the phone. I don't know at what moment I may get the real chance to expose Van Houton, but I'll learn of victims and I'll come to you. You trust me?"

"Absolutely," said Vee Brown.

"Then give me a key. I can't chance waiting in the hall or downstairs."

Brown dug a hand in his pocket and handed her his key. Then he walked across the room and followed her to the door.

"You and I are going to get Van Houton, aren't we?"

"Yes," she said, "I hope so. But you are anyway."

I heard her refuse Brown's suggestion that he see her home, or that I should. She said: "It would be worth my life to be seen with you; recognized with you."

"Van Houton knows you, of course?" I guess Brown was fishing, for the girl had never even once hinted at what her connection was with Van Houton.

"It's not Van Houton that I fear now." And I think her voice trembled. "It's Johnny Casserelie. If he exposed me to Van Houton, I—I—"

"I know," Brown said. "But have no fear of Johnny Casserelie. I'm taking care of him."

A moment of silence, high heels beating across the stone floor; then the door closed and Brown was back with me.

"I never thought I'd be giving a key to a woman." He grinned at me. "You wouldn't think it was a trick, would you, Dean?"

"No," I told him simply. "I can see her point, and certainly she's done enough to convince us she's on our side of the fence."

"It might be a trap—an elaborate trap." He shook his head several times. "Sometimes, I guess, I think like a story-book detective. But if it were a trap, now; if they came here and took me prisoner, they'd question me—where? Why, in the big chair under the light. The very one she sat in. I just want to strum out a few bars that are singing in my head. *Girl of the Night!* It fits her well, Dean."

It must have been hours later and long after I had heard Brown go to his room that I heard footsteps again in the hall, going to the living room. Brown's steps, I thought, but I called out to him.

He answered at once. "I was just thinking, Dean—of the big chair under the light."

CHAPTER FOUR
THE SILVER GLADES

WE WERE up fairly early the next morning. We had to be. Mortimer Doran, the big district attorney, called on us and talked while Brown had his breakfast. Inspector Ramsey had trailed along and scowled at Brown while Vee ate his grape fruit.

The D.A. cleared his throat, looked first at Ramsey, then at Brown, and finally said: "I give you your way in things, Vee, but I did expect a report. Ramsey, here, tells me that you went straight from Mrs. Moore's to Tony Straus."

Vee Brown looked over at Ramsey. "I thought," he said, "I was working alone. How did Ramsey know?"

Ramsey's lips curled up, his big shoulders raised slightly. "After all," he said, "I am working for the police department, even if you and Mr. Doran don't think so. When two men—two damn good men are assigned to special and secret work, I like to know why. Last night a man of mine saw you and Condon, here, go into Straus's apartment house. He reported to me of course."

"It's too bad," said Vee, "that he didn't wait around and see who came out after the murder." And suddenly, "I don't like it, Mr. Doran. You don't believe in my ideas on the Black Death, yet you have given me free rein on the thing, or so you say. Now—you want reports."

Mortimer Doran spread his hands far apart. He smiled appreciatively at Brown. "After all," he said, "when the best detective in the city is on the spot when a man is shot to death, the department does expect some sort of an explanation. Ramsey, of course, is working independent of my office. Naturally he wants to know what's going on. This blackmail ring is as important to others in the police system as it is to you, Vee."

"Then why doesn't Ramsey find out for himself? Why does he sit by a telephone and wait for someone to tell him what I'm doing? God! Must he get all his information through having me trailed? He'll get so dependent on me that he'll have to throw up his job if I should quit."

Ramsey came to his feet and set a closed fist on the table. "Can that sort of stuff." He glared at Brown. "All you do is go around annoying people. This Van Houton, for instance. He's complaining now about you." And to the D.A., "I've had Van Houton watched every minute of the twenty-four hours of each day. He doesn't make a move that I don't know about."

"He made one yesterday," said Brown. "In a restaurant just after the theatre."

"Coincidence." Ramsey shrugged. "If he planned your death he'd hardly be in the restaurant a few minutes before the shooting started."

"That's right," nodded Doran. "If he is half the man you think him, Brown, he'd hardly be that crude."

"Crude!" Brown smiled. "That's the cleverness of the man. He could even say I knew he was going to be there and preceded him there."

"And didn't you?" Ramsey demanded.

"Maybe I did," agreed Brown, and I remembered Vee's statement that he expected Van Houton. "But he left without eating a thing."

"Maybe." Ramsey sneered. "Well, I questioned Van Houton shortly after your shooting. He admitted leaving because you were there. He said you continually annoy him. He's thinking of making an official complaint. He's only afraid the thing will reach the papers."

MORTIMER DORAN came to his feet now and smiled down at both Brown and Ramsey. "Gentlemen. Gentlemen! We're not here to wrangle about Van Houton. I'm on Ramsey's side about him, but as long as you don't embarrass the department, Vee, you can work your own way. The thing is this. Ramsey pointed it out to me and I must admit he's right. You were in the room when Tony Straus was shot to death. He was not a criminal. That is, he hasn't any criminal record. Did he have anything to do with this blackmail business?"

"He did," said Brown emphatically.

"In a small way, eh?" Ramsey questioned.

"In a big enough way to have himself killed."

"He knew who the Black Death is?" This from Mortimer Doran.

"No," said Brown. "But he knew the man who worked directly from this blackmailer."

"Do you know who shot him?" Ramsey demanded.

Brown just looked at Ramsey, stirred his coffee, then lifted the cup to his lips, ignoring the question.

"You're not answering that?" Mortimer Doran leaned forward. "Now—I say, Brown. It looks bad for the department; bad for you. The papers, of course, don't know you were there."

"All right." Brown nodded grimly. "Give me a little time, Mr. Doran, and I'll produce the murderer of Tony Straus. Either the man who actually shot him or the man that caused him to be shot."

"You mean this blackmailer—the Black Death. You mean—"

"I mean exactly that. The man who did the killing or the one who sent him."

"The Black Death, eh?" Ramsey sneered. "Van Houton, I suppose."

"Exactly," said Vee Brown. "The Black Death. Vincent Van Houton!"

Mortimer Doran shook his head. "This thing is becoming an obsession with you, Vee. We've checked up Van Houton; right back to his birth. He's always been respectable."

"That's the trouble with the police system," Brown said. "The confusion of respectability with honesty. Van Houton hasn't got any record because the police were too stupid, or he was too clever to have anything pinned on him."

"Well," said Mortimer Doran, "I'll be satisfied if you produce the murderer of Tony Straus. You know who he is?"

Brown hesitated, and then: "Yes, I do."

"You do!" Ramsey's voice was loud now. "Well, who was he? Come! Who was he? You haven't got any idea that this is a one-man police department." And when Brown just looked at him, "Come, come! Mr. Doran, here this dick sits and eats a late breakfast and reads his newspaper while a murderer collects his resources and makes a getaway."

Mortimer Doran looked at Vee Brown, and stroked his chin. "Well, Brown, what do you say?"

"You're the boss," said Brown. "Give me twenty-four hours and I'll deliver the murderer. Either the hand or the brain."

"Cripes!" said Ramsey in disgust. "He's at that again. If he knows, Mr. Doran, make him tell. Don't let him wait twenty-four hours and then make us a long speech that it's this society jumping jack, Van Houton, and forget to tell us why."

MORTIMER DORAN looked long and earnestly at Vee Brown. Then ignoring Ramsey's speech, "It would make Ramsey and me look silly if you were right about Van Houton." He shook his head. "But I'll be satisfied with the head of the man who killed this Tony."

Brown grinned at the D.A. He didn't look at Ramsey when he spoke.

"It might make you look silly, Mr. Doran." His voice was very serious. "But I'm afraid it's rather late to do anything about that for Inspector Ramsey. He's already attended to it himself, over and over."

Ramsey didn't speak. He couldn't, I guess. He just glared at Brown as the two men departed.

When they had left, Brown said: "After all, Dean, the drama of life is very much like the drama of the stage and screen. We must have our comic relief." And with a shake of his head, "It's lucky I'm working for the D.A.'s office. How long do you think I'd last in the department with

Ramsey my superior officer? Damn my soul, Dean! Did you see his face? What a temper the man has! But there! I've got to do some telephoning."

And he did. From his face, the results he got were disappointing. At three o'clock he said to me: "Ramsey may be right. Johnny Casserelie is not in his usual haunts. Can he suspect I know? Has he taken a run-out powder?" Then he shook his head. "Impossible! The papers all carried the story that Tony died instantly."

At six o'clock Brown got a call that sent him whistling up and down the room.

"He's with us, Dean. Johnny is back on the Avenue again. I was right. He has no suspicions; is not worried." He wrinkled up his face. "Do you know, Dean, for a moment I had grave doubts of a certain young lady—Maria."

"But why would she double on you? Good Lord, Vee, you see the bad side of everyone. She tipped you off to Mrs. Moore in the beginning. She saved me from Pete Stokes. Why—"

"Women change their minds," he said half seriously, half jokingly. "But we're going out to dinner. Going to dine at the Silver Glades. Johnny Casserelie owns it, by the way. Business hasn't been over-good. Perhaps he'll appreciate the few dollars we turn into his till before our little talk."

"Won't that warn him?"

"In a way." Vee nodded. "More, alarm him, I hope. Since he's close to Van Houton he'll know, of course, that I'm interested. But it will give him something to think about. And Johnny's quite a thinker, quite a schemer and planner. None better on the Avenue, unless of course it's Van Houton. But then, he's not of the Avenue. You know who he'll think of, Dean?"

"Who?" I picked up my hat.

"Of Johnny Casserelie—just Johnny Casserelie."

THE DINNER hour brought only a small number to the Silver Glades, and I didn't wonder. The food was poorly cooked, badly served, and the prices ridiculous.

"This is what I've got to put up with in the way of duty." Vee made a particularly wry face over a bit of half-cooked chicken. "But it will all serve its purpose; perhaps give me indigestion and make me that much more bitter against Johnny Casserelie. He is one of the brainiest if not the biggest of the racketeers. Watch me put him over the hurdles. It'll do you good. He has probably beaten the rap, or never been arrested for some really big shootings. What a comedown to be threatened with a jolt of lightning for knocking off a punk like Tony Straus."

Vee Brown paused a moment and whispered across to me.

"Don't look now, Dean, but Johnny Casserelie has just come out of his office behind the dining room. He's been told that we are here, of course, but he pretends not to see us." Vee Brown folded the evening paper he had bought outside to the theatrical pages, peered at them a moment and said: "I see that Gertrude la Palatin did not appear for her matinée today. She's indisposed. And I don't wonder at it, after being with Van Houton after last night's performance. It's her stomach, I'll bet, and—"

He broke off and looked up. A man was leaning on the table. He was a big man; broad of body and broad of features. Nose, mouth and ears were big. But there was something in his face. Not just criminal, not just coarseness, not even sinister. The face was just—well—just wicked. I can't describe it any other way.

"Hello, Brown," he said. "Haven't seen you in some time. Just wanted good food, or here on business?"

"The food," Brown said, "was terrible."

"That's right." Johnny Casserelie's smile broadened. "I send out to the cafeteria around the corner for my dinner. So it's business then."

"You guessed it." Brown nodded.

"About Tony Straus, eh?"

Brown laid down the knife with which he was buttering a hard roll.

"You guessed it again. You're good at guessing, Johnny."

Casserelie laughed, and it sounded like a natural laugh. "Not so good," he said. "Ramsey and a couple of boys were around not so long ago."

"You knew Tony Straus then?"

"Sure. He came here a lot. Wasn't particular about the food; liked the lights and the pretty girls, and the liquor too. There's a lot of them that like to kick the snow off the moon once in a while. Sometimes he was a nuisance, but nothing bad about him. Can't think who would want to knock him over."

"You should," said Brown, but there was nothing of accusation in his voice.

"Yeah? Why?" The smile left Casserelie's face but there was nothing of guilt in it. Just puzzlement.

"Because you're so good at guessing. Did he pay his bills?"

"Sure. Why?" The grin came back to Casserelie's face.

"Heard he was broke."

"Well, he paid me. I'm running no charitable institution. They all pay."

"That's right," said Brown. "They all pay. But they don't all pay like Tony did."

"Say—what are you driving at? I had nothing against this Tony, nor I didn't have any special yen for him. Just a good customer. Ramsey wanted to get a line on him. Who he met! Who he brought in! If he seemed to be dough heavy! Oh, the regular stuff. Anything you want to know?"

BROWN SHOOK his head. "Not any questions to ask you, since the efficient Ramsey covered all that." And as Johnny shrugged his broad shoulders and turned from the table, "But I'd like to tell you something, Johnny. In your private office, as soon as we finish our coffee."

Johnny Casserelie turned back to the table, opened his mouth, closed it again, eyed us a moment and finally said: "O.K., Brown. I'll be in the office for a bit."

Then he moved from the table, stopped to pat a man on the back, bowed to a lady with a plaster-of-Paris face and enough jewelry to sink a battleship, and went slowly into his office.

"Not like friend Pete Stokes, eh?" Brown laughed. "Yet they both came from the same school; the same gutter. The Black Death. Van Houton is improving in his selection of men. Smooth, eh?"

And I agreed with that. Johnny Casserelie was smooth; polished to a fine glossiness, at least on the surface. But I had seen many types of men since being with Vee; and somehow I thought, with Brown, that underneath that polish was the same gutter that had bred both him and Pete Stokes. Yes, Pete Stokes, who had threatened to kill me, who very nearly did kill me. If I had my choice of meeting either one of them up a dark alley at night, I think I would have picked Stokes.

Vee took his own sweet time over the coffee, which was vile—and I knew how particular he was about coffee.

"Ramsey!" he mused. "Well, of course the trail would lead him here. It wouldn't take long to catch up on Tony's former activities. A nice little business, that. Tony could meet Johnny here and get his orders. I hope Ramsey won't drag Mrs. Moore's name through the newspapers. He's a hound for publicity." And stroking his chin, "But not on these Black Death cases. I must give the devil his due there. He's kept his mouth pretty tight, and with that mouth it's a real accomplishment."

"You don't think Ramsey suspects Johnny Casserelie?" I asked.

"No, no. He couldn't. Just routine work, Dean. After all, the Silver Glades is as popular as any night club after the theatre. I wonder if Johnny really owns it, or if Van Houton is back of it."

"You've certainly got Van Houten in everything." I smiled.

"Everything evil." Brown nodded grimly. And after a moment's thought, "Perhaps Mortimer Doran is right. An obsession! Well maybe more. A fetish with me." His hands clenched on the table, his lips set grimly, those black eyes flashed. "After all, Johnny Casserelie is a big part of the Black Death. God, Dean, he shot that man at my feet, through the back of the head. It would be funny now if I lost my head and popped over Mr. Johnny Casserelie. But that will hardly be possible. He'll receive us with his two bodyguards. Ike and Mike, the boys call them. Twin brothers. Remarkable resemblance."

But Vee Brown was wrong. Casserelie received us alone in his nicely appointed office down a little hall behind the dining room.

Casserelie opened up a silver humidor, took out a cigar and shoved the big box across the desk. Then he bit off the end of the cigar, shot it from between his teeth onto the thick rug, and sticking his thumbs in the armholes of his vest, said: "Well, Brown—just what's on your chest?"

Brown closed the top of the humidor, lifted a box of matches from the desk, struck the one and offered Casserelie a light. Casserelie bent forward, drew the flame into the end of his cigar, nodded his head in thanks; and Vee Brown spoke. His voice was low, conversational. There was nothing of his words in his face. He said simply: "Tony Straus spoke before he died. An *ante-mortem* statement. You're wanted for murder, Johnny."

CHAPTER FIVE
CRIME MACHINE

IF VEE BROWN expected Casserelie to keel over, even turn pale or shake the knees, he was badly mistaken.

Gray eyes blinked once or twice; lines came into Casserelie's face from his mouth to his nose. He removed the cigar from his mouth, blew a ring of smoke out into the room, and said very slowly: "So that's how it is, eh?"

"That," said Brown, "is just how it is."

For a moment the big man and the little one eyed each other. It was like a boy threatening a man. Johnny Casserelie could have stretched forth those great hands and crushed Brown in a vise grip; could have, I mean, if his hands had ever reached Vee. But I wasn't afraid for Brown as he stood there, his hands swinging easily at his sides. From experience I knew that Vee could move either hand with such rapidity that one hardly saw the gun appear before it was spouting flame.

Johnny Casserelie sucked his lower lip under his upper teeth. His eyes narrowed; he looked down at the end of his cigar, flicked the ash off with his little finger, then said through a half-closed mouth: "Well, got the warrant?"

"No," said Brown, "I haven't."

"I see," said Casserelie. He jerked his cigar toward a chair. "Sit down." He sank into the chair behind the desk, but both his hands were visible. And when Brown dropped into the leather chair across from him, Casserelie nodded toward me. "I suppose this guy's a witness to the frame."

"No frame," Brown told him. And to me, "Show him the book, Dean. What you wrote down before Tony went out."

Johnny Casserelie's hand was steady as he took the notebook from me, held his thumb between the pages, and after carefully reading it returned the book to me.

"So—" he said. "He lived a rat and died one. No warrant, eh?" Shrewd eyes studied Brown.

"No. And we won't bother to hold you on the Moore blackmail. Murder is the rap this time, Johnny. As for Tony! It didn't matter. I saw you through the curtains."

Johnny Casserelie grinned. Certainly he knew how to take it.

"So you'd even go that far to roast me. Don't like me much, eh?"

"Not much; but the man behind you less. The Black Death. I'd give a lot to fry him." Vee leaned forward now. "A whole lot, Johnny."

"Humph!" said Casserelie. "You'd even destroy that book, eh? And the boy friend's memory."

"And my own."

Johnny Casserelie's eyes gleamed brightly. He waited for Brown to say more, and when he didn't, "Well, let us have it. I'm a good listener. It won't be the first deal I've made with a cop."

"It'll be the last, though, if you don't see it my way. But here's the ticket. I want the Black Death. You can deliver him. Give me the evidence that will convict Van Houton and I'll forget about you. We don't have to use the Moore case. There was Mrs. Townsend; a dozen or more others. Suicides. Murders. The state can only roast him once."

"Van Houton, eh?" Johnny Casserelie scratched his head. "Yeah, I know him. A nice guy. Gets in here once in a while, but too high-toned; too respectable for us to make money out of." And coming to his feet and his soft voice turning harsh as he closed both hands into fists and held them on the flat desk, "You want me to rat out on a guy, eh—and you come here with a crooked frame! Well, take your book and your boy friend and get your warrant." He leaned far forward now and his lips quivered and his gray eyes were ugly and evil. "Understand, copper. Get out!"

BROWN WAS surprised. I saw it for a moment in his face. He hesitated, then motioning to me turned toward the door.

"I didn't think you were a fool, Johnny," he said. "You can't take a run-out powder because the place is watched. And, if you think a moment—you can't beat this rap. I'll wait outside for five minutes. Then," Brown shook his head, "I'm not going to get any warrant. I'm going to put the cuffs on you and take you along." And as Casserelie's hand maybe half unconsciously moved toward his left armpit,

"Or if you want it that way, I'm willing to save the state the expense of the juice."

"Yeah?" Johnny Casserelie's lips quivered with the effort he made to control his passion. "Well, do some thinking of your own. The minute you snap them cuffs on me, the little lady gets it." He raised his right hand drew it across his neck.

Almost at the door, Brown swung, and I guess I stopped with him.

"What little lady?" Brown seemed puzzled.

"What little lady!" Casserelie sneered the words. "The leak. The one who saved Condon's life, gave you the Moore tip, like as not tipped you off to me. Oh, the big guy doesn't know her. No one knows her—no one but me. What would the big shot do with her if I blew to him? But that isn't the question. The question is: what will I do with her? I'm not the fool you think me. I picked up that dirty little tart. She's with a couple of the boys now; boys that know what to do with her if I don't tip them off otherwise. Now, stick on them cuffs, Mr. Wise Dick." And with a great flourish he stuck his hands out across the desk.

Brown moved quickly; he always moved quickly. Just a few steps, his hands flashed up, and silver steel showed on the wrists of Johnny Casserelie. And that wasn't all that showed. Johnny's face went suddenly white; his mouth opened and closed.

"You—you don't understand." He half stammered the words. "I'm not bluffing. Before you have me booked they'll knock her off."

"Well," Brown shrugged his shoulders, "she should have thought of that. I'm no wet nurse for a dame who ate her cake, didn't like the taste of it, then came to me to cure her belly ache. Come on, Johnny."

"Vee!" I had grasped him by the arm. "It's not human. This girl—" I started to say, "saved my life," but he swung on me so violently that I stopped.

"Save your breath," he snapped. "I'm not supposed to be human. I'm a machine—a crime machine, employed by the state, and this man is wanted for murder." His gun jerked into his hand, making a half-circle from Johnny Casserelie to the door. "Come on!" he said. "Step on it."

And Johnny Casserelie broke.

Beads of sweat appeared on his forehead, his face turned from a dull white to a pasty yellow and then back to white again. His hands came out and clutched at Brown's arm. Saliva hung on his lips when he talked.

"Geez! Brown. Geez! Give a guy a chance to think. You come on me so suddenly. I'll— God! Don't take me through the dining room like this."

"What the hell!" said Brown, his hand on the doorknob. "They're going to burn you anyway. Going to burn you because you won't talk—won't talk of the guy who put you on the spot. Won't—"

"What do you want me to do? Say— wait!" And Johnny Casserelie's legs were trembling now; he was wavering on his feet. And I thought of Brown's repeated statement— "They're all yellow when the smell of burning flesh is in their nostrils."

Vee Brown paused. He half turned the knob, and then, "I want this man, Johnny. If you can deliver the evidence that gets him, you can go free. If you can't—"

"But the girl!" Johnny Casserelie was steadier now. "I ain't kidding about her. She's in real danger. I expected you'd have a heart and beat it. In case you had doubts she was to call you later at your apartment and let you know the jam she's in."

Brown's shoulders went up and down. "The question is; are you going to spill it? Yes or no!"

JOHNNY CASSERELIE looked at the ceiling. His thick lips set tightly. His chin came forward, then dropped on his chest.

"Yes," he said grimly. "After all, he put me on this spot. But not here. I've got friends coming in. Come up to my house and—"

Brown cut in with a grin. "Don't be a sap, Casserelie; or don't think I'm one."

"Well, your place then; or Condon's. Any place but here."

"That's better," said Brown. "Let's get moving."

"Take these damned cuffs off me." Casserelie was growing more confident now that he had taken the step. "I can't go through the dining room like this."

"I don't want you to." Brown stepped forward and snapped off the cuffs. He pushed them into a jacket pocket and frisked Johnny. Just a single heavy German Luger and a long-bladed knife.

"So—" Vee examined the knife, ran his finger along the edge of it. "You too. The Black Death likes steel." He nodded grimly. "Twice as much advertising in a knife; something terrible and horrible about dying that way."

"Yeah." Casserelie eyed Brown shrewdly as Vee tossed the knife and gun into a drawer of the desk. "I suppose you don't care what happens to the girl."

Brown grinned. "We'll take that up afterwards. The important thing is the Black Death. You're not stalling, Johnny?"

Casserelie laughed. "I can tell you plenty. Enough to roast him over and over. I suppose I'll have to duck out for a while."

"That's for you to decide." Brown flung open the door. "Just do it natural now. Only a few people outside."

So we passed out into the narrow hall and to the dining room. Casserelie preceded us, nodding and smiling as he passed the three or four occupied tables. I had a chance to clutch Brown's left arm; his right hand was in his pocket.

"The girl!" I said. "God, Brown! You've seen how others died."

"*Shh*—" Brown warned me. "We must wait until after Casserelie talks. The fool! If he had stuck to the point, about the girl—I'd of had to let him go." And half in anger, I thought, "Maybe I haven't any heart; any conscience, but I've got a sense of loyalty—or at least, sportsmanship. Besides, the girl knows my secret." He drew in a deep breath. "Damn clever of her, that."

"Yet only last night you were thinking that—" And I stopped. We had caught up to Casserelie at the cloakroom.

Brown and I received our hats; the big racketeer had taken his from the costumer in his office. Together, the three of us reached the street, walked up to the corner and around to the side street. Brown's big Rolls was there at the curb, Wong, stiff and straight, behind the wheel.

Casserelie talked on the way uptown to our thirty-odd-story apartment house. Brown was right. The man was a schemer. And he was thinking of one thing. Johnny Casserelie! His thoughts ran to the best way to protect himself.

"It's got to be the real thing, Johnny," Brown advised him. "Evidence that'll stand up with a judge and jury, and against the assault of the best criminal lawyers."

Casserelie grinned and nodded. "As long as I'm going to do it I'll do it right," he said. "You've waited a long time for this night, eh?"

Brown's black eyes sparkled in the flash of a passing electric light. "Yes," he admitted, "I have."

"And so have I," said Johnny Casserelie, very low. But Brown wasn't listening. I knew that he was thinking. This was the big moment of his whole career. "Wong," Brown said as we drew up before the apartment, "do you know any nice little Chinese girl?"

Wong's unexpressive face lighted up. "Nice, but not little. Good cook; maybe better than Wong."

"Does she like a Rolls?" And not waiting for an answer, "Take her out driving, and don't come back before twelve. Then—a midnight supper, Wong. Almost a feast. It's a big night; the biggest night of my life."

CHAPTER SIX
UNDER THE LIGHT

THERE WERE times when Brown was like a boy. This was one of them. His step was brisk as we entered the lobby, passed the operated elevators and went to the automatic lifts.

He was whistling when we left the elevator, walked to our door and stuck the key in the lock. A moment's pause and he pushed the door open, reached in a hand and snapped on the light.

"You first, Mr. Johnny Casserelie." Brown's voice rang with triumph as Johnny preceded us down the hall and the door closed with a bang. "Right through the curtains to the living room," he went on. Johnny Casserelie pushed back the curtains and stepped into the living room. We followed on his heels.

Then all hell seemed to break loose. I saw the shadows; the bulky figures that moved from either side of those curtains.

I heard the warning voice, tried desperately to reach for my gun, knew that Casserelie had swung and knocked me against the wall. Then I was struggling with him. I heard the shot too, knew that white hands clutched at curtains and that they came down; knew too that a body—a human body, living or dead, had fallen into the darkened living room.

Johnny Casserelie was a big man, a strong man; but so was I. His attack had been a surprise. His hands were on my throat, his body pressed so close to mine that I could not draw my gun. And I cursed Brown for teaching me to wear it in a shoulder holster beneath my left armpit, and cursed myself for not having it in my hand when we entered the apartment.

No more such thoughts. Just the thought that a shot had been fired and Brown was dead and I was fighting for my life, or maybe fighting so that others in that apartment would kill me, rather than Casserelie.

I tore at the hands upon my throat, kicked the man in the shins, twisted and turned, and then realizing the uselessness of such tactics, threw both my arms about him, twisted a kg between his—and we both hit the floor. I was on top.

For the moment, then, I forgot that others were there. I remembered only that Brown was dead and that the man, at least responsible, was beneath me, his fingers still upon my throat; biting, squeezing, cutting off my wind. Hate—passion—the lust to kill. Call it what you will. Both my hands lifted Casserelie's head and pounded it back on the floor. The fingers on my throat loosened. I lifted his head again, and—

Someone said: "Cripes! A picnic, eh? One dead—and look at this." Then a dull thud, a pain in the back of my head, and I rolled over on my side and for a moment forgot everything. Just blackness.

THE STORM was terrific, the thunder almost blocked out by the whistling of the wind. But inside my head I felt it, tearing at my ear drums, throbbing in my temples. The lightning; great flashes of it, that made me close my eyes.

Men called to one another. One man cursed. He said: "He was my brother, and he's dead. Give me back the knife and I'll slit his throat where he lies. Not a soul heard the shot."

Another man said, a long ways off it seemed: "Nothing seems to surprise this Brown. He shot through his pocket, and then—"

I opened my eyes. Things cleared. I was in the big chair directly under the lamp. The thunder was just the roaring in my head; the lightning my blinking eyes beneath the lamp. The voices— And I looked around the room, before I fully knew that I was bound hand and foot.

Brown lay on the floor. His face was very white. He was half on his side, but I could see the cut on his forehead and the tiny trickle of blood running from it. I could also see the steel cuffs; his own cuffs, that held his hands behind his back. My hands were tied with strong rope, clothes line, I thought. And there, not far from Brown, was the body of a man. The dead man they were talking about. They—

And I looked straight into the face of Johnny Casserelie and the man he was talking to; then I looked down at the dead man on the floor. It was a shock to my already aching head, shattered nerves. For the man upon the floor and the one standing were exactly alike. And I shook my head. The standing man had a scar upon his cheek that the dead man didn't have.

I knew them of course; the bodyguard that Brown had spoken of. Mike and Ike, the Avenue had dubbed them.

Casserelie and the man were still talking. Casserelie was saying: "You can have Brown later, the dirty skunk." He kicked the silent figure of Brown upon the floor. "I tell you, Ike, I expected things to break different. I thought to get Brown to come here to hear the girl call up; thought that I would be running the party and be armed. But the dirty rat didn't give a damn about her. He took my rod. Where's the girl?"

"Inside. One of the bedrooms, trussed up and gagged."

"Well, fetch her out, and take the gag off her. We'll let her squeal a bit. Damn it! this place is sound-proof; not a soul heard the shot."

"Hardly," said Ike. "It's on the roof. Don't think you'd hear a shot even if it was fired on the terrace." He walked toward the door, paused a moment and kicked Brown viciously in the head. "The lousy bum." He cursed. "Never gave Mike a chance."

I could have grinned at that one as he passed out of the door, but I didn't. I was looking at Brown. I was wondering if he were alive or dead. He must be alive; these men talked as if he were.

And then Johnny Casserelie turned and spoke to me. "So you're coming to and ready to see the show," he sneered. Then looking down at Brown, "The great detective. The Crime Machine. What a sucker! As soon as you left here tonight I had the girl brought in. Convenient too. No lock to pick, no evidence to show you and Brown that people were inside. The little lady furnished the key."

"She told you about the key?" The words just came from my lips without any order from my brain.

"Not exactly. She's a tough little piece. Thinks more of Brown that he does of her. Even a couple of belts in the mouth wouldn't make her talk. But she carried the key on a chain around her neck." He shrugged his shoulders. "We ain't all dumb dicks, you know. I—" and with a grin as the girl stumbled into the room, only her hands bound now, but her stockings torn at the ankles and the marks from tight ropes plainly visible, "Here's the little lady now. Meet Vee Brown, the great Vee. He's the lad on the floor." And as the girl just glared at him, he stepped forward, turned her roughly around, and pushing the heel of his hand under her chin almost sent her from her feet as he crashed her onto the couch.

THE GIRL'S head cracked against the back of the couch. But it was a low soft couch of fine down. She straightened. Green eyes; tired green eyes looked over at Johnny Casserelie, then at me and back to Casserelie again. She spoke, and her voice was different than I had heard it before.

"What are you going to do?" she said. "Turn me over to him; or are you going to—to do it?"

Casserelie laughed. "Both," he said. "I'm going to do it, and then turn you over to him. He's a fool. He never suspected you. If you even mention his name I'll gag you, and it will be worse for you. The big boss won't even know a thing about you until you're dead."

She nodded, resignedly, hopelessly. And then Brown turned over and opened his eyes.

"Well, well." Johnny Casserelie stepped forward and pushed Ike back. "So you came around. The show couldn't commence without you. It was rather clever, bringing the girl here to your apartment, wasn't it?" He leaned down and grasped Brown, one hand on his coat, the other on his tie. Brown gasped for breath as he was jerked to his feet.

There was another chair to the left; a lamp set far back from it. I could see the hesitancy in Casserelie's face. Then he spoke.

"Throw that big bum out of that chair." He held Brown steady with his left hand and jerked his right toward me. "We'll put the wise dick; the killer dick—the Crime Machine smack under the light." And as Ike half helped me, half dragged me, and mostly threw me from one chair into another, Casserelie said: "I want to see Brown's face. I want to see how he likes watching a woman die—and the boy friend die. I want him in a good light for the feast. Yeah, that was it. That's what Brown said." And as he hurled Brown into the big chair, "Feast, eh? A death feast!"

I can't describe my feelings just at mat minute. I don't think I felt fear; I don't know if it was exactly horror. Yet I knew—knew that all three of us were going to die. Die! And I saw the knife in Casserelie's hand; the knife I learned later he had taken from his dead guard. Die? Yes, die horribly. The knife—the sign of the Black Death.

And Brown sat there his hands behind his back; bound with his own cuffs; his feet tightly tied together. His face was very white and the trickle of blood had dried on his forehead. But his eyes were wide open, staring straight before him. If he saw anything, I don't know, but occasionally he would shake his head as if to clear it. Clear it! Clear it for what? So that he might the better watch the girl and me die?

Then Brown turned his head and looked at the girl. Slowly he turned it again and looked at me. The dazed glare went out of his eyes. He set them hard on me. Was his mind—was— And I knew the truth. Brown was trying to give me some message. What message?

I looked about the room. The windows were closed tight; there was no use to cry out. I knew that no sound could be heard outside that room; at least, outside our spacious bungalow apartment. What was the message? What—

And Johnny Casserelie was running a sharp edge of that two-edged knife along the end of his thumb and walking toward the girl.

He said over his shoulder to the man he called Ike: "Stand close to Brown and cheer him up. There's no chance of an interruption, but keep your gun in your hand. Under no circumstances hurt Brown yet. Yes, like—I know. He killed your brother. Your chance is coming later."

Ike walked across the room and sat down on the edge of Brown's chair. He talked rapidly, in a low voice. Part of it, only, I got. But it was about his brother.

"Watch her die, you dirty murderer," he said. "See how she takes it. Steel is mean, and it hurts. Then watch him die." He nodded toward me. "And as bad as it may seem, it'll be nothing compared to the way you'll go out. I'll throw water in your face to bring you to, to make you feel it again. To— Damn it! Keep your head up."

Brown had leaned sideways, his head upon the arm of the huge chair; or he had fallen there just as Johnny Casserelie leaned over the girl, grabbing her hair in his left hand.

Ike jerked up Brown's head as Casserelie looked over at Brown and grinned evilly. Then, as Casserelie pulled back the girl's head, exposing her slender head, exposing her slender throat, Brown's head dropped forward again.

"He can't take it," Casserelie sneered. "Yellow when the showdown comes. We'll see how the jane likes it." He paused a moment, the knife held out in his right hand. "Well, here's the vengeance of the Black Death."

CHAPTER SEVEN
DEATH FEAST

IT WAS to be a brutal and a terrible murder. I tried to close my eyes and couldn't. Then the hand moved. A minute; a second now, and that white throat would— would— The knife swept back, then down—and stopped suddenly, hardly an inch from the girl's head.

A shot. A single shot had burst through the silence of that room like the roar of a cannon. I looked at Ike. He was leaning far over behind Brown, as if to pull his head up again. And I looked at Brown. He was leaning forward, toppling out of the chair onto the floor.

Johnny Casserelie was looking too. I think the girl screamed once, but can not be sure. Anyway, her eyes were staring wildly at the slowly toppling form of Vee Brown.

Casserelie cursed and called out. "What did you do that for, you fool? You killed him and—and— Ike. Ike!" he shrieked wildly.

Brown had fallen off the chair. He was on his knees upon the floor, and Ike—Ike had dropped across that chair, stretched his huge body across it so that his chin rested upon the other arm. I didn't get it all at first, and then I did. I looked at Brown and understanding was forced upon me.

He was kneeling there on the floor. His whole body was bending; twisting at the waist, twisting from the knees, the handcuffs behind his back bending upward. Bending upward! And I saw the hands; the right hand was clutching a heavy automatic. Brown was turning so that the nose of that gun was pointing upward; slowly pointing toward Johnny Casserelie. And I knew that from the nose of that gun had come the slug that had buried itself some place in Ike's huge carcass.

For a moment I saw Brown's face. His lips were thin, grim and tightly set. No whimsical smile there now; perhaps a slight quivering twist at the end. But his eyes! Narrow slits of black hatred; deadly, malignant eyes. No Vivian, Master of Melody, now. Just Detective Vee Brown, Killer of Men. Yes, the will, the desire, perhaps even the lust to kill was in his eyes. Would he—could he do it?

Johnny Casserelie recognized the danger as soon as I did. He turned and faced Brown, drew back his right hand and hurled that knife.

I think Brown's head lowered for a split second, but if it did it was up again almost at once. And his body hadn't moved with his head. It remained motionless. Johnny Casserelie jumped forward, huge hands outstretched, reaching for Brown's throat; as if in a single throw of his body he'd pin Brown's frail form to the floor.

As Casserelie hurled himself forward I saw the knuckle of Brown's index finger turn white. I heard the crash of the gun and raised my eyes; raised them to see Johnny Casserelie. This was the moment. Was he hit? Would the bullet stop his mad rush?

Johnny Casserelie paused almost in mid-air, rocked a bit, then settled back on his heels. His face turned white, then red. His eyes blazed and his right hand shot to his left armpit as his body moved quickly away from that gun.

Brown's body twisted with the moving murderer; his knees turned too, as if he were on a revolving platform.

Casserelie fired. I could see the flame belch from his gun, and Brown still knelt there on the floor. Once, twice, three times Brown closed a finger on that trigger. Casserelie fired again too, I think. Wildly, blindly. There was fear in his eyes, in his quivering lips. Then he dropped his right hand to his side, his fingers opened and his gun crashed to the floor.

There wasn't fear any more in Casserelie's face; only a sort of hurt surprise. He tried twice to raise his hand, finally got it to his chest, jerked his other hand up quickly; then both hands clutched at his chest.

JOHNNY CASSERELIE had lived hard and he died hard. He went slowly to his knees still clutching at his chest. Then he fell forward on his face. He lay still a moment, then lifted his head, saw his gun and started for it, clawing at the carpet with the nails of his right hand.

And Brown! The expression on his face never changed. His knees moved and his body turned and his gun sought that crawling, cringing, now whining man. There was agony in every line of Johnny Casserelie's face. I didn't think he'd make it. I didn't think there was a possible chance. And he fell forward, reached the gun, raised it in his right hand. Turning slowly he drew a bead directly on Vee Brown.

It was all over then. Vee squeezed lead once more and shot him straight between the eyes. Johnny Casserelie dropped like a log; he didn't move again.

Powder filled the room, got into my nostrils. Through the haze of smoke and my own dulled vision I saw Brown swaying there on his knees. His head moved and he looked at the girl. She was very still upon the couch, her eyes closed. Then his head swung and he looked at me. For a long moment he stared, hard and cold and cruel. Then his eyes softened, his lips parted, and damn it, he winked over at me.

"That last shot," he said slowly, "was damn good shooting, Dean. No one could deny that."

"It was terrible, horrible, revolting," I said. "The man was half dead."

"It would have been revolting if I had missed; for me, for you, for the girl. We've got to get out of this mess." He swung on his knees and looked at Ike, spread there across the arms of the chair. His lips parted again. "Never trust a woman, Dean, even though our Maria turned out as straight as a die. It was not trusting her that made me put that gun there early this morning. Oh, you'll say I got a break, and I did; but it was the logical place to put me. Of course I never thought it would happen, but if it did I thought it would be Van Houton who'd watch my face beneath the light. The Black Death likes a knife, you know. I sneaked the gun up from behind the thick cushion. It wasn't more than six inches from Ike's stomach when I fired. It must have ripped him to pieces."

I never could understand Brown and I'm not claiming to understand him now. At times there was something terrible about him in the presence of death. It was there now.

He looked from one dead bodyguard on the floor to the other upon the chair.

"Ike and Mike!" he said with a grin. "They look alike now all right." And with an effort he struggled to his feet and stood there trying to keep his balance.

And the girl came to, came to with a scream; sat bolt upright on the edge of the couch.

"There, there!" Brown spoke to her. "You missed the most of it, and we need you now."

"I saw it all," she cried. "I saw it all. I thought— He didn't even hit you?"

"No, no—of course not." Brown's voice was very calm now. "Dean will tell you that they all turn yellow when the big moment comes. That's why I'm alive and the others are dead. Boys like Johnny Casserelie believe that it is better to give than to receive. He couldn't face the music, that was all."

I WON'T go into details of how the girl acted. She was the only one of us whose feet were not bound and she was the only one of us whose hands were bound in front. Brown directed her and she did find the knife stuck in the chair below the body of Ike, and she did manage to cross the room, and holding the knife between her hands, set me free. Then it was a simple matter for me to cut her loose.

Not so easy about Brown. I cut the ropes from his legs. But it was my job to go through the pockets of both Casserelie and Ike before I found the key to the cuffs in the vest pocket of the latter. But I did get it and did manage, despite my trembling fingers, to finally get it in the lock and snap open the cuffs that held Brown.

Things are a bit hazy after that. I know we had drinks all around in the music room, and I know that Brown served them and chatted and laughed and perhaps studied the girl, but I can't be sure. Then I heard Brown out in the living room at the phone. He came back in a minute.

"Just had Mortimer Doran on the wire." He grinned, then frowned. "I'm sorry it happened that way. I was a fool.

I should have had Van Houton. But Doran wanted the murderer of Tony Straus, so I told him to bring Ramsey along and have a look." And to the girl, as she pulled at his arm. "What's the matter?"

"What time is it?" she asked.

Brown smiled and looked at his watch. "Twenty minutes of nine," he said. "The evening's just beginning, and I've ordered supper for twelve o'clock. Surely you're not going."

"But I must—I must," she pleaded, when he stood before the door. "I must carry on, and Inspector Ramsey must not see me."

"I see." Brown placed both hands on her shoulders. "Yes, it's a big thing, Maria. You—we must carry on. And you've forgotten your part; forgot it for a bit tonight. Your face was—well, rather too good." And he started in to hum.

She jarred erect and drew back from him.

"I thought," she said, "I was going to die." And after looking directly into Brown's eyes a moment, "You and I, Vee Brown, both lead double lives. I like you, Vee. I like you lots. But—but I'm in love with Vivian." And she suddenly threw her arms about his neck and kissed him on the mouth.

Then she was gone, running quickly through the living room and across the hall beyond. We waited a moment. The door slammed.

I said, just for something to say: "She sure had her nerve with her."

"You think so?" Brown looked from one dead body to the other, then with that little twisted smile, "Do you know, Dean, I rather liked it."

THE DEATH MASK

"IT'S JUST A MATTER OF TIMING—
THIS KILLING JOB," BROWN
TOLD CONDON. "SO I'VE BOUGHT
MYSELF A NEW WATCH AND WILL
GO INTO TRAINING AS A BOXER
WOULD BEFORE A FIGHT." THE
ONLY DIFFERENCE WAS THAT
ALL THE CITY WAS THE BATTLE
RING. AND BROWN'S OPPONENT
A BLACK-MASKED MONSTER
WHO HAD ALREADY COLLECTED
HIS SHARE, OF THE GATE IN
ADVANCE—A HUNDRED, GRAND
FOR ONE SHOT THROUGH THE
BACK OF VEE'S HEAD!

CHAPTER ONE
MURDER FOR CASH

V **EE BROWN** was interesting when he talked about crime, music—and certainly, firearms. He had a small room in the rear of the apartment which I called the gunroom, though Brown always spoke of it as "the morgue."

"You see," he explained, "they're all trophies of the hunt; and most of them taken from the dead." He was sitting on the floor in the living room now with a heavy, long-barreled, ugly-looking automatic, the parts of which were scattered over a large square sheet of white paper; a tiny oil can balanced perilously as he cleaned each part carefully before replacing it.

"A German Luger." He nodded his head. "And oddly enough, taken from the body of a half-breed just over the Mexican border. A deadly weapon. An accurate weapon." He raised it and looked along the barrel. "You mustn't confuse it with the cheap, rebuilt army Lugers or the inferior models that were rushed into the country shortly after the war. A little cumbersome for my work but great stuff in case of a siege in a lonely shack on a Mexican desert. There's a story there, Dean." He shook his head. "At the time I was very young and my life was despaired of."

"Here's a story now!" I cut in. "What about this Vincent Van Houton? You haven't forgotten him, Vee?"

Vee's lips parted in that crooked smile.

"No," he said, "I haven't. And he hasn't forgotten me; and I'm going to see that he doesn't." He paused a minute, looking toward the ceiling humming softly; the tune of the new piece he was working on. "Unless we can make him forget

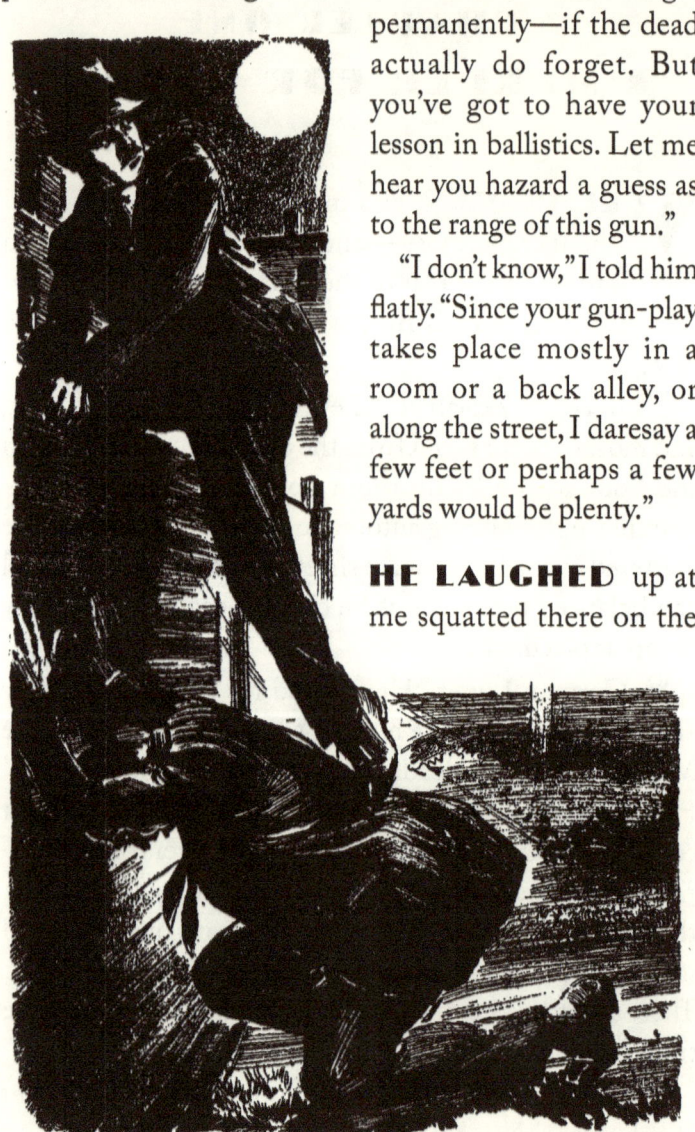

permanently—if the dead actually do forget. But you've got to have your lesson in ballistics. Let me hear you hazard a guess as to the range of this gun."

"I don't know," I told him flatly. "Since your gun-play takes place mostly in a room or a back alley, or along the street, I daresay a few feet or perhaps a few yards would be plenty."

HE LAUGHED up at me squatted there on the

floor, his legs folded under him, his figure boyish—even delicate. But this lack of strength—that is, physical strength—was taboo with Brown. It was one of his very sensitive subjects.

Without losing stride, I landed on that rising back.

"It's surprising, almost unbelievable; but the range of this gun is slightly over a mile. Think of it. Twenty city blocks! An indispensable sort of a weapon for the man who can handle it. But what a curse to the untrained officer of the law; the criminal who desperately uses it in an attempted escape! Stray bullets with twenty city blocks in which to deal death to helpless, defenseless women and children. The law's a joke. The State forbids firearms, and they come to you by the United States mail. Oh, we'll have it in time. A federal law that—"

Brown stopped. The lock in the hall door had clicked audibly. He smiled too as he twirled the now cleaned gun and jerked a cartridge home.

"It would be funny," he said, "if we were attacked while I sat here on the floor with such a weapon facing the foyer. But, no. Only one person has a key."

"The girl, Maria. After Casserelie so nearly killed you— you still let her carry a key!"

"Certainly. Johnny Casserelie was the only one who knew she brought me information about the Black Death—Vincent Van Houton. He was the only one who knew her real identity, and he's dead. The girl, Maria—" And as feet beat quickly across the hall, "Something stirring, Dean. She's—"

Brown lowered the gun. Maria stood in the dim light of the hall, by the parted curtains that led to the living room. Small? Yes. No taller than Brown, even. Sometimes I thought that was why he liked her; he was so conscious of his own small stature. Her face was set; hard, cruel; a curve to her lips, a narrowness to her eyes so that the green of them were just two slits of brightness. I looked at her then and couldn't see what Brown saw; what Wong, our Chinese servant, saw back of the hardness of her face—as if, inside, she was good.

She nodded first at me, then at Brown; jerked her little hat tighter down over her left eye and walked straight to the big chair beneath the light. She snapped out the light and sat down. There was nothing in her face or her attitude to make me remember, but I did remember that when last she left us she had flung her arms around Brown in parting.

BROWN PEERED at her long and earnestly though her face was in the shadows. She spoke quickly, as if she had been running.

"Don't watch me like that," she said. "I can read Dean like a book. I can read most men. But you bother me. I don't know what you're thinking; at least I hope I don't—Vivian."

And the smile that had been on Vee's face faded, then returned again almost at once. Beside myself, and even including his publisher, no one except this girl knew that Detective Vee Brown, assigned to the district attorney's office, and Vivian, the season's greatest success in popular song hits, were one and the same man.

"I was thinking," Brown said very slowly, "that you are very beautiful, Maria." And when green eyes widened, "I mean, inside. So different—so—"

"Aren't we all?" Slim shoulders moved in the vastness of the chair. "We all carry a veneer; a—"

Brown smiled. "A polish, certainly; which differentiates our actions with friends, acquaintances and enemies. But not necessarily cold cream, grease paint, theatrical—"

"Please!" she cut in quickly. "I'm here on business, terrible business. The life of a woman."

"Vincent Van Houton? Blackmail?"

"Vincent Van Houton, yes." She looked questioningly toward the door to the music room, and when Brown assured her we were quite alone, "Worse than blackmail. Of course it starts with that; finishes with that, too, unless a very fine woman risks her own happiness, her husband's career, her baby's—" She laughed shrilly, and then, "I never was a sentimentalist and mustn't kid myself that I'm doing the big squeal for anything but hate." And she broke into that coarse voice again, that was bred of the underworld; as Brown called it, "of the night."

"And I can be of use to this 'fine woman?'" Brown asked.

She shrugged her shoulders. "I don't know that you can pin it smack on Van Houton, though I think he's working it himself. You've upended his props, have destroyed all but his biggest assistant." She seemed to think a moment. "No, I can't lay a finger on that assistant yet. It's too unbelievable."

"Maybe not. I'm a sucker for unbelievable things. At least, the district attorney and Inspector Ramsey think I am. Neither one of them believes for an instant that Van Houton is behind this Black Death; murder, suicide, that follows the—his blackmail. So why not let me have it?"

She shook her head; full red lips parted. "Not yet," she said. "It's really too fantastic. But I've got enough for you. This master blackmailer, Vincent Van Houton; Emperor of Evil," and she fairly sneered out the words, "has missed the assistants you have eliminated—especially Johnny Casserelie. So he has decided to seek to enlarge his present organization; greatly enlarge it. He has decided to use George T. Moffet, political leader."

I SMILED as Brown did, for I knew as well as Vee knew that George T. Moffet was through. The district attorney had tipped Brown the information. His brightest, his best, his straightest man, Assistant District Attorney Edward Bainton, was handling that matter and the skids were under Mr. George T. Moffet; skids that would finally drop him for a twenty-year jolt. The conviction was in the bag.

"Use Moffet!" Vee's black eyes widened. "Why, don't you know? Of course it hasn't been in the papers, but an indictment is certain; a conviction sure to follow. This young Bainton dug all the evidence up himself; I understand, in fact I know it's complete."

"Yes," the girl said in a tired voice, "I know all about that. But, you see, the Black Death has promised Moffet that that evidence will not be produced—if Moffet is a 'reasonable man.'"

"The Black Death; Van Houton will—can destroy that evidence!"

"No, he won't destroy it. He may say he will, but it'll be the whip he'll hold over Moffet's head. Just more blackmail. And, Moffet! What an ally, with all his political powers, his great influence back again; and his feelings toward those who tried to get him."

"But—" I stammered, and Brown looked over and shook his head.

The girl smiled. It was a sad, tired sort of smile that made her face almost gentle. "Dean's right." She bobbed her head up and down in the shadows. "I can't help going in for drama. My life is drama. Like the stage, except perhaps that there can't be a happy ending." And quickly, "But I didn't come here to squawk. Van Houton is in a fair way; more than a fair way of getting all this evidence against Moffet that this Assistant District Attorney Edward Bainton has collected in the last two years, since his marriage."

Brown shook his head. "Bainton's honest. He can't be bought; certainly he can't be intimidated, and even if the skeleton rattles some place back in his family closet, he's the kind who'll sink with the ship and not bend even to a blackmail that means disaster."

"You misunderstand the significance of my last words," the girl said slowly. "I said, 'since his marriage.'"

"The wife!" Brown came to his feet and started toward the girl, stopped and dropped into a chair. "It's to come through her, eh?"

"Exactly. You see, the evidence is kept in a safe-deposit box in her name. Nothing strange in that; she helped in collecting it. Indeed, I believe she directed the collecting of it."

"But how—" Brown was puzzled. "Her husband—"

"Her husband believed it was her nose for crime; her instinct; a natural ability to understand things he brought to her and to explain them. At least, something like that. But certainly he never believed, nor those working through him, that hers was knowledge; the knowledge of long experience. That's right!" She nodded her head even before Brown could get out the question on his lips. "Like me, she was of the night."

"Bainton—her husband knows that?"

"Part of it." The girl shrugged. "He knows that she rose above her environment. But his family doesn't; his—" her lips parted—"do you call them his constituents? Well, they don't know it. And her husband doesn't know that, if a certain letter found its way to the police, his wife would do a jolt in the big house. Which all has its moral." She grinned, and this time her face was not beautiful. "The moral is—that crime catches up on you, even if you are living straight."

"What sort of a letter did she write, and who has it?"

"She gay-catted a job a few years back; took a position as maid in a house. Then she made an outline of that house, put it on paper together with a letter of explanation and mailed it to a certain party. Van Houton has that letter."

"And how bad was the robbery; how influential the people?"

"What difference does it make? Her home, her child, her husband's career, her happiness; her whole house of cards goes tumbling as soon as that letter is produced. So, even if she beat the rap, which she couldn't, for a man was shot to death that night, what good would it do her?"

"I see," said Brown. "You want me to talk to her." His lips curved at the ends. "Convince her that the citizens come first; before herself, her child, her husband. Convince a woman of the underworld, who has risen above her environment."

GREEN EYES looked steadily at him. "I wonder," she said, "if the absence of a heart is just a pose with you. I have given you her name, I have told you the circumstances. You can go and see her."

"And threaten her into handing that evidence over to me." And suddenly, "It will be a jolt to the administration; the people; Mortimer Doran, the D.A. himself, if Moffet doesn't take the ride. Just what do you expect me to do?"

"That," she said, "is up to you. But I expect you to strike at Van Houton and protect this woman."

Brown came to his feet, looking down at her. She curled far back in the chair and although she was in a very dull light pulled her little hat, or tried to pull it, down even further over her face.

"You're a great little partner," he said, "and it's not all built of hate for Van Houton." He paused, and with that whimsical smile, "And you—the grip Van Houton must have on you! When can I strike for you?"

She hesitated a long moment. "What he holds over me is not written on paper, it's stamped in his head. It can't be destroyed or burned. It's brains; his brains."

Vee Brown looked down at the long ugly gun still clutched in his hand. "Brains have been burned before; been destroyed before," he said, only half aloud.

She shook her head. "He never carries a gun, has no weapon in his house. Your methods of extermination would be useless against him."

"Why?" Brown was still smiling.

"It would be murder," she said simply.

Brown's thin lips became a single narrow gash. "Murdered men are just as dead, and have been known to remain just as silent, as those who shoot back. But the woman; this Mrs. Bainton. We'll see her now."

"You. Not me." She shook her head. "I have arranged for her to see you at ten o'clock tonight. Her husband's out attending a dinner."

"I see." Brown grinned boyishly. "If a man answers, hang up." And suddenly, "Don't move. Sit so." He stood looking down at her. "For the moment you had it. Hard, sinister, cruel. A determination that was swept away almost the moment it came. A determination to—" He stopped again, and then, "You thought of killing Van Houton; you've often thought of it." And putting a hand upon her shoulder, "Don't, Maria; don't entertain such thoughts. They are dangerous. Still, you couldn't do it. You lack the—"

She flashed to her feet. Green eyes blazed; lips parted. She said—and if she were acting before; if her heavy make-

up was to hide her real identity, she was not acting now—
"Guts! Guts is the word." She flung open her bag and held
it tilted. Plainly the pearl handle of a revolver showed; a
small weapon. "I have thought of it, often thought of it;
gripped this firmly when he has used the phone; used it to
send some unfortunate victim to death. I—"

Brown's black eyes blazed too. Not with hatred; not with
the lust to kill, but with that sparkle of creative genius he
so often displayed.

"Don't move. So!" He began to hum softly. Low; a weird
sort of chant. Then his hand tightened upon her wrist and
he half led her, half dragged her to the music room. "I've
been stumped on it. The inspiration wouldn't come, and
now— Listen!"

The girl didn't speak. I saw her draw back slightly from
the piano as Brown almost jumped onto the stool. Then
the notes; the soft notes that grew louder; his voice above
the music.

"The song's for you, Maria. *Girl of the Night!* I—"

The phone rang. I lifted the receiver. Then with my hand
over the mouthpiece I called to Brown.

Maybe my voice was hoarse, even strained. But I said:
"Vincent Van Houton is on the wire."

CHAPTER TWO
A LIVING DEAD MAN

THINK the girl had started to sing but I cannot be
sure. If she had, her voice died. Brown swung from the
stool and stood in the doorway. The girl said, and her voice
was a whisper: "He—Van Houten—he—he can't know
about me—being here."

"Of course he can't." Vee was emphatic. "If he did he would not telephone me like this. If— You acted as if you were running, hurrying, when you came in. You think you were followed?"

"No." She shook her head. And then more thoughtfully, "Not by Van Houton anyway. But there was a man across the street; he disappeared in a doorway. I'm not sure, but I think it was Inspector Ramsey." And after a moment, "I think everyone who follows me now is Ramsey."

"Sure." Brown nodded. "He watched me for a bit, until I complained to Mortimer Doran, the district attorney, that it interfered with my work. Ramsey is jealous and suspects that I get information which he doesn't get, and he'd like to know who gives it to me. He didn't know you, of course."

"Hardly." She jerked a thumb toward the phone. "Better see what Van Houton wants."

And Brown did. The conversation was hard to follow. Brown's words were cryptic. "How interesting" and "Really, I appreciate your efforts." A moment of hesitation, and then, "Very well, I'll come right over. With Dean Condon, of course."

"He wants," Brown explained when he hung up the receiver, "me to come over and visit him."

"You're not going!" the girl said, clutching at his arm. "Don't you see, Vee? Don't go. He's planning your death. I know, Vee." And when Brown only smiled and jiggled her shoulder, "He's sure this time. If you could see his smile you'd understand."

"He takes you greatly into his confidence."

"Yes," she nodded, "he does. Once, terribly so—and his eyes were so peculiar at the time. I think he killed once, Vee. And I think he would kill again if I— Don't go!"

"Mortimer Doran knows my suspicions of Van Houton; Inspector Ramsey knows my suspicions. And Van Houton knows that I have confided in them; no bones have been made about that. Now—the safest place in the world for me is at Van Houton's house. Nothing could happen to me there. It is quite possible that he may speak out of turn." And his eyes narrowing, "You think he killed once? You think—God! Maria, if we could only pin something on him; murder on him. If you could prove that! If—"

"The moment I can prove that I'll let you know." She set her lips very tightly. "I know it will end me; finish me, but I'm willing."

"You are very, very close to him?" Brown looked at her sharply, and she moved from the light.

"Yes," she said. "Very, very close. He—he likes me in my peculiar way."

"I thought," Brown was not looking at her now—"it was Gertrude la Palatin, the actress. That's the rumor around. That she's—the one."

"Yes," she said, "that's the rumor. You may wonder what he can see in me"—her face had gone very white in the shadows—"but he likes cats; almost worships them. He struck me once, for, despite his languid attitude he's very strong, very alert, very— But he likes cats; they have very beautiful, soft bodies."

SHE WAS walking toward the door now and I watched her, recalling the first time I had seen her and her soft catlike tread that had impressed me then.

She stopped. The door bell rang—the bell of our private entrance. That meant that someone had slipped above in one of the automatic lifts, or that we were having a visit from Mortimer Doran. No one was permitted above who was not first announced; that is, no one who inquired at the desk below. But the apartment itself was too big to prevent visitors entirely though the attendants tried very hard and succeeded in most cases. The girl, Maria, of course, was always admitted—day or night.

"Mortimer Doran." Brown nodded. And at the girl's alarm, "Hop into the music room until he's gone."

Maria, safely in the music room, the door closed behind her, Brown walked to the hall, and heavy feet followed him back into the room.

Mortimer Doran's huge bulk led the procession. Behind him, just as tall and just as huge, but with a muscular strength the district attorney's flabby body lacked, was Inspector Ramsey; and behind him came a stranger.

"Well," Brown pointed to chairs as he addressed Mortimer Doran, "something important, to bring you and the old sleuth along!" He grinned at Ramsey, who scowled in return.

Mortimer Doran did not smile as he introduced the stocky, shock-haired stranger.

"Detective Tom Haskin, from Chicago. Got an eye for faces."

"He won't have much trouble in remembering Ramsey's," Vee said as he shook hands with the grinning detective from Chicago.

"I don't think," Ramsey dropped easily into a chair and put his eyes straight on Brown, "that he'll have much trouble remembering your face either after you find out what brought us here."

"Really!" said Brown. "Well, put on your show."

It was Mortimer Doran who spoke, and his fat, many-chinned face was very somber.

"The matter is very serious; extremely serious Brown. You've heard about 'Spot' Kelly, the unknown killer from Chicago."

"Sure. Sure!" Brown nodded, and as if thinking aloud. "That is, in a way."

"In a way!" said Detective Haskin. "God! man, he's Chicago's greatest menace; maybe the nation's greatest menace. He's put on a new show; a new racket, and as far as we can make out, works it alone. He's made the crime of murder a business. For a certain sum; an amount according to the importance of the victim, he'll undertake to murder anyone." And after an emphatic pause, "To date, he hasn't failed once."

"Ah!" said Brown, "you can't be sure of that You can only know of his successes—not his failures."

"There are no failures. He marks his victims before they die. Lets it be known in criminal circles just who is to die. Of course we of the police have our secret channels for such information. You see, men dying so shortly after he marks them for death helps him to receive future clients. Once he puts up a man's number that man is as good as dead."

"I see." Brown nodded. "And how do people pay for such murders?"

"That, we don't know. But that they pay, and cash on the line in advance, we do know. Who collects for him is something we have never figured out. Most of his victims have been underworld characters, but lately he has gone into— more legitimate business. Less than a month ago Lieutenant Duff, of the police, was murdered by him; shot right through the back of the head."

"Well, well—how distressing!" Brown was facetious and clearly showed it. "And now you're here from Chicago to ask me to come out and hunt him down."

THE GOOD-NATURED detective scowled for the first time. If he resented Brown's attitude, I think he had good cause to. I had heard of this man, "On-the-spot Kelly," and knew that he was anything but a joke to the Chicago police. Detective Haskin set his lips tightly when he spoke.

"No," he said. "I've come here to warn you." And rather dramatically, "Pack your bags, Mr. Vee Brown, and get a hide-away. Your number's up. You're listed as Spot Kelly's next victim." And when Brown still smiled at him, "Don't you understand? Someone has paid cash for your death."

"Hell!" said Brown, "someone has been paying cash for my death most of my life." And the annoyed expression leaving his face, "Not that I don't appreciate your—"

"You mean," the detective pushed to the edge of his chair, "you won't hide out and—"

"No!" Brown snapped. And the fire that started into his eyes and the curl to his lips suddenly vanishing, "I suppose it's that fish-face there," he jerked a thumb at Ramsey, "who put such an idea into your head. But let me tell you this, copper—copper from Chicago, and without meaning any offense; when the cops in New York jump, they jump forward and not backward."

"So you mean—"

"I mean that, after all, I'm just a New York cop."

"But, Brown," Mortimer Doran's voice was soft and wheedling, "for the moment, until we can locate this killer. There—there's no disgrace in being careful. Every one of Spot Kelly's victims has been found dead, with a bullet right through the back of his head."

"Yeah?" said Vee. "When they pick up Kelly they'll find my bullet in the front of his head."

And to Haskin, from Chicago, "Now—why are you here? Surely not just to tell me to skip town!"

"Well—no, Mr. Brown. We've heard of you out our way and we felt you'd stick. I've come to offer my services." And with a grin when Brown would have cut in, "Oh, not in the way of shooting, though I can do a bit of that—but in way of identification. You have my chief's letter." And when Doran nodded, "I'm the only man in the world who has ever seen Spot Kelly's face."

"Only living man," said Vee.

Detective Haskin shook his head. "Living or dead. His murders are all dramatic; that helps his business. There are generally several witnesses, so he always wears a mask. The papers have called him 'The Masked Death.' Now—have you any enemy? Oh, I know there are hundreds who would be glad to see you knocked over, but I mean—any particular one, with the jack for such a deal. Spot Kelly charges big rates." He looked at the ceiling. "I wouldn't be surprised if a man like you would rate a hundred grand; at least, that's the rumor."

"You flatter me," said Vee. "And I have such an enemy, with just as appropriate a name as your Masked Death, and with just the same yen for advertising his business. We call him, here, the Black Death. Vincent Van Houton. He gives out little cards and—"

"Bosh!" Inspector Ramsey cut in. "That's one of Brown's pet delusions. You know, Mr. Doran, I've had Van Houton shadowed and have watched him personally for weeks. Why—damn it!—he's even trying to run down this Black Death himself. Naturally being along with the social set; the wealthy set, he has had friends who—"

"The Black Death. Cards, eh?" The detective from Chicago was stroking his chin as he cut in. "Well, this

Masked Death, on big occasions, sends out letters. You see, it's mostly in murders of vengeance, to let the victim know directly; make him suffer a hundred deaths before the actual one. Fiendish in its way. The victim knows Kelly has never failed; knows that any moment death may strike; knows—" He shook his head. "If such an enemy wanted you dead there should have been a letter, or—"

"And there was—I think there was." Brown nodded vigorously and going directly to the waste basket started to paw through it. "Did it come yesterday or today?" He seemed to think aloud. "Wong emptied the basket only— Ah!" He straightened "the very thing. I remember now. There was a threat in it."

I TOOK the letter and read it to the others before I passed it around. A warning of death, a threat of death, a promise of death. In its way, perhaps, it was not as dramatic as the cards the Black Death sent his victims or left on their bodies. Certainly not as melodramatic, if there is such a thing as melodrama in today's criminal reign. For, as Brown says, 'Melodrama has simply become drama and drama has simply become life.' But the message was perhaps more deadly, certainly more business-like than those sent by the Black Death.

> Dear Mr. Brown:—
> Your number's up. Straighten out your affairs.
> > Very truly yours,
> > > Spot Kelly.

"No monkey business about that," said Haskin with a certain pride it seemed. As if Chicago should be credited for breeding such a criminal. "You don't have men like that in New York. You don't know what it is to meet such—" He coughed behind his hand and broke off. "My apologies, gentlemen! But you can see from that document that the Windy City is unjustly accused of laxity. There's nothing missing from that letter."

"Only the return address." Brown smiled crookedly. "Now—just what do you want to do about it; you and the Chicago police?"

"I'll be honest with you." The good-natured smile left Haskin's face. "The D.A., here, or Ramsey, spoke to the chief on long distance. I know this killer and he doesn't know me. That was a break I had. If you will get out of town, when I say—get out. If you won't, let me hang around with you; sort of follow you. Now"—he shook his head— "this lad shoots them through the back of the head. He's no Robin Hood. It's just business—the business of producing a corpse at a certain price. I see no hope; not one chance in a hundred of saving your life. But I do see a chance of getting Spot Kelly for your murder."

"We could give you a police guard—night and day," Ramsey started, and stopped when Brown turned on him.

Then to the D.A. Brown said, "My God! What has come over all you people? A hood from Chicago walks into town and you all go ga-ga. After all, if there is to be a corpse— I'm that corpse. Why worry?"

"Many men," said Mortimer Doran, "have received many such letters and every one of them is dead. How many more died by this man's hand it is impossible to tell. This Spot Kelly has no criminal record. Twice his fingerprints have been found, but there are no corresponding prints anywhere in the country. You know well, Brown, that when an unknown takes up a life of crime, of murder, and has no former acquaintance or dealings with, or even knowledge of the man he intends to kill, it is impossible to get him—unless you get him right in the act."

"Then that's settled," Brown said. "I'll shoot him to death for you—right in the act, and since Chicago is a little short of funds at present, I'll receive as a reward the key to the city."

"And the gratitude of every cop on the force," said Haskin.

"Sure!" Vee grinned, and suddenly growing serious, "And Dean, here, is— Maybe he'd better take a trip."

I started to cut in when Haskin said: "Your friend is in no danger." His lips parted and his white teeth showed; his colorless eyes even flashed. "This Spot Kelly is a business man." He pointed a finger at Brown. "He's been paid only to get you."

"And you think he will, eh?"

The man shook his head. "I know he will."

MORTIMER DORAN laid a hand on Vee's shoulder. "God! Vee," he said, "take care of yourself. You're such a fool for courage. This man knows the murderer, has actually seen him. Better listen to him."

"Certainly." Brown glanced at the clock. "And now—I'm sorry, Mr. Doran, but I've got some important business, very important business." And to the dick from Chicago, "If you'll tell me the hotel you're stopping at I'll get in touch with you. You're a cop and know how things are. Can't let these little side issues interfere with duty."

"Side issues!" The man's eyes opened wide, and as Brown led the way to the hall, "If I hadn't heard about you, Vee Brown, I'd think you were a—"

And Brown laughed. The others didn't understand, but I did. Brown's pride was almost a fetish with him. "Don't you worry about me. If the letter really means business I'll pop this lad over for you."

"He's bad," said Doran, at the door.

"No, not bad," Brown shook his head. "Just rotten. We'll go along down with you."

Halfway to the elevator Vee turned. "See them below, Dean. I'll join you at the door. Telephone call." And to Haskin, "Don't forget to give Dean your phone number. We'll want you to identify the body."

I tried to carry on a light conversation as the three men remained silent in the elevator. In the hall below I button-holed Mortimer Doran. Their silence, their seriousness! Even the sneering derision was gone from Ramsey's face. It got me.

"Vee always has been able to take care of himself," I told Mortimer Doran. "Now—why this sudden alarm?"

The district attorney shook his head. "I don't know. I don't know. When I was last in Chicago I talked with their chief of police about this very man. And now—God! Dean, how can anyone protect himself from such— Why, if Brown only knew the man or—"

When he broke off I turned to Detective Tom Haskin. "If you knew Brown you wouldn't be so worried and—"

"And you're not worried!" Colorless eyes glared at me. "Listen, buddy. Your pal's number is up, just as that letter said. Look up Tom Haskin, in Chicago. See if there's anyone, even his worst enemy, who'll say he's yellow—has even the thinnest stripe of yellow. Yet—" He picked his teeth with a match. "Oh, hell! can't you see it? A sure killer. On the street, in the theatre, at dinner, in a speak, entering or leaving a building! Just a single shot from a stranger, through the head. I don't know what I'd do. Your friend has guts, but that's the best I can say for him. Many fools— dead fools had guts."

"But if this killer comes out in the open he should be easy to catch."

"Sure! That's what you think. That's what we thought. But you don't know how people act when a man is shot to death; murdered before their eyes. Besides"—his shoulders moved—"if he were caught; if I caught him, what good will that do Brown if he is dead?"

"He's always been able to handle these—"

"Sure. Sure!" The strong fingers of Tom Haskin tightened on my shoulder. "And I hope he will this time. Give me a buzz—or I'll give you one later. If Brown's going anywhere that looks to you as if it might be a trap, and that conceit of his drives him into it, ring me up. I might help out." And his head going up, "I don't mind telling you it would make me rate a sergeant out in Chi if I go this Spot Kelly."

"It's not so much the saving of Brown's life then?"

"Hell!" said Haskin. "You don't know this Spot Kelly." His hand left my shoulder and a particularly hard finger pounded against my chest as Ramsey called to him from the D.A.'s car at the curb. "You're walking around with a dead man, Mr. Condon. A living dead man. Night!" And he dashed across the sidewalk and climbed into the car.

CHAPTER THREE
BLACK WARNING

IT WAS nearly fifteen minutes later that Brown and I were speeding in a taxi to Vincent Van Houton's. Brown was talking.

"The girl will stay above," he told me, "until we come back. She likes the new piece, Dean." And he frowned slightly. "I'm glad of that. For the moment I thought that she wouldn't. Not that it isn't good. In its way, I think it's the best thing I've ever done. But women are funny—"

"God! Vee!" I couldn't keep quiet. "What about this killer from Chicago?"

"Well—" Black eyes regarded me coldly—"what about him?"

"Why—" I guess I stammered at first; then I came out with it. "You can talk about music—a song, when the deadliest killer in the country has threatened you with death!"

"Hell," said Vee, "we've buried a few in our day! And perhaps I'll live to dance on Spot Kelly's grave, too." And when, I guess, I shuddered visibly, "Snap out of it, Dean. We're not children, to be frightened by this bogie man of death. Why, nine tenths of his asset is the fear he inspires."

"But Mortimer Doran said—"

"And that's it!" Brown fairly snapped his words now. "The psychology of the thing. I don't mind the dick from Chicago. He doesn't know me. I don't mind Ramsey—he hates my guts. But I do mind Doran and I do mind you. My friends! Doran knows me. You have seen me in every conceivable danger; you've seen how I handle my guns and— Damn it, if I didn't have any more pride in myself; trust in myself than my two best friends have in me I'd be dead long ago!"

"It isn't that," I tried to tell him. "But what are you going to do?"

"Do!" he said. "Do what I always do. Shoot this Spot Kelly to death, of course. He's invaded New York now, and it's my duty. It's what I'm paid for."

"But how?… Vee, you haven't the proper respect for this man."

"But I have." He nodded. "And, like any fighter going into the ring, I'll go into training for Mr. Spot Kelly." And looking suddenly at me as my eyes knitted, "And for God's sake, Dean, don't try to help me out. Don't get meddling in things like this."

I GUESS I stiffened. "Meddling!" And when Brown squeezed my arm and laughed, "I suppose you consider this detective from Chicago a meddler."

"He'd like to cash in on my death, and I don't blame him for that. But we'll leave him out of it. It's my job, my honor. And, by God, I don't think Van Houton can well afford the loss of a hundred grand at this time!"

"You think he—"

"I'm sure of it." Brown straightened against the rear seat. "A hundred grand! I don't know but I'm flattered. But here's Van Houton's now and—" He jerked out a gun and thrust it into my hand, reached for his other, then took the gun back from me and jammed it into his shoulder holster again. "I'm a fool, Dean," he said quickly. "A sentimental fool."

"But I don't need the gun. I'm armed," I told him. "Besides you said nothing could possibly happen to us at Van Houton's."

"It isn't what could happen to us"—I had never heard his voice quite so serious—"it's what might happen to Van Houton. I didn't tell you, Dean; but another woman committed suicide this afternoon. You see, Van Houton could have spared her but he didn't."

"What's that got to do with giving me your gun?" I was slightly bewildered as we climbed from the taxi.

"Nothing. Only that there are times when I'm afraid of Van Houton, afraid that I may just raise my gun and shoot him to death. A weakness? Certainly. But even that would not explain my bullet in his forehead. Don't you see, Dean? If I thought as you think; Doran thinks; Haskin thinks"—and with a twisted grin—"Ramsey hopes-why, I'd pop off Van Houton just as a friendly gesture; a final gesture."

There was no chance to say more. The taxi pulled to the curb. And I could just look my disapproval of Brown for his loose talk as he pushed the button of Van Houton's residence.

The butler who opened the door was the same as on our first visit some time back. He was just as stiff, just as formal, and just as polite.

"Certainly. To be sure, gentlemen. Mr. Van Houton is expecting you, but I think a bit earlier. However, he'll be down directly. This way, please."

He led us into a dimly lighted room; pushed a button, flooding it in a bright glare, and stiffened slightly. Three of the big, comfortable chairs were occupied by fluffy balls of fur. One of the cats raised its head and stared at us unblinkingly.

The butler drew back. "I'll take you to the library," he announced in what seemed hurt pride. "Mr. Van Houton, sir, won't have the—the animals disturbed."

"You'd like to hoist one of them, eh?" Brown put that boyish smile on the butler when we were in the library. "I mean—put a toe to them."

For a moment the butler's face cracked, his lips parted, his tongue protruded slightly and moistened his upper lip. If it was a smile it was gone almost at once. He turned toward the door; then I guess he just had to say something. His words were not very heavy but his tone was expressive.

"It would be worth my position, sir," was all he said, but what he left unsaid was—that his position might be worth it.

Five minutes, and Van Houton did not come. Brown walked about the room. Cats! Pictures of cats, photographs, paintings, books on cats. And by the fireplace, close to a steel screen where logs burned despite the heat of the room, a round ball of silver—a huge living cat.

TEN MINUTES, and Brown consulted his watch. "Ten o'clock," he said. "Really, Dean"—he spotted the bell on the wall and pressed it— "Van Houton is quite a man. His servants, now. I spent weeks tracing every one of them. Not the sort of servants you'd think such a man would hire. Every one of them with an enviable reputation of long service in the best families. Clever villain, this cat-man. Doesn't let the breath of suspicion enter his home."

"But I should think he'd need bodyguards if he mixes with racketeers and—"

"None of them know him except a very chosen few, and now even a smaller group since I had the pleasure of shooting a few to death." And to the butler who entered the room, "Well, where's Van Houton? Did you tell him we were here?"

"Yes, sir. I did, sir." He looked about the room. "He hasn't been here—isn't here?"

"Hasn't and isn't." Brown's eyes narrowed. "What did he say?"

"Why, he didn't say anything. At least I don't think he did. He— I tapped on his door, sir. The study, upstairs, and announced your arrival. I'll go up again, sir."

It was close to five minutes later that the butler, slightly red of face, informed us that Van Houton must have gone out.

"I can't understand it, and—"

But we were out the door, into the waiting taxi and speeding to the address of the assistant district attorney, Edward Bainton.

"This Spot Kelly—"I started, and stopped.

"God in heaven, Dean,"Brown cut in, "are you still harping on that? I'm just a cog in a big police machine and am paid to face death, paid to protect others from death. Now this woman—the one in whose hands lies the destiny of the city's leading political crook! Don't you see? Van Houton has known for some time that there has been a leak to me. But he can't place it. He can't even be sure it isn't luck or downright cleverness on my part. Tonight! Well, perhaps he wanted to be certain where we were for a certain length of time. Why?"

"You think he had her murdered?"

"Without obtaining that evidence? Ridiculous."

And for once Brown made a mistake, if it was a mistake. He seldom, on such delicate business, drove directly to a house. And this time was no exception. We left the taxi around the corner and walked down the block. Walked down it as a man descended the steps of the very house we sought. As the chauffeur of the big car at the curb held open the door the tall figure turned and looked back along the walk toward us, his face almost directly beneath the light.

"Van Houton!"The words choked in my throat. "Vincent Van Houton."

I almost started to run forward but Brown clutched me by the arm.

"If he wanted to get away we'd be too late," he said. "And if he didn't we'd make fools of ourselves. But he is in a hurry."

The door closed. The chauffeur climbed behind the wheel and the big high-powered black car pulled from the curb.

Brown sighed. "His visit will make it that much harder for us, Dean. We'll have to threaten the woman, of course. We have nearly as much information about Mrs. Bainton as Van Houton, without, of course, the evidence. But he'll have made it harder for us, be assured of that."

THE WOMAN who opened the door was slender and dark, and not as tall as she seemed to appear; that is, measured by my height, which is a good six feet. And she wasn't the type who would appear an easy victim of blackmail. She met us with a straightforward look, an upward shoot of her head, and gray steady eyes that were certainly capable of a direct stare.

"Mr. Brown and Mr. Condon, of course." She closed the door and led us into a side room. "I'm playing servant and—" She shrugged her shoulders, turned and faced us in the better light. "You're rather late, Mr. Brown."

"We were unavoidably delayed," Vee told her. And when she just stared at him, "I'm sorry, very sorry."

"Yes." She nodded then. "You would be; you will be. As for myself, I don't know."

"You don't know?" Brown said, and though there was a question in his voice she did not explain her meaning then. "That was Mr. Van Houton who just left your house. He advises you, I suppose, that to listen to me would be most disastrous to you—tragic to you."

"That was Mr. Van Houton." She repeated his words but not in the monotone of a distracted and confused woman. Her voice was very clear. "And, as you say, he advised me that to listen to you would be both disastrous and tragic. But those were not his exact words."

"I hope, for your sake, that he has not made things harder for me—for the people I represent. I am here to help you, Mrs. Bainton."

"Yes." She nodded. "Just how?"

And for once Brown was stumped. Here was no cringing, frightened, lying woman, looking for a loophole of escape.

"Help you to remember that there are over six million people counting on your husband," Brown said. "That perhaps their fate hangs on your decision to be an honest woman."

Her lips curled slightly at the ends. "Go on," she said.

"You're not a fool, Mrs. Bainton." Brown fairly threw the words at her now. "Moffet is a crook, the most dangerous kind of a criminal—a politician. Grafting, rotten politicians have done more to take the bread out of the mouths of little children than any other single thing. You know that. Blackmail is ruin to a few, perhaps even death to a few. But you are playing with the millions and—"

"What did the millions ever do for me?" Gray eyes were steel now. "I— I—" She stopped suddenly. "I'm talking like a fool, Mr. Brown. But look at me. I've come from the gutter, the real gutter—not the story-book kind. And I climbed out of it; yes, fought every inch of the way out of it. I didn't ask anyone to give me anything; anyone to help me even. And no one did—except one man, maybe. The man I married. And later—" She stopped again and her eyes raised slightly. "Well, I used to think women who had kids were fools, until I had one."

I LOOKED at Brown. He didn't like the line and neither did I. It looked bad. Brown said: "I've come for something; something you are to give me. That you are to get out of the safe-deposit box for me"—and his lips narrowing—"or an order from you to open that box."

"I have nothing for you," she said. "Maybe I was strong enough—or weak enough, to be willing to go back into that gutter. But I wasn't weak enough to drag Ed and the baby down into it. I have nothing for you."

"But it isn't as bad as all that, Mrs. Bainton." Brown grew smooth. "You want to know how I can help you. I have great influence with Mortimer Doran, the district attorney; he will do anything I ask. And he is very close to the governor. You'll have a full pardon, and a clean conscience—a right to live—"

"A right to know that I wrecked my husband's chance in life. A right to know that my baby will grow to a boy who comes home from school because the other children have pointed the finger of shame at him; a boy whose mother was a crook; who declared she was a crook to save the face of a lax administration. And for what? For the law. The law that left me without food or clothes, without air or sunshine; with dirt and filth, and kicked me back in the gutter when I tried to climb out of it."

"And how," said Brown, "will you explain to your husband and child the betrayal of the trust that husband placed in you?"

"I'll say I was afraid of the vault; afraid of the influence Moffet might exert, and I took out the document and it was stolen."

"And he'll believe that?"

She laughed. "He'll believe it," she told Brown. "You see, when he looks at me he doesn't see the gutter and filth. He loves me."

"If it is necessary for me to tell him the truth, what then?" Brown's face was very hard.

"So you are the man I was advised to trust; you are the man I decided to turn over that evidence to. You are—" She looked at him a long time. "No, you won't talk. Come!"

Brown and I followed her into the hall and up the stairs. On the landing at the rear of the first floor she took a key which she must have held in her hand and unlocked a door. A dim light burned in the corner of that room.

"I warn you," Brown said as he looked at the little crib, "that I am not a sentimentalist. You're making a mistake in—"

"*Shs!*" she cautioned. "The baby doesn't as a rule wake up no matter how many look at him." And in a lower voice, "He hasn't got the fear of eyes, nor of a heavy hand. He didn't inherit that from his mother." She preceded us across the room. "You don't have to look at the baby if you're afraid. Just look there!"

Brown and I looked together. There, pinned on the blanket close to a soft chubby hand that hung out and almost gripped its hard surface, was a small oblong card. I guess my breath whistled into my throat. Maybe Brown's did too. Though the light was dim, I read plainly what was printed in black type on that card—

THE BLACK DEATH

No. 3

MRS. BAINTON spoke, though she didn't need to—I understood well enough. "Number Three," she said. "I have had such a card myself, but I didn't care. You know what it means. It's the final warning. The last warning of the Black Death. There is only one card that follows it, Mr. Vee Brown. That reads Number Four." She hesitated; her voice was husky but it did not break. "That final card is found only on the bodies of the dead." And turning and facing Brown, and very low and without emotion—certainly without any hysteria, "I didn't want that card found on the dead body of my baby."

"No, no; of course not." Brown gulped. He was thrown all right. "But a threat; simply a threat, that—"

"I have read the papers and I am not a fool. If you had arrived here on time my baby would be dead."

"What do you mean?"

"I mean," she said, "that I was afraid of temptation. I took that evidence from the vault today and brought it here to give you tonight."

"And you have it here now?" Brown barely breathed the words.

"No." She faced Brown, head high. "I gave it to Van Houton; standing by this crib I gave it to him." She leaned down quickly and snatched the card away. "Nothing can harm my baby now—nothing."

"But—" Brown stammered, "your— The letter that he had. You trusted him, and—"

She pointed to a large tray and the burnt ashes upon it. "That is my past," she said. "The woman I used to be lived hard. She died there tonight. Come!"

She preceded us from the room, and this time she did not lock the door behind her. Back in the room below, she faced Brown. "Well, what are you going to do?"

Brown shrugged, and his smile was anything but whimsical. "What can I do? Van Houton, then, was in that room tonight. He—he put that card there?"

"At least," she answered, "he pointed it out to me and told me then that these blackmailers had trusted him with my letter, for that evidence. Otherwise— That was when he pointed to the card."

"And you let him up in the baby's room! You—"

"You forget. Up to that moment Vincent Van Houton was just a friend; rather, an acquaintance. He said that he too had been blackmailed. It wasn't until tonight that he showed his hand. And even now there is nothing to prove—against him. Another woman might not have understood even then. But I have lived a full life. I knew when he looked at the baby. He could have—" She shuddered slightly.

"Van Houton never strikes, himself."

"No? I saw his eyes tonight, and I made a bid for happiness and freedom—and a deal for my baby's life."

Brown just stood and looked at her. Stunned, I think. Then he smiled. "You're sure you got your letter—the right one?" His smile was not a bad one; at least, a bad try—and when she nodded, "Well, you're free as far as I am concerned. That's a nice-looking kid, Mrs. Bainton. And, after all, he's your kid."

"Then you won't talk."

"No. I'm hired by the six million, not you. It's my job. Van Houton—" Suddenly, "He—he let you know he was the Black Death?"

"No, no." She shook her head. "There would be no proof of that; none at all. We were very discreet; both playing a game. We got what we wanted. He let me understand that he was giving me something he was asked to deliver, and in return was taking a letter from me."

Brown nodded. "It took nerve. He must need Moffet desperately or Moffet must have offered him a fortune and he's badly in need of funds, especially after paying out one hundred thousand dollars for—" He broke off as he walked to the front door. "Don't you worry, Mrs. Bainton. You'll bring up that kid to be a fine young man. But don't tell your husband anything yet. Wait until the Moffet trial is ready or he insists on that evidence."

"Good night!" she said. "My friend was right. You're just a—a regular guy."

CHAPTER FOUR
GIRL OF THE NIGHT

A S WE turned down the street I said to Brown: "Why in the world did you tell her to wait? What possible good can that—"

"We're going to see Van Houton. I know he won't scare easily, but he may have that evidence still on him. God Dean, but that's a blow to the city!"

"Yes." I knew how badly Brown took it when he felt that he had failed. "It's too bad you were late."

"Too bad? Hell Dean, there's a woman who deserves what she can get out of life. I'm glad I was late."

He was silent for a long time after that, and we were in the taxi before he spoke again. Then he picked up his words from where he had left off.

"Perhaps I mean I am glad I was not too early, and took the evidence from the woman." And then exactly what I was thinking, "But if we had driven straight to the door we'd have caught him coming down the steps, with the evidence in his pocket. But here we are, at Van Houton's again."

This time Van Houton stood behind the butler when the door was opened.

"Detective Vee Brown." His big blue eyes widened and he ran a hand through blond wavy hair. "And your shadow, of course," as he nodded at me. "I'm deuced sorry I wasn't here when you called." He smiled broadly. "But I'm a stickler for punctuality; I just thought you weren't coming."

"You were out, eh?" Brown followed him across the hall.

"Yes. Visiting a friend—a friend in trouble." And looking at the butler and touching his lips with a well-manicured finger as he lowered his voice, "I don't mind telling you that it's this very blackmail business that you still pretend to think I'm connected with."

We were in the library again now. Van Houton indicated chairs as Brown said: "I know. You visited Mrs. Bainton; took a certain envelope from her. Held us here so that—"

"Damn it! Brown, we don't appreciate you," Van Houton interrupted, his blue eyes shining. "I guess it's because you're so small; so frail, and we connect police achievements with strong masculine frames, keen brisk minds. And now you turn out a regular Sherlock Holmes!"

"Then you admit taking an envelope from Mrs. Bainton."

"Admit it? Certainly." Eyebrows raised.

"And got me to come here to be sure I would not interfere."

"To be sure you wouldn't interfere!" Amazement was written on Van Houton's face—blank, theatrical amazement. "What an absurd idea, after asking you to come here."

"Then, just why did you ask me to come here; tell me it was very important?"

"Mrs. Bainton." Van Houton cleared his throat. His thin lips set tightly; his voice was very serious, but he had difficulty in keeping the twinkle out of his eyes. "You see, I had a note to deliver to Mrs. Bainton. In exchange I was to receive an envelope of some sort from her. Blackmail? Yes, I thought of that. I called you to come here and take my place."

"You—you"—Brown fairly stammered—"wanted me to take the note to Mrs. Bainton; receive the one—the envelope in exchange!"

"Certainly. It went against my pride, of course; but after all, you were more experienced." He shrugged his shoulders. "But you didn't come. Your lack of interest was no doubt caused by your pride in not wishing to receive help from me."

"A beautiful lie!" Brown stared straight at him. "And you couldn't wait a few minutes for me. It was a matter of minutes, eh?"

VAN HOUTON grew very dignified. "It was a matter of seconds. The man who brought me that letter informed me of the time he would come. He came; insisted that I depart with him. What could I do?" And when Brown would have interrupted him, "You being a— well, what you are, you can not understand." He drew himself fully erect. "But a gentleman does not hesitate when a woman's honor is at stake."

"Baloney!" said Vee Brown. And the scowl leaving his face and his lips twisting at the ends, "But damn good baloney, Van Houton. Baloney that might very easily be digested by the police." Vee looked toward the door, saw that it was, closed, and looked back at Van Houton. "I wonder," it was as if he thought aloud, "if you've got the thing on you."

"The thing. The thing! Oh, that envelope. I passed my word to drop it in the first mail box." But his eyes sought the safe at the far end of the room, by the fireplace. I made a mental note of that action; that covert glance.

"So you passed your word." Brown was on his feet now, moving toward Van Houton who stood leaning on the flat desk.

"Exactly. You see, that's why I thought of you. You might give—" And suddenly, his voice rising, "I warn you, Brown. Any gun-play here won't go." A finger bore down heavily on a desk button.

I too was on my feet. The soft glow of the Master of Melody was not in Brown's black eyes, nor was there exactly that burning hatred that made his eyes malignant deadly orbs when he was the Killer of Men. But the light was coming there.

Maybe Brown got hold of himself, maybe my hand upon his arm jarred him back, maybe it was the feet across the hall and the butler opening the door. Anyway his arms dropped to his sides, his hands sort of spread; hopelessly spread. Then that little crooked twist at the corners of his mouth. But he didn't speak until we were out the front door and Van Houton stood on the steps behind us.

"You don't fool me, Van Houton," he said then. "I know everything that happened—everything you did tonight. No one needed to tell me. The card"—and looking back over his shoulder—"the number-three card on the baby's crib; how you tricked me into waiting here. Yes, I understand it all. Good night!"

"Remarkable!" Van Houton rubbed his hands together. "I am glad to see, Mr. Brown, that you are one of those bright young men who understand just how the cards should be played—after the game is won. Not good night, but good-by!"

As we climbed back into the taxi I said to Brown: "That last—the 'good-by.' Did you notice the emphasis on the words; the—the almost finality? I wonder what he meant."

"He meant," said Vee very slowly, "Spot Kelly and the one hundred grand he put on the line for my death." And after a moment, "He's clever, Dean—very clever. If— I wonder where that evidence is."

"I know," I said quickly. "He looked toward the safe; he couldn't help it. People always do that. I've read—"

"You've read!" Brown snapped in. "Have you ever read of anyone paying a hundred thousand dollars cash in advance to have a man shot through the back of the head?"

"It's a lot of money. Spot Kelly must be pretty sure to—to—" and I bit my lower lip sharply. That was hardly tactful. But if I stopped to spare Vee Brown any nervousness I had wasted my time. He was thinking of something else.

"If I were sure it was in the safe. If—" He rubbed his chin. "I studied that safe, Dean. It's new—it's good." And sharply, "I suppose you've read too that any detective worth his salt, in books, can rub sandpaper on his fingers and open the very latest steel model safe in three minutes and ten seconds. Well, I can't do it with my hands and I'd have damned hard work doing it with a drill—an electric drill. But I could blow hell out of it with some nitro-glycerine." He laughed gruffly. "It's a job for an expert box man. Now, our good fence, Mr. Irving Small, would know the one— the very man." He leaned forward and called to the driver.

The taxi turned toward the river at once and shot downtown.

I DIDN'T go in with Brown but waited a good forty-five minutes before the little pawn shop that hid Irving Small's real business—the receiving of stolen goods. Brown knew that; could send Small up for twenty years on charges he had never pressed. And in return for Brown's silence and also Brown's pay, which was more than generous when he wanted information, Irving Small sold out friend or enemy, or through the grapevine service of the underworld got information that went to Vee Brown. "Not good ethics," Brown had said. "But damn good sense. Most of the breaks astute detectives get in criminal cases come first through the tip-off of some favorite stool pigeon. An evil, to be sure—but a necessary evil."

I saw Irving Small in the doorway when Vee came out. His emaciated, long form; his bent shoulders; his clawlike fingers; the parchment hands which seemed to be continually washing, as if with invisible soap.

"What luck?" I asked Brown.

"None. None at all." Vee pushed himself back in the seat after giving the driver our Park Avenue address. "I tell you, Dean, I hate this rat, Van Houton but one must admire his shrewdness. Mind you, not a breath of suspicion about him in the entire underworld; not a word that he's the least bit off color, even to Irving Small, who knows everything. Yet— Well, the fact is that Van Houton's taboo in the underworld. Once Van Houton's name was mentioned, Small told me he couldn't get a first-rate box man to touch the job. Of course we could send out of town. But that'll take time, too much time." He shook his head. "We can't expect that evidence to stay there more than over night—

"Damn it all, Dean, I'll do the job myself!"

I looked at him there in the darkness of the cab, and I knew that he meant it. "You can't, Vee," I told him. "It's not your line. It's not— Good God, man! Don't you know what it means? Not only your job but your freedom. Van Houton would like nothing better than that." And when he didn't speak, "Besides, you couldn't."

"No?" Black eyes fairly glared at me from that white face. "I'll get that document, Dean, if I have to blast my way into the safe. No more—no more of it now. I'll think on it."

I thought on it too. Vincent Van Houton was getting under Vee's skin. Van Houton had laughed at him that night. Van Houton had stolen—at least had taken that evidence right from under his nose; even made him lose his temper. Van Houton had fooled him. And Vee Brown! Yes, it was getting him. He was going to sacrifice that cool, calculating daring for—for wild reckless vengeance.

We entered our apartment to the soft notes of a piano and a voice. I stopped dead. The voice was good. The voice was—I looked at Brown. Damn it, the girl had a trained voice; a professional voice. And it stopped; stopped on the final note—the final words. Brown's new song. *Girl of the Night.*

Brown's eyes shone. "It will make her, Dean. Any musical—" He stopped, hummed softly a moment. "I'll change it just a bit there. I didn't realize she'd be so proficient, so professional. And no make-up"—his lips curved in that crooked smile—"that is, no more make-up than she uses now." And suddenly, "Do you like her hair?"

"Why, I don't know. Why?" The question just startled me. I was thinking of other things. I never could get used to Brown's sudden shifts from a detective who shot to kill, to a composer of songs that very often just dripped with sentiment.

"No reason especially." Thin shoulders shrugged. "She's a clever woman. Notice how she avoids the light. I was just wondering if the hair is her own, that was all."

The girl came from the music room. For a moment she was very young, very eager, very glad, too—and relieved, I thought, to see Vee.

"You saw her—you saw Mrs. Bainton?" And dropping the hands she had placed on his shoulders, "You didn't get the evidence; her promise, even?"

"That's right." Brown nodded. "I didn't get it yet. But I'll get it tonight or make a stab at it. Van Houton has it."

"He's crazy. Plumb loco, Maria." I blurted it out. "He's going to rob Van Houton's safe."

Brown told her then all that had happened. He trusted the girl absolutely—at least, in matters she brought to him. And he had to. She had insisted upon that—insisted that she must know everything, even to the smallest detail. And somehow she left the impression with me that her insistence on being thoroughly posted was not only to keep her informed so that she could help Brown, but that her own safety, maybe her life, depended upon it.

"You can't do it." The girl looked long and steadily at Brown. "The safe is not a big one, but it's a specially constructed one."

Brown grinned. Not a pleasant grin, but a determined one. "I have made my arrangements." He nodded grimly. "Tonight I turn burglar—box man. Within the hour will be delivered to me enough soup to rip open the old can. Soup, Dean," when my eyes opened. "Just the professional box man's term for nitro-glycerine. I described the safe and Irving Small is taking care of the amount to be used."

The girl shook her head. "You can't get away with it—that way."

"Why?" demanded Brown. "He doesn't have strong-arm men around the house. A quick blow, a hand in the safe, a threat with a gun—and a drop from the window."

"Not that safe. You'd be caught, sure. Van Houton has influence. Now, with Moffet behind him—" And suddenly, her green eyes blazing, "It's big, Vee—means a lot to you?"

"It means everything to the city, to the administration, to Mortimer Doran. Not only Moffet being free to rule as he has ruled, but the power it will give the man who by suppressing that evidence lets Moffet rule—Vincent Van Houton. Why, it will give him a power for evil that—"

"Yes, I know," the girl cut in, her green eyes fastened on Brown, "I hate him. But hate isn't as strong as—" She bit her lip; and then, "Never mind Van Houton, the citizens, Mortimer Doran. Just what does it mean to you personally—to you, Vee Brown?"

VEE WASN'T looking at her. His thoughts, perhaps, were far away. But if he had talked for five minutes he could not have been more impressive than with the few simple words he spoke. "It means everything—everything to me," was all he said.

I was looking at the girl; looking at those cruel green eyes—eyes that were no longer cruel. They were soft—very soft for a second. And then maybe still soft as the mist obscured them.

The girl nodded her head. Her voice was very low. "Everything to you," she said. "Then I'll give you the combination of the safe."

And Brown was at the flat desk, a pencil and paper in his hand; his black eyes eager, his voice boyish. So for once he missed a trick, for he didn't see what I had seen, nor catch in her voice and her eyes what I caught—though maybe I was wrong and it was not there. But to me it was as if the girl had said, "Very well. For you, Vee Brown, I'll risk my life."

She was leaving after that; leaving while her eyes were still soft, after those small white hands had rested for a moment on the back of Brown's long slender fingers. He did not notice the eyes nor the caress of those hands. He was busy memorizing those figures; the combination of the safe. But he did call to her at the door; to both of us at the door, for I was taking her downstairs.

"Don't worry, Maria. Van Houton will never know how the safe was opened. I'll see that hell is blown out of it after I leave."

"It might—might kill him," she said.

Vee laughed. "We can't hope to have all the luck," he said. And I led her into the hall.

Downstairs, I left her while I examined the court behind the servants' entrance. No one watching; no one there. Her departure was quite safe. As I led her down the steps and through the rear court I thought of her as very young, very much alone, and very far from being hard, cruel, cold—and even vicious.

"Don't mind Brown," I told her; she was so silent. "It's his way. But inside he's grateful, very grateful for what you are doing."

"Grateful!" Green eyes shone in the darkness, accentuated now, rather than dimmed by—by the mist. Or was it a mist—a mist or tiny globules of water? "Good-by!" Her hand was warm. "I don't need Vee's gratitude; I don't want his gratitude. Somehow or other, Dean, I think you and I discovered the same thing at once. You won't tell Vee."

"What—what do you mean?"

"Why," she said simply, "that I love him; love him very, very much."

She was gone. Just a moving shadow in the night; then not even a shadow. Just gone.

CHAPTER FIVE
I DO MY STUFF

BACK IN the apartment Brown was humming softly. On the table beside him was a black mask, a tiny flash, a jimmy and a long slender pair of nippers, and rubber gloves.

"I think that's the whole show." He grinned at me. "I've just buzzed Irving Small and he'll fix up some stuff for me and send it along. I'll blow hell out of the safe after I'm finished with it. Cause confusion and fear and leave no clue that someone had the combination. The— Maria need have no worry. It'll certainly be a surprise to Van Houton when he misses the envelope."

"Maria's doing a lot for you, Vee."

"Sure. Sure." He nodded absently. "And she won't be sorry. If she can act a bit, with that singing—singing like we heard tonight, I'll make her a sensation. Why, she'll be an over-night find and—" He looked toward the music room, looked at the clock, hesitated and finally said: "Damn that Spot Kelly, from Chicago. Here I've got a couple of hours to kill, and instead of going on with the song I'll have to think of him."

"How?" I said. "What do you intend to do?"

"Practice up in the gun room."

"Practice! You practice with a gun?"

"Certainly. Why not? There's nothing strange in that. The world's boxing champion practices and calls it 'training.' Besides, this is different. Spot Kelly doesn't fancy shooting it out with a man. He likes to put a bullet in the back of a lad's head."

"But you can draw, turn and shoot in—"

"Yes, if I can turn. But that's why I was so long in Irving Small's. My business about a box man for Van Houton's safe was over in two minutes, but Irving Small had quite a collection of newspaper clippings which furnished plenty of information on the way Spot Kelly's victims die. Interesting, Dean. Kelly has a system and sticks to it." He grinned at me now. "By the way, in his younger days Irving Small was a jeweler—a real one." He snapped out his watch. "I had him look at my watch while I looked at the clippings."

"And what has your watch to do with Spot Kelly?"

"Maybe nothing, maybe a lot. But we're going to consult that watch always from now on. You'll be surprised. You see, Dean, we'll call it a matter of timing, or at least a matter of a time piece." He left the room quickly and turned into the little hall that led to the Morgue—the gun room—which was steel-lined and soundproof, and contained everything from tiny targets to birthday-cake candles that Brown could snuff out drawing from the hip or from under his arm. "Call me at once if Irving Small's messenger comes," he shouted back to me before the steel door banged closed.

Several times I walked down the hall to the gun room. It was well built. Just a dull *pop* came to me as I listened close to the door. Now, if he didn't have a real respect for this Spot Kelly, why— And I felt for the moment a certain chill of fear. It was the first time since I had been associated with Brown that he had ever—well, admitted, let alone stated, that he was practicing because of threatened death by a gunman.

IT WAS one o'clock when the package came. Gingerly I placed it on the desk in the living room and went to the gun room. I listened a moment, opened the door a crack and waited. I didn't want to stop a slug.

"Come in—come in," Brown called cheerfully.

I entered and sniffed the irritating aroma of burnt powder. Vee rose from the stiff-backed chair by a small table and stood there, a gun in his hand. "Well," he extended his hand, "let's have it. The package, I mean."

"I didn't bring it here," I told him. "It's on the desk outside."

He started toward the door, then turned back. For a moment I saw his watch, the case open as it lay upon the table. So he had been timing himself, I thought. But he snatched up the watch and followed me from the room.

"One o'clock, eh?" Brown put on his overcoat and began to slip things into various pockets. "I should really carry a satchel. It's a little early for the job, but a good burglar gives himself lots of time, and— Damn my soul, Dean, where do you think you're going? Take off that coat!"

"Why, I'm going with you, Vee! I couldn't let you go alone." And when he shook his head, "We first booked up under that agreement when I contracted to write up your cases for The Globe and prove that you didn't kill except when necessary."

"But you don't write for The Globe now, and"—with that whimsical smile—"where's your sense of drama, Dean? If you ever did write this up, how much more interesting—dramatic even—for you to be pacing the room here, wondering how—or if—I'll come out."

When I still insisted Vee grew serious. "Nonsense, Dean Condon. I want you with me, but it's a one-man job. Just the opening of a window and the spinning of a dial. Amateurish, almost childish even." And as he reached the door and pushed me back into the apartment, "Besides, I'll need you here. An alibi in case of trouble later. Van Houton will suspect, of course." And with a twist of his mouth, "I may need you to pick me up some place, a hunted, slinking criminal in the night. No, no, Dean. Van Houton's strength is his weakness tonight. No firearms, no bodyguard that might convince Mortimer Doran and Ramsey that I was right about his being the Black Death. Why, damn it! Dean, I might even stick a gun in his stomach and press the trigger, and sleep with the easy conscience of a newborn babe. Night!"

The door closed. I was alone. Vee Brown had gone to rob the house of his enemy—the city's enemy. Vincent Van Houton—the Black Death—Emperor of Evil.

There you are! Those are the thoughts Brown left with me. And he was right. It would be much easier to be with him, sharing his danger. In a way, I was with him. Mentally I stepped from that taxi, walked along the sidewalk across the street, spotted the dismal aristocratic brown-stone front, slipped to the block behind and through the alley of a house there, over a high fence, and hanging close in the shadows reached a basement window. A basement window! Barred certainly. Then the ash barrel up-ended, the uneasy balancing of it and Vee Brown cutting a round hole close to the window lock or jimmying the window from the bottom. In the house then, across the library, and—the flash of light—the roar of a gun—the laugh of the killer and Vee's slim body—

I SNUFFED out my cigarette in the ash tray and immediately lit another. What nonsense! In the first place, Vee was hardly more than in the taxi now. In the second place, Vincent Van Houton would have no guards. And besides, he hardly would suspect that Brown was going to rob his safe.

Then the phone rang.

I jerked up the receiver. It was Maria; I knew that. Not that she gave her name, not that I recognized her voice—but from the message that she whispered, breathed over the wire.

"Dean, tell Vee it will be suicide for him to come to Van Houton's tonight. There, don't question me! I'm risking my freedom, my life—even for these few seconds. The house is watched. Van Houton is expecting him. His glance at the safe was a trick to make you— But don't let him come."

Question her. Talk. Damn it! I couldn't talk! I was stunned, thrown completely. And then I could talk—did talk, I must have cried out the words. I said: "He's gone. Vee's gone. God, Maria! Vee's there!"

Did the click of the receiver across that wire reach me before I spoke, while I was speaking, or after I had finished—or did it even reach me at all? I didn't know. Just one thought, one thing clearly as I dropped the phone back into its cradle. Van Houton had fooled Brown again; fooled me with that glance toward the safe. Yes, the Black Death had set his trap and Brown had walked into it.

What should I do—what could I do? And even while I asked myself such questions I was putting on my coat, getting a gun, jamming a flashlight into my pocket. No

THE DEATH MASK 111

thoughts! I'll admit that. At least, constructive thoughts. But I'm big and strong and can shoot if I have a gun in my hand and the distance isn't too great. And then I did have one thought. If it was a trap; if that house was watched, it was watched by ruthless desperate gunmen; the kind that would kill in a moment. And Vee! Well, I didn't know how he'd plan it if I were in the same position, but I did know what he'd do. He'd come for me. My duty, my desire, my one driving force was plain enough. I was going to Vincent Van Houton's house. I was going to Vee Brown.

I was in the hall, near the door when Wong suddenly appeared from the rear of the penthouse. He had an uncanny way of sensing trouble, or maybe after he saw my face it was not exactly uncanny.

"Trouble, Mr. Dean! You go out? Much trouble?"

I hesitated, and then, "Much trouble, Wong. Real trouble."

"Mr. Vee?" There was no expression in that yellow face; those slanting eyes. But there was emotion. Not in his voice, but in his fingers that opened and shut.

"Yes. Mr. Vee." I nodded quickly. Stay awake, Wong," I said, needlessly of course. He'd give his life for Brown. "We—Mr. Vee may need you, though God knows what—"

"And the phone, Mr. Dean? If others call I am to say what?"

"Others! But who else will call?"

"It is the instrument of trouble." His head bobbed up and down solemnly. "Always it brings first the bad news as well as the good. Where will I say you are— Mr. Vee—"

"Say—" And two things struck me at once. That I didn't know what message Wong was to give and that time was passing. "Say anything," I finished lamely and dashed out the door.

A TAXI sped me to the block behind Van Houton's. I guess I scraped my feet impatiently until it drove away. Then I was in the narrow alley that ran along one side of the house. I ran across the rear yard to the high wooden fence. Ugly and black, over that fence loomed the dull outline of the Van Houton residence. No light showed; just inky blackness.

I reached for the fence with my left hand. Then, shoving the gun into my pocket, I grasped it with both hands, bent my body slightly for the spring—and froze where I was. My hands dropped from the fence, my breath sucked far back in my throat and held there. A voice had spoken on the other side of that fence; a voice that was so close that—

But the voice said clearly enough, gruffly enough: "Certainly the man has gone into the house or we wouldn't be here. The flash in the window was our signal. You better get moving. There's only the alley on the left for you to cover; better go well down it. I'll stick here close to the fence. If he tries to escape from the back—well, that's my job."

The answering voice was eager; the voice of a younger man, I thought. "And the orders. To shoot to kill!"

"Sure. Now get to your post before the big crash. There will be real things happening in a minute, when the boys show up."

The soft tread of feet as one man left the other; feet that died out almost the minute they started. The house was evidently surrounded. They had let Brown enter, trapped him in the house, and when he tried to escape would—would—

My gun was in my hand again, my heart in my mouth—and Brown was in the trap, unless—unless— And I remember the words of the man—"Real things happening when the boys show up."

A man guarded the back of the house, another the side alley. There would be others at the front. The watchers, now, were in case of an emergency only; they were waiting for the arrival of more. Men who would enter by the front door, shoot Brown down or drive him out into the yard for— And there was only one man between me and a warning to Brown; one man between minutes—maybe seconds—and Brown's death. One man—

And I did it. Moved down a couple of feet, gripped the top of the fence, held my breath as the gun in my right hand caught for a moment and I thought I'd lost it. Then I raised myself slowly. My hat reached the top of the fence. A split second of agony, then the top of my head. I wondered if it was going to be shot off. Then my eyes were above the fence and I saw the man. Almost directly below me was a soft black hat; at least it seemed black in the darkness.

Now what? Brown, perhaps, with his precision and calmness might have leaned down and struck with his gun; struck the man directly behind the ear and jumped from the fence in time to ease his unconscious body to the hard stone. Brown might have—but I was not Brown.

But I had to strike. Just once; viciously once. A single cry would be disastrous. Hard? Yes. I realized in that moment the courage it takes to strike a defenseless man. He was far below me. I hoisted myself further up on the fence, my stomach on the hard boards, my knees desperately trying to find a resting place, my gun in my right hand, held out—ready. Ready! And then came trouble.

THE MAN raised his head and turned it. A white blotch in the blackness; that was his face. A sudden start on my part, a slip, and I lost my balance.

I knew it then. All my plans were gone; gone in that single split second that I hurtled from that fence. And they weren't gone. The man's head shot far back, a white throat showed. The gun fell from my fingers and I was on him, my hands upon that throat.

I'm a heavy man; a strong man. I've kept myself fit. As my fingers closed about that neck the man's knees gave and we crashed to the hard stone. A single thud; a dull thud, and I was on top of him, fingers biting into that throat to choke off his cry. And there was no cry.

My fingers loosened, my hands dropped from that throat. He was lying there very quiet, his left hand by his side, his right hand beneath his body. I understood. The single thud above the fall of our bodies had been his head striking the flagstones.

For a moment panic struck me. I had killed a man! I had— But he wasn't dead. His breathing was regular enough but for little gasps in it. Should I leave him there? Would he be unconscious long enough for me to reach the house and warn Brown? Should I tie him? And I picked up my gun and was running toward the rear of Van Houton's house. How much better Vee would have planned things! I had nothing to tie the man with.

My entrance to the house was simple. It was all there as I had pictured it. The up-ended ash barrel with a box upon it, the window above it, now wide open; the window through which Brown must have entered.

Courage? No, I don't think it was courage. I may have been reckless, foolish, even downright stupid. But Brown had saved my life many times, and now I wanted to be with him; wanted to warn him that his death was planned; wanted to—

And I was in that window, my foot upon the porcelain sink as I slid noiselessly to the kitchen floor.

The library—the safe? Where would they be from the kitchen? It was dark, deadly quiet too in that house. I remembered my flash, wondered if I had lost it in the dive from the fence and breathed with relief when I drew it from my pocket and it still worked.

Just a single flash and I found the door—a swing door. I chanced the light again. I was in the butler's pantry. The dining room must be beyond then, to the left of it the hall and across that hall the library.

Cautiously I moved to the dining-room door—another swing door. Carefully, and I hoped noiselessly, I opened it. I say 'hoped noiselessly' because my breathing seemed so loud that I could not tell if the door squeaked or not.

Did I hear something? Did a man breath loudly in that dining room or was it just my own breathing? So, with that door held open by my left foot, I stood waiting, undecided; and any minute, any second even, the man in the back yard might come to life and shout his warning. Shout it? I nodded at that thought. Perhaps Van Houton's men had no more desire for noise than I had. But the man had said, "Shoot to kill!" out there in the back.

I THOUGHT of calling out Brown's name but saw the folly of that almost at once. He wouldn't be in the dining room anyway. He— And I started forward and stopped. It would be foolhardy to try and cross that room quickly without a light. Chairs, table, sideboard! Why, I would have to feel my way every inch to the hall. I'd chance it—one stab of light and the furniture would be stamped in my mind for the few quick steps to the hall.

The door shielded my body when I pressed the button of the flash. A single pencil of light splashed upon a round table, the legs of that table and then— Yes, on the low tan shoes of feet; human feet.

Maybe if took several seconds, maybe it took only a split second. But before I could even release my paralyzed finger from the switch of the torch, a voice cried out. A shot crashed in the somber stillness of that room. There was a tingling in my hand; the stab of light disappeared; the flash left my numbed fingers, the metal cylinder ringing as it struck hard polished wood.

Men were calling from some place in the front of the house. Someone pounded on the front door, or at least on wood. But I don't know for sure. I only know that panic gripped me. I turned, jumped across that length of pantry, crashed against the other swing door and was in the kitchen again.

Luck, that, in the darkness? Sure! I'm not denying that. But after I reached the kitchen it was just speed. The white of the sink stood out vividly, and above it the open window. I don't know if I crawled through that window or jumped through it, but I do know that I was through it and that I missed completely the up-turned barrel with the box on it in my hurtle to the ground. And I do know that I landed with my knees beneath me, that I toppled forward, caught my balance and was away across that open court like a sprinter with a clean start.

Guns blazed from behind me, at least window.

A man shouted from the alley behind the house. Someone called, "Get him!" And when I thought I had a chance of making that fence a dark object loomed up before me close to the fence, moving like a huge dog in the darkness.

Then I understood. The dark object was a man coming to his feet—the man I had fallen upon a few short minutes before. I raised my right hand with the gun to strike him down—and didn't. For he was on his hands and knees, struggling to come erect. What did I do? Well, I did as well as Brown could ever do. Better maybe, because I was quite an athlete in my day. Without even losing my stride I landed on that rising back, gripped at the fence and in a single leap landed in the yard beyond.

Close? Maybe I have been closer to death before but I don't think so. I heard the shot and I think I heard too the splint of wood between my fingers. Vee smiles at that story, but I did have a splinter in my finger to prove it.

CHAPTER SIX
THE LOCKED DOOR

FOR MEN who, I thought, wanted silence, they certainly were making one hell of a racket. Somewhere, out on the street before Van Houton's house, a whistle blew shrilly; then another and another. Far distant came the sudden screech of a siren. And I was on the street behind, running along it. For the first time I thought of Brown, my mission there and the mess I had made of it. Vee was dead now—or perhaps I had saved him. Those sirens, the whistles, meant only one thing. The police. Brown saved? I shook my head. The thing would drive him out of the city, if it didn't actually put him in jail. Why had he gone? Why—

I jerked erect. A car had come along the block, pulled silently to the curb beside me. A big expensive Rolls, like Vee's car. And a voice spoke. "Please, Mr. Dean, put away the lethal weapon and step into the car. You are expected at Mr. Van Houton's."

And it was Vee's car, with Wong, placid as usual, behind the wheel. I looked down at my right hand and for the first time realized that I still clutched a gun in it. I smiled, too. Then I thought of Vee and the smile went. I asked anxiously as I climbed into the car: "Vee! Mr. Vee, Wong? He's all right? He's at Van Houton's?"

"No can tell." Wong slipped silently into gear and moved down the block. "Police make much disturbance. Mr. Mortimer Doran, he call up and want Mr. Vee and you to go to Mr. Van Houton's house. He is very much from dignity, and I tell him that I tell you right away. So I drive here, for where big trouble is you and Mr. Vee must be."

"There is big trouble, Wong," I told him as we went down five blocks and turned right. "I think Mr. Vee is there, where the shooting was. I got away. But I'm afraid for him."

There was nothing of sarcasm or even depreciation in Wong's words or his voice when he spoke again. It was as if he uttered a great universal truth. "Where you get away Mr. Vee get away. In trouble I am alibi for you. You could not be at house of trouble, for I went from phone to your room and you got dressed and drive here. Mr. Vee sends you, and if needed he come later. It is good?"

I shook my head. Things did not seem as simple as that. I had great faith in Vee, but not the simple absolute faith Wong had. There had been nothing clever about my escape. Besides, I was not expected and came after the trap was sprung. But the police! How would Van Houton explain to them the gunmen who guarded his house? How—

A small police car that must have picked us up a block or two before was edging us to the curb. But it didn't matter. We were almost at Van Houton's. Another car sped by and drew up with a grinding of brakes before Van Houton's door. Wong brought us to a stop just behind it.

I was out of the car and moving toward Van Houton's residence, for I had seen Mortimer Doran step from the big car and I had seen, too, the policeman who hopped quickly from the other car that had followed us.

"Hey there!" The cop had me by the arm with his left hand, his right was under his coat close to his belt. "Where did you come from?"

Mortimer Doran saw me and turned. "What's this? What's this?" he said irritably.

"This man may have something to do with the racket," the cop said. "His car came along just—"

"Nonsense, Sergeant!" Doran snapped. "That is Mr. Condon. I telephoned him to come." And to me, "Where's Vee?" He took me by the arm and led me toward the house.

"Why—why—" I guess I stammered a little. "He— Well, when I got to the phone you had hung up, and Wong wasn't sure of your voice, and I thought—" and in sudden inspiration, "I thought it was that Spot Kelly, laying a trap for him, and I didn't tell Vee."

A sneering voice spoke from above me. "But you walked into the trap, eh?"

I LOOKED up surprised. Inspector Ramsey was standing by the door looking down at us.

"There was no danger for me," I said quietly. "Beside, once I saw the cars here and heard the police sirens I knew it was all right."

"So you heard the sirens and—"

"My God enough of this wrangling!" When Doran was in a bad temper, which I must say was seldom, he was in a very bad one. "Come, come, Inspector. I telephoned Condon and he came at once. Surely you don't suspect that Dean was here robbing the house!"

Ramsey showed his teeth. "No, I guess not. Condon wouldn't have the stomach for it. But Brown, now. He—"

"Yes, yes," Mortimer Doran cut in. "You hinted as much as that over the phone, and I came right down. Now—let me have it. You said Van Houton called you, for police protection; had an anonymous note he would be robbed tonight."

"That's right—only more." Ramsey nodded. "He told me he thought Brown wanted to get a look into his safe. You know, Mr. Doran, how Brown's been annoying Van Houton and telling us that he's this master blackmailer but offering no proof. Now"—he leaned forward—"what would you do if Brown did go as far as entering Van Houton's house for the purpose of robbery?"

"I'd break him, of course." Doran looked straight at Ramsey. "You'd see to that, Inspector—you hate him enough. But, God! What a scandal for the—the administration at this time."

"That's right," said Ramsey. "What a scandal! If Brown did do it—it might be better if he got himself shot to death."

Doran's eyebrows raised. "You left orders that men were to shoot—shoot to kill—shoot, suspecting that—"

Ramsey straightened. "Vincent Van Houton is spending money to discover this blackmailer, the Black Death. I know that. His suspicion that Brown would rob his house may be, and certainly should be, as unfounded as I believe Brown's suspicions of Van Houton are. As an inspector of police I can not believe that a detective of the force—a first-grade detective—even one assigned to your office, would commit a felony. It was only a hint from Van Houton. I can not jeopardize the lives of my men on such a hint and perhaps have them shot down by a desperate killer." Ramsey leaned forward and spoke very low. "And you won't deny that even Brown can at times, and has been, a desperate killer."

"Enough of this nonsense." Mortimer Doran pushed through the vestibule and into the now lighted hall. "Now—just what has happened? We're having too much guess work." Ramsey shrugged his shoulders. "Something has happened. I stuck her in the front. There was a shooting in the rear; a shooting in the dining room by the man I planted there. He said he saw a light and saw a man jump from the kitchen window." And with a smile, "I don't think our man can escape. He's probably a prisoner now, or dead there in the yard."

Van Houton suddenly appeared.

"Where have you been while all this racket was going on?" Mortimer Doran demanded. His temper had not improved.

Vincent Van Houton ran a hand through his wavy blond hair, stroked the cat he held in his arms, spoke to it softly. "It's poor little body is trembling and—"

"Never mind that damn cat!" Doran snapped, and I saw Van Houton's lips tighten, his soft eyes blaze; he was touchy about his pets. "What did you do? What did you hear? What did you see?"

"Me?" Van Houton's blue eyes widened. "Why, I went to my room shortly after Mr. Brown visited me this evening—say, eleven o'clock. I locked my door after advising the servants to do the same."

"Why?"

Vincent Van Houton looked at Inspector Ramsey. "On the inspector's advice; almost command. It seems he thought it best to let this burglar enter the house, then catch him red-handed. I—I—well, I didn't like it. I'm afraid I'm rather timid, Mr. Doran. But it seemed a duty, and my door has a strong lock."

"That's right," said Ramsey. "The arrangements were mine. Ah—Sergeant Twait! What now?"

I WON'T go into the details of what happened as told by individual policemen and detectives. In the questioning by Ramsey and Doran it came out as a whole.

Ramsey had instructed Van Houton and the servants to lock themselves in their rooms. Van Houton, it appears, had an alarm in his own room that gave him silent warning if any of the windows were forced. There was also such an alarm placed under the rug close to the safe. As soon as anyone entered that house Van Houton was to flash a light from his window. Then Ramsey's men would close in and prevent the burglar's escape. Everything until that alarm was given was done to make the entrance of the burglar easy and assured. Not a policeman or detective was watching the outside of that house. But two men were inside the house; one on the front stairs and one in the coat closet in the hall.

The man who had been in the hall said: "I had no way of knowing when the signal for the boys to close in would come. But when the time came to strike I would open the front door and let the inspector and the men in. As much as I know I have told to the inspector."

"Tell it again," said Doran.

"Well, I never heard a sound and it appears now from what happened later that this man had entered the house a good—well, maybe ten minutes before I knew it. I first discovered him when I started to move around, saw the flash in the dining room and fired at it. The flash is there on the table."

He pointed to the table—we were all in the library now—and there was my flash.

"And the prowler made a run for it," the detective went on. "I followed him to the kitchen, took another shot, missed him, hit the glass and fired twice more as he crossed the yard. I guess I hit him then all right, and—"

"We'll soon find that out, if there's blood in the yard. What next?"

"That's all. He jumped on Hannigan's back by the fence. Then—I don't know. It was too dark."

"And Hannigan! Hannigan got him—shot him? He's—" Ramsey gripped the man by the arm. He didn't know of my escape then! "Where's Hannigan?" he finished.

Hannigan was brought in. Two men were supporting him; a plainclothesman and one in harness. I felt sorry for Hannigan and I felt alarmed too. This was the big moment. Would Hannigan recognize me? I looked straight at him. Fear left me. I grinned. I didn't recognize him—how could he recognize me? But his story would give the show away. They hadn't found Brown. He must still be in the house. Once they learned that Hannigan was attacked from behind after the warning that the man was in the house had been given, they'd know the truth. A search of that house would begin and Brown would be found.

Hannigan told his story. It was straightforward enough and told without flourishes, by a man who'd been long on the force and knew how to make his report.

"The warning was given," he said, "and young Dillon and myself went to the back of the house. I gave him his instructions as ordered and he went into the alley. I don't know just where he stood for I couldn't see him." Hannigan hesitated a long moment there.

"You fired and missed, eh?" Ramsey sneered. "With the man right on top of you!"

Hannigan caught the tone of the inspector's voice and recognized the danger in it. The danger to himself.

"No—" he said slowly. "I pressed the trigger and the gun jammed; then the running figure struck me down." And in sudden defense, "I complained about that gun before." And at Ramsey's deepening scowl, "My complaint's in black and white down at headquarters, for anyone to read—and nothing was done about it."

I SMILED inside. Hannigan was not a young man. He knew the ropes. He had lied, to his own advantage. At least, he had lied about that gun. About my dropping on him from the fence—I don't know. Later I was to learn that Hannigan lied in self-protection. He had not seen me drop on him from the fence. He couldn't explain anything that had happened. He had heard shots in a distant sort of way—men shouting, too. But he didn't know how or when he was struck down; he simply told the best story he could.

Mortimer Doran, if not exactly pleased, was relieved. Two men, at least, had seen the fleeing figure cross the rear yard, and both were convinced that the man was of powerful build. Mortimer Doran had them repeat that description several times. And Ramsey, try as he might, had to admit the truth of it. Both the men knew Vee Brown and laughed when Ramsey tried to get them to say that "the fleeing figure might be about the build of—say, Vee Brown."

Vincent Van Houton looked at Ramsey. "Much thanks for your protection tonight." His lips curled at one end. "And for the good—the very good advice. I suppose my servants and myself are fortunate in not being murdered in our beds."

"You didn't lose anything, did you?" Ramsey turned to the safe. "Better open it and have a look."

"I have had a look," said Vincent Van Houton. "There is nothing missing. Absolutely nothing."

"And I presume," said Doran, "the whole house has been carefully searched."

"Thoroughly searched," nodded Van Houton. "Inspector Ramsey attended to that while the burglar escaped."

"Sure!" said Ramsey. "Gone over with a fine-tooth comb."

"All but that one room that's locked," said a young detective.

"How's that?" Mortimer Doran swung quickly as he was moving toward the door. "What room?"

Van Houton glared at the young detective. He said to the D.A.: "A room on the third floor. In fact, a suite of rooms. But the door is always locked, and since there is no ladder on the outside the searching of it was quite unnecessary. I explained it to Ramsey."

"Well!" Doran turned on Ramsey.

"What he says is true." Ramsey nodded, and when Mortimer Doran eyed him steadily Van Houton cut in.

"It's a suite that on occasion is occupied by a very dear friend; a friend who would not like it gone over."

"Well, we'll have a look in it," Doran said, and I thought he half looked at me. Was it possible that after all he did take some stock in Vee Brown's continued accusation that Vincent Van Houton was really the blackmailer—the Black Death? And did he now see the opportunity of discovering some hidden secret?

"Hell!" said Ramsey, before Van Houton could speak, "you might as well have it. A dame-a lady uses it."

"Humph!" said Doran.

"On occasions—on occasions. Properly chaperoned, of course." Van Houton spoke behind his hand. "A friendship. Mutual artistic understandings. Entirely platonic."

"She's there now—there tonight, when you knew—"

"No, no. The rooms are quite empty. I simply thought that, under the circumstances, the fact that the door is locked and—"

"Of course," I cut in with a laugh, "if the door is locked and—" I stopped.

CHAPTER SEVEN
FOR A PRICE

ALL THREE men turned and looked at me. Why had I spoken? What business was it of mine? And why did I bite my words off before they were finished? Oh, I knew what I was thinking all right. I was thinking how easily Vee Brown could open that locked door and slip inside; I was thinking—But were the others thinking the same thing? Van Houton—Ramsey! And Ramsey said abruptly and sharply to Van Houton: "Well, the thing's out now. We're all gentlemen here, and it'll go no further. Come on! We better have a look in that room."

Van Houton's eyebrows went up. "But the man escaped; the burglar fled out the back and—"

"There might have been two; a little man as well as a big man." And when Doran looked at him, Ramsey added: "That's the way crooks work, often. At least, that's the way eye witnesses always describe them."

"If that's true," said Van Houton, "if there was another— if he was able to pick that lock, then he's in the room now. He couldn't have—"

"Couldn't have—" Ramsey turned quickly and gave sharp orders to his men to get outside the house. "Damn it! He may have escaped while we talked here. Every man, nearly, has been inside and—"

"It's too big a drop," Van Houton said, and he seemed excited. "By God, Inspector, we may catch one of them yet! My hunch may be right."

"Hunches are dangerous things, Mr. Van Houton," Doran said. "If you have any direct accusations to make against anyone, why—"

"Or," Van Houton straightened, "if anyone has direct accusations to make against me."

And that was all. The police scattered quickly. The front door slammed, the kitchen one too. And I— Well, if Brown was in that room, or those rooms, he was caught. And this time it wasn't Van Houton who had trapped him, but I. My words—the words I should never have spoken. Yes, I couldn't tell myself differently. I had read the suspicion in Ramsey's eyes almost before the words were out of my mouth.

Six of us went up those stairs. At the second floor Ramsey paused. "You stay here, Jenks," he said to the young detective. "Maybe you spoke out of turn at the right time."

"And me?" said Hannigan, who was rubbing his head.

"You!" sneered Ramsey. "You go to the kitchen and soak your head in the sink, or get someone to do it for you."

Doran, Van Houton, Ramsey and myself mounted those stairs to the third floor. There was one floor above that; shadows moved back on the stairs.

"The servants!" Van Houton explained, and to the butler who stepped forward and held his ground, "There's no further cause for alarm. I told you there would be some excitement tonight and to stay in your rooms."

"Yes, sir. You did, sir. But the police insisted on searching each room. Quite unnecessarily, since we did that most carefully before locking our doors." And suddenly, gripping Van Houton's arm, "I have something to tell you, sir."

"Well," said Van Houton, shaking off his arm, "out with it!"

"With all these men present and—" The butler jerked his head and rolled his eyes at a door down the hall close to the servants' stairs.

"Yes, yes." Van Houton nodded. "This is police business. We must not interfere with the law. They know. Now, what is it?"

"Well—" the butler straightened. "Did Miss—did—is she—you didn't say she'd be here tonight."

"And she's not here. Come! Out with it, man."

"There's someone in her rooms," said the butler dramatically. "I heard the feet and I saw the—the light."

"So—" Ramsey nodded grimly. He turned, a triumphant smile; a sneering smile. "How long ago?"

"Not five minutes ago," the butler whispered as he followed us down the hall. "The light's there now. You can see it through the keyhole."

RAMSEY BENT to the keyhole. We were all silent, listening. Just dead silence and then feet; soft, careful feet; nervous feet. As if someone paced up and down.

"A light, all right." Ramsey came to his feet. "And it looks like we have our bird cornered. It may be a shock to you, Mr. Doran," and he held out his hand to Van Houton as he asked for the key.

"I haven't any key," Van Houton said. "I assure you, gentlemen, that—" He stopped. Ramsey grinned, turned the knob slowly, then quickly jumped back clutching for his gun.

Someone inside had jerked the door open; a small figure was framed in the light; a small bag was in her hand; her face was almost buried in an ermine wrap. Just that flash of a white face as she spoke in a high-pitched, half-hysterical voice.

"I've been scared to death. Guns—shots—men! What's happened?" And for the first time realizing that several figures stood in the hall she rushed forward, buried her blond head against Van Houton's chest and cried: "Vince—Vince! You're all right? What happened? These men—these men!"

And I heard Mortimer Doran, who hardly ever missed a first night and was quite an admirer of stage celebrities, say: "The actress, Gertrude la Palatin."

I nodded my head in understanding. Brown had known she was very friendly with Van Houton—if this friendly, I didn't know. I had seen her once or twice on the stage, but before she had become so famous as an impersonator and mimic.

Van Houton said, over the girl's shoulder: "There'll be no need to search the rooms now. She's been here all evening."

Ramsey half looked into the room then looked at Mortimer Doran. Then he said: "Well—as long as we're here. A guy might have slipped in while she was in the bedroom or otherwise disposed."

Mortimer Doran entered the room at once, discreetly missing the little scene between Van Houton and the actress. Ramsey stared at the man and the woman for some time; heard part of their conversation as did I. For I just stood there gaping at the back of that blond head.

Van Houton said to her: "I didn't know you were coming; didn't know you were here."

And the woman answered: "I never left my rooms. I didn't play tonight. I have a new piece; these rooms create the atmosphere and— What happened? I was so frightened!"

There was more, of course. But I didn't get it, for Van Houton led the woman down the hall. Ramsey chewed on a match, watched them start down the front stairs, then with a shrug turned into the room.

I FOLLOWED Ramsey about those beautiful rooms. They must have been done by Durio, of Fifth Avenue. And the pictures! Rare works of art. I even recognized a— But Ramsey! I had sucked in my breath each time he opened a closet.

The search was completed, and no Brown. Maybe all my fears were groundless. I might have stayed at home and gone to bed. No doubt Brown had discovered the trap and avoided it. When I got home I'd find him there.

Downstairs, Ramsey's mouth hung open, and so did mine. The woman, Gertrude la Palatin, had gone. But that wasn't what caused Ramsey's mouth to hang open. A little figure stood by the open front door.

"You should know me," the slim figure was saying to the policeman who blocked his entrance. "I'm Vee Brown— Detective Vee Brown." And suddenly pushing by the policeman and stepping into the hall, "Why, there's Inspector Ramsey."

"You! You, eh?" Ramsey gasped. "Where did you come from?"

"From home." And turning to me Vee said somewhat sternly, though I saw the slightest twist at the corners of his mouth: "I've got a bone to pick with you, Dean. Why didn't you tell me that Mr. Doran telephoned for me?" And when I just looked blankly at him, "There, there! We won't wash our dirty linen before the inspector. I—"

"How did you happen to come here?" Ramsey snapped.

"Why," Vee fairly gasped, "Dean sent Wong back in the car for me."

And when Ramsey and Doran looked at me, "Why, yes," I said, "I did—when I saw you were here and things were on the up-and-up."

"Why didn't you tell us?" Ramsey grabbed at my arm.

Brown stepped forward, knocked Ramsey's hand from my arm. It was not a hard blow; not exactly a friendly gesture either. He said sharply: "I'm not responsible for my actions to you, Ramsey—and certainly Dean is not for his."

VEE BROWN moved quickly into the library; looked at the safe. "So this was the drawing card." He spoke to Vincent Van Houton, who was leaning against the mantel piece smoking a cigarette. "Nothing valuable gone, I trust. At least, not that precious document you were discussing with me this evening."

"No, no." Vincent Van Houton turned and put those mild blue eyes on Brown. "Nothing missing. The document was taken care of and the safe was not even opened."

"Good!" Brown nodded as the others entered the room. And to Mortimer Doran, "This seems a simple police matter, complicated perhaps by the elaborate methods of—of—" He stroked his chin, grinned at Ramsey and winked at me. "Really, Mr. Doran, I don't know why you sent for me."

"Nor do I," said Doran sharply, but he wasn't looking at Brown. He was looking at Ramsey.

And Ramsey said nothing. His eyes narrowed. He was looking at Van Houton. For the first time, was suspicion that things were not right there entering Ramsey's head?

We moved into the hall. Van Houton still stayed in the library, still leaning against the mantel above the fireplace. He called to Ramsey: "I will have the police guard for the rest of the night, of course." And I didn't think there was sarcasm in his voice when he said: "You might even stay yourself, Inspector."

"I might," said Ramsey. And, again, I was unable to discover sarcasm in Ramsey's return.

Ramsey followed us down the stone steps to Mortimer Doran's car. Twice he would have spoken and twice he changed his mind. Then just before Doran drove away he did say, and I thought in a sort of defense: "I'm sorry I got you out of bed, Mr. Doran, but things aren't hopeless yet. There's the flashlight metal. Might be some fingerprints on it."

"Sure!" Brown cut in. "Maybe mine."

"Maybe," said Ramsey very seriously and very slowly.

"Or maybe Dean's," Brown suggested with a smile.

"Yes," said Ramsey very seriously. "Or maybe Dean's."

I guess I turned red at that; at least, I felt the blood rush
into my face. But Doran said just before the car left the
curb: "You're worse than a couple of children, Vee—you
and Ramsey. Funny at times"—he laughed mirthlessly—
"but not quite so funny at this time of the morning. Good
night!"

RAMSEY STOOD on the curb watching us as Wong
moved the big car silently down the street. I said to Brown:
"That crack about the flashlight may not prove so humor-
ous. You might have familiarized yourself with what had
happened before—"

"Now, now, Dean. There's been enough goat-getting for
one evening. Here!" He ducked his hand quickly into his
coat pocket and out again, leaving a long cylinder of cold
metal in my hand. "I recognized your flash of course, and
removed it from the library table. As for being familiar
with the situation—well, I heard enough from the cops
and guessed the rest. You rather—" And slamming his
hand down upon my knee, "I wouldn't have you any other
way, Dean. Your blundering methods saved, if not my life,
at least my face tonight—and surely the life and career of
Miss Gertrude la Palatin."

"You were there then—in the house?"

"Yes." Brown nodded. "I was a stupid, blundering idiot.
Imagine Van Houton notifying the police! Of course the
evidence was not in the safe."

"You opened it?"

"No. But if I were caught red-handed I'd make a statement that might force the opening of the safe. But you did
it, Dean. Your escape; your dash through the window
convinced the police that the burglar had left the house. I

think you were all in the library when I slid down the rope and got away."

"Slid down what rope—from where?"

"Why"—he nodded—"from Gertrude la Palatin's rooms. We must see that Wong gets rid of the rope and also the flashlight."

"She—she didn't know you were there?"

"Now, now, Dean. I couldn't very well slide down the rope and drag it after me. She dropped it to me. You see, she found me in the kitchen. She came down the back stairs. I was lying close to the house a long time before going in. I was very careful of a trap." And with a grin, "At least I thought I was.

"You see, Dean, I lingered a long time in the kitchen too, listening and watching—watching out into the back yard. And I saw Hannigan come and young Jenkins. How many more I don't know. So I never reached the library. And then the woman!"

"She was willing to save you?"

"Yes, at a price. By God, Dean, I was in a blue funk for the first time in my life! Not that I feared death, though all of us do, of course. But I didn't think of death, nor did I think so much of the public disgrace and the sneering lips of Ramsey, nor the hurt eyes of Doran, nor even the triumphant ones of Van Houton. You know! After all I'm somewhat like Van Houton. God. Dean, I feared most being made ridiculous!"

"And the woman! What do you mean—'a price?'"

"Just that—a price. She led me up the servants' stairs and through the darkened hall to her rooms—kept me there in the darkness, then produced the rope. Where did she get it? I don't know. Why did she have it? I can only guess at that. Maybe she kept it in case she had to leave suddenly without disturbing Van Houton. But she did have it. And I dropped to the ground, picked up Wong cruising a few blocks away, and went back there in style."

"And the price?" I demanded again.

"Oh"—and Brown grew serious—"she's a great actress, of course. But somehow I don't think she's exactly happy in Van Houton's love. She made me promise that, in return for 'my life' as she called it, I would, if necessary, some day later chance that life for her."

"You think she knew you were coming, to rob that safe?"

Brown shrugged. "I'm rather practical. It's hard for me to believe that blind chance led her to the kitchen; that blind chance kept her from telling Van Houton that she was in her rooms; that blind chance made her think of naming such a price—an unknown price. No, Dean, she's a clever woman. Maybe she loves Van Houton and the price has nothing to do with him. Maybe she fears him and hopes I will help her. But she knew—knew of the trap. Waited for me to walk into it, then got my promise."

"And you'd keep such a promise—such a blind promise?"

He held his chin in his hand a long time, and then, "I think so, Dean, I think so. It was a close squeeze tonight."

CHAPTER EIGHT
FIVE GRAND A MINUTE

BACK IN our apartment Brown paced the room. His easy talk was gone, his smiling lips were set grimly and his black eyes were narrow—uneasy.

"I've failed, Dean—failed again," he said. "This man beats me at every trick; yet I pride myself, pat myself on the back tonight because of—what? Because through blind luck, the help of Gertrude la Palatin, and your mad episode I'm a free man. Nothing but a free man. It wouldn't be failure if I had obtained that evidence, for if a man reaches his objective; obtains his goal, it doesn't matter how he accomplished it. Call it 'the breaks' if you wish. But life is full of good and bad breaks. It's the persistent lad who gets the good breaks. If you're not plugging; not on the job, you won't be around when what we call 'the breaks' come." He smiled somewhat grimly. "I guess I'm trying too much to be a master mind, but certainly I've managed to be around; around when the bad breaks were handed out by fate."

Of course I had to tell him of my experience; of Maria's telephone warning and of my going at once to Van Houton's.

Then we went to bed and to sleep. Or at least I went to sleep. For twice when my dreams, with the spitting lead in them, snapped me awake I knew that Brown was up and around.

It was close to five o'clock when the phone rang. I lifted the receiver from a phone by the bed and got quick sharp words. It was Maria.

"Vee! He's all right?"

"Yes, and you? I'll call him. Where—"

"No. No time. Take this address." I picked up a pencil and scribbled down a street and number far downtown, on the East side. "Now—the name is Cordinia—Carlo Cordinia—C-O-R—"

"I got it," I cut in quickly.

"Good. Have Vee there at two o'clock tonight, tomorrow night, every night—or rather, every morning until I come. It's a lunch room. Just ask for Carlo and— Got it?"

"But—"

"Every night."

"Here's Vee now," I cut in quickly as I saw Brown enter the room.

But the receiver clicked and she was gone.

"It's a queer message." Vee shook his head. "I wonder what she wants to see me about. Another case, no doubt." His shoulders moved up and down. "The Moffet case is dead now. I wonder how long it will take Mortimer Doran to discover that. Tomorrow maybe. A discreet word to 'drop it all,' then an investigation and young Bainton discovering his loss. It's a nasty blow, Dean."

"But Mortimer Doran—others, they won't know the part you played in it."

"But I know the part I played." Brown's eyes flashed; he fairly snapped the words, and turning went to his own room.

WE HAD dinner out that day and we were well through our meal before I noticed the watch Brown had laid upon the table, open, by his coffee cup, the back of the case toward me. I didn't mention it at first. Certainly he was not expecting to go any place in a hurry, for he lingered over his food.

I talked of inconsequential things, then of music. But it was hard to interest him. Mortimer Doran had called on us and talked for an hour about the case Bainton was building up against Moffet.

"It'll knock Moffet clean off his feet. Oh, he suspects it, I guess, but the papers don't. This young Bainton's a marvel and is going to go far." And with a broad grin, "I wouldn't be surprised—that is, if they don't shove me up to the governor's mansion too soon—if Edward Bainton gets my job." And although his tone conveyed that the gubernatorial nomination was referred to jokingly, his glance at both of us was speculative.

"A great chap, Bainton," he went on. "Modest and all that. Says his wife had a lot to do with it. Well, drop into the club and have dinner with me, Vee—and Dean, of course. Bainton tells me the evidence is now quite complete and safe, if this master blackmailer of yours—Van Houton—" he shoved his stick against Brown's chest and laughed—"doesn't bust into the bank's vault where he keeps it."

Now—in the restaurant, Brown saw me looking at the watch at which he continually glanced. "The matter of timing I told you about," he explained. "And always remind me of it, Dean. Seriously"—he tapped the open watch with a finger—"it's a matter of life and death."

And I didn't know if he meant that or was joking. Joking? Hardly. All day he had been very serious.

THAT EVENING after we returned home, along about eight o'clock we had a visitor at our apartment. Brown repeated the name that was sent up and knitted his brows.

"Theodore Lessinger, Dean—of the law firm, Lessinger, Levy and Bryant. A few years ago we'd call them shysters. Today they are big names in the legal profession. And the reason? Politics; crime; money, which three words combined mean—power."

A few minutes later Wong bowed in Theodore Lessinger. He was a tall man who bent slightly, and although smooth, low and cultured of tone he had never gotten over the ingratiating manner of his younger days.

Now he shook his head at Wong, placed his hat on the floor beside him, laid his brief case upon his knees, neatly folded his yellow gloves and held them tightly with both hands on the silver top of his dark cane. So—he assumed a position slightly forward and said: "Nice place, Mr. Brown—delightful place. You have taste, my boy—real taste."

He let his eyes drift back and forth; bulging eyes they seemed through the heavy thickness of his black-rimmed nose glasses. And suddenly bobbing his head at me, "My talk is quite confidential. Mr. Condon is to stay?"

"Yes," said Brown. "He always stays. I have a bad memory."

"Ah! A bad memory. A liability that very often becomes an asset. You are very busy with your police duties, Mr. Brown?"

"Why?" Vee grinned. "You wish to hire me?"

"Quite correct." Lessinger did not smile in return. "That is, I have a client who desires your services; a very little of your time, Mr. Brown. Say—five minutes." He seemed to bend further forward then. "Say—twenty-five thousand dollars for that five minutes. Five thousand dollars a minute! What do you say to that?"

"Your client," said Vee, "is very generous." And although Vee's voice was even, there was the slightest, almost imperceptible movement of his eyelashes, a sign that he was surprised.

"And how," questioned Vee, after a silence, "would I spend those five minutes?"

"You would spend them," said Lessinger very slowly, "looking for a certain envelope—a rather bulky envelope."

"And just what is in this envelope, and where would I look?" Brown's eyes flashed.

"My dear Mr. Brown"—Lessinger never changed his voice—"a man worth such a price for so short a period of time should know what to look for and what to find. My client believes you are that man."

"And your client's name?"

Theodore Lessinger hesitated a moment, and then, "That same man who is worth twenty-five thousand dollars for five minutes is clever enough to guess the name. Let us be done with talk, Mr. Brown." He removed his hands from the cane for the first time, balanced it between his knees, and opening the brief case took out a thick package of bills, held it in his hand a moment, looked at Brown and said: "This package contains five thousand dollars. It—" He stopped, and without taking his eyes off Brown again dug his hand into the brief case and drew out another bundle of bills of similar size, "I'll not quibble, Mr. Brown. I am authorized to pay you ten thousand dollars on your promise to start looking"—and his lips parting slightly—"and, of course, your assurance of a successful search."

BROWN REACHED out his hand, took the money, ran his slender fingers through the bills. Then he wiped the grin that was beginning to form on Lessinger's face clean off it when he handed back the money and said: "No dice, Lessinger. I just wanted to see if it was real. A lot of money in these times!"

"You mean it's not enough. You mean—"

"I mean there's nothing doing." Brown shook his head. "There, there! Don't raise your price. You're breaking my heart now." And with great assurance, "I mean that that envelope, full of evidence, will go to the district attorney."

"Will go—" The words just slipped out of Lessinger's mouth when he came to his feet. "Despite all this luxury—" He caught himself up quickly. "I understand you are not a rich man, Mr. Brown; that Mr. Condon is the one who has the golden touch of Midas. Now—" and stiffly as Brown yawned—"I can offer you any sum within reason—or out of reason for that matter. I—"

"Nothing doing!" Brown was on his feet. "You'll show Mr. Lessinger to the door, Dean, and watch his departure, giving a careful eye to any umbrellas that may be in the hall stand."

Lessinger didn't speak as he gathered up his brief case, hat, gloves and stick and passed out of the living room, across the wide foyer and into the narrow hall beyond the turn. But when I held open the door for him, he set those fishlike eyes on me and said: "Perhaps later you and I can do business, Dean Condon—later."

"Later?" I said inanely. I was greatly puzzled.

"Yes, later. Mr. Brown looks delicate—quite delicate, I should say. He looks like a man who won't live long. So, then—I will see you later."

He was gone. I watched him down the hall to the elevators. His steps were slow, measured and pompous. He looked just what he was—just what he was to the rest of the city—a successful, clever and dignified lawyer.

Vee Brown was pacing the floor and humming when I returned to the living room. His chin was up, his black eyes alive—vividly bright.

"Why"—I burst out—"Why did you let Lessinger believe you had that evidence? He can find out from Van Houton that—"

"Don't you see?" Brown gripped me tightly by the shoulder. "He's already found out from Van Houton; found out that the evidence is missing. And Van Houton— Well, he thinks I have it, Dean; is convinced that I have it."

"But who stole the evidence?"

"Maria." Vee nodded emphatically, and reading the question forming on my lips cut in before I could ask it. "Don't ask me how. It's not how you do things in this life of crime, Dean—it's what you do; what results you get."

"But you don't know that she—"

"She wants to see me—see me badly. And she doesn't know if she can make it or when she can make it. So—two o'clock each morning until she arrives. It may be tonight. I'd—damn it! I'd give my next song to get that evidence and be even with Van Houton."

"But there's Spot Kelly," I said. Then I told Brown what Lessinger had said about his dying.

Brown frowned. "Just his little legal joke; neither very funny nor very alarming. I let Lessinger believe that I had it because—he might be fishing. He watched me closely, Dean. I hope I didn't give the show away—and I hope you didn't. He was watching you too. It wouldn't do for him to suspect Maria." His lips set very gravely. "We mustn't fall into any more traps."

"No," I said. "Be careful."

"Careful!" Vee laughed. He was humming, boyish, different, since Lessinger had come and he saw a chance to get that evidence again. "That's great advice to give a cop. But the breaks have been against us, Dean. That can't last; our turn will have to come." He looked toward the ceiling. "Through Maria, tonight—tomorrow night—the night after. But it must come—soon."

AGAIN VEE wouldn't let me go with him when he left the house that night shortly before one o'clock. He explained his not taking me. "It isn't as if I were going into danger. It's simply a waiting game. Two of us might complicate matters. Again, conditions are such that you should be here at night. Her plans may change; she might chance a visit here."

"But why so early? She said 'two'." I looked at the clock.

"I might be followed and it would take time to throw a shadow off my trail. Besides— Hell, Dean, to my shame I must confess that tonight I'm as nervous and excited as a young school girl at graduation. It's like my first case. I've got to be moving." And just before the door closed, "To be fair and honest I'm very much afraid that this Van Houton gets in my hair."

Waiting hours are long hours. I tried to read, tried to keep from pacing the floor. Just one thing that wasn't difficult. It wasn't hard to stay awake. Thoughts attended to that.

It was ten minutes after five when Brown rolled in and threw himself into a chair. There was no need to ask him if the girl, Maria, had showed up. I knew that she hadn't.

"She'd come if she could," he said after he asked about a telephone call. "It would be terrible if Van Houton found out about Maria. He hates me, Dean; he'd kill her horribly."

"I waited until close to five. I expect, if she can come, she'll be very close to the hour of two." He took the drink I handed him and smiled up at me. "You look white and drawn. Long hours, eh? Or painting horrible pictures of my demise? What could happen to me through Maria?"

"I wasn't thinking of Maria or Van Houton," I told him. "I was thinking of you alone on the streets—the deserted East Side—and of Spot Kelly."

"Hell!" Vee gulped his drink. "I wasn't even followed, and lucky I wasn't; at least, on my way home. I was in a particularly vicious mood."

I listened to his description of the place. "It's an all-night lunch room, Dean—a respectable one. Carlo Cordinia is a fat, greasy gentleman, to whom the name of Maria is magic. He asks no questions and expects no confidences. He has given me a key to the little room above and to the back of the restaurant. It's a small room that might have been used for cards and perhaps drinks, but free for me now that Maria has spoken. Free for you too, Dean, if I ever should send for you—need you. And I may Dean—I may."

CHAPTER NINE
DEAD BEFORE BREAKFAST

THREE CONSECUTIVE mornings after that Brown returned and dropped into the chair. Maria had not yet come. They were quiet days. Always, when we ate out, Brown's watch—a new one now, with a much larger case—was on the table hidden by his coffee cup or his glass. Once or twice I asked him about it. He grinned and smiled.

"The watch is to kill, Dean." And when my eyes opened wide, "I've told you it was a question of time; killing time—maybe, killing by time."

Twice in those days we had a call from Detective Tom Haskin of Chicago. He was not encouraging—at least, to me. Each time when he came, Brown was in the gun room and each time when I went for him there, he lifted the huge, cumbersome timepiece from the table and shoved it into his pocket. Funny that! I never really got a good look at it, and somehow I began to connect it up with a superstition—like a rabbit's foot.

The last time Detective Haskin called, Brown came from the gun room, said, spreading out his hands. "Here I am in the flesh. You've always seemed surprised; disappointed, maybe. The hometown boy, Spot Kelly, has not made good in the big city!"

Detective Haskin did not smile in return. He shook his head, tapped a letter he held in his hand. "From my buddy in Chicago," he said seriously. "You can expect it any time now. God, Brown, I'm a good shot! I know this guy, Kelly's, map. Why not let me tag along with you? Especially on these early-morning excursions."

"No." Brown shook his head. "And I saw you at five this morning, when I came in. Don't you ever sleep?"

"You make it hard." Haskin shook his head. "I didn't try especially to hide from you. Park Avenue's a lonely street, and five in the morning would be the time for it. There's no use in trying to tail you. I'm working alone, and you know the ropes." He put a hand across his mouth. "As for watching this apartment all night! Hell, I've got to sleep some time and Kelly's just as apt to go after you in broad daylight, right on Broadway."

"Forget it!" Vee told him. "I'd as soon pal around with an undertaker as you." But he grinned when he said: "Good-by, Sunshine."

And that last visit of the detective was on Friday night, rather early in the evening. As for myself—Well, Haskin was certainly a somber bird. But he knew Spot Kelly, and seemed sincere in his efforts to see that Brown did not discount Kelly's ability, almost genius for carrying through a murder.

But Brown said: "He's an old woman, Dean. Imagine his being sent to guard a banker or a broker or even a clergyman! Why, he'd have the poor men dead of fright long before Spot Kelly even got a chance to draw a gun on them."

THAT NIGHT—OR rather, early that Saturday morning—I was more nervous than usual as I waited for Brown. It was just two o'clock—two o'clock to the minute—when the phone rang.

I grasped the instrument. Brown sending for me? Or Maria with a message? And it was neither of them. I recognized that gruff voice over the phone even before I got the name.

"Brown there? Damned important. Haskin speaking—Detective Haskin."

"He's—he's out." I guess I Stammered. The man's voice seemed even more ominous than usual.

"Well, get in touch with him; give him a buzz. Tell him either to lock himself in the apartment and send for help or hide out all night."

"Why?"

"Why!" he said. "I just got a phone call from Chicago. They are betting three to one in the right circles that Brown will be dead before breakfast. Now listen, Condon. You've got sense—sense that isn't overshadowed by a false idea of Brown's charmed life. Spot Kelly has taken Brown's past performances into consideration. I understand he's imported a load of gunmen, and they're to blast Brown out."

"But—" I stammered. "I thought Spot Kelly always worked alone."

"Have it your own way—if you know more than I do," he cut in gruffly. "There's no use trying to help or advise you New York guys; you're too wise."

"But they won't be able to find Vee, and—"

"No?" he said. "I found him the other morning—could have popped him off too."

"Oh, he saw you and—"

"All right, all right. Tell me the same thing at his funeral. We'll have lots of time then to talk it over. Good night!"

The phone banged up. I was mad. Then—I didn't know. After all, we had not treated this detective over well. Brown, I guess, resented his assurance that Kelly would get him. And Haskin! He made no bones about his mission in the city. It was to get Spot Kelly—not to save Brown. Still, he had called up and—

I went to the phone, and remembered that Vee had given me no number to call. I grabbed the telephone book and started to wade through it for Carlo Cordinia. But I only started. Suppose he had a phone. Who would answer it? Would Brown want to be called to the phone? Where would the phone be, and—I was into my hat and coat and shoving the button for the automatic lift! I must warn Brown, of course. A speeding car along Park Avenue; spitting lead from machine guns, and he'd— But enough of such thoughts.

I HAD no difficulty in finding the little lunch room with its dingy, smoke-covered window and its faded, gilded sign which bore the letters *Carlo Cordmia.*

I didn't enter the lunch room itself. I turned to the little door a few feet down the block that led to the hall, the stairs and the room at the top, to the left, where Brown waited. He had described it to me well enough. I'd have little difficulty if the door—the heavy outside door, that led to the dingy unlighted vestibule, was open. I passed in, paused, saw the dirty glass of the inside door and the dull light that burned behind it. My hand turned upon the knob. Would the inside door be locked; would— I pushed forward and the door gave.

So this was the place Brown waited, I thought; waited for the coming of Maria. Anyone might enter; anyone might sneak in and—I was in the hall. Dirty, damp, sticky! An ill-smelling place. My feet made no sound on heavy carpet. The dull light came from a rear hall. Dimly I made out a flight of steps; at least the first two or three steps. The room at the top of those steps, to the lefts—and Brown!

Cautiously my foot went out, silently it landed on that carpeted step. Why, anyone could—

I stopped dead and fell back a step. A broad figure had risen from the darkness; something hard was pounded against my stomach. A voice said: "What you do here? What you want here? Come! Speak fast, or this gun blow a great hole in your middle."

"Brown. Vee. I'm—" The man was backing me toward the rear, nearer the light. Was he going to shoot? This man must be Carlo Cordinia, from Vee's description. Quickly I said: "Maria—Maria. I'm her friend. Brown's friend."

"Oh!" the man said, but the gun did not lower. "Maria." He had a way of stretching out the name. "You are lucky I'm a careful, slow man. You are the other one then." And when I would have put my hands down, which had mechanically jarred above my head when the gun bore into my stomach, "Maybe you lie, eh? Maybe not. Turn! Go above! We have the identification for sure—certain. Carlo is no fool. Maria tell you that."

My appearance before Brown was not the strong, silent one I had expected. Instead, I was marched up those stairs with a gun; the muzzle of a sawed-off gun stuck in my back.

Narrow stairs, the turn to the left, the room at the back, and Carlo's tap on the door. Then Brown's smile when he opened that door and saw me.

"All right, Carlo." He laughed. "You're a good guard." He turned back to the table with the red-and-black-checked cloth upon it and sat down. "Close the door, Dean. Carlo can find his way in the dark."

I CLOSED the door, started to say something about locking it, then didn't. My mouth just hung open in amazement. Seated at that table, facing the door, was the girl, Maria. There was a veil covering most of her face, but I thought I caught the green of her eyes.

"Sit down," Brown directed me to a chair so that my back was directly to the window. "A fire escape," he explained. "I like to face it. Spot Kelly is making me a careful man, even here. There's a door behind me, of course, but you found out how well the stairs to it are guarded."

"I did," I said, and looking at the papers scattered about the table that Brown was placing in an envelope, "Maria had it then. That's the evidence?"

Vee nodded. "All of it. Not a thing missing, Dean," And with a quizzical look in his eyes as he shoved the envelope into his inside coat pocket, "Not even you."

"Not even the watch," I said as I saw it on the table, close to a glass of red wine.

He laughed. "No need for it here in this hideaway. But I must make it a habit." His thin shoulders shrugged as his hand came down and moved the watch slightly. He looked at it, moved it again and nodded, took a drink from the glass of red liquid. "Bah!" he said. "Bitter. But it would offend our good host, Carlo, and there's no place to throw it. Now—why your visit, Dean? Nerves, or—"

I told him.

"Nonsense!" He smiled over at the girl as he leaned forward, his chin in his hands, his elbows on the table. "A car load of guns are easier to spot than a single man with a single purpose. No, that has been tried before and— What's the matter, Dean?"

And there was something the matter. The door directly behind Brown; the door by which I had entered had silently opened. A man stood there. There was a slouch hat far down on his forehead. A black mask covered his eyes and nose and part of his chin. But his hands! Both his hands were extended; one moving slightly between the girl and myself, the other trained smack on the back of Brown's head; and both of those hands held guns, menacing black guns. I recognized the make—the long barrel, the fine dull steel. They were German Lugers.

"Never mind getting advice from your buddy, Brown." The masked figure spoke. "Keep your elbows on the table— just as they are. I like to talk, brother. But one movement of your arms will interrupt the conversation. As for the dame! She better leave that hand bag lay. Yep, it's Spot Kelly talking. Try and laugh that off, Mr. Vee Brown— Killer of Men."

"So," Brown spoke, "you've come at last. How did you work it?"

"You'd like to know, eh? Well, I'd like you to know. Just keep them little white fingers of yours on the table, Condon. If you're a good boy and she's a good girl you're in no danger, if I don't get nervous. I kill for cash, and cash only. How did I get here? Well, I found I couldn't trail you, Brown, so I trailed your friend, Condon. Followed him and the grease ball up the stairs, waited in the dark and knocked the grease ball on the head and let him fall easy. Then—just walked in."

I LOOKED at Brown. Would I see reproach in his eyes? I had led the killer directly to him. But I saw nothing in Brown's eyes. He was looking down on the table; looking—yes, staring, almost fascinated, straight at that watch; at the open, peculiarly slanted case of that watch. He never took his eyes from it as he spoke.

"So that's how it was." Vee's head seemed to move slightly, but his eyes never raised. Mine did. They raised from the watch on the table to Brown's face—well, not quite to his face. They stopped. I saw Vee's right hand; his right hand that was coming slowly out from under his coat, crawling out with but a movement of the wrist, so that his elbow never moved upon the table. A gun—a snub-nosed automatic—was appearing from under his left armpit. And his body and his arm were rigid. Just his hand and wrist were moving—moving so stealthily that the masked figure behind him could not know.

What did he expect to do? What did he hope to do? Spin and fire? Fire before that man could close a finger on a gun; a gun that could shoot twenty city blocks; a gun in the hand of a paid murderer; a man who had killed over and over again?

"Well!" said Kelly. "Ready to take it?"

"Are you ready to give it?" Brown's voice was very calm. "Oh, you've got me clean enough. But how about your getaway?"

"Out the window—down the fire escape." The masked figure shrugged broad shoulders.

Fascinated, I watched Brown. His eyes—black, pointed balls; glaring balls—never left that watch. And I saw his hand. The gun was turned now and creeping up his left side, to his shoulder, moving steadily, close—very close to his chin, unseen of course by the masked figure.

But he didn't have a chance. Spot Kelly had extended his right hand, closer to Brown's head. Six feet away, no more. He couldn't miss, no matter— And I saw his fingers tightening. Spot Kelly was going to— And Brown spoke; to gain time, I thought.

"You don't know who the girl is then? You're not going to—"

"The girl?" The words just came from behind that mask. Metallic, plainly without any attempt to appear natural. And in sudden determination, "But you take it first."

Brown's eyes narrowed. His lips set to a thin red gash, then curled cruelly at the right corner. I saw that in the split second and recognized what it meant. But it couldn't be. It was impossible. For that look always meant that Vee was on the kill.

CHAPTER TEN
BEHIND THE MADE

OF JUST what happened for that split second I can never be sure. I saw Brown's right hand dart like a striking snake up over his shoulder as his slender body fell forward and he crashed upon the table.

I heard the shot. Two shots? Yes, it seemed like two shots. And I heard the glass in the window behind me crack just as orange-blue flame darted from that German Luger.

Then I saw things. I was looking directly at Spot Kelly; that black mask. Plainly, high up on that mask, almost in the center of the man's forehead was a white hole in the black. Then it wasn't white. It was purple.

Spot Kelly straightened, half bent backward. Both his hands dropped to his sides. Then his left hand came up, very slowly; dropped again lifelessly. His whole body spun and he crashed to the floor.

Through it all Maria hadn't moved. I knew that. She sat there as if paralyzed. Now, as Brown came to his feet, spun around, his gun ready, she sank slowly onto the table.

Brown spoke—and his voice was eager, his words quick. Pride in them? Yes, there was that all right "Now, that's shooting. Oh, I couldn't very well have missed him—I had practice enough. But a bull's eye!"

"It was a close call, Vee; a split second— If he had shot a split second sooner! You were pretty lucky. The breaks came at—"

"The breaks!" He cut in on me. "No breaks in that. He saw my gun—that's what caused him to shoot. I couldn't see his face, behind the mask, but I knew what was there. Fear, terror, horror. Rats are all the same, if they come from Chicago or Philly, or right from our own town. He just didn't have the guts for it when the time came. I counted partly on that, though I'd have shot him to death before he ever could close a finger on the trigger if he hadn't seen my gun. That's why I kept him talking. The breaks!" He scoffed in that childish, hurt way of his. "If there were any breaks in this shooting, Spot Kelly got them. But we'll have a look behind that mask."

"How did you do it, Vee? Somehow—"

He was half on his knee by the still body when he turned his head and came quickly to the table. Maria was leaning on her hands; queer sounds were deep down in her chest.

Vee went to her, slipped an arm under her shoulder, lifted up her head. Her cheeks were wet below the veil. Maria; hard, sinister and—

"Maria!" was all Brown said, but there was something in his voice that was new.

"I'm all right." She came to her feet, staggered slightly, clutched at the table as Brown gripped her arm.

"Don't look at him if—" I started, as I got between her and the dead man on the floor.

"It isn't that. It isn't that," she said. "It's new—something new. I didn't think I'd ever be able to cry again." And suddenly clutching at Vee, holding tight to him, "I—my eyes closed for a moment. I thought"—she looked down at the silent figure—"I thought it was you, Vee."

POUNDING FEET on the stairs outside that door, a commanding voice. Then the voice of Carlo Cordinia, whom I found out later had recovered and staggered erect. Then plainly, the first voice again—a voice I knew, recognized.

"Is that the door? Damn it! I heard the shots. Out of the way."

The girl jerked from Brown, leaped across the room. "Ramsey—Inspector Ramsey," she gasped the words, ran to the window and all but her legs disappeared behind the shade. I heard the window go up as the door flew open and Ramsey was in the room. Behind him I saw Cordinia, his eyes wide.

"Hell!" said Brown. "A little late, as usual, Ramsey." And to me, "The window, Dean."

I was too late or Ramsey was too strong. His great hand shot out, smacking me back against the wall. He was across the room, lunging forward, tripping suddenly over Vee's foot and stretching himself full length on the floor.

He was on his feet at once. Anger blazed in his eyes. He half stepped toward the window, saw Brown's grinning face and turned toward him, his hands raised, his face red, his lip bleeding where his teeth had bit into it. The girl was gone.

Ramsey's left hand held a gun. It dropped to his side. Two steps he took forward, and stretching out his right hand hammered it down on Brown's shoulder.

Vee's face paled, his lips twisted. Ramsey was a strong man. I knew his fingers were biting into Brown's shoulder; the pain was plainly stamped on his face. In that moment of triumph—Brown's success, I saw tragedy. I cried out: "Don't Ramsey! Take your hand off Vee!"

I knew how Brown hated, almost to an obsession, anyone placing a hand on him; an unfriendly hand, especially a violent hand; one that gave physical pain. I wasn't thinking of Brown, afraid for Brown when I shouted. My fear was for Ramsey—Inspector Ramsey.

"So the little man doesn't like some of his own medicine," Ramsey started—and stopped. His eyes bulged. Vee had whipped out a gun and thrust it against his stomach so violently that Ramsey finished his sentence with a gasp.

"Drop your hand, Ramsey, or—"

Inspector Ramsey's hand dropped to his side as if it had been struck from Brown's shoulder. He stepped back a pace. His eyes were fastened on those glaring black ones of Brown. His tongue came out and licked at his lips. He said: "By God, Brown! I believe you meant—meant to kill me."

"By God!" said Vee very slowly, "I did."

For a full minute they faced each other. Neither man spoke. Then Ramsey said: "You tripped me on purpose. You're not denying that."

"I saved your life," lied Brown. "A girl with a gun was on that fire escape. Spot Kelly had a girl with him. But no matter. Kelly's dead and the girl got away. Now—how did you find your way here?"

"I got a tip," said Ramsey. "Like you get tips. And I don't believe that one about the girl. The tip was that you were to be shot to death here tonight."

"Well, I wasn't," said Brown. He walked to the window, carefully raised the shade and peered out into the night. "Others heard you and beat in when the girl went through the window. You certainly throw the fear of the law into the criminal, Ramsey. We'd better have a look at the stiff."

VEE WALKED across the room and again he dropped to one knee by the body of the dead gunman; the man who made a business of murder. I was looking down at the squat figure when Brown jerked off the mask, and I was the one who gasped the words.

"Tom Haskin. Detective Tom Haskin, from Chicago."

Brown looked long and steadily at the dead face, with the round hole in the center of his forehead. Then he turned to Ramsey with a sneer. "You made a, fine job of investigating his credentials. Not surprised, eh?"

"I know." Ramsey seemed really contrite for a moment. And then, "Doran and I both were careless. But he had Haskin's papers. And I'm not surprised, because the body of Tom Haskin was identified by a dentist—his dentist in Chicago—tonight. I got a wire that told that this Haskin was a fake. The Chicago police thought he was here."

"Oh!" Brown nodded. "So he wasn't just a cop, gone wrong."

"No," said Ramsey. "Tom Haskin was sent on to New York, but he never got started. We were advised of his coming. This man, Spot Kelly, murdered him and left his body on the railroad tracks. It was horribly mutilated when found a week ago. The identification by the police was just good detective work. It finally came through his teeth. That's why I came here tonight. To find you—warn you." Ramsey gulped. "It's hardly believable, but I came to protect you."

"Yeah—it is hardly believable. How did you find your way here?"

"Well," said Ramsey. "I've had you shadowed, clever as you are. I knew you'd been coming here for the last three mornings at least."

"So—" Vee Brown stroked his chin. "Then you know I haven't had much sleep. The corpse is yours. Good night!"

"But"—Ramsey followed us to the door—"how did this man die?"

Brown's eyes opened wide. "I'll ring up the D.A. and make a full report, of course. But for your own enlightenment—he was shot with a gun, straight between the eyes."

And to me when we had walked nearly a half dozen blocks before finding a cab, "Ramsey hates me, Dean. I don't believe that story of his that he came to protect me. I'd rather believe that he was downstairs and waited until he heard the shots. But then, he doesn't believe my story about the girl, so we're even." He leaned back and lighted a cigarette. "Imagine a man on the force as long as he's been wanting to know how Spot Kelly died."

"Well—" I couldn't wait until Brown explained it himself. "How did he; how did you, over your shoulder, you know? It was some shot; some—"

"Don't say it," Vee cut in. "Don't say 'some break.' If there was a break, it was your bringing Spot Kelly to me tonight. Simple, that, though. He telephoned you to warn me, then followed you there, entered the front door and was almost on your heels when you and Carlo Cordinia went up the stairs. After that— He simply waited in the dark and struck Cordinia down.

"No, I didn't have any break. I knew that Spot Kelly always shot his man through the back of his head, and some time he would try to get me that way. Therefore, I also knew that Spot Kelly wasn't used to facing a gun. He wasn't used to seeing threatening death from another man's hand. That would be in my favor; and it was, for his hand trembled when the big moment came. Hell, Dean, you're too good to be true! Didn't you guess how I did it; planned his death just as he planned mine? I've often shot at targets back over my shoulder while looking in a mirror; you've seen me do that. But I couldn't carry a mirror around with me. I thought of the watch. It took practice, of course, but with the small case of my own watch it was too uncertain. So I bought the new one and took it in to Irving Small." He lifted the large timepiece from his pocket and slapped it into the palm of his hand. "That turned the trick. In the gun room I made a bull's eye every time, from all angles, all positions. Difficult at first? Well—yes. For as 'Alice' might say: 'In Looking Glass Land everything is backward!'"

IT WAS looking at the watch, striking a match the better to see the highly polished mirror that Irving Small had placed in the back of the now open case.

Brown was saying: "There's just one thing I don't believe, and can't understand. Ramsey never tailed me or had me tailed."

"But I was followed—" I started.

"Bah!" Vee sat up stiff on the edge of the seat. "You and I are two different people, Dean." And then he burst out laughing.

"I don't see anything so funny in—"

"I'm not laughing at you." He threw himself far back in the corner of the cab. "I'm laughing at Van Houton. A hundred grand smack on the line! He can't afford it, Dean—not after losing that evidence. A hundred grand. And Spot Kelly missed me by a good foot."

THE SWINGING CORPSE

THERE IT HUNG AT THE CROSS
ROADS OF THE WORLD—FIFTH
AVENUE AND FORTY-SECOND
STREET—A GHASTLY, MUTILATED
CORPSE. AND ON ITS CHEST WAS
PINNED THE BLACK DEATH'S
FINAL WARNING. HOW HAD IT GOT
THERE THROUGH THE MIDNIGHT
FOG? WHY HAD THE CAT MAN
SWUNG IT FROM A LAMP POST ON
THE BEST-KNOWN CORNER IN ALL
NEW YORK?

CHAPTER ONE
A QUESTION OF HONOR

MARIA, THE girl with the green eyes, sat beneath the darkened lamp seeking the shadows, as she always did when visiting us. Her hands rested very gently in her lap. Her lips were a deep scarlet, her lashes and eyes heavily treated; all plainly visible despite the dimness. Maria—girl of mystery—who hated Vincent Van Houton, the man Detective Vee Brown was convinced was the blackmailer who preyed upon the unfortunate, the weak, even those who were simply indiscreet.

Her green eyes watched Vee from the darkness. Finally her head bobbed back, then forward again. She half looked at me but spoke to Vee.

"Vivian!" she said slowly. "The greatest of song writers—Master of Melody. Detective Vee Brown—Killer of Men. You're licked as Detective Vee Brown. Quit this hunt for Vincent Van Houton." And as his dark eyes narrowed and his lips twisted at the corners, "Why not?" Her shoulders shrugged. "Super-men come and go. Sports, politics, crime; even the greatest national leaders must finally step down for a still greater man." And suddenly, "Gertrude la Palatin, the actress, saved your life. You made her a promise."

"Yes." Vee nodded. "You are very well informed. I made her a promise. Do you know what that promise was?"

THE GIRL laughed harshly, putting herself back in character; for surely, just now, her well chosen and well spoken words had hardly been those of the underworld— of the night, as Brown called it. She had suddenly, in speech and manner, if not in her appearance which still remained sinister, stepped out of her environment.

She hesitated before she spoke again, and then; "Yes, I do. You were trapped in Van Houton's house, trapped like a common burglar. Men hunted you with drawn guns, men who had orders to shoot to kill. She saved you then. You promised her your life if she demands it."

"But," said Brown, "she doesn't demand it."

"She demands that you give up your pursuit of Vincent Van Houton. Don't smile. You saved some lives, forestalled many of his plots and plans, deprived him of great amounts of money in his blackmail schemes. But he has defeated you. He's still active, still as unsuspected by the law, by the district attorney. You have simply made things worse."

"How—worse?" Brown asked.

"You cut down his income. You lost him a hundred thousand dollars that he had paid a hired killer to murder you. You took from his pocket many other thousands of dollars, and took from him the information that would free the big political leader, George F. Moffet, who, behind Van Houton, would have made him another fortune. That evidence was turned over to the district attorney. Moffet is already indicted; Vincent Van Houton is desperate. His need of money to keep his organization intact is great. Crooks, gangsters, murderers are crying for funds or blood, and he has not the money to give them."

"But they don't know him, these people whom he hires through others—through those leaders I have eliminated. How can they threaten him?"

"In one way—through one man. Through his biggest connection with the underworld—that is, in person. This is the only man who knows that Van Houton is the Black Death, the Emperor of Evil. The Frankenstein which Van Houton created is back-firing on this one man. Every penny of his vast fortune has been drained by your activities. Van Houton will give him no more; has no more to give the murderers, the thieves, the gangsters, and even the smaller crooked servants—taxi drivers, waiters and gigolos—that produce the information necessary for Van Houton's operations."

"Sounds interesting, and it's true," Brown said. "I worked up from the bottom, cut off those Van Houton trusted. Now, if we can eliminate this final connection, Van Houton can no longer remain unknown. He can still advise his friends in his own social circle, whom he fleeces through his hired murderers and blackmailers. But to those hired criminals he must make himself known, and once he does"—Brown tapped the side of the chair—"his secret will be a secret no longer and I'll get him sure."

"There are no others he can trust," the girl said. "He won't come out in the open himself."

"Ah!" said Brown. "Then he must go out of business, and as we say in chess—it would be a stale mate. I would not have the pleasure of seeing Van Houton burnt to death, of course. But I would see him beaten and no longer a menace to society."

"You are wrong." The girl was very serious. "Contrary to the opinion of Van Houton's closest connection—this sole remaining man who knows him—Van Houton still has some money. Not enough, of course, to carry on against your activity; not enough, of course, to keep paying out more to these scores—perhaps hundreds—of hirelings.

The Cat Man's face twisted in anger
as the animal squealed.

But enough to live comfortably himself until you are driven
out, killed, or quit hounding him."

"That'll be a long time," Brown mused.

I HAD never seen Maria quite so serious as she answered: "I hope not. It will be an evil time, a time of wrecked homes. It will be a period of divorces, children torn from parents, mental torture and death." She leaned forward. Her lips were tightly set, her green eyes narrow. "For during this period when he cannot increase his income Van Houton will tear down the characters of many people. He will begin with the wife of a college friend of yours, perhaps more a friend of Dean's. Thomas D. Wilson's wife is caught in his net. I telephoned you about her this morning. She has no more money to meet the Black Death's demands. Will she welcome death rather than face her husband and two young daughters, to whom she has more than atoned for a past folly?"

Brown stroked his chin. "And I am to quit cold, so that Van Houton may pick out the ones with money to fleece; so that he will not cause destruction to those who cannot pay! Is that your advice, Maria; you who have hated this man; you who have given me the names of those he would blackmail? Now you want me to walk out, so he may rebuild his crumbling horror; build again a great fortune through the misery of the unfortunate!"

"I bring you that message from Gertrude la Palatin."

"You're a strange girl. You know everything connected with this Black Death, everything except the evidence that will— But the song I have written for you! Let's go over it again."

"But your promise to Miss La Palatin?"

"I offered her my life, if necessary, in return for saving mine." Vee came to his feet, let his lips curve into that whimsical, twisted smile and bowed as he said half mockingly: "I did not offer her my honor."

"Your honor would not have been worth much that night at Van Houton's if Inspector Ramsey and the district attorney had found you there, attempting to rob Van Houton's safe. Remember—they have not the same belief in Van Houton being the Black Death that you have. You're licked, Vee, and you're not a big enough man to see it. You're without fear. Put a gun in your hand and one in the hand of a criminal, and you're invincible. But this time! Van Houton never carries a gun, won't have one in his house. You haven't got a man who'll shoot it out with you. Your honor—"

"Very well, then"—and this time Vee was serious—"I owe my life and my honor both to Gertrude la Palatin. If necessary—understand, only if necessary—I will sacrifice both that honor and that life for her."

"Then you'll—you'll quit; not bother Van Houton again?"

"No, I won't quit. Don't you see, Maria? I can't. After all I'm just a cop—a common cop. Personally I hate this Van Houton; personally I owe much to this Gertrude la Palatin." And after a moment's pause, "But above all I'm simply a machine—a crime machine—hired and paid by the State, the people of that State. I can not promise the lives nor the honor of those people."

"Not even—even for—if you loved a woman?"

Maria was on her feet now, facing him. Brown took a step forward; he was very close, his slender body not much bigger than hers. He stretched out those small hands with the long strong fingers—fingers that could pick melody worth thousands of dollars out of the air and strum it on the piano—fingers that could close upon a trigger and place lead straight between a criminal's eyes. He spoke very slowly and his words jarred me, surprised me. Silly that, for I'm not sure I fully understood them.

"Not even for a woman I love."

THEY STOOD looking at each other for a long moment. Oh, I knew that Maria loved Vee. But I didn't know before, and—damn it!—I didn't know now, that Vee loved her.

Maria half leaned forward. Beautiful? Yes. There were times when that cold cruel mouth became soft, those sinister green eyes almost kindly.

Vee laughed and said: "Damn it! Maria, we're treating Dean like the furniture—like an overstuffed chair." Unconsciously, I think, and resentful of his own lack of physical strength, he often made fun of mine.

Maria looked straight at him. "I guess," she said very slowly, "it's Vivian, the song writer, I'm in love with. Why do you think this Gertrude la Palatin wants you to quit?"

"To save her own hide, of course." Vee shrugged his shoulders.

Green eyes blazed. "And why do you think I want you to quit?"

"To save my hide," said Vee. "You have altogether too much respect for Mr. Vincent Van Houton and too little for me. But since it's Vivian now, let's have a last rehearsal of that song. Damn it! Maria, I'll see that my publishers find you a spot—a big spot. That song will make you, and you will make the song."

Vee winked over at me, and taking the girl by the arm passed from the living room to the music room, leaving the door open but swinging the curtains closed behind them.

I heard him say: "It's a tough, rough number and you'll have to get someone who'll know how to put the steps over. *Girl of the Night!* You won't need any make-up"—and so low I hardly caught the words—"that is, any more than you already wear. When, Maria, are we—to see the real woman beneath the paint and cement?"

CHAPTER TWO
CAT MAN

UNLIKE THE close friend and biographer of many great detectives I am unable to sit and think over a pipe. It goes out on me every few minutes. Bits of tobacco gather on my lips; burning, ill-tasting juice drops back into my throat. But usually I do fairly well with cigarettes—And now my thoughts, as Maria's voice, slightly husky but with a professional touch that even I could not miss, came from the music room— Well, maybe it was the lack of a pipe, but they did not fit like the well-placed pieces of a jig-saw puzzle. On the contrary, they were disordered, jumpy, unpleasant thoughts.

Brown's many victories over Van Houton did not stand up so well in a future picture. Certainly Vee went directly after men he wanted, pushed them into a corner, drove them to fight for their lives; or they attempted to take his, and death followed; quick and sudden—and sure.

Here was Van Houton; blackmailer, murderer—yes, as much a murderer as if he had pressed the trigger of the gun or driven the knife home! I shuddered. The knife! That was the method of the Black Death when killers did their work. And always on the body of a victim, mostly pierced by the knife that struck death, was a tiny card. THE BLACK DEATH. The warning to other victims that another unfortunate could not or did not pay.

Back in his beautiful home, with its well-trained, high-class and perfectly referenced servants, sat the Emperor of Evil, as Brown had called him. Quiet, serene, soft-spoken Vincent Van Houton—society man, lover of cats; and with a benevolent attitude toward his social associates who were threatened by his blackmailers. There were even stories that he had lent people money to pay this Black Death, that he was spending money to hunt down this criminal; and he had admitted to being blackmailed himself.

No one but Brown believed that Van Houton was this Black Death. Mortimer Doran, the district attorney, smiled condescendingly. Doran felt that Brown was getting results even if Van Houton was not part of those results. As for Inspector Ramsey! He was a shrewd, clever, efficient police officer. But he disliked Brown and so tore apart all of his theories.

And Gertrude la Palatin, the mimic; probably the greatest female impersonator on the stage today! Where did she fit? Did she love Van Houton? Hardly, for she had freed Brown. Did she hate him? Hardly, for— And I stopped there. She might very easily hate him or fear him; just another of his victims.

And Maria, who knew so much; knew so many of Van Houton's moves before he fairly started them! Where did she—

And she was singing again. I raised my head. It seemed different; as if she had played a part before and now let herself go. It was the voice of the Maria we had first met; low, harsh, hard and cruel, perhaps, but yet with a certain—

The door bell buzzed far back in the apartment. Wong was out. I walked quietly into the foyer so as not to disturb Vee, turned into the narrow hall, opened the front door— and stepped back, my eyes wide, my mouth open. If a gun had been shoved into my stomach I could not have been more surprised.

But no gun was shoved into my stomach. I was looking into the soft blue eyes of Vincent Van Houton. Not only looking, but I had allowed him to slip through the open door, even pass me and go down the narrow hall, his cane dangling on his arm, his hat in his hand, his curly blond head just turning toward the living room.

I CAME to myself, stepped quickly after him, grabbed his arm and swung him back into the narrow hall. "What do you want?" I raised my voice almost to a shout; scraped my feet. The singing had suddenly stopped.

"Really!" He jerked his arm free of my grip, brushed carefully at his sleeve. "This is hardly the way to treat a guest. When you and our esteemed friend, Brown, call on me, you are better received."

"How did you get upstairs?" I demanded, now blocking his way to the living room.

"Get upstairs! Upon my word, Mr. Condon, you speak as if you were running a night club—and in these times!" And when I did not smile in return, "There! I won't make a mystery of it. I simply paid more for the elevator ride up than you evidently offer to keep the unannounced rider down. But don't misunderstand me. I am not hinting that you and Brown are cheap. Indeed, I was forced to be more than generous."

Did I hear him? Of course I heard every word of what he said. It's stamped in my memory now. But only unconsciously was it stamped there then. For, paying no attention to him, I called out loudly for Brown. Maria was there. Maria, who gave us so much information. Did Van Houton suspect that? Did he know that? Would Maria and Vee walk directly from the music room? I called again.

"Vee! It's Van Houton. He's here—inside."

Silly that? It sounds silly now and it sounded silly then. But what could I do? I couldn't run to the curtains and whisper to Brown; I couldn't be sure that Van Houton wouldn't follow and look through the curtains too. But silly or not silly, that's what I did.

Vee heard me and Vee came. There was no surprise in his face. He did not offer to shake hands with Van Houton, nor did Van Houton raise his hand. He said simply: "I appear to be, if not an unwelcome guest, at least an alarming one; a most alarming one."

"Hardly that." Brown faced him. "You know what I think of you and I can guess what you think of me. I have been outspoken."

"Delightfully so." Van Houton nodded. "But really, outside your—well, impossible delusions about me, I think you are an efficient detective."

"I'm costing you money, anyway." Brown smiled slightly. "Now—why am I insulted by this visit?"

Van Houton stiffened slightly. "I have something to say to you that will take a few minutes. May I come in the living room and sit down?" And when Brown hesitated, "Or perhaps you have another visitor."

"Come in," Vee finally said, and as he took up a position by the music-room door, "Is it a threat—or just bribery this time?"

Van Houton sat down in the chair, raised his head and sniffed the air. His eyes narrowed slightly; he seemed to sniff again. Then he said: "One would hardly threaten such a courageous man as you, Mr. Brown. As for bribery! I am afraid I am not in a financial position for such an attempt."

"No," said Brown, "you're not." He smiled slightly. I guess he was thinking also of the one hundred thousand dollars that Van Houton had paid Kelly to kill Vee; paid him in advance. "At least I've been stepping on your financial toes."

VAN HOUTON'S head went up again. His mouth was closed tightly, his nose sucked in air sharply, as he sniffed once more.

"If anything offends you," Brown said brusquely, "you don't have to stay."

"No, no," Van Houton said softly. "I am very sensitive; like the cats I admire. At times I doubt that it is entirely nasal; perhaps simply the same instinct of those soft, warm animals."

"Cats," sneered Brown, for he knew that was the one thing that got under the skin of Van Houton, "take everything and give nothing."

"Somewhat like a woman," Van Houton said as he watched the curtains. "It seems that I feel another presence here, now." He looked directly toward the music room.

Brown showed no alarm. He said simply: "If you expect me to clean out my place because you sense an alien presence, why—"

"Not an alien one," Van Houton cut in, "but a friendly one." And lips setting tight, his eyes growing hard, "Or perhaps I should say a familiar one."

"It's no go with us." Brown's face never changed, except to smile perhaps. "Dean and I both read the advertisements."

"Not you nor Dean"—and Van Houton turned his head suddenly and set his eyes directly on me—"but Gertrude la Palatin."

If he had turned from Brown to catch me off my guard, maybe he succeeded. That is, he may have read surprise in my face, perhaps; too, a touch of fear. For if he suspected Gertrude la Palatin of visiting here, then he must know that some woman had preceded him to our penthouse and—maybe he suspected Gertrude la Palatin of letting Brown escape that night. He might—

The curtains of the music room suddenly parted. Maria stood there between them. There was a cigarette dangling from her lips; her eyes were very narrow. So narrow, in fact, that the green did not show at all; just slits of flashing, indistinguishable color. A small hat hung partly down over one eye. She spoke, and her words fairly snapped through tight lips.

"I didn't get all the gent's words"—she shot a finger toward Van Houton—"but I got enough to tell me he's fussy about his company." And to Brown, "I'm on my way. I got the fifty and you got the talk."

She walked across the room; no catlike steps now but long, manish strides. Her face twisted into a grin; more, a smirk. As she passed Van Houton she snapped up his head with her closed right hand.

"Look me up sometime, brother." She jerked a thumb toward Vee and myself. "The boys will give you my number"—and swinging just before she reached the turn in the foyer—"or maybe that educated beak of yours can hunt me out." And she was gone, slamming the door closed behind her.

"Maybe it can." Van Houton's words were more a spoken thought. He half came to his feet, then dropped back in the chair again. He spoke lightly enough but he was thinking, and he was puzzled. "You have strange company, Mr. Brown."

"Sure. Sure." Vee nodded. "I get around. It pays."

"She's what you might call a stool-pigeon?"

"She's what you might call—whatever you want to," Brown snapped. "You didn't come here to discuss the oddities or the necessities of my profession."

"No, no—" Van Houton said very slowly. "It's strange, that's all. It might be such a person as that who supplied you with information about this blackmailer; as you would say, 'about me?'"

"It might." Vee nodded and looked directly at Van Houton.

It was a full minute before Van Houton spoke.

"You know, I was once blackmailed by this same Black Death. I have bent every effort in my small way to apprehend him. Tonight he telephoned and warned me that my further interference and advice to those dear friends who have been unfortunate was dangerous to them."

"Yes," said Brown, his eyes narrowing; no more humor in his voice. I knew how he hated this man.

VAN HOUTON nodded, "I believed him, took his warning and am ready to cease my activities. I did it particularly to save the life of Mrs. Thomas Wilson." And looking quickly at me, "I understand her husband was at college with you and Brown. This blackmailer"—he shuddered— "this hideous criminal also demands that you too cease annoying him; that you stop entirely trying to convict him. Otherwise this woman—this mother married to Dean's friend and your friend will die. Diabolical! Imagine simply taking a human life because of his dislike for you or through the necessity of convincing you that he means business. But what do you say?"

"I say—I'll get this blackmailer, this Black Death; and won't quit until I do."

"Shall I tell him that if he should call again?"

"There's no need to tell him." Brown leaned forward. "I have already told him—told you."

"Why—"And Vincent Van Houton switched suddenly. "Then the woman dies?"

"No, the woman won't die. I'll protect her; be sure of that."

"Really, I wish I could be sure of that. As sure as you are." He ran white, manicured fingers across his mouth. "I wonder, Mr. Brown, if you can protect her."

The phone rang. At a nod from Brown I answered it. Half surprised, I turned. "It's for Mr. Van Houton," I said slowly-

"With your permission." Van Houton came slowly to his feet, walked to the flat table and lifted the instrument.

"Van Houton. Vincent— Yes." A moment's pause, and his voice still lower; a touch of sympathy apparently in it, "Yes. I understand exactly, but I can do nothing for you. No. No one can do anything for you."

He started to lower the phone slowly back in its cradle, then shoved it quickly down. Did I hear a dull sound, or was it just the sudden click mingled with the jar of the replaced telephone?

"You'll excuse me." Van Houton did not sit down again but walked directly toward the door. "I am depressed today. I came here on an errand that I hoped would be one of mercy. There is no use in trying to change your mind now?"

"No use. Now or later," Brown said.

"Dear me!" said Vincent Van Houton as I followed him to the door. "I fear I have failed—failed miserably. A woman's death!"

"You don't need to worry about her death," said Brown. "I can assure you of her safety."

"I hope so. I hope so. And I won't try to influence you further—yet."

CHAPTER THREE
MURDER BY TELEPHONE

WHEN VAN HOUTON was gone I asked Brown point blank how he could sit there and be so sure about the woman.

"Maria told me that Mrs. Wilson had received the final warning since she had no money to pay. I have surrounded the place with detectives. But perhaps we had better go to the Wilson home and have a talk with her."

"But, Maria! That was strange; her coming from the music room like that, and stranger still the fact that Van Houton didn't know her. I thought she was—She said— But she must be very close to him to bring you so much information."

Brown's eyes narrowed. "She might be very close to someone who is close to Van Houton."

"But why did she walk out like that?"

"To protect another. Van Houton knew someone was in that room. He voiced the thought that it was Gertrude la Palatin. Maria might have made her dramatic exit to convince him that it wasn't."

"I can't believe in that sniffing, or that 'instinct.' It sounded too—"

"Improbable! Yes." There was no humor in Brown's voice now. "But it's possible, Dean. Some people are very sensitive to perfume, perhaps even to personalities. As for me, I can sense danger on occasions. But I think Van Houton suspected someone was here before he came up."

"Yes." I agreed wholly to that; I'm a practical man. "Since it wasn't Gertrude la Palatin his senses played him false. He was simply guessing."

"Was he?" Brown's black eyes were on me now, though I think he was looking through and beyond me. "He must have suspected her; suspected that she helped my escape that other night." He raised his eyes to the ceiling, shook his head, then nodded. "Maria did the only thing she could do; that is, if the protection of Gertrude la Palatin is so important to her. And— By God, Dean, I think I've got it! I think—" And stopping again, "No, no. I hope not. For if I got it certainly Van Houton got it."

"What—what do you think?"

Vee looked at me a long time before he spoke. Then, "I think that Maria and Gertrude la Palatin are very close." And breaking off suddenly, "Somehow Van Houton was very convincing tonight. I mean about the death of Mrs. Wilson. But he couldn't know then that her house was surrounded. Still, we'll go at once and have a talk with the woman."

We had lifted our hats from the costumer; were almost at the door when the phone rang.

"Answer it!" he told me. "Take the message, unless of course—"

I lifted the phone, gasped something about being right down, replaced it and turned to Vee.

"Mrs. Thomas Wilson," I said, "was shot to death less than five minutes ago."

NOT A word was spoken until we were downstairs, into a taxi and on our way to the Wilson residence. Then it was I who said: "How—how could it happen?"

He looked at me in the darkness. "How did she die? You were on the phone."

"I—I don't know," I gasped. "She was shot to death. I was too surprised; too stunned to ask any questions."

"I know. That's why I didn't ask you for details. We'll find out shortly. She's dead; that's certain."

"Yes, that's certain." I guess I was just talking to hear the sound of my own voice. "But, maybe it wasn't the Black Death at all. Maybe— You see, they—the Black Death favors a knife."

Brown's eyes seemed to pierce the darkness. "You think," he said, "that it was done by someone else; just a coincidence that the woman was killed five minutes after Van Houton visited us, threatened us, even told us?"

"But how could he—"

"So a stranger slipped by an elaborate police net and killed her! Just passing and dropped in."

I didn't like the irony in his voice; in his words. I tried: "They can't blame you, Vee. It won't hurt you?"

"Hurt me!" His laugh was not pleasant. "No, not in the way of giving me a black eye in the Department. It's Ramsey's headache. I told him the woman's life was in danger. It was his job to guard her; his responsibility. I didn't mean to, but I did pass the buck to him; the official buck. But the personal one! Hurt me?"—and it was one of the few times I had ever heard his voice break—

"Yes, it tears and rips inside me."

"But how—" I started again.

"We'll know in five minutes—less." And as the taxi pulled to the curb, "I see the medical examiner has beaten us to it; and there's Mortimer Doran's car."

"They—must feel it's important," I stammered.

"Important! After the woman had received the final notice of death! After I told them her life was in danger!" He shook his head as he muttered something to the uniformed man at the door and said to me: "If Ramsey's to blame for this he should be broken. It'll be his own carelessness or his stubborn, vindictive indifference because the warning came from me.

The room of death was in the front of the house, up one flight. A large bedroom. A cop stepped aside as we entered. Mortimer Doran stood over by the window, leaning against the wall; Inspector Ramsey was close to the door. He grinned at us unpleasantly. A man, leaning over a dressing table and partly shielding the body of a woman slumped there, turned suddenly. It was the assistant medical examiner.

"You're right, of course, Ramsey," he said to the inspector. "This woman shot herself just below the right ear. I can't be positive that's the gun clutched in her right hand until after the autopsy and the ballistic boys have done their job, but it's sure enough."

He whistled very softly as he picked up his bag and crossed to the door. Poking Brown in the ribs as he passed, his lips parted and his eyes twinkled. "Hello, Vee," the doctor said. "It's nice to find one that doesn't belong to you. Good-night."

"So it was suicide." Brown went over and examined the body. He lifted the hand that held the gun, felt of the fingers, pulled one back slightly. His shoulders shrugged, his hands came apart. He looked at her other hand; the colored French telephone.

"You can't make anything else out of this." Ramsey came and stood beside him. "Six men outside, protecting her from what? From firing a shot into her own head. You can't lay this to the Black Death."

BROWN'S VOICE was very tired. "No? I guess I can't lay it to your carelessness either, Ramsey. Just my own." He was opening and closing drawers. "She wouldn't keep them around." And to Mortimer Doran, "She had her third warning from this blackmailer. The fourth! This time they couldn't leave it with the body."

"How do you know she had a warning?" Mortimer Doran asked. And when Brown shrugged thin shoulders, "She was telephoning when it happened. At least, she was found dead with the receiver off. Ramsey's guess is that she lived long enough to wish she hadn't done it; tried to call for help but couldn't make it."

"That's right," Ramsey agreed. "The doc says she kicked right out, but it only takes a second to lift a receiver. I've seen guys, dead—or about dead, do strange things."

"We're checking up with the telephone company." Doran nodded. "It's a cinch someone noticed the receiver was off. They were buzzing hell out of it when we got here."

"What did the company say?" Brown's eyes were wide now.

"Housemire is downstairs on the other phone now." Inspector Ramsey looked directly at Brown. "Why don't you come clean? What's the racket this time? Why have the boys outside? You're not going to blame this on your Van Houton myth!" And when Brown just stood and looked at him, "I suppose I'll have to check up on him; test his alibi for tonight."

"No. I'll be his alibi for tonight," Brown said listlessly. "He was at my apartment when the woman was murdered."

"Was murdered!" Mortimer Doran walked across the room and took Brown by the shoulder. "Come, come, Brown! You've got eyes. She shot herself."

"Yes, she did. But the Black Death is just as responsible as if he pressed the trigger himself."

"Sort of hypnotism?"

"In a way." Brown ignored Ramsey's sneer. "The hypnotism of fear. This woman was afraid to live; afraid to face it, and— Where's her husband?"

Mortimer Doran answered. "He's downstairs, in the back; the library. It knocked him. There's two daughters; two kids in bed, who didn't hear the shot. What was it she had to face, Vee?"

"The same as the others. Something that crept out of her past. This Black Death bled her of all she could raise; then—well—something snapped in her head and—"

A long, bony man walked into the room. His eyes peered through thick glasses. Ramsey said: "Let's have it, House-mire."

The bony man coughed, half read it from a small note book.

"She was calling Two-O-O-two-two," and he gave the exchange. "They'll give me the name as soon as—" He raised his eyes, broke off. His eyes bulged through thick glasses.

"What's the matter?"

But we all knew what was the matter. The number was familiar. It was the number of our apartment. Vee Brown's phone number.

"That's right." Vee was the only one who didn't seem surprised. And to me, "I think I knew, Dean, as soon as we learned it was suicide. She called Van Houton, asked if there was any hope, I suppose. Remember what he said? 'No one can do anything for you.'"

"What the hell is all this?" Ramsey demanded. "This woman called Van Houton at your place, and then—"

"That's right. That's right," I cut in excitedly. "There was a queer sound just before Van Houton hung up. I thought it was his jamming down the receiver, but I know now it was a shot—the shot."

VEE BROWN looked at me a long moment, then at the insistence of Mortimer Doran he told him of Van Houton's visit. He didn't mention Maria.

He said: "It's quite plain, though I know neither one of you will agree with me. Van Houton is beginning to fear me; he wants me out of it. Can't you see? This woman's husband went to college with me, was very close to Dean. Van Houton told her that I might help her; she threatened to kill herself if I couldn't. Then she called him at my place, by appointment of course. And he simply—not his exact words, of course—but he told her to go ahead and kill herself. He murdered her just as if he tightened a finger upon the trigger of that gun and—"

"Murder by suggestion, eh?" Ramsey laughed harshly. "A nice case for a jury, that; with you the witness to his whereabouts when the death took place."

"I say, Vee!" Mortimer Doran seemed disturbed. "You've harped about this Van Houton now for months. But there's never been the least shade of suspicion about his actions. He was even blackmailed himself."

"Sure," Ramsey cut in. "He's known a lot of people who have been blackmailed by this gang. But that's natural. He's known around as a sort of sucker for a hard luck story. It's known too, that he rather fancies himself as an amateur detective. Lots of people confide in him; especially the women. He's that kind of a duck. Now, probably he didn't know anything about this woman's idea of doing the Dutch act. When she called up he told her the truth."

"What truth?" I demanded. I didn't like the quiet way Brown took it.

"Why—about Brown. Didn't Van Houton say he was scared out of the racket; this hunt of his against the black-mailer? And wasn't he to bring down the message that this Black Death wanted Brown out of it, and wasn't this message—that this woman would suffer? He told her he was going to Brown. Then she called and he gave her that message."

"The death message!" I said.

"But what else could an honest man tell her?" Mortimer Doran came in, turning to Brown. "After all, Dean, this Black Death has proved himself a real menace. Van Houton had to tell the woman the truth; had to warn her that— You see, Vee, the thing wouldn't hold water if it were true. We'll go and talk with him, of course." And raising his voice slightly, "Damn it! He should keep his nose out of this anyway. He's interfering with the law; obstructing the course of justice. I'll—"

"Leave him alone," Brown said quietly. "There's no evidence against him yet. I wouldn't be surprised if this Black Death promised her that her death would wipe the slate clean; that her husband would never know; her children would never know."

"And they won't," said Ramsey, "if we don't find anything; if there's nothing to find. So far it's all in your head."

"But why," said Doran, "would this Black Death wish her dead? In other cases there was the card with the message on it; the card of death, that would be reprinted on the first page of every newspaper and naturally frighten others into meeting his demands by fearing the same fate. But here there is nothing; no advantage to him. Absolutely nothing."

BROWN SEEMED to think that out a long moment. Then he crossed the room again, and lifting the face of the dead woman looked at it.

"There couldn't be much of bad inside her," he said slowly, "and a great deal of good. I wonder just how many of us—if our lives, our minds, our souls were laid bare—wouldn't, perhaps, prefer to go like that. I don't think I'd want my inner thoughts spread out in the morning papers." He smiled but it wasn't whimsical; rather, bitter; perhaps, sad.

Mortimer Doran laughed uneasily. "But we don't all put our thoughts in writing or allow our indiscretions to become public. Now—why should the man force this suicide? There's nothing to denote the work of the Black Death. Always, before, he's let the public know that the Black Death has struck."

"Because"—Brown turned on him suddenly—"this was not a public crime, not a warning to his victims. It was a warning to me. A warning and a hate—a private hate." And straightening slightly, "And perhaps a little fear."

Mortimer Doran grabbed Brown by the shoulders. "Sometimes you make me believe you," he said. "Damn it! Ramsey, if Brown's right about this Van Houton we're fools, and the man's too foul to—"

Ramsey nodded. "There's someone at the head of the Black Death, of course. But I can't believe it's this lad who keeps a houseful of cats and a roomful of pictures of them. That he happens to know five or six people who have been blackmailed seems reasonable enough. Let Brown work up that alley if he wants to. I'll admit the thing is beginning to smell to high heaven down at headquarters. Van Houton's got money and he's got influence. If you want to drag him in, go ahead. Tonight! Well, the worst possible thing you could stick on him would be bad judgment in sizing up a woman, and who hasn't been guilty of that?"

For once Brown agreed with Ramsey. He said: "Ramsey's right on that. Leave Van Houton to me, Mr. Doran."

"Sure. Sure!" Ramsey grinned broadly. He liked seeing Brown down in the mouth. "Only, if Brown's suspicions are true I'd advise having his telephone disconnected." And he walked over to the corner and started picking his teeth with a match.

Vee Brown, with his snappy comebacks; his quick wit that used to make Ramsey fairly bluster with anger! There was none of it now.

"I don't know. I don't know!" Mortimer Doran said, a hand on Vee's shoulder. "You've always come through before. This Black Death has given us an awful shellacking in the press. I don't mind saying that if a card had been found on this body— Well—damn it! Brown, don't you think you need help? You've always played a lone hand, I know; but that was a hand with a gun in it. Now—"

"It's brain work." Vee's laugh sounded more like a gargle. "I'm sorry this happened—damn good and sorry. I'll give you the Black Death—Vincent Van Houton—within a week."

"Now, that's talking," said Ramsey from the corner. "And if you don't will you give us a rest?"

"After all," Vee said quietly, "I'm not the only cop on the force."

Inspector Ramsey's face reddened. "After all," he said, "you're the only cop on the force who asked particularly for this job, and you're making it a life's work."

Vee said nothing. He took me by the arm and led me into the hall and down the stairs.

"Go in and see Tommy Wilson," he said at the front door. "He was your friend more than mine, and I don't think he'll want to see me after this."

"But he won't know that Van Houton came to you and—"

"Yes, he will." Vee nodded. "I feel that Van Houton would see that he does. You know, Dean—Van Houton knows character; knows men. I think he even knows me and knows that if I am beaten I must be terribly beaten."

CHAPTER FOUR
TWO HUNDRED GRAND

M **Y TALK** with Thomas Wilson, if it can be called a talk, was not pleasant. It is sufficient to say that he loved his wife very much, knew that she was in some trouble and that Van Houton had been advising her. That it could not be any great wrong he was sure of. I thought of the two children; the dead woman upstairs with the gun in her hand, and was not so sure. But I didn't dodge the issue. I told Brown the truth when I came out; I thought he would want it that way.

"You were right," I said as we walked slowly to the corner. "Van Houton is after you. I'm not sure if he wishes to drive you off his tracks by fear or remorse, or simply to break down—"

"My morale," Brown finished for me when I stopped lamely. "I hope he can't do that. I've given it, Dean; given it again and again. Now let me have the truth and see how I'll take it."

"Huh!" I gulped. "Vincent Houton rang Wilson up. He told him he was alarmed about Mrs. Wilson; that she was very morbid and should be watched."

"When was this?"

"A short while ago. If you mean—was she already dead? Yes. When Van Houton learned that she was dead he appeared greatly shocked; at least that's what Wilson said. I didn't disillusion Wilson about Van Houton. I wasn't sure you wanted that."

"No, I didn't. What else?"

"Well," I let him have it, "Van Houton told Wilson that he visited you; that Mrs. Wilson was in great trouble, and you—well, you did nothing. There's no use to go into it, Vee. I had dinner with the Wilsons a few months back. He's a different man now. It's been a terrible shock to him."

"Yes," said Brown. "She was picked first for the slaughter because of me—of us."

"It's not your fault. You're not to blame."

We paused under a light, hailed a passing taxi. I had never seen Brown so white. His face was drawn.

"No. Legally I'm not to blame; that's true," Brown said when we were in the cab and he had mumbled directions I did not get. "But neither is Van Houton legally responsible. I can't see sticking a gun to ones head and taking an 'out.' Poor, unfortunate devil; she must have lived through hell to do that. And, Dean, I happen to know it was a very silly affair. She magnified its importance in fearful days and terrifying, sleepless nights. And Van Houton! He drove her to it. No doubt assured her that with her death the thing could not be made public because of the blame of her death attaching itself to the blackmailers. Think of it, Dean! He sat there in our apartment, took the message over the phone and calmly pronounced her death. Heard the shot too, as you seem to have heard it; then walked calmly from the room.

And the law I'm supposed to serve would no doubt disapprove of me if I went to his house tonight and shot him to death."

"Don't talk like that. Don't—"

"It's not one woman's life, Dean; it's many. Do you know what he may be planning now? He may be planning to take hundreds of letters, affidavits, proofs—and make them all public. The slaughter of the innocents along with the guilty. Racketeering, kidnaping, murder. Why—they amount to nothing when the blackmailer; the master fiend of crime steps into the picture. Broken homes, broken lives, the hundred agonies that precede the self-inflicted death. And those too strong to end it that way? He hires someone to stick a knife in them for fear that some knowledge may ruin him. Do you know why I don't go to his house and shoot him to death?"

"Why—you couldn't, Vee. You're just not built that way. It would be murder."

HE SAID: "Would it? I wonder. But maybe you're right and I wouldn't have the guts for it when the time came. But I like to think that the reason is—because it is unnecessary. At last I am in a fair way to turn Van Houton up." His hands clasped together, his fingers opened and closed, and he said almost viciously: "Yes, turn him up to the law; maybe roast him for murder."

"How—you didn't tell me of this."

"No. I kept it until the time came to strike. And the time has come. You recall our visitor, Theodore Lessenger, the lawyer; the lawyer Van Houton or Moffet, the crooked politician, sent to us, trying to bribe me when they wanted that evidence against Moffet. Well, Lessenger is Van Houton's man; the man these criminals recognize as their leader; whose orders they take."

"How did you find that out?"

"I guessed it." He smiled slightly. "At least I worked on him. Remember, in the Mandozza affair, I decided not to work against Mandozza but collected instead evidence against his lawyer, and by suppressing that evidence got the lawyer to furnish me with evidence against Mandozza!"

"Yes, yes." I was eager now. "You've got something on this lawyer then."

"No, I haven't." Brown shook his head. "Lessenger is a shrewd man. I could not find a thing against him, not one scrap of evidence. He is too clever. My guess in that direction had been wrong."

"Then what good did it do you?"

"I found out that Lessenger, who had been a rich man, was now a poor one, heavily in debt; and that it was not because of unwise investments, but because he was drawing his money in cash from the bank, turning every available security into cash, raising notes where he could. But all honest and above board. Now, what was he doing with that money?"

"He was hoarding it, turning it into gold and—"

"Not gold, but blood. He was turning it into blood—his blood. He was paying out his own money to a vast organization of criminals so they would not use the knife on him; the knife he had hired and paid them to use on others. He was paying this organization to keep the blood in his body.

These creatures who served him demanded money. He was giving it to them to avoid the very death he dealt to others—the Black Death."

"You mean—mean that Lessenger is the—is Van Houton's last link?"

"Exactly. He is a criminal lawyer, therefore can openly associate with crooks. Van Houton controls him, probably through the same channels he uses on others—blackmail. Common sense should have told us before that there must be one big known leader; a leader with many lieutenants in such a vast scheme. Well, that leader is Theodore Lessenger. Influence, politics—he had everything that Van Houton needed."

"And you have proof that he—"

"Proof? No, no proof. Not one bit of evidence against him. But it's from him that I hope to get the proof against Van Houton. Indeed, I am certain of it. But here we are at Irving Small's."

IRVING SMALL, the cleverest fence in the city, let us in the side door of his little shop, bowing and rubbing his hands ingratiatingly. Although his head was down his eyes never left us. Brown always said he was his most valuable asset in crime. Small knew every criminal in the underworld and sold much information to Brown. That Vee could at any time send him up for a twenty-year stretch was true. But he considered Small a far too valuable asset to lose.

"The stool-pigeon—the necessity of every detective worth his salt!" Vee had explained. "I could make him talk for nothing, Dean, but I don't. I pay him well. I imagine he is a very rich man, but he loves money, and his love of money makes me seem as necessary to him as he is to me.

Otherwise"—he had grinned at the time—"Irving Small might be interested in seeing my throat slit some night."

Irving Small led us through a small unlighted vestibule and into a dull hall beyond. "He's come," he whispered to Brown. "In the room now; gave me the signal and I let him in. How you got a man like that to meet you here and—"

"You—you know who he is?" Brown cut in.

"I know everyone." Irving Small bobbed his old head up and down. "He is the most dangerous man in New York today."

"Not the most dangerous."

Irving Small cocked his head. "Perhaps not," he said. "But this other you think of! You must strike quick, Mr. Brown. He is not to be so easily beaten. And where I see your reason for the gent inside, I can tell you this. The Black Death may not much longer need the man in that room." He stopped suddenly, then spoke rather loudly. "The unknown gentleman has come, sir, and is waiting."

I was looking over Irving Small's head and had not heard the door open nor seen the thin sliver of light that came from the long crack. But Irving Small, with his back to it, had heard it. Without another word we walked to that door. Brown pushed it open and I followed him into the room. Irving Small turned and passed through another door.

I saw Theodore Lessenger again. Tall, slim; yellow-gloved hands; the slight stoop to his shoulders and even the silver-headed cane. He had the same poise, the same assurance and polish—or had he? For the eyes that watched us through the black-rimmed glasses seemed to bulge more and were not as capable of a direct look. But most of all, he needed a shave; the black stubble was in strange contrast to his careful appearance.

"I see"—Brown spoke to him at once—"that you are all ready to accept my offer, and beginning a beard to start off with. A natural disguise when you flee the city—the country."

"So"—Lessenger looked at me—"he is to be in on our little talk."

"Sure!" said Brown. "You had no objection to his presence when you tried to bribe me."

"Bribe?" Lessenger raised his eyebrows. "This is hardly a bribe, Mr. Brown. You want certain letters, certain affidavits." He leaned forward on his cane. "I can tell you where Van Houton keeps every document, every letter he intends to use to bleed people; accumulated at great expense, through years of work."

"But the proof that he is the head of this Black Death! You can prove that?"

Lessenger laughed. "Certainly. By sitting in the witness stand; a witness stand that will later turn into an electric chair for me. I am not a fool, Mr. Brown, and—frankly, I have no desire to help anyone but myself. You offered me fifty thousand dollars for that evidence. I refused. Now you had me meet you here. I presume that you are ready to meet my price. That price was two hundred and fifty thousand in cash or a certified check."

And when Brown only looked at him, "Come, come! Let us not quibble. It's a lot of money, of course. For my part, I could not use those letters. This— Well— Van Houton, if you'll have it that way, can do things to me; knows things about me that are not kept with those documents. Frankly, I can't make use of the documents; not while you're so close. As for you! They would be worth millions to you. Of course, played carefully over a period of—"

"I am not interested in making money out of them."

"Well, then—in saving lives, aiding society, protecting the weak and unfortunate." Lessenger's lips curved sarcastically. "I am not built that way, Mr. Brown, nor did I understand that you were. I'm a man of few words, and perhaps a man who may find time valuable. My life may hang on wasted time."

"All right." Brown spoke quickly. "When I sent you word to meet me here I was willing to raise the price, but only on the condition that you would convict Van Houton for me. Now something has changed my mind. I want to buy all this evidence that Van Houton has collected. I have been able to raise two hundred thousand dollars in cash. I offer you that for the letters—Van Houton's information."

LESSENGER LOOKED for a long time at the ceiling. He twisted the head of his cane in his hand, then finally snapped: "Done! I'll take it. You know, Mr. Brown, I always suspected a man of your talents wasn't simply in this detective racket for—" And seeing Brown's face. "We'll forget that. And don't misunderstand me. I would not double-cross any man, least of all such a power as Van Houton, except to save my life."

"And without you he has no power?"

"No? You think not? I thought that too. I didn't think he'd dare leave me to face the wolves of the night. I admire his brains, his keen understanding of human nature, his quick decisive method of striking or ignoring. If he had stuck to me I would have stuck to him. But I have paid out every cent I owned to protect this organization and save my own life; every cent I could borrow, thinking that he would—would eliminate all obstacles."

"Eliminate me, eh?"

"Perhaps." Lessenger smiled and the smile was really pleasant. "You must strike quick, Mr. Brown. Van Houton has been building another organization; building it from the inside of the organization I spent years to raise for him. A sort of new idea; a richer soil, that will eliminate the weeds. I am selling out because I am one of those weeds. A day, a week, a month even; then someone puts the knife in my chest. No. I'm too clever for this Van Houton. But we waste time! I have accepted your offer. It will be paid— how and when?"

"A certified check when the documents are in my hand and I am convinced that they are authentic."

"Placed in your hand. Exactly!" Lessenger nodded. "I think that is far better than telling you where they are. Since it is necessary that I have access to them I will obtain them and deliver them to you at your apartment tomorrow night, say—eight o'clock."

"You think that safe—my apartment?"

"Quite safe. I am to call on you anyway tomorrow night, at the suggestion of this Black Death, whom we now both refer to as Vincent Van Houton. I am to suggest that your further activities against this society will cause the death of another of your friends."

"Who?" Brown looked startled.

"I am not sure; not sure at all. I might guess at it, but just guess." He was turning his coat up around his neck, tightening a heavy muffler, pulling his slouch hat well over his face when I broke in for the first time.

"But, Vee. You're giving this man every cent you have. For what? Simply to delay Van Houton. In time he will have built up more victims and—"

"Exactly!" Lessenger said to me. "But your friend, Mr. Brown, is a clever man. He has already directed suspicion to Van Houton. If this evidence, this list of victims with their letters and so on, should be found in Van Houton's house, I think that would prove embarrassing."

"The letters are there—at Van Houton's?" I gasped.

"No, no; not yet. But a clever man like Mr. Brown might see that they were found there. Most damaging—most convincing."

"Wait!" Brown stopped Lessenger at the door. "Will you kindly guess—just guess—who this next victim, a friend of mine, might be?"

Lessenger shrugged his shoulders. "I know a very charming, very intelligent, and yet a very dangerous woman. But I am not in love with her. Love deadens the keenness of the mind toward danger. Van Houton is—or maybe was in love with her. This charming lady I have suspected for some time. She is called Gertrude la Palatin." He smiled, bowed and was gone.

"So—" I turned to Brown. "That's why you've been attending to your own finances lately; selling, borrowing. Lord, man, that's every penny you have in the world! Why should you use it?"

"That's what I asked myself—until tonight," Brown said very slowly. "Until tonight, when I looked into the eyes of that dead woman. Now—Gertrude la Palatin."

"But two hundred thousand dollars." I whistled.

"A lot of money—a high-priced squeal. I guess that will go as an all-time record for any stool-pigeon, for that's all Lessenger is. Just a stool-pigeon—a glorified stool-pigeon!"

WE STEPPED out of the little room and turned toward the back of Irving Small's pawn shop, which for years had hidden his real activities.

Brown said: "We'll talk with Irving for a bit. He always has some news. Besides, we've got to give Lessenger a start. He's smooth. He was a good man for Van Houton until he went broke. Somehow, they've fallen out. I am the cause of it, I guess. Van Houton seeks vengeance; Lessenger seeks compensation. He strikes before he is struck, which makes him that much shrewder than Van Houton."

Brown tapped on the locked door and Irving Small opened it.

"Come in. Come in!" Irving Small returned quickly to the old flat desk with its many deep drawers on either side of it and placed his hand over a large object. A gun, I thought.

"Not going to kill a man, I hope." And Brown's voice was better; some of his—well, morbidness gone.

"No, no." Irving Small started to put the gun in the drawer.

"A hot rod, eh?" Vee asked.

A small head twisted, shoulders hunched, shrewd little eyes watched us. For a moment Irving Small slipped that gun toward the drawer, then he stopped and shoved it quickly into Vee's hand.

"You like guns. I wonder you never carried one like this. They say a man who knows his hardware can do wonders with it."

Brown took the gun, hefted it in his hand. "A nice rod," he said. "I don't use it for the same reason gunmen don't use it. Too easy to trace down if a lad wants quiet shooting." He hesitated a moment, laid it on the desk and repeated, "Quiet shooting!"

Irving Small shook his head. "I suppose I'll never get rid of it now. The boys won't fancy it. But the price was right and I took it. It belonged to Pete Stokes. You remember him. You should, Mr. Brown. You killed him."

"Of course. You remember, Dean." Brown nodded at me. "Peter Stokes. I shot him to death in a cellar in the first real attack we made against Van Houton. He made money as a bootlegger—when money was made that way. He visited Van Houton often." Brown stroked his chin. "It was the only real connection that could actually link Van Houton with the Black Death. But that was when Van Houton claimed he too was being blackmailed."

"Yes," I said, "I remember him well." And I shivered slightly. I had been close to death the night Stokes died.

"Could the police trace this automatic revolver; trace it to Pete Stokes?" Vee asked Irving Small.

"Sure!" Small pointed to a mark on the gun. "Pete, when he was young, was a fool. He put that mark on it. I think he quit carrying it, but everyone knew Pete's gun. It would be easy for the police to trace it to him. That is why I'll never sell it."

"Vee"—I sort of grinned at him. I knew he was upset but I meant it for just good-natured raillery. It wasn't often one caught Vee up on guns—"there are automatic pistols and there are revolvers. If you read your detective-story magazine you would see how easily readers are annoyed by careless authors who speak of 'automatic revolvers.'"

"Not this time, Dean!" Vee lifted the gun and handed it to me. That was how I came to examine it so carefully. And see the peculiar mark on it; the rough chipped, five-pointed star on the grip. "This time it is the reader who would be careless. That gun is actually an automatic revolver. I think it's the only one of its kind, but I'm not sure. It's a Webley-Fosbery."

"But an 'automatic revolver.' I never heard of such a thing. What's the point of it?"

"Not just to show up the annoyed reader, anyway; for I doubt if the makers thought of that. I'm thinking of using such a gun myself. There are many people who fancy a revolver and yet would like the speed of the automatic. That gun there is the fastest shooting revolver that I know of today. I would ask for nothing more in speed and accuracy than that automatic revolver."

"It looks like a heavy, dangerous gun," I said as he took the gun from me.

"Yes, yes." Brown put the gun down on the desk and we started toward the door. "It uses Remington revolver cartridges—four fifty-five, I believe. It—" And stopping as I passed out the door, "I'll be right with you; just one more word with Irving Small."

I heard Brown say to Small: "Does anyone know Pete Stokes left that gun with you?" And I heard, too, Small's answer, "No."

After that I heard nothing, for I had walked down the hall to the vestibule and the little door and was peering or trying to peer through the dirty glass out into the deserted darkness of shabby tenements. Three minutes later Brown joined me.

CHAPTER FIVE
GIRL OF THE NIGHT

IT WAS close to eleven o'clock when we reached home. Brown picked up the phone, called the President Theatre, where Gertrude la Palatin headed the musical show. He seemed relieved to discover that she had not yet gone and in a few minutes was connected with her in her dressing room. The one-sided conversation was annoying.

"I had to call you," he said. "Have you had any threats from the Black Death?" A moment's pause, and then, "That's strange, or perhaps it isn't. You must let me know the very moment it happens. Good!"

He hung up the receiver and turned to me. "The Black Death is not running true to form. Miss la Palatin has not received any threats. Or perhaps Lessenger lied to us."

"Or was misinformed," I tried.

Vee shook his head, walked the floor, then swung on me. "I'm a fool, Dean. Of course she would not receive a card. She's too close to Van Houton. She even has an apartment at his house. Why—" He grinned for a moment, and then, "But I don't think that would cover it altogether. She helped me to escape from his house; therefore she either recognized him as the Black Death or that he was very close to the Black Death, or—" He shook his head again. "But he would let her know when her time came to die. His fiendish cruelty would see to that."

"But if she knew the truth about him, then he wouldn't warn her. Just strike."

"Why?" Vee demanded.

"Afraid she would talk; would—"

"But we can talk. Lessenger can talk. Perhaps many others can talk. It's the same old story. We know, but talk is not evidence. If it were, our prison population would go up by a thousand percent. Hundreds of electricians would be put to work pulling switches on wired chairs. Don't you know, Dean, that we have a murder every hour in the United States? But you don't hear of the states working overtime on the death penalty."

"Back to where we were, Vee. How will Miss la Palatin let you know?"

"In a way that will surprise me. That was how she put it." He rubbed his hands together. "Tomorrow night at eight. Not much longer. Not much longer."

"You think—you're sure Lessinger's on the level?" I couldn't help blurting it out.

"On the level!" He swung and faced me. "Did you see his face, his eyes? Why, it means everything to him. Greed and need. He'll be able to leave the country with that money, live abroad. And Van Houton can't expose him; that is, without exposing himself."

"I was only thinking that, after all your work—the months you have spent—it comes pretty easy at the end. Too easy."

"That's life." Vee nodded. "I knew a detective once who looked for a man half around the world, only to find when he was far off in China that a rookie cop had arrested that man in a lunch room; a lunch room that the detective had made a habit of eating in for years. Inventors work for a lifetime, unrewarded, and at the end stumble by chance upon the little trick that makes them world famous. Why—"

"But what good will all this do you?" I cut in. "Van Houton will start right up again."

"Perhaps." Vee nodded. "Things are not ending as I'd like them to end, of course. But you saw that dead woman's eyes and you heard the shot that killed her. At least the city will not be shocked by suicides, murders and—"

"But Van Houton is building up a new organization. Even now he may have other and worse murderers that he controls. He's starting over."

BROWN CUT in: "And I'll start over. There'll be an even break there. If he's thrust into the open I'll get him."

"But Gertrude la Palatin! If he suspects her, then—"

"Her letters will be with the other letters, and will be destroyed."

"But what he knows about Lessenger isn't with those letters."

"That's because he never intended to sell his evidence against Lessenger to Lessenger. He intended to keep that over his head."

"Then isn't that same thing true of this famous actress; hasn't he been friendly with her? Won't he—?"

"God in heaven! Dean, stop it," Vee cried out. "What can I do; what shall I do? Should I take those letters to Van Houton, make a deal with him, allow him to destroy the many to save the one? Gertrude la Palatin saved one life—mine. Am I to sacrifice a hundred lives, maybe more, to save hers? Am I—am I—" he put both his hands to his head. "Am I a cop, or a song writer?" And he turned and dashed into the music room.

For a while I heard the piano, the deep notes, the strange eery melody. *Girl of the Night!*

As for myself, I read or tried to read the evening papers. But all I remember was the hurricane in the south, the floods and destruction along the Atlantic coast, and the promise that New York would get the real force of the storm some time "tomorrow night."

All the next day Vee Brown was on edge. And after dinner he was worse, as the hands of the clock moved toward eight. It was ten minutes of eight when the phone rang. Vee jumped to it. It was not Lessenger—it was Vincent Van Houton.

Van Houton had two very fine seats for *Celebrities on Review,* Gertrude la Palatin's show, and he wanted Brown to take them. Vee hesitated, then said he was busy and hung up. But he was bothered by the phone call and paced the room, snuffing out butt after butt in the different ash trays. At eight fifteen we had another telephone call. This time it was Lessenger. Brown turned from the phone.

"He's lost his nerve, Dean. He didn't get his instructions from Van Houton to visit me here. I thought perhaps he hadn't when Van Houton rang up about the tickets. Lessenger won't come to our apartment. He's in a blue funk and I don't know that I blame him. But he's got the letters and will deliver them to me at one o'clock tonight—or rather, tomorrow morning. He's picked a prominent place. No, no, Dean. I can't even tell you the spot—he made me promise that. The man's frightened. But you're to go with me. I have the certified check, of course, for two hundred thousand dollars." He walked to the wide French windows and looked out. "It's a night for it," he said as the rain pounded against the glass. "It seems as if the promised hurricane from the south is making good this time."

For the third time the phone rang. This time I answered it. It was Vincent Van Houton again.

"Will you tell Mr. Brown about those tickets? I'm sending them around to him. He'll have to hustle."

"But he said he couldn't—"

"Maybe," said Van Houton very slowly, "he'll change his mind when he learns that this is Gertrude la Palatin's last appearance."

"For—for the season?" I half stammered.

"Forever!" said Van Houton and hung up.

That was Thursday night, and the show was—was—I turned and told Brown; was still telling him when the messenger arrived with the tickets.

"He—he had already sent them, "I stammered. "What does he mean—'forever?'"

Brown's thin lips were a single straight line as he got into his coat. "You know what he means, Dean. Van Houton has never bluffed us. He—But come on. We'll see the show."

AT THE stage door we were stopped. Yes, Miss la Palatin was expecting us; hoped to see us after the show. She had left a note for "Mr. Brown." Vee tore it open and read it.

> Don't come to see me until the last curtain. This card that I received, explains.
>
> > Gertrude la Palatin.

And the card did explain. In the center in large type were the dreaded words, and below them but in smaller type—a message.

> THE BLACK DEATH.
> This is your last performance. You are playing tonight to Vee Brown and Death. I wonder if you can give it and if he can take it.

That was all. We didn't talk. We didn't need to. Vee took me by the arm and led me around to the front of the theatre. The play had begun.

As we slid into our seats Vee half whispered to me or to himself: "We'll see first if she can give it."

And she did give it. There was no doubt that she was America's foremost impersonator. I won't mention the different actresses she took off, except to say that as usual her impersonation of Marie Dressler was almost startling, considering her slim figure. As for Marion Davies— But when she pulled off her wig and rubbed the grease paint from her face she was a most charming little woman; no more than a girl it seemed.

"Is that her real self?" I asked Brown. "At Van Houton's that night her hair seemed different. But you saw her and—"

"I saw her only in the darkness of that room before I slipped down the rope to safety," he said. "But tonight we see the real la Palatin, I think. Her hair is so short and clipped so close to her head—but they do say that on the street she wears a wig, though no one could tell it."

Yes, she could give it. Certainly no one in that vast audience, and the place was filled despite the rain and the storm, could possibly realize the strain she must have been under.

I looked at Brown. When Gertrude la Palatin was on the stage and she was on often for the show was built around her, his eyes were glued on hers. I wonder that she didn't feel them, there from the fourth row. But she didn't, or if she did she made no sign. She was giving just a wonderful—a finished performance. Finished! I didn't like the taste of that thought.

Between her appearances Brown's eyes searched the theatre. It was after we had returned from the lobby for the last act and just before the curtain went up that Brown nudged me and I looked in the upper box to the right.

The man must have just come in. His top hat was lying crown down on the flat surface of the box, a white muffler sticking from it, and he was just tossing his gloves into it. Blond hair, broad shoulders, fine features. Yes, it was

Vincent Van Houton. Begrudgingly I admitted he made quite a distinguished figure. Others were looking too, for Brown told me that Van Houton often occupied that box; had engaged it for the entire run of the show. More than one columnist had linked his name with a "famous impersonator."

Gertrude la Palatin saw him, almost as soon as the curtain went up. For a moment only she hesitated; for a moment only her low throaty voice broke while imitating a well-known radio star, then it was as if he had never appeared.

I am not going to describe that performance, except the end of it. Brown had sighed with relief the moment Van Houton had entered. He had whispered to me: "She's safe for the time, anyway. Do you know, Dean, I'm almost beginning to fear that man. When we got the tickets, his message, and hers! I was afraid something spectacular was going to happen; yes, happen right on the stage, before our eyes. But not now; he wouldn't be here. His alibis are always so perfect. We may expect nothing spectacular tonight."

IN THAT Brown proved a poor oracle, for to me perhaps the most spectacular episode or at least the most startling one—in the whole case of the Cat Man, the Black Death— was about to take place. And when it came, it came with a suddenness; too quickly for me to realize that—that—

The manager had appeared from the wings. He spoke loudly in a sudden lull in the music. "La Palatin, the great. A new creation—a new impersonation—a new triumph."

There was the music, the low notes ever rising—weird, eery. And she was there, slipping, gliding from the wings. That was when I came to my feet, started to open my mouth and felt Brown jerk me back into the seat again.

Gertrude la Palatin was gone, her fine impersonation of famous personages was gone, and now the slim figure that swept catlike across that stage was— The same green eyes, the same curved lips with the cruel twist to them. Yes, there was no doubt. I was looking at Maria, the girl who brought us the information about the Black Death; the girl who— who— And there was the music—Brown's music— Brown's lyric. *Girl of the Night!*

"It's—Brown! Vee! How did—" And though I must have known it the very minute she stepped upon that stage; the very moment the strange familiar notes came, I certainly didn't realize it fully. At least, it didn't register in my whirling head.

"Yes," Vee whispered, "Gertrude la Palatin and our Maria are one and the same person. I should have known it. I asked you once if you noticed her hair. But truth is truth. I didn't know it. So now she lets me know, like thousands of others in the great city, what a great actress she is." And after a moment's pause, "And she lets me know too that Van Houton has struck."

"Van Houton!" I clutched Vee's arm. "He must suspect, must— God, Vee, he saw her in our apartment only yesterday!"

"Yes, yes. He's been cleverer than I again. Maybe he's right. I'm just a gunman."

Brown was absorbed in the girl. There is no doubt that the song was a hit, a stupendous success. Three times she had to repeat the final chorus. And Brown—

For the moment anyway he forgot the thing he faced; she faced. He clapped me on the back. "I knew it. I told her so. But partly I lied to her, Dean. I told her she would make the song, but I believed that the song would make her. Now she's made it and she'll keep it. No one else will ever sing it. No one—" He stopped.

The curtain was going up and down amid the enthusiastic applause. Maria, or Gertrude la Palatin, was bowing and smiling; smiling right down at us; waving and— Not once did she look at Van Houton, and then she did. Looked straight up at him. Was there a defiance to the sudden tilt of her head; to the sharp twist of cruel lips before she tore the black wig and the little hat from her head? I don't know; I think there was. But Van Houton only clapped and nodded, then tossed upon the stage a great bouquet of orchids.

They lay there as the curtain dropped for the last time. The lights went on, the people were leaving. The show was over—was over!

CHAPTER SIX
CITY OF THE DEAD

NEWSPAPER MEN! Admirers! She saw them all. It was some time before Vee and I were admitted to her dressing room. She dismissed the maid at once, was across the room and in Vee's arms; and Brown was holding her too. Nothing strange about that? No, there seemed nothing strange about it at the time; nothing strange in their talk either. It was of the song; her performance; a few arguments over some words—and all this in the shadow of death, the death that had never failed to strike on time.

And their talk was mainly a discussion of Brown's insistence that the name of the piece and the words of the chorus should be changed from *Girl of the Night* to *Girl of the Shadows*.

"Of course. Of Course!" She finally agreed. "You're Vivian now—just a sentimental song writer. I understand. You remember me so. Always in the shadows!"

"Always in the shadows." Vee echoed her words, and then holding her at arm's length, looked at her. "Wong was right. He saw, too, the inside of you."

"And you like me so? The red hair!" And with a laugh, "Even that is not true; it is really black. Simply henna. But you like me, now?"

"I liked you always—inside. I think I always saw you as I see you now."

"But you never suspected?"

"That you were la Palatin—the great la Palatin? No. No one could suspect that who had never really seen la Palatin close. Of course I knew you were heavily made up, that your hair was not real. Plainly you were disguised, but with that art that made the disguise very real. But I always knew you were playing a part."

She threw back her head and laughed. "You are wrong. I was not playing a part. You were seeing the real me, the only me. Made up? Yes. But the girl of the night, the girl I was born. Originally I came from the very underworld you hunt in. Even inside I was not disguised as a crook. I was one. I helped Van Hounton with his dirty blackmail until—until I understood what it meant."

"You have paid for all that." Brown stiffened suddenly and said: "This card! Van Houton knows, of course, that you brought me the information."

"He knows everything." She nodded. "That's why I did that song tonight. I wanted you to know; to see it—just once. There is nothing: you can do for me."

"There may be much I can do for you," Brown told her.

She shook her head. "I can—will never play again."

"You will play tomorrow night."

"I—"

The dressing-room door opened. We all swung and faced it. Van Houton was standing there; he was smiling. He walked over to a huge vase, lifted some flowers from it and tossed them into the waste basket. Then he placed the orchids he was carrying in their place.

"The excitement made you forget them." He lifted her hand and touched it with his lips. "You were gorgeous tonight—divine. So—you will rest tomorrow; you will not play tomorrow night."

THE THING was ghastly. The blood left the girl's face. She opened her mouth but no words came. Here was a man who carried a message of death. But nothing could be done about it. Nothing—

Brown spoke very quietly. "I think you're wrong, Mr. Van Houton. Anyway I must thank you for the tickets. I never had the pleasure of seeing Miss la Palatin quite so perfect. She has promised me to play tomorrow night."

"Really! How charming. But, as her friend I must forbid it. I fear it would be a great mistake." He shook his head, knitted his brows. "Miss la Palatin loves nothing more than her art; sets nothing above it—not even me. Now, I may be wrong; she may set another above it. But, no. It is very sad. Such a great actress! Her health comes first. She must give up the biggest thing in her life. She will never play again.

And Maria! She looked at Van Houton—at Brown. Vee spoke and his voice didn't shake, but his lips were very tight.

"I think that Miss la Palatin will play tomorrow night, and I think she will be quite safe. I will call on you tomorrow, Mr. Van Houton, and I feel sure that you will advise Miss la Palatin to play."

"Indeed!" Van Houton spoke easily, free from restraint. "In a way I am Miss la Palatin's personal manager, but I am also her friend. Still—" he hesitated, looked at Vee and smiled— "since you wish it I will permit her to play tomorrow night, but only until the final number."

"You mean—not the—the *Girl of the Night!*" Somehow I just had to say it.

"I mean—not the *Girl of the Night,* as you so quaintly express it, Mr. Condon. Miss la Palatin, perhaps, does not think so much of her health. Like all great artists she thinks only of her art; the name she has made in that art; the advancement she has contributed to it. She would do nothing to drag down that name. Indeed, I am sure she would prefer death first." He turned to Maria. "By all means, my dear, play tomorrow night. Telephone me how you feel just before the final number—the new number. I will tell you then exactly what to do."

And as the door opened now and the manager stood there, red of face, broad of grin, enthusiasm in his moving hands and sparkling eyes, Van Houton ran on easily: "I understand, my dear Gertrude, that tonight you will not be using the little apartment at my house, which I set up to assure you absolute quiet; that you are going to your hotel. Very well. You will be quite safe. This—er—Detective Brown here is evidently alarmed that your great success tonight may cause the envious to harm you in some way. At least, I noted several plainclothesmen outside. You won't need me further. Good-ni—" Van Houton hesitated, lifted her hand and held his lips to it a long moment…. "Good-bye!" he said, dropped the hand, and pleasantly tapping the manager on the back, and with a nod and a smile to us, left the dressing room.

"These detectives! It is a good thing." The manager jerked his head up and down at Brown. "She will need this protection. I was about to—" And to Maria, "But, there! You were magnificent. You surpassed yourself tonight, Miss la Palatin. Crowds gather even in the rain to see you leave."

RAIN WAS right. The tropical storm that had been for so many days sweeping up from the south had arrived. The theatres were already emptied, the people swept to their homes. As Vee and I drove back home, Fifth Avenue was as deserted as a country town. Just a cop now and then, the whiteness of his face hardly visible through the slit in the rubber helmet; only the toes of his great boots showed from beneath the long rubber coat.

An occasional figure slunk into a doorway. Homeless derelicts. But otherwise the wind and rain in ever increasing velocity produced a silent city. Silent! Well, yes—as far as human silence goes. But the wind whistled and the rain beat upon the cab, and occasionally signs rattled in their stanchions or, breaking loose, flopped against the side of a building.

Safely at our apartment, a few drinks under our belts, I stood behind the glass door of our private terrace and looked out at the storm; felt or thought that I felt the building rock.

"A bad night for a meeting," I told Vee. "You think this Lessenger will show up?"

"A good night for it. A man in a doorway with a suitcase in his hand could remain unseen for hours. Of course he'll show up."

"Bad, about Maria!" I raised my glass, twirled it so that the ice clicked pleasantly against the sides; more pleasantly as I looked out at the storm. "Think you can help her? Strange that she could so fool us!"

"Think that I can save her?" His lips smacked together. "I must. She and la Palatin are one. And I owed so much to both! Now, to just one. But it isn't strange that she fooled us, Dean. She's paid an enormous sum each week to fool thousands; thousands who are looking to be fooled; critical about being fooled, while we— No. I knew she was not the real thing. Maybe I should have guessed the truth. Once I was very close—very close indeed. Of course, if you'll check back you'll see that several nights she hurried from here, quite evidently to reach the theatre. There were times too when Maria was with us, and la Palatin did not play. I remarked about it once to you. But of course it explains all Maria's information. As Gertrude la Palatin she worked in with Van Houton; he gave her his confidence. As Maria she gave that confidence to us. He won't be the first man-the first clever, even great man who made a fool of himself over a woman—" He drained his glass. "I wonder," he said, "if I will."

At twenty minutes of one we left the apartment again. And what a wind! Twice I gripped Brown's arm as his frail form was almost swept from the sidewalk and Wong bent his body against the open car door.

"God, what a night!" I said when we were in the car.

"Not so bad. Not so bad," Brown muttered. "I remember a night—" And again self-conscious of his physical frailness he related some wild story of a tropical storm.

The car turned into Fifth Avenue. Big and powerful and heavy as it was I thought we were going to turn over. If the wind, before, had been terrific, it was worse now. And Fifth

Avenue! Not a cop in sight. Perhaps there were many in doorways, who still guarded the city. But we didn't see them.

"I hope the car holds out," I told Brown as the front wheels dashed water over the hood like a wave at sea. "We'd never make it on foot."

"But we'll make the last of it on foot." He nodded grimly. "Or we'll crawl it. Even tonight I can't chance the car to our final destination." And he lifted the speaking tube and called to Wong.

We swung over to Madison Avenue. An occasional light in a window stood out vaguely between the gusts of wind-driven rain like a beacon at sea. Again a turn, another burst of wind that I thought would drive the side of the car in, and we were creeping again downtown; passing Forty-sixth Street.

"One more swing like that," I said, "and we crawl from under."

"We could have gone straight down Park Avenue or even Fifth," Vee told me, "but I thought it would be better to twist and turn a bit. It wouldn't be hard to spot a car following us tonight. Not many on the road."

"Not many! Not one. Not a human being even. It's just a city of the dead." I felt Vee flung up against me. The car came to a stop on Forty-third Street, a few feet from Fifth Avenue.

WE CLIMBED out into the storm. Down the block, around the corner. We made Fifth Avenue all right, but at the turn the rain grew worse.

"Where do we meet him?" I shouted against the wind.

"Down— Only a block," Vee shouted back over his shoulder as we fought our way along Fifth Avenue.

Peculiar, that storm. There would be great breaks in it, where you could see the rain swirling all around you; hear the whistling of the wind, yet feel yourself in a dead spot.

We pushed on, hugging close to the buildings. Once above the wind and rain there was a crash behind us, just about at the corner we had left. We huddled for an instant in a doorway, turned and looked back. There in the dimness was a figure; a hooded, coated figure desperately fighting his way across the Avenue to the scene of that crash.

"A window," Brown shouted. "And a cop! You can't beat it, Dean. The minute he is needed he appears. A jewelry store, maybe, that needs guarding."

"No crooks would be out tonight. None but fools—like us," I shouted as I pushed forward.

Little visibility ahead; little behind, I guess—except for the single moment when we saw the cop. Heads down upon our chests, we fought every inch of the way.

I felt like a ship going to answer an S.O.S. at sea. But I plodded on, pushing Brown as much as following him, as his body would suddenly be swept up and crashed back against me.

And in that deluge, in that storm, straight into the heart of it came flashing lights. A bus. A bus that sent up waves on each side of it, splashed them over the curb and onto our feet; like a small steamer passing a bathing beach on the Sound. Then it was gone; gone as I half turned my head to see its disappearing lights.

I looked ahead again—straight ahead. I saw the man, of course. The crouching figure, the shabby figure. Plainly a poor unfortunate creature, without a home—on the streets a night like this. And in the glare of the street light I saw his face, the fear and terror in it. He stood against the wind, right on the corner—glued, riveted to the spot in horror.

His head was flung back over his crouching body, his eyes followed his pointing finger.

My eyes also raised. Feet! I saw feet, just feet, hanging in the air. Then I saw it all, and gasped—cried out loudly. And my scream sounded but a whisper in my own ears.

A MAN was hanging there on the corner of Fifth Avenue. His body that had been held against the pole by the force of the wind was now beginning to swing grotesquely back and forth. And driven almost into the very center of his chest was a huge knife, and held there by that knife was a square of cardboard; cardboard on which plainly and in large letters was printed the message—

BLACK DEATH—4

I guess I knew the truth before I saw his face; was close enough to recognize that face; the matted, storm-soaked hair, the stubble of a beard. The man was Lessenger. Theodore Lessenger, the stool-pigeon—the glorified stool-pigeon. The man who was afraid to come to our apartment but must pick a safer place. A safer place! There in white letters against the blackness of the stanchion above the man's head glared the phrase W. 42 ST. and above it 5th AVE!

I tried to shout again, saw that Brown had bent low and was holding the man who pointed, forcing him with the aid of the wind toward the sign post. The wind sucked into my throat and choked my words. But they came just the same. At least, the thought was there.

"City of the Dead."

A whistle blew, a cop was there. Two, three—half a dozen, maybe. A siren shrieked, a car jumped the sidewalk, skidded or was blown half around. Men climbed from it.

The city was alive again. That great police system, which we so little respect but welcome so at such a time, was on the job.

After that, what? Just what I didn't know. The body was cut down all right; an ambulance was there. Somehow Wong had swung the corner and I was in the car—and Brown was gone. To headquarters, I thought.

Maybe the storm was just as bad when Wong drove me back to the apartment; maybe it wasn't. I didn't know. But even after a stiff hooker and the warmth of our great open fire in the penthouse living room, I still shivered. The thing was terrible, certainly a defiant challenge. I gulped, thought of the information Brown had expected from Lessenger, and realized that it was a challenge that could not be answered.

CHAPTER SEVEN
STORMY WEATHER

I DON'T know what time Brown came in. I had changed my clothes and was in a lounging robe, trying to be calm and collected. But it didn't work. Brown threw his hat and coat in a corner of the foyer and slouched into the room.

"Good God!" I cried out, "how did it happen? How could it happen? How long was he hanging there; stabbed before or after? Maybe there in the storm for hours, and—"

"Nonsense!" Vee went and stood with his back to the fire and dripped water over the floor. "He was stabbed to death some other place and brought there. No one on the street to be sure, Dean; not in such a storm. But after all, New York is not the back woods and Forty-second Street and

Fifth Avenue are the cross roads of the world, not of Wampus Junction. A bus had just gone by; people must have passed, cops may duck into doorways for a few minutes, but— Well, I'll hazard the guess that he wasn't hanging there over three minutes at the most. Even that poor unfortunate who had no home and was slinking from doorway to doorway saw him."

"Did he have anything to do with it?"

"No, certainly not. They're holding him of course, but he didn't even see it, though he thinks a car left the curb just before the lights of the bus came into view down Fifth Avenue. The driver of the bus saw nothing. Who would on such a night?"

"You think—think the message from Lessenger that he'd meet you there was a fake; that someone else sent it?"

"No." Brown shook his head. "It was Lessenger who telephoned me. He is—" he smiled grimly— "or was—a clever man. If the message was a forced one; if he was made to send it, he would have slipped me some hint; something in his voice. Damn it! I would have known." And then, with a shrug of his shoulders as he poured a stiff drink down, "Van Houton got him tonight. I went over the body. We won't go into detail, Dean." And I saw his shoulders tighten. "It's too ghastly even for me. Lessenger was tortured horribly before he died; I think, even after he told Van Houton where I was to meet him. The thing was—just fiendish. Lessenger was slowly tortured to death."

"What are you going to do?" I asked.

"I—" he hesitated. "I doubled the guard on Miss la Pala- tin—Maria."

"Vee—" I took him by the shoulders, half shook him; there was a peculiar, staring look in his eyes. "That— But what about Van Houton; what about him?"

He looked blankly at me. "I don't want her to die like that." And his eyes suddenly blazing back to life, "I promised her that I'd take care of her. I thought—I was sure—I'd have those letters." He walked to the phone, stood by it, stretched out a hand and held it there.

"What are you going to do?"

"Do?" he said. "Tell her—tell her. Tell her what Van Houton told the other one. I—I can do nothing for her. I—"

I was across the room and reaching for his hand, but he had turned and swung back to the fire. "One more night of peace for her," he said. "One more night. She's safe with the guard I've got."

"Mrs. Wilson had a guard too, and—"

I stopped. That was not the thing I wished to say. But his lips twisted at the ends. It wasn't a smile exactly; it wasn't—I guess it was just a twisted grimace.

"She couldn't do that," he told me. "She's built of better stuff. She'd face it."

"But we don't know what she has to face, Vee."

"That doesn't matter." Again he shook his head. "Van Houton has beaten me perhaps, but not Maria—not that girl. If she was built that way, why—why, Dean, I couldn't feel like I do about her."

AND THERE it was. His conceit. Even beaten at every trick, his pride came to the surface, unconsciously perhaps. It was not in his voice or even in his words, for they were spoken naturally; free from any such impression. But the pride was there, far back inside of him.

I tried to encourage him; tried to tell him that perhaps the information Lessenger was to give him wouldn't do any good anyway; couldn't convict Van Houton; couldn't—

And he said simply: "It's contrary to my whole life, Dean; contrary to every thought I ever had about being a servant of the State. I have never even admitted it to myself up to this very moment; this moment when it's an impossibility. But I am afraid I might have betrayed my trust; forgotten the millions I serve for the one—the one woman. Yes, I would have sold them all out; would have offered those letters for the freedom, for the life of Maria."

"No!" I said. And for the moment I rather liked what he had said. It was so different from the Vee Brown I knew—so human. But I shook my head. "You couldn't have done that. You couldn't have."

"That's what I thought until—until just now. But truth is truth, Dean. There's something about the girl that—"

The house phone rang. I lifted the receiver. We were to have guests at that time of the morning, and in that storm!

I turned to Vee. Mortimer Doran, the district attorney, and Inspector Ramsey were coming up.

Vee simply nodded and said: "You know, Dean—Van Houton has simply been a picture in a frame. Tonight he stepped out of that picture and hung a dead body on a lamp post. For I think he was with the boys who did it."

"But what a foolish thing—what a desperate thing! What purpose could he have in taking such a—"

"Purpose!" Brown laughed. "I told you that he knew I'd have to be terribly beaten. He laughed in my face tonight, Dean; laughed through the sightless, agonized eyes and twisted tortured lips of Theodore Lessenger. You should have seen his face beneath the arc light in the morgue. Yes, Van Houton stepped out of his frame and murdered this man himself. It's hard to believe that he could find another human who could so horribly mutilate his victim before killing him."

"He must be mad."

"Mad." Vee looked at me. "Well, yes—if you mean that he is without a soul; that some satanic agency has sucked all the blood of human feeling from his body. But if you mean his mind, his brain, then—no. I never was one to swallow the sob stuff that cruelty, viciousness and even fiendishness is in the literal sense madness." He shook his head. "But I couldn't convince Ramsey and certainly won't be able to convince Mortimer Doran that Van Houton pulled this job tonight." And as the bell of our private door rang, "We'll have a storm inside now that will make our hurricane a gentle zephyr. For I was there almost the very moment the body was strung up."

And we did have a storm.

RAMSEY STARTED it and for once Mortimer Doran stood by, gravely silent. "There's been enough of them; too damn many of them, Brown." Ramsey blustered now. "Mrs. Wilson—and you're not even surprised to find that she kicked herself in. Now Theodore Lessenger. But you're on the job almost the very moment he's strung up. A great detective you've turned out to be! Killer of Men, eh? Finder of Corpses, more like it. Always late. Some day it'll be you, the late Mr. Brown, we'll be cutting down. In front of the New York Stock Exchange at the lunch hour, I suppose."

"That would give you some pleasure in an otherwise drab career. You're never late, Ramsey, because you never know where you're going."

"Come, come!" Mortimer Doran came in at last. "You see, Vee—the knife and the card. Theodore Lessenger isn't much loss to the community, of course. But the Black Death again! What a riding the papers will give us tomorrow on this. Surely you're not going to tell us that Vincent Van Houton—smug, snobbish society man—stepped out in a hurricane just to string this body up at Fifth Avenue and Forty-second Street."

"I'm going to tell you just that," Vee Brown said. "And the reason? Well, it's not in defiance of and jeering at the police. It was in defiance of me; a jeer at me; perhaps a warning to me."

"Pretty important, ain't you?" Ramsey started, and stopped.

Mortimer Doran had raised his hand. I never saw him quite so serious. "Put everything on the table, Vee—all of it. You knew this man was to be hung there and went out in the storm and found the body? That's it?"

"Not exactly. I expected to meet him there—yes, meet Theodore Lessenger there. He was afraid to come here. He was the Black Death's right hand man; I knew that. Theodore Lessenger was ready to hang out the white flag; deliver to me—" He hesitated there, and then, "Or point out to me the place where I could find all the letters, information, documents, scandal about people that the Black Death has accumulated. He also told me—which I knew—that Vincent Van Houton was the Black Death."

"Yeah! You've told us that. Did he give you any evidence; anything more than you've already told us?"

"I might add that Dean Condon—" he looked at me— "was with me and heard what Theodore Lessenger said."

Mortimer Doran tightened his lips, stroked his chin, made clicking sounds in his throat. "It's the same stuff, Vee—has been for months. Lessenger, who makes the accusation, is dead. Dean, of course, is a prejudiced witness; and even if he wasn't, Lessenger's story is hardly evidence." And suddenly, partly in anger, partly incredulously, but mostly just spontaneously, "My God! Vee, what has come over you? If it is Van Houton, he's made a monkey out of you at every turn."

"But a live monkey," said Vee. "Was Vincent Van Houton's house watched tonight?"

Mortimer Doran looked at Ramsey. "Yes," Ramsey said after a bit. "There was a man there but he saw nothing."

"One man!" Vee cut in quickly. "There's a yard and a fence and an alley leading from the house to the other street. You should know that, Ramsey. The man was in front of course!"

"Of course," said Ramsey. "Van Houton's been tailed plenty. He complained to the commissioner. He's got friends, he's got money—so he's got influence. I couldn't give any reason for watching his house; I didn't even have any right to have a man in the front."

"Of course," Vee nodded, "they carried the body out the back, took it down to Forty-second Street and hung it to the stanchion. By God! Every paper will have streamers about it."

"You can't lay it on me." Ramsey pounded a finger against Brown's chest. "If a guy made a live monkey out of me I'd make a dead monkey out of him."

"You'd like to see him a dead monkey, eh?" Vee said, and I felt better when I saw that little whimsical twist to his mouth. "It isn't often that you and I agree on anything, Ramsey."

THERE WAS more of course, much more. Mortimer Doran blustered, threatened too, perhaps. He was worried. Not the hearty friend he always had been to Vee, yet he seemed as if he wanted to be.

"You said to give you a week and you'd clear this Black Death up," Mortimer Doran said just before they left.

"When I said that—" Brown started and stopped. And then suddenly, "the week isn't up yet."

They were gone.

"What did you mean—the week isn't up?" I asked Vee. "You have some plan?"

"No plan; and I meant nothing. I guess I'm beaten, Dean, and didn't have the guts to admit it. You are looking at the real man now; the real Brown, stripped of his guns and the chance to use them. No headlines in the papers now about my courage and glory. No bombastical boast on my part of my guts—the guts that others lack. I'm like the others—the rats I hunt. I can see my course, see it clearly—but I haven't got the guts for it."

He lifted his wallet from his pocket, pulled a check from it, looked at it a long moment, then tossed it into the fire. "Two hundred grand," he said slowly. "I'm a great one for saving money anyway."

He took another drink, flopped into a chair and put his head in his hands. I had never seen Brown like that before. I tried to read the papers, kept going to the window and looking out at the storm. Then I told him that it had let up considerably.

Vee jumped to his feet.

"I can't sleep." He fairly spat out the words. "And I can't go in that damned music room and lock the door on you; I can't go in there and think—think of her. For God's sake, Dean, go to bed! Leave me. I want to think. I've got to think." I had to leave him. But I knew I'd never sleep; knew it positively as I gulped down that final drink and without a word went to my bedroom. But I was asleep ten minutes later. Was it confidence in Vee—that he would finally work it out some way? No, I don't think so. Was it that I didn't have the same interest that he had in this—this—whatever the end was to be? No, I'm quite sure it wasn't that. I was tired, worn out—and I slept. And in my dreams a man swung back and forth—a man who hung at the end of a rope—and protruding from the center of his chest was a knife. A knife that pinned to that grotesque body a huge square card which read—BLACK DEATH 4.

CHAPTER EIGHT
THE LEATHER BOX

WHEN I woke up Brown was gone. It was late in the morning and there was still a light rain. Wong served me with breakfast.

"Mr. Brown, Wong?" I finally asked.

"Mr. Vee go out," Wong explained. "He tell me tell you no worry about him. But in your place I would worry—worry very much."

"But, why?" I asked. "Why should I worry, Wong?"

"Well—"Wong seemed to give the matter considerable thought—"because he is not the man you know and Wong knows."

"Did he say when he'd return, or what I am to do—or can do?"

"He said nothing. But he looks like a man who walks alone with his thoughts and knows not of the rain."

And that was that.

At three o'clock Maria telephoned. Her voice trembled over the wire. "I can feel it," she said. "I can feel it. The Black Death—just as it must have settled on others. I am to die too, Dean."

"Why talk such nonsense?" I told her. "You're well guarded. Vee has taken care of that."

"But Mrs. Wilson was well guarded." Her words were hardly audible but I got them, for they were the very words I had spoken to Brown earlier that morning. I guess I took a full minute before I spoke. Then I decided that it would be silly to try and ignore her meaning.

"Vee said you would not; could not— You understand. The stuff in you wouldn't permit it."

Badly expressed? Sure. But she understood it.

"Better that than the other," she said. "What is Vee doing?"

"I don't know."

"But he is to see Van Houton this evening. I heard him say so." And when I did not answer at once, "He is, isn't he?"

"I don't know," I said again. I couldn't tell her he had nothing to see Van Houton about—nothing to threaten him with—nothing to— But she cut in.

"Van Houton called me up. He told me that Brown was coming to see him tonight, at nine o'clock. He— Why don't you say something?"

What could I say? Tell her the truth? But, no. I said simply, and without sense: "I'll tell Vee you called when he comes in." But I didn't quite add the words that hovered on my lips. If he does come in.

This time it was the girl who hesitated before she spoke.

"No, don't tell him; don't tell him I called. I think I know. I've read the papers. He's failed. Don't make it harder for him. There's nothing he can do. Please, later, tell him 'Good-bye.'"

There was a click. I sat there for a long time with the phone in my hand. She had said simply, "Good-bye." But it had brought a lump up into my throat, to drop back almost at once with a dull thud in the pit of my stomach.

IT WAS ghastly, unbelievable. New York! The city of millions. Twenty thousand policemen; Vee Brown, Killer of Men. And Vincent Van Houton, sitting back in his easy chair lifts his phone and condemns someone to death. Vincent Van Houton, who—

A voice spoke so suddenly in my ear that I half jumped from the chair. Then I realized that I was still holding the instrument to my ear and that the operator had said: "There's a party trying to get you; will I put them on now?"

And my own voice answered mechanically, probably naturally, for we are creatures of habit: "Thank you. Please do."

It was Vincent Van Houton.

"Condon, eh? Well, you'll do." Van Houton's voice was soft and quiet. "Don't bother Brown if he's resting. I've read the papers and understand that he had a very busy night— a very busy night, indeed. Must have been disturbing to even such a hard-boiled killer of men. I understand the papers don't dare print the full details of Theodore Lessenger's death. Horrible. Horrible!"

"Yes." I could hardly speak. "What do you want?"

"Oh, yes. Brown, and I presume you, since you always travel with him, were to honor me with a visit tonight. There, there. Don't tell me you're not coming; that you have no reason to call on me. This is an invitation, now. I will be pleased to receive you both at nine o'clock. Indeed, you might tell Mr. Brown that it is imperative that he come." And very low and in sarcastic awe, "I've had a message from this Black Death—a message to give Mr. Brown. Nine o'clock, then." And though I never said a word, "Fine! I'll be expecting you."

This time I did not sit there with the phone in my hand. I dropped it back in its cradle as I turned and faced the door. Vee Brown stood there; swollen eyes looked at me.

"Where have you been?" I started toward him, turned quickly as he came into the room, and hurriedly tossed a stiff drink into a glass and handed it to him.

He half raised it to his lips, paused, grinned a rather ghastly sort of grin, then laid the glass down on the table. Though the rain still poured down his face he licked at his lips before he spoke.

"No. I need a shower and a bed. The whisky would be good for me but I can't take it now."

"Vee," I put an arm about him as he walked toward the bathroom, "where have you been? Just walking around? You're not—you haven't let Van Houton get you?"

He was tearing off his wet things, tossing them in the hall before the bathroom door. "No. Almost beaten— beaten to my knees, Dean. But not quite licked. I have made a decision. That's why I won't take the liquor. I don't want afterward to think— But there! Don't say anything— not now. That was Van Houton of course. He's expecting us tonight."

"Nine o'clock." I nodded.

"Good! We'll go, and we'll have a surprise for him." A moment's pause. "A surprise for you too, I think, Dean."

For a moment his drawn face was there. Then the bathroom door closed.

IT WAS ten minutes after three that afternoon when Brown went to bed. Just before eight o'clock I was thinking of awakening him—when Irving Small came. He just slid into the apartment—*oozed* in is perhaps a better word. He always seemed to slip or glide or ooze along. But now his hands were not rubbing together ingratiatingly. They couldn't. He was carrying a heavy black case—a peculiar, long, and evidently heavy container of leather.

He slid into the living room, placed himself on the edge of a chair and grinned at me as he cocked his head. "I want to see Brown," he said. "I've got something better for him than bodies hanging to posts."

Brown was wide awake, but now very grim in his long dressing gown. Though the bleariness had gone somewhat from his eyes, the pouches and black lines, even if not so marked, were still beneath them. His tight lips parted slightly when he saw the long black box at Irving Small's feet.

"You should'a' told me sooner," Small said. "I didn't see the papers until this afternoon. Being a careful man, I went to the morgue and had a look at the body. It was Lessenger all right."

"Well, what about it?" Brown demanded, but there was excitement in his voice and his eyes were riveted on the black leather.

"He was a clever man, though hanging to a post at Fifth Avenue and Forty-second Street may not look like it. But he knew I recognized him last night, and he came back—came back and left this box with me. You see, he got a call to go and see a certain party. He was afraid. If anything should happen to him, he asked me to give this box to you." Irving Small paused, licked his lips. "No one would deny that something certainly happened to Lessenger." He rubbed his hands together and chuckled gurgling sounds at his own gruesome mirth.

Brown, with a visible effort, lifted the heavy box and put it on the table. He made quick work of the small brass lock at the end and threw up the lid. It was a long filing cabinet. Cards inserted; names neatly typed below the printed letters of the alphabet.

Vee was running his fingers quickly over those cards, pulling out an occasional letter, a typewritten sheet. Then he shook his head at me.

"No 'Lessenger' and no—the girl. But it should serve its purpose." He clapped the fence on the back.

"Small, old child," he said, "there'll be a grand piece of change in this for you."

"Yes?" Irving Small's eyes widened. "You didn't know he left it with me? He didn't tell—drop a note even—didn't give you a hint?"

"Not a hint," said Brown.

"I guessed what it was. I knew what it was." Irving Small's head dropped. "I could have made a fortune out of it, sold it to the Black Death for a great deal of money. Lessenger led me to believe that you would expect it if anything happened to him."

"He knew you." Brown glanced toward the clock. "I'd have found out if you had tried any tricks, Small." And after Small had gone, "He would cut my throat in a minute, Dean. That is, if he could see the cash value of it."

Vee whistled now as he ran his fingers through the long row of cards in the case, before closing the lid.

"Vee," I said, "you're going to turn this box over to Van Houton for the girl's—for Maria's freedom?"

The brightness went out of his eyes; they seemed to suddenly grow lifeless and glassy. There was a peculiar choking sound in his voice.

"I hope so. I hope so." And with almost a plea in his voice, "I don't know what I am going to do tonight."

It didn't take Vee long to dress. He was back in that room again, at that file of letters—going over and over them.

"Vee," I said at last, "there must be some other way. Some evidence—something you can—"

"Not a scrap—not a scrap of evidence against him," he rasped. "I've been through it a dozen times. If I plant it in his place and you and I swear we found it there, we might get him. But we'd get Maria too."

"But we couldn't do that—it would be perjury."

"Perjury!" His laugh sent chills up my back. "I've heard enough perjury in my day not to be bothered about that. Don't you see, Dean? It's not the city, it's not the State. It's Maria I'm thinking about. And, damn it! This whelp from hell knows it."

NOT ANOTHER word did he speak until we arrived at Vincent Van Houton's and I preceded him up the steps, the long leather box under my arm. Then, just before putting my finger to the bell button, I said: "This is a mighty precious package to carry with us. Yes, I know Vincent Van Houton hires only servants with the highest references and formerly with the best families. But, now— if he carted that body from here last night he must be using some pretty hard characters."

"That's right." Vee nodded. "Some pretty hard characters. Let us hope this box may tempt him to use them tonight." Then he shook his head. "But I'm afraid we'll have no such luck. He's too clever for that. He knows that my strength is in my right hand and the finger that closes upon the trigger. He'll play against my weakness."

"Your weakness!"

"Yes." Brown grinned crookedly and tapped his head. "The old think box. Most men I've hunted have gambled their quick shooting against my quick shooting. He gambles his brains against my brains, and so far— But give the button a dig."

It was the same butler we had seen on other occasions who now let us in. The same dignity—perhaps, worried dignity—and the same politeness. He closed the door carefully and said: "Mr. Van Houton, sir, is on the telephone. He is expecting you and wishes you to wait a few minutes only, then he will receive you in his study above. He—"

The butler broke off suddenly. Brown and I both turned toward a closed door to our right. The same door that Ramsey stuck his head in when we had first visited the house. It was the room with the pictures of cats. We listened.

Queer sounds came from behind that door, like the frightened shrill shriek of a bird.

Vee Brown stretched out a hand and turned the knob. The door was locked. He looked at the butler. "What was that?" he demanded.

The butler stiffened. "I don't know, sir."

"But you can guess, sir; and I never speak of—of my employer. I might add, sir, that Mr. Van Houton has had my notice for the past two weeks."

"You're leaving! What did he say to that?"

"He doubled my salary, sir. Doubled a most generous salary. But the notice still stands. I—well, I don't like the new type of servant coming in."

"New servants, and undesirable?" Brown kept his black eyes on the man. "Then why does he want you?"

"I am sure I don't know, sir." And without the trace of a smile, "Unless, sir, he wishes to retain an air of unquestioned respectability in the establishment."

The shriek of a bird again, and Brown held out his hand to the butler. "The key to this door! A simple lock," he said.

"I have no key to that door." The butler stood straighter, if that were possible. Then, without the least appearance of unbending in speech or manner, "A simple lock, as you say, sir—and you a detective. I could take a few minutes outside the study before announcing you, sir."

He turned, and walking straight to the stairs went slowly up then, not once looking back.

"And me a detective." Brown seemed to think aloud. "Old Butts is right, Dean." He dug a hand in his inside jacket pocket, produced a long skeleton key and with a few deft turns of his wrist unlocked the door.

He swung it open quickly. Darkness—and a form that darted by our feet and up the stairs, but not before I had recognized it as a cat. A huge gray ball that—that held something yellow in its mouth.

I was looking over Brown's shoulder when he snapped on the light and peered into that room. Yes, pictures of cats; but it wasn't that which made me gasp. It was the miniature trees and the half dozen living cats that wandered about in the dull light. Wandered? No! Skulked. Hunted their prey in a tiny forest—a forest that meant death for the victims.

"Don't bother to look, Dean." Brown clicked out the light, pushed me back and closed the door. Then seeing my face, "You saw it. The birds had no chance. Poor things! Their deaths were as horrible and as certain as the victims of their master."

I said nothing; the thing nauseated me. I had to pull myself together. The butler was coming down the stairs.

"God!" I finally said to Brown as we followed the servant up the stairs, "the man deserves death—a hundred deaths."

"Yes." Brown nodded, then he spread his hands apart. "We would hardly feel elated, Dean, if we got him a twenty-five-dollar fine on a cruelty-to-animals charge."

CHAPTER NINE
EMPEROR OF EVIL

VINCENT VAN HOUTON met us in his study. He did not rise—just indicated chairs for us. His mild blue eyes that rested on the long box which I held turned for a moment to sharp daggerlike points. I was looking, as Brown was looking at the gray ball that lay on his lap, and at the yellow feather that Van Houton plucked from the purring mouth and let glide easily to the floor.

"We happened to look in the room downstairs," Vee said abruptly, "and saw the cats—and the birds."

"Really!" smiled Van Houton. "I'm afraid someone left the door open again. But no matter. I am training the birds to get used to those pictures of the cats first. You've seen cats and mice friendly; at least in circus performances. I have a theory that cats and birds could very easily be—"

"I might have killed those cats," Brown cut in.

"You didn't dare. You—" Van Houton came to the edge of his chair so suddenly that the big gray ball was thrown from his knees, landed almost at Brown's feet and clawed viciously at his leg. Brown's foot shot forward and up. The cat hung for a moment on the end of his toe, turned over once in the air, and with a squeal of rage or pain struck against the tongs by the open fire.

Van Houton was on his feet, his hands clenched at his sides; hands that rose suddenly and half stretched toward Vee. I had never seen such passion; such hate in a human face. Every fine feature of that face was gone; every line now was cruel, the lips snarling, twisted; the eyes burning like an animal's; the hands—

The hands fell to his sides. Van Houton turned and put another log on the fire, brushed some loose hairs from his jacket and dropped into the chair again. He was smiling. The real man, that had showed for a moment, was gone. He wore again that usual mask of the pleasant, perhaps slightly lazy but kindly gentleman.

"You are rather clever, Mr. Brown," he said softly. "I have strong hands, could very easily choke you to death. Anyone would believe that; and anyone would believe that to save your own life you were forced to shoot me to death." He shrugged broad shoulders. "What does it matter now? Your opportunity has passed." He looked at the cat that was sulking in a far corner of the room. "I am afraid that kick will cost you much heartache." He laughed slightly. "I have found your weakness, Mr. Brown; discovered something inside of you that no one else suspected. You have a heart, my friend."

"I have more than that." Brown looked at the watch on his wrist. "But we haven't much time. Dean, give that box to Mr. Van Houton."

Van Houton took the box and placed it on the long flat desk beside him, leaning from his comfortable chair to run fingers through the contents. His face never changed. He nodded once or twice, then to Brown, "Not the collection of the Black Death, surely. But it must be. Why show this to me? It will cost me many friends; people I had thought beyond reproach, and in the hands of an unscrupulous man might—"

"That box," said Vee Brown, "can send you to jail—perhaps to the chair."

VAN HOUTON looked startled, then he laughed. "Me! I see. You still believe I am this Black Death, this—is it 'Emperor of Evil'? So—for the moment and for our amusement let us pretend that I am. There is nothing in this quite complete collection to connect this Black Death with any murder or even suicide. I note that those names have been withdrawn and no doubt destroyed. As for the rest of the documents, I deny of course any knowledge of them, and I there is nothing to connect any individual with them. I presume"—and his smile was really pleasant now—"this box is a present from our dear departed friend, Theodore Lessenger."

"That's right," said Brown. "You're not afraid of its contents?"

"No, I am not afraid of its contents. But I recognize, of course, its value in dollars and cents, and I understand why you brought it here." Vincent Van Houton leaned forward now. "Still pretending, Mr. Brown, that I am the Black Death, you are offering me this box in return for the freedom, for the life, of Gertrude la Palatin—really Myra Johnson, christened perhaps Maria—Maria St. John."

"You are well informed," Brown said. "But there is no evidence against her in that box."

"No." Van Houton came suddenly to his feet, walked over to the fireplace, and sliding back a panel beside it dug in his hand and drew out two envelopes. He left the panel open, revealing a compartment which might have accommodated the long box upon the desk. One of the envelopes which he had taken out he tossed into the fire.

"Don't worry about that," he turned to Vee, holding the other envelope in his hand. "The document in the fire concerns one, Theodore Lessenger. Let us not malign the dead. You represent justice, Mr. Brown—stern and quick justice. I can assure you that Theodore Lessenger received all of that. Society has been avenged for his wrongs. But glance through this." He thrust the long envelope into Vee's hand.

Vee opened it, spread out the single sheet and looked at it. Van Houton went on talking.

"Just her name—a simple matter. Nothing like the others. You will see that she was convicted under the name of Myra Johnson. Poor Myra! She was a product of what we call Environment. Born to poor but honest parents in Cleveland, she was sent to relatives in New York. They could not keep her. They were poor too, but not quite so honest. A reformatory before she was twelve years old! Later, a conviction; no matter the offense, she will deny it. But the State found her guilty. You'll see, Mr. Brown, that our great Gertrude la Palatin's mistake was in leaving prison—leaving it a few years before her sentence had expired and without bothering with the formality of a pardon. And as Vee glanced toward the fire, "Toss it in; the memory is unpleasant."

Brown did toss the paper and envelope into the fire.

"Poor kid!" he said. "Her record doesn't show much chance in earlier years. I suppose you have a copy of that, which is why you let me destroy it."

"No. No copy. Only the words so indelibly stamped upon my mind. I believe I am the only living man who knows who Gertrude La Palatin really is, except you and your friend—now."

"But I never keep written records of the dead."

"The dead!" I jarred in. "She— Why, she's not dead."

"No, no." Van Houton seemed to choose his words very carefully. "To me she is dead. A few more hours, then to you and the world she will be dead. She will wish it that way."

"You hate the girl, don't you?" Brown's voice was low.

VAN HOUTON seemed really startled. "Hate her? You do not understand life and death and love. I love her, Mr. Brown. No woman can ever take her place. Her catlike tread; the smoothness of her arms; her hair, so like the fur of a cat! The warm breath. No, no. I could never hate her. I shall miss her when she's dead."

"Why," Brown asked, and he seemed very calm and cool now, "are you so sure of the girl's death?"

"Her art—her great love for the name that she made." Van Houton leaned far forward now. His lips were tighter, his eyes not so kindly. "She wants to leave an honest name for Gertrude la Palatin—a name that I can not destroy. She was in this blackmail business as deep as—as the Black Death. Then she changed, and was so clever about it that I did not for a moment suspect that it was she who struck so effectively at the Black Death. Sometimes I think it was something inside of her; sometimes I think it was the first time a victim died. But always I fear; always I wake up in the night and believe it was you. You"—his face was white now—"you love her, or at least she loves you. So—she dies."

"You expect her to kill herself?" Brown's voice was very steady now though I saw his hands tighten upon his knees.

"What good would that do her? How would it save her name for her to take her own life?"

"Overwork. The strain on a great actress; ill health that forbade her to act. I know her well; am recognized as her friend. I will make the story protect her name. The thousands that have admired her will pity, understand, and have nothing but the kindest memories."

"You won't bring up her past, then—if— You promised her that; gave her your word on that, eh? Will she take that word?"

"She will take that word, and I will keep it. I have spoken to her at some length, tried to make the going easy. She will call me here on the phone tonight. It will be my duty, my very sad duty, to tell her that Vee Brown can do nothing for her, then"—he paused, spread his hands slightly—"she will shoot herself to death. Very simple."

"Yes, with some." Brown nodded. "But she's got too much stuff in her to take that way out." And when Van Houton's eyes grew hard, "Perhaps you may not answer the phone when she calls."

Van Houton shrugged. "I daresay you can arrange that. But if I do not answer, she does not need the answer. She knows that she may play until the final number—your number. After that—living, I will disclose her to the law. She has often said she would rather die than return to prison."

Brown looked at the file on the desk, toward the hidden length of oblong where it had at one time evidently been kept, nodded slightly and asked: "There is no alternative—no deal you'd like to make with me?"

"Well"—Van Houton stroked his chin—"love and hate are very close. The girl is to die because a man loves her; perhaps because she loves a man. But tonight—let us say that just before you came I had a message from the Black Death. I hope it doesn't strike you as rather silly! But he told me, if you should leave her here tonight, go at once to your apartment and blow out your brains, the girl— Then I could tell the girl on the phone that Vee Brown could— was doing something for her."

"God!" I shot in, "what an absurd idea. You must be mad."

BROWN KEPT his eyes on Van Houton. "No, no. Original, revolutionary, perhaps—but not mad. There are two other alternatives. One—that the girl won't, at the final moment, press the trigger."

"Possible!" Van Houton cut in. "But it will not matter. The suggestion about yourself I suppose you will not entertain."

"Hardly," said Vee. "A woman wouldn't think much of a man who, given a problem to solve, solved it by shooting out his brains. Brains! I think you flatter me there. And a man"—slender shoulders moved—"could not believe that a woman he thinks a lot of could turn the same trick. I tell you, Mr. Van Houton, Mr. Emperor of Evil, Mr. Black Death—I am going to do a lot for that girl, for the citizens of this city, for the department that pays me."

"Good God!" I cried, "you're not going to do as he suggests and—"

"Hell, no!" said Brown, and his voice rang with his old time vigor. "Do you think I'd shoot myself and make a musical-comedy ending out of the city's greatest tragedy? I—"

The phone rang. Van Houton reached toward it. "That will be Gertrude la Palatin now."

"Wait!" Brown was on his feet, clutching at his arm. "I'll call your bluff for you, Mr. Van Houton. That girl can take it. I can't believe she's yellow. There's a chance of her going on the stand and convicting you. Let me tell her that Vee Brown can do nothing for her—personally."

"You know what that means. If I can't answer the phone, she understands—"

Brown knocked his hand from the phone—grabbed it up. "Yes? Vee Brown talking, Maria. That's right; I'm telling you in place of Van Houton. I can do nothing for you."

"Vee!" I forgot my promise to Maria. "She'll do it. She'll—" But it was useless. Vee had jammed down the phone.

"Will she?" he said. "I hope not. That would be the biggest let-down of the whole case. No, no—Dean. I have something else up my sleeve."

"Ah!" Van Houton clasped his hands, his elbows on his knees. "I'm afraid it's too late now. You might hurry to the theatre and stop her, of course; but then—there's the information still in my head, you know. Now let us hear the other alternative; the one instead of putting a bullet in your head."

Brown swung on me. I had never seen his eyes blaze as they were blazing then, except when he had completed a case; when he was about to complete it. But he was pushing me toward the door, throwing it open.

"Outside, Dean. Outside!" His voice was quick, throaty. "I have something to say to Van Houton—something even too private for you."

"But Vee, I— Of course, if you insist. But the box!"

"We're going to let Van Houton keep his box."

The door slammed, the key turned and I was left standing alone in the hall.

CHAPTER TEN
BEHIND THE DOOR

SO BROWN had something up his sleeve. What was it? At the last minute would he make good? Would—but what could he do? The girl, too! Why, he had been almost brutal to her. Was it possible that he didn't—didn't care? Would he, as he said, make some deal with Van Houton to sacrifice the many for Maria? But Van Houton wouldn't do that. Greed and love and hate! And hate had won out. He hated Brown. He—Maria had saved Vee's life. Maria had—But Vee had already told her on the phone that he could do nothing. I should have told Brown; told him of her call, what she said. There might be time yet! I raised my hand to pound heavily upon the door, and held it there without striking.

Voices from below—the slam of the front door. A gruff, loud voice that I knew well drowned out the well-modulated tones of the butler.

"So Van Houton's got company and cannot be disturbed, eh? Well, we'll go up and join him. Make a real party out of it—a surprise party. Who's he entertaining?"

A mumble from the butler that I did not get and then the voice I knew again.

"You're not permitted to tell. So that's it, eh? Come! Get that fat carcass of yours out of the way or you won't be able to tell anything for the next two or three hours. Come on, sir! I hate to take it on the chin like this from Brown, but the law's the law and there's some satisfaction in beating him to— Damn my soul! If it ain't Brown's little playmate, Dean Condon."

This last as I stood on the stairs blocking the passage of Inspector Ramsey and seeing behind him the huge, if not so muscular, Mortimer Doran, the district attorney.

"So the boy detective's with Van Houton," Ramsey said, and suddenly, "Has Brown got him this time?"

"Got him!" I guess I stammered. But I did grab Ramsey by the arm as he thrust me aside and started up those stairs. "Wait"—I pleaded. "Vee's with him now. He's talking to him."

Ramsey shook me off. He shot his face forward, his chin thrust out. "I want to talk to him too. What's Brown—"

He stopped, raised his head, listened. Plainly came the report of a gun, dulled perhaps by the curve in the hall and the closed door, but unmistakable and certainly from Van Houton's study.

I didn't try to hold Ramsey then. I simply tried to beat him up those stairs and down that hall. But he kept ahead of me. Back of us came Mortimer Doran, panting heavily though he had run but a few steps. What had happened behind the closed door of the study? What did the shot mean? Perhaps I had those thoughts; perhaps I had other thoughts—many of them. But I don't remember them now. Just one single thought. Vee Brown and Vincent Van Houton were in that room alone, and a single shot had come from that room.

A single shot!

And it wasn't a single shot. Almost the moment we reached that locked door; almost the moment Ramsey had grasped the knob and found the door locked; almost the moment his huge shoulder had crashed against it, there was another shot; another roar of a gun. Louder this time. A moment of silence, and I was helping Ramsey; throwing my body madly with his against that door.

Splintered wood, groaning hinges! The sudden snap as the lock gave and the door crashed. We were in the room, Ramsey half on his knees as I stumbled against him.

Then Ramsey was on his feet, his gun dangling in his hand. Mine? In my pocket, of course. I had never even thought to drag it out.

VEE BROWN half sat, half crouched in front of the large flat desk. There was a gun in his hand, a surprised look on his face, smears of powder and a slight trickle of blood along his left cheek. He staggered to his feet; I half supported him. Then I looked at—at the body.

Yes, Van Houton was slumped over the desk. Under his right hand was the nose of the gun. Mortimer Doran gasped; Ramsey lifted up Van Houton's head. It wobbled slightly, hung to one side. The eyes were open, staring, glassy, and just between those eyes was a dull red hole.

"Dead?" There was no sense to the question I asked.

"As stiff as a mackerel." Ramsey let the dead man fall forward on the desk again, none too gently either. I shuddered as the body jarred the long leather filing case on the desk.

"Let us have it, Vee." Mortimer Doran finally spoke as Ramsey wandered about the room, jumped aside as the cat darted from under the chair that held the dead body and fled into the hall.

"I had Van Houton—had him on the Lessenger murder—had him cold." Brown wiped burnt powder and blood from his face with his handkerchief and looked over toward me. "Dean will tell you. But there was something else. This man, admittedly the Black Death, held hidden someplace letters, documents, information that would cause hundreds to suffer, perhaps take their own lives. So I wanted to know where those documents were."

"You mean you wanted to make a deal with him." Ramsey's mouth hung open.

"In a way." Vee turned to Mortimer Doran. "I chased Dean out of the room, then promised Van Houton that I'd get you to go easy on him if he delivered to me all this information which Lessenger said he had."

"Go on!" said Mortimer Doran.

"Van Houton agreed." I listened to Brown continue with my mouth wide open. "He told me all his information was in a leather filing case hidden in a secret compartment by the fireplace." Vee pointed to the long yawning hole. "For the moment I guess I was off my guard. You know the story that he never had a gun—wouldn't even think of keeping one in his house. Well, I swung back, with that heavy file of papers there on the desk in my hands—when he did it. He whipped a gun out from beneath the desk some place." Brown wiped his forehead now and shook his head. "It was my closest call."

"You must have been pretty close; there's powder on your cheek." Ramsey was staring at Vee, running his fingers along the file of letters. "Just what happened?"

"I was stunned, of course." Brown told the story easily. "Both my hands held the heavy leather file. I dropped it to the desk, leaned forward, clutched at his gun with my left hand and knocked it aside as it blazed. I thought I was gone. Powder burnt my face, a bullet creased my cheek. I was thrown back onto the floor. Then, before he could fire again I let him have it."

"Before he could fire again," Ramsey mused aloud. "There was a good seven seconds between those shots—

maybe ten." He sneered slightly. "You were always pretty slow getting out a gun. Everybody knows that."

Brown was very calm. "Seven seconds, you say? Perhaps you're right. It seemed to me all in an instant. I must have been stunned—dazed there on the floor. Van Houton, I guess, thought I was dead. Maybe that's what happened." And nodding his head, "Yes, that must have been what happened. I remember the fear in his face when I raised my gun, just as he tried to fire again."

RAMSEY LIFTED Van Houton's head again. A single look and I turned my eyes away. Yes, there was fear in the dead face—terror—horror.

"Yeah, he saw it coming." Ramsey dropped the head back again. "And I guess he didn't like it. But it's—it's—You had a lucky break, Brown."

"Come, come!" Mortimer Doran was the efficient official now. "Take the phone and get on the job, Ramsey. As for Vee! He saved the State some money."

Brown wasn't listening. He was at the desk when Ramsey was telephoning, had lifted the box of letters, put them in my hands.

"Feel the weight of it, Dean. That's what got me. Now—hold it by the strap. Heavy, isn't it?" And putting the box down again and turning to Doran, "What brought you here?"

"We came to apologize to you, Brown. Ramsey and I." Doran jerked a thumb toward Ramsey, who scowled as he talked into the phone. "Lessenger left a letter with one of his law partners, to be sent to me if he died by violence. I got the letter an hour ago. I don't know if it would convict Van Houton or not—that is, with a jury. But with these letters, that file you discovered here, and Van Houton's attempt on your life it will certainly convict him with the public. Damn it! Vee, I never believed it; never really believed it."

Ramsey hung up the phone, strutted across the room. "Damn lucky you found those letters here and we had that note, Brown," he said. "Otherwise I might think you just staged this thing and simply shot him to death. That gun of his! We'll see if we can trace it to him. He always let it be known that he hated firearms."

"Don't be a fool," said Mortimer Doran.

"He's not a fool," Vee said. "I too believed that story that he abhorred firearms. Everyone believed it—his servants too. It was that belief that very nearly cost me my life. Damn it, if I hadn't believed it, I'd of had Van Houton for you! We'd have roasted him sure. And I wanted the law to—to have him."

"It's better as it turned out." Doran said. "He might have beaten the case."

"Vee—" I tugged at his arm and whispered. "Maria—the theatre. It's after ten. She—she—"

"Unfinished business." Brown looked at Doran. "And I want to have this scratch—" he touched his left cheek— "fixed up."

"Sure. Sure! Run along." But Doran grabbed Vee before he reached the door. "That stuff there." He pointed to the file of letters. "Dynamite!" He half looked toward the fire.

"I'd chuck them in," Vee said, "if you don't need them as evidence."

"Hell!" said Mortimer Doran, "you don't think we're going to put a dead man on trial. We've got enough to convict him in the newspapers certainly, after his attempt to kill you."

"Telephone the theatre. Let Maria know," I told Brown as we went down the stairs. "There's a phone in—"

He held me back as I turned toward the library. "No, Dean. No!" He shook his head. "You won't understand; maybe I don't even understand myself. But I never could feel the same way about that girl again if—if—"

I didn't understand and told him so. But he never answered me. Then I tried something else. "Why didn't you tell them the truth? Why those lies of finding the documents there?"

"I didn't know why they had come then," he explained. "I wanted them to be sure of his guilt." He smiled wanly up at me. "As for handing you the box—the file! The fingerprint boys would have found your prints all over it." He dabbed at his face. "I'll have that burn fixed up later."

DESPITE ALL my pleadings and even my threats he wouldn't go to Gertrude la Palatin's dressing room and tell her she was safe; and what's more, he wouldn't let me do it.

"You may be making a terrible mistake," I told him when we entered the front of the theatre and Brown, after locating the head usher, insisted upon being escorted to Van Houton's box. "This is the time of that long interval, when the *Dance of the Fans* precedes the—that number—your number."

"*Girl of the Night. Girl of the Shadows.*" His words were calm; his voice was natural, but the hand that he unconsciously placed on the back of mine was wet and cold.

The manager was on the stage. He was talking. It was about the final number. *Girl of the Night!* I didn't catch his words, but subconsciously the enthusiasm in his voice reached me. I was looking about the crowded house.

Crowded? Yes, every seat was taken; everyone was expectant. Gertrude la Palatin's conquest of the night before had been featured in every theatrical page.

The music came—Brown's music. The manager disappeared in the wings. A minute passed—two—three. The orchestra leader leaned forward; people grew restless. The manager came from the wings, he raised his hand. The music stopped. People were quiet. The whiteness of his face, his whole attitude, his two attempts to speak that failed! And then his voice rang out.

"I regret that Miss La Palatin, due—due to—"

Brown was on his feet; his fingers bit into my arm. "I was wrong—" He started to speak, dropped back into his chair again, and finished, "I was right, of course."

The manager waved to the orchestra. The music started. Far back in the wings we could see Gertrude la Palatin. Slowly, with head down, she was walking toward the lights; then into the lights. And it was Maria—Girl of the Night.

"Guts," said Brown. "I knew it. Guts!"

And she sang. Never once did she raise her eyes or even turn her eyes toward our box. And then, just at the end of the chorus—the words—*Girl of the Night,* she did. She turned her head slowly and looked straight up; straight up at Vee Brown, who was leaning far forward, his elbows on the rail.

For one single moment her left hand went to her throat; her right clutched at the drapes behind her as her knees sagged. Then she straightened, nodded to the orchestra leader and swung into the chorus again.

"She's singing to bring down the house tonight." Brown's eyes were alive, dancing; the old twist was back in the corners of his mouth.

This time, when she reached the final chorus, she looked up at the box. And the words were changed—at least, the last word was changed. It was—*Girl of the Shadows.*

"She's not singing to bring down the house," I told Vee and meant it. "She's singing to you tonight. Somehow, she knows!"

"Somehow she knows," echoed Brown as we left the box to go back stage.

IT MUST have been a week later when Vee was in the music room with Maria and so was "out" to everyone, that Mortimer Doran called.

"Brown home?" he asked, and when I shook my head, doubtful if I should tell him, he went on. "Good! I've got a present for him. We won't need it anymore and I know how he likes to collect trophies of the hunt." He thrust a package into my hand. "Open it after I go and stick it up in his gun room as a surprise. It's the gun Van Houton used, and I guess it was Vee's closest call."

Mortimer Doran nodded. "I think the Van Houton case was Vee's greatest success. How he stuck to that man despite everything! And at the end he killed him." He grew very grave. "Do you know that the happiness of hundreds; the deaths of many lay in Van Houton's hands? Damn it! I gave it to Ramsey good and plenty after we had traced the gun and learned how Van Houton got it. Ramsey more than hinted that it was a set-up; that Vee smoked his own cheek after he had deliberately shot Van Houton dead. Not that Van Houton didn't deserve it. But the discovery of how the gun must have come to Van Houton silenced Ramsey on that. Still, you know how Ramsey dislikes Vee."

"Sure!" I held open the door as Mortimer Doran was leaving. "But where did Van Houton get the gun?"

"It came from a racketeer; a man who used to call on Van Houton some time back. Why, damn it, you were with Brown when he killed him! That gun belonged to Pete Stokes. Van Houton must have gotten it from him months ago. So that dislike of his for fire arms was just bluff!"

The door closed and I walked into the gun room. I laid the queer-shaped package down on the table. I didn't open it at once. I thought of the woman, months back, who had died with a knife in her chest; of Wilson's wife, who had shot herself just below the right ear; of the knife driven into Lessenger's body through the card that read—BLACK DEATH. I thought too of the birds and cats, and even of the tiny hole in the center of Vincent Van Houton's forehead. And of Maria, of course; of the gun that she had left lying in her dressing room; the gun that she didn't—couldn't use when the big moment came.

Then I slowly opened the package.

It was an automatic revolver, and there was a nick on the grip shaped like a five-pointed star.

MAKE YOUR OWN CORPSE!

THE MURDER SYNDICATE—
THAT WAS HOW THE DEATH
NOTES WERE SIGNED. AND ONLY
DETECTIVE VEE BROWN—CRIME
MACHINE—KILLER OF MEN, KNEW
THE GHASTLY MENACE THAT LAY
BACK OF THEM—KNEW THAT
CRIMELAND'S NEWEST POST-
REPEAL VENTURE COULD BE MET
WITH HIS OWN BULLETS AND HIS
ALONE.

CHAPTER ONE
DEATH INTERVIEW

VEE BROWN lay far back on the couch, his hands stretched above his head and under the pillows. He looked almost like a boy. Slim-waisted, narrow-shouldered; small—very small. But this same diminutive detective was the envy of the entire police department and feared by every criminal in the city.

Killer of Men he was called—ever anxious to shoot it out with desperate criminals. His ability to draw quicker, shoot faster than they, and to hit what he shot at was best demonstrated by the fact that he was still alive and so many public enemies were dead. The underworld feared and hated him. And Brown, though he called himself simply a crime machine controlled by the State, hated the criminal; the murderer, with a bitterness that had become almost an obsession.

And his hands; those fingers that could squeeze a trigger so rapidly, were the same fingers that strummed the sentimental songs that earned him a fortune and paid the rent of our Park Avenue penthouse apartment, the lease of which was in my name. For few knew—not even his music publisher—that Vivian, Master of Melody and Vee Brown, Killer of Men were the same man. Yes, those fingers— But I could not see his fingers; both his hands were out of sight beneath the pillows.

After a long silence I said to Vee: "Do we take the vacation? Will you tackle the whole review?"

"We! What do you mean—we?" His lips twisted in that little whimsical smile. "You hunt and fish and read by the fire—and I write music."

"Then you won't do it."

"I didn't say that either," he snapped. "I've got to do it sooner or later. It's for Gertrude la Palatin, you know. Why shouldn't I write the music for a play in which she'll star? She certainly did enough for me, Dean; was willing to sacrifice her career—her life, even."

HE WAS referring, of course, to Vincent Van Houton, the cat man, blackmailer and murderer, who was now dead. And Gertrude la Palatin! Environment had started her off badly in life. She had been in prison, had escaped; started life under a new name, and now her secret had died with Van Houton.

"She must be pretty happy," I said.

Vee shook his head. "On the contrary, she still talks of paying a debt to society. Damn it! Dean, she wants to help me in my cases." He grinned.

"There's nothing to laugh at in that." I nodded. "She's the world's greatest impersonator; fooled us for months as to her real identity, and can handle a gun like any woman of the night."

"Girl of the night!" Vee half corrected, half mused. "It was a good name for her. But it isn't that—not that she isn't capable. It's that she's too close to me. You see, we don't know if we love each other or not."

"She knows." I smiled. "Maybe you don't."

"It's our careers. We both have that to think of." And when I continued to smile, "I see too much of her now. If it were known; even suspected by some big criminal who hated and feared me, he'd strike at me through her; maybe even dig up her past. At one time the underworld knew her well."

"I thought you were arranging through District Attorney Doran to clean the past up for her, and—"

"I am. I am!" he said impatiently. "But I must be careful. I can't let him know yet. It's Inspector Ramsey, you see. He hates me, Dean." The crooked grin again. "I don't know that I blame him; I've shown him up enough, and gone out of my way to do it, too. It's a good thing I'm assigned straight to the D.A.'s office or I wouldn't last ten minutes—no, not even as a cop."

"You're not just sure you love the girl, Vee." I told him plainly what was on my mind. "You're afraid of being—well, perhaps 'compromised' is not the word, but it's as near as I can strike it. You pretend your neglect is caused by the thought of her danger. There, don't laugh! There isn't a big thing breaking in the city today; nothing for you to work on. So why not trot up to the mountains and do the words and music for the review?"

"Because," he snapped, "I don't think I can work. Hunting criminals and hunting melodies is my life, and the one is so interlocked with the other that I can't separate them. Criminals stimulate me to write music; music stimulates me to hunt criminals. They are not two separate parts of me, as I thought. The one is necessary to the other."

"If things don't pick up in a criminal way, then blooey goes the review!" I spread my hands apart. "Nothing but a few scattered murders; a dead man here and a dead man there. Nothing for you in that!"

"No?" Vee's voice raised doubtfully.

"No!" I insisted. "These bodies have been found in different parts of the city. One stabbed, one choked, one shot to death. The police have traced down each victim. No love, no hate angles. Nothing in their business. Not vengeance.

The second splash brought
Clausen around.

Certainly not robbery. They had insurance, of course—at least, two of them; but that was traced down, and blew up. Not a motive!"

"Not an apparent motive, you mean. And 'no apparent motive' is the biggest motive of all. We'll have more victims, Dean. Mark my word. And one of them will give away the secret of these apparently unrelated crimes."

"You think there is something behind these murders?"

"Yes, I do."

"Then you did give that statement to the press that you knew, and would shortly lay your hands on the murderer of Henderson in the Bronx."

"Something like that. If I'm wrong, then 'the mountains.' No crime, no music, and perhaps I won't be strong on the hunting. But I'll chuck rocks in the lake and disturb your fish, and take the best seat by the fire."

"You're giving out another interview?" I didn't look at him when I said that.

"Yes." I felt that black eyes were on me. "A detective-story writer, I believe. A publisher is sending him to me tonight. He's due here shortly."

ALL I said was, "I see," but I didn't like it. Vee Brown had always refused to be interviewed on his work. That was how I first hooked up with him. Even now, when criticisms of his methods; his "loose shootings," as editorials called them, got too hot, I came to his defense in the *Morning Globe.*

"You're jealous as a young school girl, Dean," he chided me. "Authors must eat, you know. But there! I'm sure you'll get more from my interview than he. Answer the phone! I refuse to move for anyone. Not so much as a foot—or a hand."

I lifted the receiver. It was Gertrude la Palatin. Lately Vee called her just Pal, for short. She didn't ask for Vee. She spoke quickly; cryptically too, I thought.

"Tell Vee," she said, "that he's right. Everything is all tied up. What does he say?"

In some surprise I gave Vee the message.

"Fine!" His black eyes flashed. "Ask Pal to give you the phone number and wait by the telephone until I call her back, and tell her she's to keep things tied up until she hears from me."

Gertrude la Palatin took the message and simply said: "Yes."

I banged up the receiver, didn't speak. Vee was grinning at me like a Cheshire cat. Maybe, as he said, I was like a young school girl; but I had been Vee's only real confidant. Yes, I resented it, though, after all it might be the most innocent exchange of messages.

"Good old stupid Dean!" Vee was being facetious. I expected his hand to creep out from under the pillow and give me one of those fatherly taps on the arm. But his hand didn't. He kept smiling as he talked. "There's no one who could take your place. Sherlock Holmes never had so naive a Watson. By God! I've done some of my best work just to see the expression on your face."

"It's a wonder," I told him, "I'm capable of any expression. Certainly you're surprising enough to—" I paused. The doorbell rang. I looked at Vee; back toward the hall where Wong, our only servant, had his rooms.

"That," said Vee, "will be our author friend. You'll have to let him in. Wong has gone for the evening. I'm anxious to see what a detective-story writer looks like."

"You have never met him?"

Brown grinned. "Never even heard of him until his publisher came to see me. And I had a devil of a time buying a couple of his books. They are on the table there. Straighten them out a bit, push them more forward. Not too pointedly, Dean, but so that he'll see them when he enters the room. Writers like flattery, you know; even a certain one who writes for the *Morning Globe* occasionally."

I didn't say anything and I didn't touch the two gaudy-jacketed books when I passed the table. I went straight to the entrance door and let the man in. He wasn't a whole lot taller than Vee Brown but he must have weighed a good fifty pounds more. He looked more like a detective than he did a writer. Everything about him was broad—his hips;

his shoulders; his face; even his nose. His eyes were set very close together. Little watchful eyes, that seemed out of place behind the heavy-rimmed glasses. And he was dressed to the minute. The purple of a handkerchief showed in his jacket pocket when his overcoat fell open.

"I'm Clarence Thompson Ward." He grinned, and it was like the sudden opening of a manhole. "The writer, you know." And when I didn't show any great enthusiasm, "The detective-story writer! Mr. Brown was kind enough to arrange an interview with me through my publishers. I'm afraid I'm early."

"Maybe." I stood aside for him to pass. "But he's expecting you."

"That's great—just great." He sounded as if he were having trouble warming up to his work. "There'll be pictures and things, of course."

"Will there?" And I half followed him, half pushed him into the living room.

HE WALKED toward Vee Brown, paused, saw the books, lifted one and raised his voice in what seemed false elation.

"Men Must Die." He read the title aloud. "One of my best, I think. And you liked it?"

Brown's lips twisted. "I must confess to not reading it. It's just window dressing. Have you read it?"

The man turned his head sharply, put down the book, looked at Vee a long moment and seeing the smile in his eyes said: "That's good! But I'm spared reading them. I've only got to write them."

"Sit down!" Vee nodded to the chair I had been occupying close to the couch. "And you, Dean, pull up one. That's right!" This as the author moved his chair slightly so as to be facing me too. "Now, Mr. Ward, remember your publisher stated that you would give me some startling information in return for this interview."

"So you're going to stick to that bargain!" And when Vee's eyes knitted, "Oh! I'm not hedging. I'm going to tell you who committed one of these peculiar murders; the one the paper quoted you as saying you'd solve. You didn't expect that?"

"Not exactly." Vee's eyes narrowed. "No, I didn't expect that."

"But," the man threw his left leg over his right, "I don't think you'll use the information I give you. Look at this for evidence!" He crossed his left hand leisurely to his inside jacket pocket.

And I gripped both the arms of my chair, half came erect and fell back in the chair again. The amiable author of a few minutes ago was now a snarling—well, a snarling villain out of one of his own stories.

"Back in the chair, Dean Condon!" he said. "You're the fool of this party." But his eyes were on Vee Brown. Vee, who never moved; never even lost the smile on his lips as that huge black automatic swung slowly between the two of us before it settled right on Vee; right on his helpless, relaxed, diminutive body.

"You see," the man smiled, "the reason, Mr. Brown, that you won't use this information is because you won't be alive to use it." His right hand moved slowly, dropped into his overcoat pocket and another gun crept into his hand. One covered Vee; one covered me. "I promised you information. Here it is. I killed the man, Henderson, who was shot in the Bronx."

"Very interesting." Vee Brown never changed his position. The half-smile never left his eyes. He lowered his gaze for a moment only, to the guns in the man's hands; then settled it on the killer's eyes again. Somehow, even in that tense moment I remembered Vee's often repeated words. "It takes only a split second for a man's finger to close upon a trigger. But the eyes! The lust to kill shows there a good second; sometimes much more, but at least a good second before that finger closes."

The man said: "You didn't know that, of course. But you knew or suspected why I did it." And as I moved slightly forward in the chair, "Put your hands high in the air, Condon. That's it! As for you, Brown. Don't change your position; don't move at all."

Brown said, and his voice was very calm; very steady: "Did you come here to talk, or to kill me?"

"I want to know," said the man, "why the man in the Bronx was killed—why I killed him."

Vee's eyes widened. "You want to know! You want me to tell you?"

"That's it." The killer nodded.

"You don't know then?"

The man laughed. It was unpleasant. "I want you to tell me. You've got five seconds."

"And then you intend to kill me—both of us."

"You guessed it." The man's lips parted; teeth showed. "I'm going to kill you—both of you."

VEE'S HEAD turned slowly toward me, but his eyes remained fixed on that sneering face. "He's going to kill us, Dean. You heard him. I wonder what he's being paid for the job."

"A damn sight more than it's worth." The killer laughed, but his hands remained steady; guns trained on both of us. "Just two saps in a sound-proof apartment. It's a natural."

Brown said very quietly: "I can't place your face. You're from out of town. Evidently you don't know much about me. If you should kill me—*if*, understand—you must remember I'm a cop. The New York police may be slow at times; indifferent at times, but they always catch a cop-killer."

"Sure. Sure! That's an old story. But they wouldn't miss you any. The cops don't like you much more than the boys along the Avenue; the wise-money boys. And what a laugh! The great Vee Brown, who shoots guys to death before they can draw a gun. I was warned about you. Now, what? Just lying there on your back, waiting for a dose of lead; waiting for some author to come and interview you. It's the easiest money I ever made."

"Yes." Vee seemed very serious—nothing more. I had seen him face what seemed sure death before. What seemed sure death! But this didn't "seem" it. It *was*. There he lay, his hands clasped over his head and under the pillows. He didn't have a chance. He didn't flinch; I never thought he would. It had to come to him, of course—some time. That it should come like this, without a chance; without—

I saw the thing in the man's eyes; the warning that Brown spoke of; the lust to kill. I saw something else too. The hand that held the gun directed on Brown had moved forward slightly. Then the whitening knuckle, as a finger tightened.

And I did it. We'd die, of course. There seemed little doubt of that. The man had only to close the trigger finger of each hand! But there was a chance. A chance that Vee might be able to jump his right hand from under that pillow to his left arm pit. Awkward, that? Sure! It was a chance in a hundred. Still, it was better than just sitting there and taking the lead; taking the final dose.

Anyway, I did it. I didn't try and reach for a gun; I knew I was no expert at that. But I'm big and strong. I shot forward from that chair. My hands came down—shot out, and I lunged straight for the man's throat.

I saw his gun jerk suddenly up. I heard the shot. Maybe I closed my eyes; maybe I didn't. I do know that I never saw the spurt of orange-blue flame, nor did I feel the pound of a bullet into my body. But I had heard that very often no pain is felt. Indeed, sometimes a wounded man does not know at once that he is shot. I had heard too—Brown had told me—that a heavy bullet at a distance of just a few feet would knock a man off his feet. Well, he was wrong— that was all. Or maybe I wasn't hit. The man had missed! But he couldn't miss. The gun must have been almost touching my chest when the shot came. Then no more thoughts. No more shots! With a cry of triumph my hands fastened on the thick neck of the killer.

"Vee!" I cried. "Vee! Quick! Before he can shoot again."

I stopped. Surprised? More than that. Bewildered, I guess. Brown had not moved from the couch. The man had not fired again. Was it possible that he had shot Brown? That was why I had not seen the flame! That was why— And my eyes popped, my mouth hung open.

My hands loosened upon the man's throat. His body went limp. I was supporting him there; the full weight of his body against my arms as I had jerked him from the chair. I saw his face; his eyes. Wide, glassy eyes that stared into mine; stared into them but did not see them. Then I saw the hole. The round purple hole that was ever widening and turning red—a vivid red.

Vee says I cried out. Maybe I did; I don't know. But I do know that my hands fell from that throat; that it was with a nauseating feeling of horror that my grip loosened. For I knew; knew suddenly that I was holding a dead man in my arms.

CHAPTER TWO
THE MAN ON THE FLOOR

THE BODY slumped to the floor with a dull, sickening thump. A thump that echoed down in the pit of my stomach, bounced into my throat, jarred back into my stomach again.

I turned my head; looked at Vee Brown. He was still lying on the couch. The whimsical smile curved up the corner of his mouth. In his right hand was a forty-five caliber revolver. As I stared at him the smile left his lips. He was turning up one corner of the pillow, looking at the marks of powder on it; the hole burned right through the silk.

"Damn it!" he said irritably. "It isn't the price of the pillow, Dean. I'm not small about that. But Madame Brevort, the opera star, gave me that pillow when I saved her from being murdered by her husband. I can't replace it, and—"

"God! Vee," I stammered, "you—you shot him and he's—he's dead?"

"What a mind. What a mind!" Vee grinned at me. "But you're right, Dean. You're always right. I shot him, and he's dead. He wanted to talk and he did talk. He talked himself to death. But I wanted to listen. I was hoping he'd talk someone else to death." And suddenly, "If you'd only held your hands a few minutes I might have heard more; much more."

"But, Vee, how was I to know you had the gun? You expected him to— You— I thought—"

"You thought I was a sap, just like he did. Yes, I knew— or, at least, I expected it. I could have shot him to death any split second from the moment he entered the room. It's those motiveless murders, Dean. I wasn't sure, myself, but I thought if I gave out a statement that I knew something and there was anything real and big behind them, there might be an attempt to silence me." He jerked suddenly to the edge of the couch, looked down—yes, indifferently down—at the dead killer. Then he was kneeling by the body, unfolding a handkerchief. "Quick, Dean. A towel; one of the big bath towels. The pillow is bad enough, but no cheap hood; living or dead, is going to ruin a thousand-dollar rug."

There you are! If you want a better picture of Vee Brown I can't give it to you. Sometimes—well, he just sickened me.

When I returned to the living room he was on the phone, talking to Gertrude la Palatin.

"Just a little bad luck, Pal—and the impetuous Dean," he was saying. "He kicked over without a word. You're right! The thing is big. You may untie the real author now, revive him with smelling salts and tell him that some day I'll give him a story that will be so gruesome and horrible that he won't be able to stay in the room with himself when he writes it." And after a rather long pause, "I wish you wouldn't Pal. I want you to be out of that life—forever."

I don't know what the girl said, but Vee banged up the receiver and turned to me. "She's stubborn—damn stubborn. She let me believe she was slipping back into the past for color. But, by God, Dean, I think she's pretty close to these murders and the reason for them!"

Then, almost in the same breath, I heard him call Mortimer Doran, the district attorney.

"Vee Brown. My apartment. Just the dead wagon.... Of course it's another body. You don't think I've been playing around with the same corpse!... Yeah, Mr. Doran, I think it would be best to keep it quiet.... Sure. Sure! It's getting so a cop has to make his own corpse."

It was in the music room, while we were waiting, that Brown told me just what was on his mind.

"You're too impulsive, Dean. You spoiled a possible solution to an especially gruesome aspect of the new crime." Then his hand resting on my shoulder, "But I wouldn't have you any other way. Your face, Dean; the expression in your eyes, and the way your mouth hung open when you discovered you were wrestling with a dead man!" And he threw back his head and laughed.

I must confess I saw nothing funny in the whole thing. And the dead man still lay on the floor.

MORTIMER DORAN and Inspector Ramsey preceded the men with the wicker basket. They were both big men, though the district attorney was given to fat while Inspector Ramsey was a giant of strength. Hard, square-jawed, with a slightly sneering mouth, and huge hands that opened and closed into two great chunks of iron bone when he was upset.

He stood looking down at the body for a long time.

"So the criminal doesn't satisfy you any more," he said, half seriously, half ironically, I thought. "You make your own corpse now. You say this man killed the lad Henderson, in the Bronx. That's your story?"

"That's right. I baited the trap with the promise of find-ing the murderer, and this is what stepped into it." Vee spoke more to Mortimer Doran than to Ramsey.

"So you think there's a motive behind these—common murders."

"I know there is." Vee nodded. "And this attempt on my life proves it beyond a doubt. Three men killed, and no motive! Too much of a coincidence."

"There's close to twelve thousand murders a year in the country," Ramsey said. "It would be more than a coinci-dence if we didn't get our share of them here in the city."

"You will!" Vee nodded sort of ominously. "I'm quite certain of that."

"You think," said Mortimer Doran, "that one man was responsible for those three deaths in different sections of the city? But this man"—he looked at the body—"told you he killed the man in the Bronx. He didn't mention the others."

"I think," said Vee, "the man responsible for those three deaths kept far away from the actual scene of the crimes. And I think that if you found the murderers of the other two it is quite likely that neither one of them heard of the other, nor were they even aware of this dead man's exis-tence."

"Humph!" said Mortimer Doran. "Sounds complicated."

"It does," Vee agreed. "It does! Yet, I think it will turn out to be very simple. Something new in the way of crime, and something that might become so far-reaching as to strike terror in the city, never before equaled by our most fiendish criminals."

"Hell!" said Ramsey. "You talk pretty words. Can you stick your finger on something tangible; something—" And to the two men who were lifting the body, "Never mind the basket. There's a clothes hamper out in the hall. He's to go down in the service elevator." He grinned at Brown. "You make your own corpse, but you don't dispose of it."

There was more talk after the body had gone. Then the phone rang. It was for Mortimer Doran.

Doran turned to us. "Brown's psychic," he said. "Come on! There's been a man murdered and his body's lying in the areaway of a house just off Central Park West. A servant returning home stumbled over it."

"Psychic?" Ramsey said, as we all moved toward the door. "I don't know as I'd call it that. I'll admit Brown called the cards, but it seems too much of a coincidence."

"It would have been more of a coincidence if it hadn't happened." Brown's eyes were bright. His lips twisted at the corner. "You see, the man behind the show wanted me dead before this happened."

"But you're not dead," said Ramsey.

"No, no. But he couldn't know that yet." And after a moment's hesitation, "And even if he did know it he'd have to go through with it. This is the big moment of the big racket. The Murder Racket."

THERE WAS a radio car down the block, an ambulance behind it. Several policemen were keeping a crowd back. We all had a look at the body that lay face down at the foot of the stone steps.

The medical examiner said to Mortimer Doran: "He's just as he was. Someone pushed a gun smack against the back of his head and shot him; two or three times, I think, though I can't be sure."

"He wasn't killed here; shot here in the areaway?"

"Hardly," said the doctor. "He's been dead for hours; four or five, maybe more. The body was put here." He lifted the dead man's head, twisted his face into the light from Vee's flash. "No abrasions, no scratches on the skin. He wasn't thrown here, but placed carefully where no one would find him."

"Come, come, Doctor!" Vee said good-naturedly. "You're getting out of your class now. Why wasn't he placed so someone *would* find him; the very returning servant who did?"

"I don't know about that." The doctor placed the dead man's head back on the stones, came to his feet, carefully brushed the knees of his trousers. "I was only hazarding an opinion," he finished rather stiffly.

Mortimer Doran brushed the doctor roughly aside, knelt quickly by the body. "Let me have that light again, Vee," he said; lifted the head; looked at the face. "By God, I thought so! It's Frank Morris, the Wall Street broker."

"So—" said Vee. "The department is going to have trouble laughing this murder off; lots of trouble."

"And you're not going to make that trouble any easier." Ramsey spoke far back in his throat. "If you know who killed this man—"

"How would he know that?" Mortimer Doran shot in irritably. "You and Brown, Ramsey, are worse than a couple of boys. Of course Vee doesn't know!"

"No," said Vee Brown, "I don't know who killed him, but I know why."

"Why?" Ramsey and Doran barked the words together.

"For two reasons," Vee said slowly. "Because he wouldn't pay, and because his death would frighten another or maybe others into paying."

In this statement Vee Brown was half wrong and half right.

DORAN AND Ramsey went into the house to question the servant who found the body and the two old ladies who occupied the house. Vee Brown hesitated on the steps when Ramsey invited him in. His eyes were fastened on the ever increasing crowd on the sidewalk. Vee was watching a man in a derby hat, who had his coat collar turned up; dividing his attention now between that man and the house across the street almost opposite the areaway where the dead broker was found.

"No, no. You and Mr. Doran can tell me what you find out, Ramsey. I'll play along the block; see if I can discover anything."

"There will be half a dozen *good* detectives doing that." Ramsey looked at Brown. "But then, you don't have to take orders from me."

"No," Brown said, "I don't have to take orders from you." And he waited there on the steps until Mortimer Doran and Ramsey had disappeared inside and the uniformed policeman had closed the door behind them.

The man with the derby hat crossed the street and went up the steps of the house opposite. Brown took me by the arm, jerked his head toward the disappearing derby.

"Watch the window there in the front. Is that a face by the side of the shade? It—" Fingers pinched my arm. "But of course it is." This as the shade flopped back and the white blotch that might have been a face disappeared.

BROWN CIRCULATED among the people gathered there on the sidewalk; people who moved a few steps this way or a few steps that, as the police ordered them away.

He was questioning them. Once or twice I saw a man shake his head as he looked at the house across the street.

Then the man in the derby came out of the house again and crossed the street. I followed Vee and was right at his elbow when he approached the man.

"Well," he said affably enough, "who are you and what do you want?"

The man looked down at Vee. "I live across the street. I'm Mr. George Rensiller's man. I'd like to know just what happened. No one seems to know."

"No?" said Vee. "I thought everyone knew. A man's been murdered. His body's in the areaway. You saw it."

"Yes. That is, I looked over the stone balustrade."

"You want to know who the man is?"

"No. No, I don't." The man started back.

"But you asked a dozen people if they knew him. Yet you don't want to know who he is?"

"No. That is—yes. Well, I wondered who he was." And straightening slightly, "I don't think I'm responsible to you for—" And as Brown laid a hand upon his arm, "You're a police officer?"

"That's right." Brown glared up at the man. "I'm a police officer. Now—Mr. Rensiller sent you out twice, particularly to find out who the murdered man was."

"No, sir. He didn't, sir. He particularly—he— I saw the people and I—"

Vee Brown took his arm and jerked his head toward me. "Very suspicious actions, Dean," he said. "We'll pay a visit to Mr. Rensiller—now."

On the stone steps of the Rensiller house the man stopped. "I'm afraid, sir, you're getting me into trouble."

And when Brown just waited, "Mr. Rensiller will not approve of my—my attracting attention."

"That," said Brown, "will be just too bad." And he shoved the man up the steps.

George V. Rensiller met us in the front hall. I didn't know the man, but later I discovered that he was vice-president of a well known bond-and-mortgage company. You'd know to look at him that he was some sort of a banker! He had the eyes for it. Stony; slightly moist, but certainly capable of a direct stare. He pulled his dark bath-robe tightly about him as he descended the final step of the stairs and looked straight at Brown.

"You're a police officer," he said abruptly, lifted his right hand and laid it carefully—almost as if it didn't belong to him, on the newel post.

"That's right." Vee nodded. "A man was murdered and his body thrown in the areaway across the street. Your servant, here, is questioning people about the man's identity."

"Am I to understand that you have arrested him for that—that natural interest?"

"We are not arresting him. His interest, perhaps, was natural, but his method of gathering information was, to say the least, furtive. Did you send him out a second time to try and find out who the dead man was?"

"I did!" said Mr. Rensiller, without hesitation.

"And did you tell him particularly not to question police officers?"

"I did!"

"Why?"

"My name is not unknown in the community. Publicity of such an unpleasant nature would hardly be desired. I didn't wish to have my name appear in the papers."

"You sent your servant out to make inquiries—persistent inquiries."

"A natural curiosity; a natural interest in the welfare of my neighbors."

"It seems to me," said Vee Brown, "that it would be most natural to seek such information from the police. Certainly you would be questioned, living directly across the street. Mr. Rensiller, you thought you knew who the murdered man was; you were afraid you knew, and you didn't wish that knowledge brought to the attention of the law. Is that correct?"

"Certainly not." The man straightened, adjusted the glasses on his nose, let his fingers toy with the broad black ribbon. "And might I ask just to whom I am indebted for this catechizing?"

"Detective Vee Brown, of the district attorney's office. And I'm not here to catechize you; rather, to relieve your mind. It was not one of your neighbors who was killed."

"No!" There was no relief in Rensiller's face. Sallow skin whitened.

"No!" said Vee Brown. "I believe the man lives on the other side of town." And quite suddenly, "It was Frank Morris, the broker."

CHAPTER THREE
THE GIRL WITH
THE GREEN EYES

THE WHITE face turned a pasty yellow. The hand upon the post opened, gripped at polished wood, nails slipping over the smooth surface. Was he surprised? That was my first impression. Then another one. He wasn't surprised. He was shocked. Prepared, perhaps, to hear the name of the murdered man, but shocked—terribly shocked when he did hear it.

"You knew him?" Vee Brown asked.

"Yes," said Rensiller, "I knew him."

"Good!" Brown nodded vigorously. "I want to talk to you alone."

For a full minute Rensiller stood there still gripping at the banister. Then he turned to his servant, half waved his hand, and without a word led us to the library on the left. A button clicked; the room was flooded with light. Rensiller turned, dropped into a chair, finally said: "Well, what is it?"

Brown went over and stood before him. "Won't you tell us what it is, Mr. Rensiller? You knew Frank Morris was to die; at least, you feared it. And his body was placed across the street for your benefit; not right in your areaway, for that might attract the attention of the police to you, and the people who were threatening you did not want that. They wanted you to know your own danger. That was it, wasn't it?"

"I don't know. I don't know anything about it."

"Mr. Rensiller, you're not only endangering your own life by your silence now; you're endangering the lives of others—maybe many others. And you are encouraging crime, if not actually aiding and abetting the criminal. You tell me you don't know anything. You knew that Frank Morris was going to die. You did, didn't you?"

"No—except that I knew he was threatened by something."

"How did you know that!"

"He told me."

"When?"

"Yesterday."

"Where?" Brown was firing the questions at him.

"At lunch. I had lunch with him. At the Spur."

"That's a lie," Brown cut in. "Morris was in Philadelphia yesterday." And when Rensiller looked up, and so did I, "That fact has already been established through a telephone call to his secretary." Brown lied with easy assurance.

"Maybe it wasn't yesterday, then."

"No," sneered Brown, "it wasn't. Nor any other day. And he didn't tell you he was threatened. And before his death there was Warren and Drake—and Henderson, in the Bronx. All dead; all murdered, and you never raised a hand to prevent their deaths."

"I—I—" Rensiller was on his feet. "Those names mean nothing to me; I never heard of them—Henderson nor Drake nor Warren." He got the names off quickly.

Brown grinned. "Those names are stamped upon your mind." He leaned forward, grasped Rensiller by the shoulder. "Come on! It's murder, Mr. Rensiller. Plain, outright murder—and you may be the next. The police will protect you."

Rensiller rubbed at his mouth; his glasses slipped from his nose; he fumbled with them awkwardly but did not put them on.

Brown went on: "Why won't you talk? What have you done? What's connected with your business? What crooked deal is it that—"

"Crooked? Crooked! How dare you talk to me that way about my business?"

"Well"—Brown stood back; his arms came far apart—"I hate to think it's just the yellow in you. You stood by and let Morris be murdered. You might have saved him. You—"

"The police didn't protect him; they didn't do anything for him. He's over there now, and he's dead. He went straight to the police and—"Rensiller's head went into his hands as he half sat, half collapsed in the chair. "I'm—I can't—I can't."

BROWN NODDED at me and grinned. Rensiller knew something, that seemed certain. It also seemed certain that he was about to talk; about to—

The front door opened and closed. Inspector Ramsey barged in. He looked at Rensiller; glared at Brown, standing over him. "What the hell is all this?"

"Inspector Ramsey"—Rensiller came to his feet again—"this detective has been threatening me; accusing me of— He thinks— My God! He's accusing me of letting people be murdered, because I knew Frank Morris."

"Everybody knew Frank Morris." Ramsey looked at Vee Brown. "That is, everybody in the financial world. And I know Mr. Rensiller." And more quietly, to Brown, "You're making trouble for yourself, and so for the department."

Vee Brown shrugged his shoulders. "Dean and I were just making the rounds, questioning people." He moved toward the door and I followed. There would be nothing forthcoming from Rensiller now. The color had come back in his face, his lips were set tightly, his chin determined. As we reached the front door I heard Ramsey saying to Rensiller: "Now, Mr. Rensiller, tell me just what you heard or saw tonight, and when you last saw Frank Morris."

Brown called back over his shoulder: "You might ask him, Ramsey, how he knew that Frank Morris was to die; and knowing it, why it was such a shock to him."

The door swung closed and Brown and I were on the sidewalk again. An ambulance was pulling from the curb across the street.

A uniformed policeman said to Vee: "Mr. Doran's across the street in the house. There's a half dozen people who say they saw a suspicious-looking car but no two of them agree on the make, and if they do they get the color or design different."

But Brown ignored the house and Mortimer Doran. Turning, we went down the street, walked across town, found a cruising taxi and sped to our apartment.

I said: "For God's sake, Vee, if you know—tell me what it's all about."

"But I don't know. All I do know is that an epidemic of murders is about to break out. And I know the motive; the only motive there could be—greed. But who is behind it or how it is worked I can't find out. Every stool-pigeon I can lay a hand on is working for me. And now—Gertrude la Palatin is back in the underworld. Of course, if they discover her identity she'll die."

"And you don't know why the murders are being committed."

"The reason is sure to come out in time. Some day a man with guts is going to walk straight to the police and blow the lid off the whole show."

"I don't understand."

"Of course you don't. I hoped that Rensiller would be that man, but he hasn't got the stomach for it." And as we entered our apartment, "We have a visitor!"

IT WAS Gertrude la Palatin. Brown had given her a key some time back, when he was working on the cat-man case, and she came and went as she pleased. But now she was not the charming actress, nor was her hair the short brilliant red the theatre goers were used to seeing when she finished her final impersonation and became herself. Now she was dark, with scarlet lips and heavily treated eyebrows and long lashes that hung over those bright green eyes.

"You're a wizard." Vee Brown put both his hands upon her shoulders as she came toward him. It might have been a friendly gesture, but to me it seemed as if she would have been in his arms and that his hands upon her shoulders held her off. He went on talking.

"You shouldn't do this, Pal. You've paid everything you owe society. You—"

"Nonsense!" She walked across the room. "I like it. That's the truth! You won't let me come and see you as Gertrude la Palatin; you say a show of friendship may endanger me." She put those green eyes on him; great brilliant depths. "Do you know, Vee, I think you're afraid of me—afraid of a woman."

Vee laughed, but said nothing. His laugh was hollow. His black eyes watched her light a cigarette; drop into an easy chair.

"Murder!" she said suddenly. "You're right, but you're only partly right. It's worse than you think. I tell you, Vee, there's a murder syndicate operating in the city. Repeal threw plenty of gunmen out of work. Now—anyone known as a killer can get a job." Her eyes narrowed, her chin went into her hands as elbows rested on her knees. "I don't understand it, Vee, but it's big. Yet there doesn't seem to be any organization. A killer simply registers his name with a certain party. Later comes the name of a man, his habits, his residence of course, and the time and place of the kill. Then the pay-off. I tell you, these actual murderers haven't any idea why they make the kill. It's just a question of money with them."

Vee looked at me. "That explains our dead man's question earlier this evening. He asked me why he killed the man in the Bronx. He thought I knew from my statement that I'd get the murderer." And Vee explained the shooting to Gertrude la Palatin.

She nodded her understanding, smiled slightly; said: "I came up the fire escape, saw the real author, Clarence Thompson Ward, strapped up in his apartment, and telephoned you. Then I waited in the store down the block until you called back, and I notified the superintendent of his apartment. I guess they cut him loose."

"We were right about that 'plant,'" Vee agreed. "But you were wrong about George V. Rensiller."

"Another man has been murdered then!" she gasped. And when Brown would have cut in, "There! don't tell me his name. Morrison or—"

"Morris." Brown grew very serious. "You're close to things, Pal—too close. Frank Morris's body was found across the street from Rensiller's house." And Vee grinned at me. "So you see, Dean, it wasn't just the keen brain of a detective that made me question Rensiller."

"I think," said the girl, "George V. Rensiller is next."

Vee Brown shook his head. "No!" he said. "They've frightened him. He's going to pay. The Morris kill decided him."

"Pay what?" The girl frowned.

"I don't know what. It's only a guess. I'm still a lot in the dark. Tomorrow I'll visit his bank and see if he drew any large sum of money. It must be money, Pal. Now—how do you get all your information?"

"Ida Trent," the girl said quickly. "She dances down in the Royal Blades. Swell name but a bad dive. I get odd jobs there, and—"

"My God!" Brown broke in. "Suppose someone should recognize the great la Palatin? It was a mistake; a big mistake for us to be seen together so often."

Her voice was very soft as she said: "We had such good times together after the death of the cat man, Vee. I—" She stiffened suddenly. "Let us get down to business. Ida Trent is used to passing notes along"—she leaned forward eagerly—"and I think those notes contain the name of the man to be murdered. I know who gives her the notes. It's Sam Clausen."

"So Clausen and I are to meet again." Brown scowled. "And I want you out of this thing, Pal." He shook her by the shoulders. "I want you out of it now. He's the worst man in the city. He kidnaped the Rierdon child and killed her brutally. He tortured that old couple on the East Side, whom he suspected of having money hidden away."

"You know this; yet he still—"

I got no further. Vee cut in.

"Knowledge, yes. Evidence, no. I know of no man I'd rather see dead than this Sam Clausen. But, Pal, if he suspected you he'd— You've got to get out of this!"

"I'm in it," the girl said defiantly. "If you won't let me work it out with you I'll go it alone. But I'll see it to the end. Want to hear the rest of my story and see how much I've accomplished? It wasn't hard for me to work back into the night. This Ida Trent! She likes to drink and likes to talk, and she was Sam Clausen's girl friend. He dropped her but he still uses her. She *knew* the day before Henderson died in the Bronx. She gave me a bum steer on Rensiller, though it may be true yet. But only tonight she told me that Morris was to die. You know the stuff! A little drink, a little knowing smirk and a sloppy statement. "I can call their numbers before they die."

"Yes, yes." Vee was eager now. For the moment he seemed to forget the girl's danger. "Is there anything else? She resents getting the air from Clausen?"

"And how!" Gertrude la Palatin nodded. "It's like old times, Vee; you and I plotting and planning again. Listen! I can't go any further with her. She's beginning to fear Clausen. I think, if you saw her; promised to get her out of the city; offered her a few thousand—well, she'd talk. But you've got to work that alone, and at once."

"Yes." Vee nodded. "Alone and tonight, eh? I've been to the Royal Blades; there will be nothing suspicious in my showing up there. Does Clausen come there often?"

"Not often, and just for a few minutes when he does come. As a rule they don't even speak. It's a good line! Cops and crooks know that he dropped the girl. They'd never suspect her as the 'go-between.'"

"We'll see her now. Come, Dean. We'll visit the Royal Blades." He took both of Gertrude la Palatin's hands in his.

"Everything is in the music room," he told her. "Clothes; your make-up box—everything. I think it's safer, much safer for you to leave here as yourself."

"Physically safer—maybe." She smiled. "But how about my reputation as an actress, and yours as a detective?"

She stood there, her hands on her hips, her feet far apart, her green eyes brilliant. When Vee Brown turned his back, at the door, she deliberately winked at me. I looked at Brown and winked back. What did I mean? I don't know. But I did know that the woman; the girl, was madly in love with Vee. And he— But we passed out the door and it closed behind us.

CHAPTER FOUR
A THREAT TO KILL

THE ROYAL BLADES had taken down its steel-latticed door and obtained a license as a restaurant; and that was its only concession to Repeal. The liquor was just as bad or just as good, according to your standing and your pocketbook and your desirability as a future patron. But the higher-class clientele, who had considered it quite the thing to visit a night club of such bad repute, had now moved up town and stormed the doors of the better hotels. They were cleaner; they were safer—and getting drunk had gone somewhat out of fashion.

Still, there was a fair crowd in the booths along the wall and at the tables around the dance floor. Fair—that is, in numbers. Prominent names along Broadway and in theatrical circles were missing.

The owner-manager spotted us almost the minute we slid into the booth. He was a sharp, ferret-faced, jerky man.

He spoke quickly, pulled at his neck and made queer sounds in his throat between sentences.

"Mr. Brown." He leaned on the table and lowered his voice. "Here on business?"

"I hope not." Vee smiled. "You've left me alone and I've left you alone. I've never made a pinch here."

"That's right. That's right!" White teeth showed. "Who are you interested in?"

Brown said: "Ida Trent. I want to talk to her."

"Nothing—nothing about the establishment; about me?"

Brown looked at him steadily. "Not unless you've changed and are going in for murder, Joe."

Joe made the queer sounds in his throat, tugged at his neck. His mouth opened and what came out of it might have been a laugh.

"Just your joke. Just your joke." Again the attempted laugh. "Surely, the girl is not—"

"Don't talk, Joe. Trot her over—now!" And as the manager turned from the table, "And keep your mouth shut! That's for your benefit, not mine."

Joe jerked his long thin body across the room, leaned over a table and spoke to a girl. I saw her look up, half push him away, then turn and look directly at us. It was not a pleasant face; not even a beautiful face, though it might have been. Hard living, hard drinking, hard thinking had cut lines in it. She stood up, took a step forward, turned back, and lifting the glass from the table drained its contents and set it down on the table again. Then she walked over to us. There was nothing uncertain about her step. She was dead sober.

"The Little Wonder, eh?" Ida Trent parted her lips at Brown; looked at me. "Move over, big boy." And when she squeezed down beside me, "Well, what's the racket? You've got nothing on me, I hope."

Brown leaned across the table, looking out into the room, lifted a napkin and wrapping something in it shoved it into her hand.

The girl showed no surprise. Furtive, blood-shot eyes looked for a moment out into the room, then her glance flashed into her lap. Fingers moved quickly; her hand came up, ducked down her bosom. "A grand," she said slowly. "That's a lot of jack. You must like me."

Brown grinned. "I hope," he said, "I'm going to like your mouth; at least, what comes out of it."

She laughed. "You should have heard the words first and paid later. You'd have hard working getting the money back." She jerked her head at me. "A witness won't help much."

Brown shrugged his shoulders. "There'll be no trouble in getting the money back if I want it. The matron at the precinct would find it the minute she searched you."

"A pinch unless I talk. That how it is?"

"That," said Vee, "is just how it is."

A MOMENT of silence; a long moment. The black eyes of Brown met the brown ones of the girl. He spoke first.

"It's like this, Ida. You call peoples' names before they take the rap; you pass notes that you shouldn't, but do. I can pull you in, get you to talk, maybe even pin a murder rap on you. Or—"

"Or—"

"Or I can listen to you talk and add four more grand to that thousand, see you safely on a nice long trip, and"—Vee leaned forward—"fry the man who threw you over."

The girl just looked at Vee, and so did I. Not that I was surprised at his offer of five thousand dollars for such information. Five thousand dollars! More than his entire year's salary as a first-grade detective. But I knew that he spent much more than that each year for information. Money from the enormous income on his song hits.

The girl said: "I like you, Brown. You make yourself so much more interesting than other men; so much clearer."

"You want time to think it over? Better not delay."

"No, I don't want time. I've been thinking it over. I worked a mind-reading act in vaudeville some years back and I learned how to open folded slips of paper and read what was on them. There'll be no delay. I've been wondering how to make money out of my knowledge and still live. And I like the idea of giving Sam Clausen the hot squat. It appeals to me."

"Have you— Do you know enough for that?"

"Yes." She knitted her eyes. "But I can earn the single grand right now. George V. Rensiller is to die tomorrow. Don't ask me why. I don't know that. But Sam Clausen puts the finger on him; I pass the name along to Rossimire, the jeweler, and he hands it to the killer." She threw her head up a bit proudly. "I spotted the name on the first kill. Clausen chucked me over; yet he needed me." And as the waiter approached the table, "A double rye, Charlie; and I'm drinking for pleasure, not for saps." And when the waiter had gone, "The dames that work here are supposed to destroy their stomach with ginger ale, colored to look like whisky. They don't play that game on me!"

"Exactly what is on these notes?" Brown asked.

"Well"—the girl sucked in her lower lip—"generally just the name of the guy who gets the dose and the price for the job. If Rossimire figures out the details or if he's tipped off to the actual killer in some other way, I don't know. But the name always turns up in the papers, dead—sometimes the next day, sometimes two or three days later, but never more than a week."

"And the price?" Brown asked.

"That changes. The price goes according to the newspaper notoriety. A lad in Brooklyn took it for one hundred and fifty berries. The next man who gets the dose—Morris, by name, will pay five thousand; right on the head. Things are looking up." She leaned forward, put those hard eyes on Vee. "You should get your money back in saving his life. I looked him up; he's got dough. I was thinking of doing it myself."

BROWN REGARDED her for a long moment. "So you don't know. Morris was murdered tonight and chucked in an areaway across the street from Rensiller's, and—"

"Cripes!" She straightened suddenly, her eyes wide, her mouth hanging open. "That was a fast one. I—"

"You," said Brown, "may be in personal danger. I'm paying you well to tell me things." He jerked a thumb at the empty whisky glass. "That stuff might make you talk—to the wrong people. You have talked, you know."

The girl laughed. "You mean Gertrude la Palatin."

Brown jerked erect in his seat. So did I.

"What of her?" he snapped.

"Hell!" said the girl. "I don't talk unless I want to. And don't worry. No one else recognized her. I always admired her; always thought I might some day become as famous as she. She came here, calling herself Myra. No, I didn't recognize her. But somehow I wanted her for a friend." Her shoulders hunched slightly. "A wise dame don't make friends in the racket without knowing about them. I tailed her; was stumped for a bit, then finally guessed it. Anyway, Gertrude la Palatin is your friend; you have a reputation for paying good money for information. I had information to sell. I simply pretended to slop over. Sam Clausen can't step on my face and throw me out for a blond tart! He'll get wise to himself some day and knock me over unless—"

"Unless—" Brown encouraged.

"If they burnt him to death, or you shot him, he couldn't hurt me."

"That's right," said Vee. "He couldn't bother you then. So you pretended to drink and talk just to get me here! Now—can you talk—talk five thousand dollars' worth? I've wanted to get Clausen for a long time."

"I can talk him smack into the electric chair."

Brown's black eyes flashed. "Let me have it—now."

"At my apartment later." And when Vee started to shake his head, "I only mean an hour. I'll jump this dump early tonight."

"You've got to jump it now, and for good. You're not dumb, Ida. Someone will tell Clausen I was here. You talk now! I'll give you the money and see that you are taken care of—protected. I'll—"

Her hard face suddenly whitened. A hand shot across the table and rested on Vee's wrist, then was back toying with her empty whisky glass. She spoke without opening her mouth.

"Sam—Sam Clausen!" she said. "He just came in. What brought him here tonight?" There was fear in her face, terror in her eyes; in the broad mouth that suddenly drooped at the ends. "If he thinks I talked you'll never get out of here alive."

"Nonsense!" Brown smiled over at her. "He won't know you talked, and we won't give him a chance to find out." And as I looked out into the room and saw the broad back of the big man who was greeting friends at a table, the back turned, the man straightened, and two hundred pounds of brutal murderer faced us.

For a full minute he stood there looking at our booth. He had the meanest, crudest face I ever saw. Thick lips, a broad sensuous mouth, and little eyes that were far too small not only for his huge head but for the other large features of his face. His nose was big, yet sharp at the end, and those round eyes were set very close to it. They were birdlike in their intensity, made even brighter and smaller by the large nose and two huge ears that stuck out on either side of his head. Then he smiled. At least, his mouth opened and white teeth showed. He moved slowly toward our table, a threat in every step he took. Explain that threat! I can't. But it was there. I felt it. The most dangerous, the crudest, the most brutal murderer in the city today! And he was free to walk the streets, unmolested.

Vee Brown spoke quickly to the girl. "For your own good, Ida, let me do the talking. To protect you I'll have to make it a pinch. Don't worry."

AND SAM CLAUSEN reached our booth. He didn't speak. He just leaned on the table, looked once at Brown, stared long at the girl, then let his eyes rest on my face. Maybe I drew back. If I did, it wasn't fear. Just revulsion. Oh, his face was cruel, ugly enough. But there was something back of it that was worse; as if he wore a mask to hide the real face behind it; the evil rottenness that lurked some place back behind his eyes.

Sam Clausen looked straight at Ida Trent. "Ida," he said very slowly, "you're keeping damn lousy company." He paused a long moment, jerked his finger back over his shoulder. "Get out—now!"

The girl stiffened, both hands on the table; flattened there. Slowly she started to come to her feet.

"You two can't work that racket." Vee leaned across the table, caught the girl by the arm, thrust her back in the seat. "I guess you don't quite get the point, Clausen. It's a pinch."

It was Clausen's turn to straighten; look down at Vee, those vulture-like eyes steady, penetrating, threatening.

Vee Brown laughed. "Sam," he said, "you should take that face of yours down to Coney Island, rent it out to the Chamber of Horrors and use it to frighten women and children."

Clausen opened his mouth but didn't speak. Then he turned and looked about the room. At length he turned back to Brown and said: "Ida's got a lot of friends here. They mightn't like it. You mightn't get out of here alive."

Vee grinned. "That's right. There might be someone here who'd take a chance on a shoot-up. But you see, it's going to be quiet and easy. No one will tell the boys it's a pinch. Dean, go with Miss Trent to her dressing room. Let her get her things, then wait for me by the entrance door."

And as I started to half help, half lead Ida Trent from the booth, Clausen said: "You'll never get her out of here alive. There's lads at the table I just left who wouldn't like it."

"Who's to tell them?" Brown laughed easily.

"I'm to tell them." There was more than just a threat now. There was a half triumph in Clausen's voice. "I know what you want the girl for. Do you think I'd let her go out of here, no matter what had to be pulled off? She's going to lie to you; try to put the finger on me. The double-crossing little rat!"

"If you suspected that"—Vee put his hand to his mouth, smothering a pretended yawn—"you waited a long time."

"By God!" said Clausen, "I didn't think you'd be here so soon. I didn't think you'd come at—at—"

Vee nodded. "You didn't think I'd come at all. You thought that cheap gun who posed as an author would wipe me out. Well, he's dead. Get going with the girl, Dean."

"Wait! You don't think I'd be willing to let the fireworks start!" Clausen swung sideways. "What makes you think I won't tell the boys?"

Brown's head turned very slowly. He looked directly at Sam Clausen.

"Because, Sam"—his words were very low but very distinct—"dead men don't talk. I believe the spot is bad enough for you to try and blast me out." And sharply, "Don't move, Sam. Sit down there or by God, I'll shoot you to death before you can take a step."

"You couldn't—you wouldn't do that," I heard Sam say, and just before we passed toward the door I heard Brown answer—answer as I saw those black eyes of his brighten to the danger point.

"Sam, you know I would. Just a pleasure long deferred."

Did Sam believe him? And Sam did. For he swung his huge body sideways and dropped into the booth; onto the seat opposite Vee Brown.

CHAPTER FIVE
RUN-OUT POWDER

A**S WE** left the dining room and went down the narrow hall to Ida Trent's dressing room, I thought—after all, that was Vee Brown's great strength in the underworld. He met gunfire with gunfire, violence with violence, death with death. Every criminal in the underworld knew that, and the Lord knows Brown had disposed of enough public enemies to make it stick in their minds. He didn't threaten just to hear himself talk. Yes, I felt; decidedly felt that Sam Clausen was right to sit down; that is, if he ever wanted to get on his feet again.

Ida Trent, for all her hard appearance and her attitude of a few minutes before, was trembling like a man after a three days' drunk. The hand with which she tried to push her key in the lock of her dressing-room door refused to find the slot. I had to open the door for her.

She hurried straight to a cabinet, jerked out a glass and a bottle, slopped whisky over the table; down her flimsy dress as she drank. Then she turned to me as I opened the window that gave on a dark court.

"I don't need air—not air!" Her laugh was harsh; went through me like scraping fingers along a wall. "So Clausen suspected, then. Brown came here just in time. Sam was going to kill me tonight." She turned and came toward me; clutched me by both shoulders. "Do you know how he'd do it? With a knife. He'd hack me to pieces inch by inch, then rub the blade across my throat. I tell you he did it with a child; a little girl. He—"

"You know about these murders, Ida?"

"No, no. That isn't what I'd tell Brown. It's the murder of that child. They could never stick it on Clausen; never will unless I talk." She held up her right hand, tried snapping the thumb and second finger together without much success. "I've got Clausen just like that and he knows it, and he'll kill me."

"Not him," I told her with emphasis. "Vee will protect you now."

She did herself another drink; none of it spilled this time. She stood with the empty glass in her hand, looking at me.

"He's going to pinch me—that's it?"

"Just to protect you; so you'll be safe."

She laughed sort of wildly. "Protect me? In jail! Listen! Vee Brown's different from other cops. He goes after what he wants; goes after the big shots; kicks the little fry aside or pays them for information, then forgets what they did when he grabs off the big fish." She licked at her lips, looked at the bottle, half extended a hand but didn't touch it. "I can't get drunk now." She shook her head. "And I can't stand going to the jug. Clausen would spring me and kill me. What I've got on him he's got on me; that's what made him feel safe all along. Don't you see? All I wanted to do was to talk to Brown, collect the jack and blow. Now— Hell! my record couldn't stand being mugged and finger-printed and—"

"Don't you worry," I cut in. "Brown's talk of a pinch might be only to throw Clausen off."

"Might be!" She stood looking at me; walked closer to me. "You're not as big as Clausen," she said, "but damn near. And you've got looks, feller. Me, too!" She nodded but watched my face. "I'm not all shot yet—not me. I just need a change. I'm young. Fear; hate; jealousy—they're all getting me." She was very close to me now. "You and me, kid! Let's skip out. Take me some place; any place. We'll telephone Brown in the morning and I'll spill over to him." She leaned against me, put her hands up to my face. "I'm afraid to be alone tonight. I'll be good company, and—"

I pushed her hands away; held them a moment. "Don't be silly, Ida. You'll be perfectly safe, and—"

"We could—" She started; stopped. "Wait outside. I'll dress."

I STEPPED out into the hall; stood close to the door which I didn't entirely close. From the dining room came music, perhaps the scraping of dancing feet. Not a soul there in the narrow dimly lit hall. At the end of it waiters passed, their white shirts flashing for an instant. As for me! I moved my gun from hip to jacket pocket; kept my hand upon it.

At last Vee was in the case he wanted. He had talked about Clausen for months. It seemed as if it were his one ambition in life; or perhaps in death. To get Clausen! Well, he was in a fair way to get Clausen now; or maybe Clausen was in a fair way to get Vee Brown. For there; was Vee, the diminutive detective, out in that dining room surrounded by a dozen enemies; desperate men, murderers and—

I gripped my gun the tighter. The girl was ready. The door opened; she beckoned me inside. She was dressed for the street now. I took my hand from my pocket.

"Listen, Dean Condon!" She closed the door with her foot and turned the key. "There's a window and an alley, and a street behind. Come on! We'll do a quick 'out.' I'd go mad in the cooler tonight. I don't want to be alone, and—"

"No, Ida." I started all over again. "Probably Vee has no intention of—"

"Come on! Will you or will you not duck with me? Yes or no!"

"No!" I said. "And you—"

I jarred back on my heels. I think the gun came out of her bag but I'm not sure. I am sure, though, that it pounded against my chest.

"Here's the lay." She threw the words in my face almost as hard as she had the gun against my chest. "I'm beating it. Tell Brown to stay in his apartment tomorrow until I call. I'll take no chances, but I'll telephone him." And when I would have remonstrated with her, "Baloney, big boy! Why, I don't even know now if Brown is going to walk out of that dining room or be carried out feet first."

"You wouldn't throw Vee over after taking his money!"

"No?" She laughed. "Say—I earned that single grand by just sitting with him. All right! Call me a rat; yellow; anything you want. And the reason? Well, I'm a peculiar woman. I don't like having my throat cut from ear to ear." And as I swayed forward, "Don't be a fool. Bullets from the gun of a woman hurt just as much as from the gun of a man. Goodby!" She backed toward the window, pushed it higher with a quick deft movement of her left hand. "Yep. Ida Trent, taking her first run-out powder!"

There was nothing unsteady about her hand now; at least, the one that held the gun while she slid over the window sill. And her mouth didn't droop.

I heard her feet thump dully on the stones below. Then, as I dashed toward the window, her face was there; her gun, too.

"Boy"—white teeth gleamed up at me—"your insurance company would call it suicide. Be sensible!" And when I was, "Listen! If anything should go wrong, Sam Clausen has a secret hangout." And she gave me the address of a small abandoned gas station and garage in the Bronx. "It's deserted. Clausen's got an office and telephone there, and meets lads who are particular about what company they are seen in. And the best part of it all is—that's one thing Sam don't think I know and would never suspect that I'd tell you. He'll be there tomorrow night from eleven to twelve."

And she was gone. A shadow in the night, then not even a shadow. As for me! I just stood there in that room with my gun in my hand. Why the gun now? I don't know. I'm just saying what I did. And Brown was outside, chancing death; yes, even inviting death with a dozen or more desperate men. And he was doing it just so that he could listen to the girl; the girl who had disappeared in the blackness of the night.

There was nothing to do now but find Brown and tell him the truth.

VEE WASN'T hard to find. He was down the hall, past the turn and beyond the door leading to the dining room. He was leaning easily against the small cigar counter, evidently laughing and talking with Clausen. At least, Brown was laughing and talking. Clausen was standing there, sour-faced, glaring along the hall. And Brown! Both his hands were clearly visible and both of them were empty.

Clausen's little eyes widened and Brown's eyebrows went up when I came along—alone.

"The girl!" Brown said quickly. "Where is she?"

"Well"—I looked at Clausen—"I'll explain that later."

Brown said quickly: "You'll never explain it. She walked out on you. And for God's sake, Dean, don't tell me that her dressing room was on the ground floor and in your modesty you waited outside, and she dropped from the window."

"Well, not exactly. But she did drop from the window." I may have stammered a bit; I'm not sure.

Clausen was smiling. At least, his mouth was open. "So that's settled in a friendly way," he said to Brown. "I ordered a broiled lobster. Oh! nothing personal, Mr. Detective Vee Brown; but I'm sure your threat to kill is no longer necessary."

"The threat to kill, Clausen," Vee said slowly, "is a promise of death. I don't know if Ida Trent would have talked. But I believe, if she did—" He paused, spread his empty hands far apart. "Well, if anything should happen to her now— Good-by, Mr. Sam Clausen."

Vee turned quickly, took me by the arm and we swung through the door and out onto the street.

"Vee," I said, "there was nothing I could do."

"I know. I know!" He nodded. "She was afraid of too much police, got her nerve back out of a bottle, stuck a gun in your chest and hopped the window."

"How—" I started and stopped.

"Nothing psychic." He grinned but it was unpleasant. "I thought of it after you left. She said she knew enough to roast Clausen, yet she lived. So Clausen must know enough to roast her, to let her live. She was afraid of the old jail."

"But I told her you wouldn't lock her up; that—"

You shouldn't have told her that for I would have. It was the only way to save her life. It was in her blood—the fear and distrust of the law. She was willing to chance me on the outside, but she was afraid of the jug. Too many things in her past life to pop up. We'll have to wait for her to telephone."

"You think she will?"

"Certainly. Greed! She'll want the money. She'll want Clausen dead. Not just vengeance now; but fear that, alive, he'll kill her."

"Clausen was bluffing about starting shooting then. You stood with him, not even covering him through your pockets."

Vee grinned. "If the girl talked, nothing would save Clausen. He knew that. He would have liked to start fireworks. It was in his mind. And that, Dean, was why I stood there with empty hands."

"I don't get it!"

"No?" The corner of his mouth twisted. "I was thinking of the Rierdon girl, so brutally murdered, so uselessly tortured. And I was hoping that Clausen would draw a gun." And when I just looked at him, "It's true, Dean. I would very much like to kill the man, and I think it's in the cards."

CHAPTER SIX
MURDER SYNDICATE

THE NEXT day we were out early. Wong had orders to sit by the phone and if Ida Trent rang up to tell her to call Vee again at exactly twelve o'clock.

"We can't wait for her call," Vee told me. "Other lives may be at stake. I've done some telephoning, Dean, and received some astounding information. Mortimer Doran tells me that Frank Morris drew fifty thousand dollars from his bank yesterday morning. It was not found at his home or at his office. Nor was anything found among his papers that could be taken as a threat. Nothing but"—and

Vee rubbed his chin—"the newspaper clippings of the murders of the three men—Henderson, Warren and Drake. Very, very significant."

At the Travelers' and Home Trust Company, where George V. Rensiller kept his account, we listened patiently to a dignified president explain the ethics of banking and that it was "impossible—absolutely impossible to divulge the transactions of our clients."

Vee said: "I am simply asking you if Mr. Rensiller drew out a large sum. Come, come, sir, it is no time for such talk! Frank Morris drew fifty thousand dollars from his bank yesterday morning and last night was shot to death. It's a question of murder. In telling me you can save George V. Rensiller's life."

The president of the bank talked and walked, and explained over and over the rules of the bank. But he wound up with a long speech about putting human life ahead of money and banking rules, and finally we left with the information that George V. Rensiller had drawn fifty thousands dollars from the bank almost the very moment the windows opened.

Outside the bank, Vee spoke. "And that should make things easier in our talk with Rensiller. I was wrong, of course, about Frank Morris not paying. The trail grows clearer but has a few added twists in it. I think we should find Rensiller at his home, unless he has already gone to his death."

"What is it, Vee? Just what is it?" I asked as we took a taxi uptown to George V. Rensiller's house.

"Why guess?" Vee's shoulders moved. "I think we'll have the whole story from Rensiller—if we're in time."

And we were in time. George V. Rensiller was coming down his front steps, a bulging brief case in his left hand.

He didn't see us until we turned directly before him; his eyes were glued on his expensive car parked at the curb.

"The death car." Vee poked a finger in Rensiller's chest. "Back, inside—Mr. Rensiller." And glancing down at the well filled brief case, "The fifty thousand is in small bills, then."

"So"—Rensiller licked his lips twice before he spoke—"you've been looking into my affairs; getting information at my bank or having me watched. Well, Mr. Vee Brown, I'm not without influence and this afternoon I'll—"

"Hell!" said Vee, "forget your importance. By this afternoon you won't be able to talk; you'll be too dead."

The man jarred slightly, but he tried to push Vee aside.

"I don't know why I'm so interested in saving your life." Vee held his ground. "Listen a minute; then go on if you want to."

"Well?" Rensiller hugged the brief case close to him, as if his life depended upon it.

"Frank Morris drew fifty thousand dollars from the bank, too," Vee told him. "Took a trip with it, paid it over—and you saw his body across the street."

"He—took money!" And leaning heavily against the stone railing, "But the police! He went to them and they didn't protect him."

"He never went to the police." And stepping aside, "I've got no orders to make you talk to me. Go ahead, if you want to." And when Rensiller hesitated, then was about to pass, "The medical examiner took Frank Morris's head apart and found three bullets in his brain. They turned the body over to his relatives this afternoon."

GEORGE V. RENSILLER'S hands opened slowly, just his fingers loosening before the brief case fell to the steps and laid there. Vee Brown picked it up while I caught the man in my arms as he toppled forward. He didn't pass right out, but he couldn't talk and he couldn't walk. He made queer gurgling noises deep down in his throat as I rang the bell and half helped, half carried him into the house.

His manservant knew what to do. "It's his heart. The digitalis! He's often this bad." And he was gone, while I threw back Rensiller's coat and vest and loosened his collar.

As for Vee Brown! He had emptied the contents of the brief case out on the low couch, and pushing the money aside was going through an envelope of papers, letters, or notes of some kind. He never once looked over at Rensiller.

The servant returned; the medicine was given, with almost instant results. Not that Rensiller came fully around right away or that he talked. But certainly he was conscious of what was going on and wanted to talk, tried desperately to talk while he made ineffectual gestures toward Vee who was still going over his papers.

I guess it was a full five minutes after that before Rensiller came completely around. Then he started in to threaten, and finally to plead. But at Brown's warning glance he dismissed his servant and I closed and locked the door.

Vee Brown came to his feet, walked slowly across the room and stood looking down at Rensiller. "Your number is up, Rensiller. I can tell from those papers that if you live through the next twenty-four hours this Murder Syndicate will have to start their reign of terror all over again. The magic chain of death will be broken. God, man, can't you see that?"

"But if I paid—if I paid!" Rensiller came to the edge of his chair. "All those who didn't pay, died. It's true. It was all in the papers. Henderson; Drake; Warren, and last night Frank Morris. He—"

"He paid and died." Brown tapped the bunch of notes he held in his hand. "The whole thing is here, Mr. Rensiller, but I'd like to hear you tell it."

"I will. I will!" Although the room was quite cool, beads of perspiration stood out on his forehead. "The thing started a few months back. Just a letter through the mail. You have it there. It stated that I must pay fifty thousand dollars or be shot to death." He cleared his throat. "It sounded like a crank letter and I paid no attention to it."

"You didn't take it to the police?" I put in that one.

"No," Vee explained as he looked at Rensiller. "There was a hint in that first letter as to some irregularities in the mortgage-company accounts."

"That meant nothing." Rensiller seemed honestly indignant. "But it made me hesitate about going to the police. At this time, with so many investigations, even a hint of such a thing would be dangerous to the welfare of my company and its thousands of investors."

"Suppose," Brown said, "now that I have all the facts, anyway, you explain in detail the steps that led up to your parting with so much money on such a threat. Remember, Mr. Rensiller, that I am interested in running down the head of this Murder Syndicate, not in the way you conduct your business."

Rensiller nodded and talked. "As I said, I paid no attention to the first letter. There was another, telling me to put an ad in the public notices if I was ready to pay. When I still ignored that, a telephone call. After that, silence for two weeks; then a list of names. Warren; Drake; Henderson. You have the list there. Two days later the list came again. This time the name of Warren was crossed off at the top, and written beside it was 'He did not pay.' There was a newspaper clipping that told of his murder in Brooklyn. Later, the list again. This time Drake's name was crossed off, with the same notation that he didn't pay. There was a clipping of his murder, but I had already seen it in the paper. Later Henderson's death, and then a new list.

"Just two names on this new list. Frank Morris and my name. And last night the two names again. This time beside the words 'He did not pay,' was the sentence 'Morris went to the police.'"

"That," said Vee, "was to forestall any such action on your part; to show you how useless it was. But Morris didn't go to the police and he did pay. And this note came this morning." Vee handed the final note to me.

IT READ simply enough. There were instructions how to deliver the money. The time Rensiller was to leave the house; the course he was to take up to Van Courtland Park; and just how he was to keep driving the car along the road by the golf course until he was stopped. And there was the final demand that he must bring, with the money, every bit of correspondence he had received from "The Murder Syndicate," as it was signed.

"You, Mr. Rensiller"—Brown nodded and his eyes shone—"have the honor of being the man who finally breaks the endless chain. There are other lists going to other victims. Today your name has been scratched off those lists. Tomorrow those victims are to read of your death and be terrorized into paying. So you see, Mr. Rensiller, they get your money and they get your influence. Your death will influence others to pay."

Vee rubbed his hands when he turned to me. "Seemed complicated in the beginning; didn't it, Dean? But I felt that it would turn out quite simple. Why kidnap people and hold them for ransom, with all the danger of being found with the snatch? Here is just a threat of death. Warren and Drake and Henderson were picked as props, just to lend color to the whole scheme. Undoubtedly they were not even threatened. They had no money to pay; none of the three could do more than meet their monthly bills. They were just names, to impress the real money—like Morris and Rensiller here." And looking down at Rensiller, "And I think, Dean, they are threatening men who have reasons for not wishing to be brought before the public notice. Of course, it had to come out in time. For even if they made the victims return all correspondence, some day someone would go straight to the police."

"And then," I said, "the thing would blow up."

"Blow up!" Brown's eyes opened wide. "But, why? The thing could grow so big that they could send out hundreds of letters; hundreds of lists. And the beauty of it was—that they didn't need any big organization. No doubt, trusted men must do the collecting. But in these times you can get a man murdered for just a few dollars. It's so effective and so simple. You pay or you die!"

"You pay and die," I corrected him.

"That," said Vee, "I think was a mistake. Maybe not in the beginning, but as the syndicate increases its business I think the man who pays will live." He stroked his chin. "Of course, they've got to murder a man every now and then to properly induce other intended victims to part with their bank roll."

"We'll go to Van Courtland Park, drive along the golf course and—"

"No, no." Vee shook his head. "You see, the thing was planned for daylight. That prevents a police trap. Besides, we must give the brain behind this new racket credit for some intelligence. Rensiller would be watched closely today, every movement he made. We were seen coming into the house, of course. There can be no question about that."

Rensiller put his head in his hands; said: "What of me? What of me now that I talked?"

Vee turned to me as if Rensiller were some specimen to be studied. "That's what fear will do, Dean. The object of this Murder Syndicate is first to create fear, turn that into terror, and turn terror into cash. If you don't think it's reasonable, look at Rensiller." And to Rensiller, "Your life is in no danger now."

But Vee went to the phone, called police headquarters and arranged to have Rensiller guarded. I was amazed myself at the precautions he took. Six of the department's crack men were detailed to that job. I met them myself as they came in, one by one, from other duties. And Brown certainly was hardly reassuring as he instructed each one of those men.

THEN WE left the house I said to him: "You're a bit finicky yourself, Vee. It looks as if this syndicate is impressing you a bit, too. Or are you impressing Rensiller with the elaborate precautions you're taking to protect him?" And when he just looked at me, "You don't really think they'd come to his house for him!"

"I don't know." Vee was very serious. "If they marked him for death; notified other victims of their extortion of his death, and he lives—their reign of terror is considerably weakened. Suppose they had ten from whom they planned to collect fifty thousand dollars each and Rensiller's murder was the final touch that would make those men pay! There you have the answer. Dead, Rensiller might be worth half a million dollars; alive"—Brown's hands came far apart—"their carefully planned plot becomes simply a bluff. No, Dean. I don't know how far these men might go for half a million, but I do know that I will prevent them getting Rensiller."

"So much for preventing the murder of Rensiller. How about these others, whose names you don't know? How will you prevent murder in that direction? How will you break up this murder gang?"

"Clausen!" Vee Brown nodded. "Ida Trent will put the finger on him."

"You think Clausen is head of this Murder Syndicate?"

"No!" Vee Brown stroked his chin. "Physically, perhaps, Clausen is the most dangerous public enemy in the city. But I don't think he has the brains to locate the proper men; find out their secret weakness or lapses in business ethics. Actively, yes. I believe that Clausen is the active head, but a bigger brain plans the details and points out the victims."

When we reached home there was no word from Ida Trent. Brown stayed by the phone. As the afternoon wore on he grew impatient, hopped from the music room to the living room, picked at the keys on the piano. Once he broke into a lively tune, jumped from the piano and rushed into the living room.

"I've got it. The curtain for the first act of the review. It'll knock them dead, Dean. No one but Pal—the great la Palatin—could possibly—" He stopped dead; and suddenly, "She should have called up, too; should have been anxious to know how I came out last night. No word from Ida Trent, who needs both money and protection. No word from Pal, who—who—" He went to the phone and called her number.

Three minutes later he jammed the instrument back in its stand.

"She went out, Dean; went out in answer to a phone call; a woman's voice. The maid said she told her not to tell anyone but me that she went to meet Ida Trent. Funny, that!"

"Not so funny," I tried to ease his alarm. "Ida Trent said she would like Gertrude la Palatin as a friend, didn't she? Maybe she's still afraid of being locked up and hopes that Pal will influence you."

"Yes, yes." Vee nodded absently. "But I don't think so. I—"

And it was at that very moment that Wong brought the note in. It had been left downstairs by a uniformed messenger. Brown tore it open. I saw his lower lip slip under his upper teeth, heard his breath swish loudly as he sucked it back in his throat. His face was very white when he handed the note to me, but the hand with which he extended it did not tremble. I read the note.

Vee Brown—

Miss la Palatin has been good enough to pay us an extended visit. This letter is to request that you cease all activities against our organization, and particularly against one of its members whom we regard highly enough to consider a human life; even the life of a woman, of slight importance in comparison. This gentleman will be particularly interested in how Miss la Palatin dies. Remember—HOW SHE DIES.

You will receive instructions as to your actions by midnight tonight.

THE MURDER SYNDICATE.

"They've got her. They've got Pal." I blurted it out inanely.

"Just as I said. Just as I said, if we continued our friendship."

"But how—"

"Ida Trent, of course. She telephoned her."

"She wouldn't do that; wouldn't double-cross her and you—like that. She—"

"She didn't do it as a double-cross, Dean." Vee's lips were very tight, his eyes very narrow. "Somehow Sam Clausen found Ida and made her telephone Pal. There, don't ask me how again! Remember—I stood over the dead body of the Rierdon child and saw the useless, horrible torture she must have suffered! No, I can't condemn Ida. I can understand why she made the call. The man is a fiend." His fingers clenched, opened, and clenched again at his side. "God!" The word just burst from his lips. "I'm a fool. I should have shot him to death last night."

"That," I said, "would have been murder."

"Would it?" I didn't like his hollow laugh. "Perhaps it would. But you could never make me believe that the killing of Clausen would be murder. And even if it would, he'd be plenty dead by now."

Brown paced across the room after that. Several times he muttered to himself. I can't be sure, but I thought the words were: "I mustn't let this get me."

"Vee!" I cried out, suddenly. "Ida Trent—Clausen. You think he did it; is behind it; knows where she is!"

"Sure. Sure! I'd send word to headquarters to pick him up, but he'd have an alibi. No." He walked into the hall and was putting on his hat and topcoat. "I must find him myself. He knows where Pal is."

"And if he does—what?"

And again that laugh. "He'll tell me, Dean. He'll tell me or I'll give him a death that the Rierdon child would not have envied."

"Vee!" I grabbed his arm at the door. "I don't know how I forgot to tell you; I was excited maybe. But Ida Trent told me where Clausen will be tonight, at eleven o'clock. It's a garage in the Bronx. Clausen meets certain people there; telephones orders from there. He doesn't know Ida knows about it." And I gave Brown the address. "Pal might be there."

I'LL NEVER forget that wild dash to the Bronx. It wasn't more than eight o'clock. Our careful entrance into the small yard was entirely unnecessary. Empty oil tins, broken wheels, torn rubber that might have once adorned those wheels. Abandoned motors, parts of cars, and an old car or two made us pick our way to that garage.

There was just one thing incongruous with its whole dilapidated appearance. That was the lock on the doors in front. Although the doors were old, the wood was still heavy and strong; but the lock was new, and the iron rings the lock fitted through also was new.

Brown picked that lock with the ease of an expert. We carefully closed the door behind us; found another lock on the inside, which might be used when the garage was occupied, and began a systematic search.

Certainly the garage—at least, on the main floor—was devoid of human fife. Upstairs— But we kept that until the last, though we listened carefully enough at the bottom of those wooden steps for any sound from above.

Brown said: "Rather clever lay-out, Dean. If you noticed the windows on the outside you'd think it was the simplest matter in the world to gain entrance to the garage. Broken windows, with boards that could be taken off without a sound, from the outside. But look there!" He pointed to a window. "On the inside the boards are strong and tightly set with huge nails. It would require some effort and plenty of noise to gain an entrance if the door were locked on the inside. But let's go above."

There was a door at the top of the stairs. With our guns in our hands, Brown turned the knob. I could see his hand moving, but under those magic fingers there was no sound. A gentle push; a muffled curse from Vee, and I knew that the door was locked.

But we had no cause for alarm there. The lock was a simple one and Brown's single twist of his skeleton key did the trick. He didn't open the door carefully after that, but standing back on the narrow landing turned the knob and kicked that door open.

Darkness—not a light. Not even a glimmer from the window. Then Vee's flash was out. Almost at once I saw the window, or rather, what I guessed to be the window. Heavy boards covered it; black drapes hung from it, as if they were simply flung there by careless masculine hands.

THERE WERE a couple of chairs, a flat wooden table and a telephone. Nothing else but a narrow door that, from the presence of the window, could be nothing more than a closet; a very shallow and narrow closet.

"Well," Vee said, "someone certainly uses this room. The phone tells us that. No one is here now, unless—" He walked to the closet door, put his hand on the knob. "But a big man could no more than squeeze into that closet, let alone breathe in it. I guess we've drawn a blank."

Brown's flash and mine were directly on that closet door when he opened it. I think Brown jarred back against me.

I know I let out a gasp and dropped both my flash and my gun to my side, but that didn't hide the gruesome sight I saw. For if Brown jarred back or not, both his gun and his light remained steady—steady upon the body of the woman that hung in that closet; hung there by a thick piece of heavy wire tied to a large curved hook in the wall.

Her face was horrible; unrecognizable, but I thought I knew just the same. Brown had been afraid of just this; afraid of just what would happen to Gertrude la Palatin if she continued close to him. Now—now I tried to look at that hideous mask of a face, beaten to a— But I couldn't look any longer. Then the closet door closed and I was leaning against the table.

I don't know how long I stood there. I don't know how long Brown stood there, his hand on the knob of that closet door, quiet, very quiet. Then he spoke. "I've got to know, Dean. I've got to know."

"Know! Know?" I cried out. "How can you know? How can—"

And Brown's voice, seemingly far away. "I've got to look at her eyes; look at her eyes and see if—if they're green."

I turned toward the closet then. I couldn't help it. Fascinated? Perhaps, if you can be fascinated with horror. Frozen? Yes. My eyes, as if twin points, fastened in ice, stayed on that circle of light as Vee opened the door again.

Things broke. My head dropped, eyelids mercifully covering my vision.

After that the sound of the closet door closing; the uncertain tread of light feet; the soft thump of Vee's small body dropping onto a chair, and I was conscious of a splash of light upon the floor.

"Well?" I finally was able to get out the single word.

Brown said, in that same distant voice: "The eyes were—were not green. It was Ida Trent. Thank God for that."

And though it was perhaps a terrible thing to say; a terrible satisfaction to express in the presence of that mangled body of the woman who had died so horribly, I echoed his words.

"Thank God for that."

CHAPTER SEVEN
THE GLADSTONE BAG

IN A dazed way I remember leaving that garage; Brown carefully looking over the room above and the floor below, making sure that things were just as we found them. I remember, too, sitting on an old barrel, watching Vee carefully remove the nails from the heavy boards before a window in the back and farthest from the stairs. As he drew each nail from the wood he placed it in his pocket.

Through dulled eyes I saw Brown stuff each hole that had held a nail with dust, dirt and oil. I don't think I got the idea until he had finished and explained it to me.

"We must have an entrance, Dean, for if Clausen should be here later the doors will be padlocked on the inside. The boards on the outside of this window can be easily removed." He stood back and looked over his work. "Now, since I've taken out the nails, the wood on the inside can be just as easily removed, set gently on the floor and afford us a silent entrance. I don't think Clausen will notice that the heavy nails are gone; all but that single loose one that holds the boards in place. No, he wouldn't see it."

We left the garage, Vee snapping the lock on the doors, and we were down the street and in our car.

"It was horrible; terrible, Vee," I said at length. "I don't see how you can be so—so indifferent. It might easily have been—" I stopped.

He turned and looked at me. His face was white; then he held his hand before the dashlight. The fingers never wavered, yet my whole body was trembling.

"Indifferent!" he said. "That's not the word, Dean. Inside, I'm a seething volcano of hatred. I don't know as I've ever felt just like this before. Yes, I can say it." His voice cracked slightly. "It might have been Pal. They've called me Killer of Men, and tonight—" He stretched out a hand; felt my arm; ran fingers over my muscles. "You're big and strong. Pull yourself together, Dean. It may be necessary for you to prevent me killing Clausen tonight; at least, before he talks."

"You think she—she's still alive!"

"Yes. Yes. I can't—I won't think anything else. She must be. She must be the bait; the living bait that is to lead me to my death. She could serve no purpose dead—while I live."

"And—what will you do now?"

"First," he said, "I will go and see Irving Small. If Ida Trent spoke the truth, Clausen will be back at that garage tonight. He must come back. He wouldn't be such a fool as to leave the body there."

"So we wait until eleven, then?"

"No. We'll spend the hours between in combing the city for Clausen." He jerked the car from the curb and started downtown. "Not a chance of finding Clausen, of course; but inactivity now would— God! I couldn't stand it when I think of how that girl died and how Pal—"

Furiously we tore toward the heart of the city. The car jerked to a stop before Irving Small's. Brown waved me back into the car and hurried to the little side door of the pawn shop. A moment later the bent shoulders; the corrugated yellow face and the rubbing hands of Irving Small appeared. Then Brown disappeared inside.

Irving Small was probably the smartest fence, and certainly the best informed in the city. Brown paid him well for information; and besides, held over his head a long trip to the Big House. Irving Small, as many bigger men have done, made one mistake—and Brown knew that mistake.

It was ten minutes later when Vee returned to the car. Irving Small followed him and leaned through the window when Vee slipped behind the wheel.

"I tell you, Mr. Brown," Irving fairly rattled the words, "the thing is impossible. Scarcely two hours, and—"

Brown turned his head as the engine roared and the car ground into a badly manipulated gear.

"It must be done!" Vee said. "I've never put anything to you like this before. But tonight—I'll pay you what you ask, but have that suitcase here when I return. You can get it. You have to get it!"

IRVING SMALL jerked his turtle-like neck from that window just in time to save his head from being torn off as the car jumped from the curb.

"You'll see!" was the only answer Brown would give to my questions,

Clausen's trail, that seemed so hot in the first few places we visited, grew cold and discouraging as time passed. There was no chance of locating Sam Clausen.

I looked at Brown. He drove now from place to place slowly; almost doggedly, his eyes ever resting upon the dashboard and the hands of the clock that crept slowly toward eleven.

He didn't talk. He didn't need to. I watched his face. Sam Clausen was right to hide out that night. I knew the signs. Vivian—Master of Melody—was entirely erased from the picture. Beside me sat Vee Brown—Killer of Men. A little lump came up into my throat, held so a moment and jarred back into my stomach. Something terrible was to happen this night. I felt it—I knew it. Vee's face was very white; his lips a single straight line; his black eyes alive, brilliant— almost to the fever point. Yes, it was there in his eyes just as he had pointed it out to me in the eyes of—of others. The lust to kill! I knew it and it frightened me.

This time, when we reached Irving Small's, Vee took me inside with him. Irving Small, for the first time since I had known him, was visibly disturbed. His head turned, bird-like, toward Brown as he took us into the room behind the shop.

None of us spoke. Irving Small indicated a black leather Gladstone bag upon the table. Brown walked to it while I waited at the door. I saw him open the bag, look into it.

"Good!" He nodded at Irving Small as he closed the bag and carefully slipped the brass catch across the top. "Russian or Italian?"

Irving Small swallowed once.

"Neither." He grinned unpleasantly. "Cuban. I had a devil of a time getting it. But it can't be traced. Listen!"

Silence. Then the ticking of a clock. Plainly it came from within the bag.

"You see!" Irving Small's head bobbed up and down. "Terrifying in its contents, but the ticking gives it away. I never favored this particular bit of—"

"No matter." Brown's lips parted as he slipped a roll of bills into Small's eager fingers. "My friend is going to hear the ticking and— Come! Dean, take a look."

As I stepped forward Brown snapped the lock and threw open the suitcase again.

I saw the ticking alarm clock; the wires that led from it, over some lengths of pipe and back to two dry cells, beside which were four lengths of pipe standing on end, and to which other wires led.

Brown snapped the bag closed, accepted the coil of heavy rope Small gave him and turned to me.

"It's heavy, Dean. I'll need all my strength tonight. You carry it"

"It looked like a bomb; a bomb of some sort," I stammered.

"And that's just what we want it to look like. You'd think it was a real bomb, wouldn't you, Dean?"

"I don't know." I scratched my head. "It was so deadly looking. More like a stage bomb. Built more to be terrifying than for actual use."

"And that," Vee patted me on the back, "is just the way we want it to look." And the rest of that thought he finished in the car when I laid the suitcase carefully down between my legs beside the rope. "Suppose, Dean, you were roped in a chair and this contraption placed beside you with the alarm set for the pipes, supposedly containing dynamite, to explode at two o'clock—would you talk then?"

"I would!" I told Vee. "But then, Clausen may know bombs and know that it's not real."

"Maybe." Vee turned the corner and shot uptown for the Bronx. "But Pal's life, my life, perhaps your life depends upon Clausen believing it real."

And that was all the conversation we held until we parked a block and a half from the abandoned garage.

ALTHOUGH I knew the bomb was not real, I carried it gingerly across the stone- and refuse-strewn lots to the deserted building. Not a light shone there as I laid the suitcase down and crouched in the deeper shadows of the garage, close to the boarded window that Brown had prepared for an entrance a few short hours before.

"It doesn't look as if he came," I said, after we listened for some time and did not hear a sound.

But I was talking to myself. Vee had slipped away in the shadows, and I was alone—alone in the blackness, while above me in a closet hung the tortured dead body of the murdered Ida Trent.

Vee Brown came silently; his hand rested on my arm.

"He's there," Vee whispered. "At least someone is, for the front doors are bolted on the inside." His hand gripped my wrist. It was cold and wet, but steady. "This is the big moment, Dean. I want you to stand by the front doors while I enter that window. There must be no chance of his hearing me and escaping by the front. Just leave the suitcase here. And, Dean. If he makes a run for it, jump him; don't shoot him. I can't chance his death."

I guess I imagined all sorts of noises as I waited by those doors. Was Clausen there? Was he above? Had he discovered that the nails had been pulled from the boards before the window? Would he be crouching there, waiting—ready—waiting to shove a gun against Brown's head, and—

One of those double doors pushed back. I slid to one side; my body stiffened. Brown never could have entered that rear window and reached those doors so quickly! But he had, for his voice came soft and low.

"Easy does it, boy. There's a man up stairs and it's Clausen. I heard his voice. Quick! The door to the room above is partly open."

"His voice! Then there're others, who—" I started.

"Sh!" Brown warned me. "I think he's alone." Cold fingers sought my face, rested against my lips for a second, and Vee had me by the wrist, guiding me in the blackness. His unerring instinct led us along the side of a huge shadow that must have been a car, in and out and around barrels, to the foot of the wooden steps. A light there. Just a flicker that became brighter as I followed Vee up those stairs. Then I saw it. The door at the top was partly open. Perhaps our steps made some noise; perhaps they didn't. Maybe they were deadened by the pounding of my heart. But the man in that room wouldn't hear us. He was talking. Just a dull, inarticulate mumble that became understandable words as Vee and I stood on the landing, our heads close to the long slit of light from the partly open door.

It was Clausen all right. His head was sideways to us. He was alone and was talking into the phone. Some of his words perhaps did not make sense, but some did. God! they did. Vee grasped my arm. We bent closer, listening to what Clausen was saying.

"I was just talking to the boss. Vee Brown will get the office any minute now. He's stuck on that la Palatin dame and will fall like a thousand of brick." A moment's pause; and then, as Clausen raised his head and let his eyes rest on the closet, "No. I won't be at the garage at all; and I don't want anybody coming to the garage. That's orders. Orders!

do you hear? No one enters this garage tonight. It's dangerous. Don't kill Brown unless you have to, until I come. Hell!
no. I hate that dumb dick's guts. He's been trying ever since
the Rierdon snatch to put the finger on me. Yeah, I'll be
down." Again his eyes went toward the closet. "May be
pretty late. But I'd like Brown alive, to see me finish off that
dame." A laugh: and, "Sure. Sure! The boss has added Vee
Brown's and la Palatin's name to the list. It should make a
sensation and be worth a lot of jack if they die tough
enough. Yeah. You'll hear from me when you see me. And
lay off the garage. Everyone! Night!" The phone dropped
back in its cradle. Sam Clausen half swung toward the
door.

And it happened. The door flew open, Vee Brown shot
into that room. For the fraction of a second, perhaps, Sam
Clausen hesitated. His huge mouth hung open; his eyes
popped, then he jumped to his feet.

CHAPTER EIGHT
KILLER OF MEN

B ROWN STRUCK; once with his left hand, once
with his right. The barrels of two heavy-caliber
revolvers tearing down Sam Clausen's face.

Clausen staggered back, knocking over his chair. Vee's
wiry little form followed. Again those guns came up and
down. Blood showed on Clausen's face; there was a deep
rip over his eyes, his lower lip was torn open. He dropped
to one knee. His left hand went up, protecting his face; his
right shot for his left armpit.

For a moment a black gun showed in his right hand,
then crashed to the floor as white knuckles were torn a

vivid red. After that an exhibition of fury, hatred, and—yes, brutality that I didn't think Brown was capable of or strong enough for.

As for me! I stood there a silent witness to Vee's flashing arms and flaying guns. How long did I stand so? I don't know. A minute; two; three! Impossible to tell. But when I did finally spring forward and clasp my arms tightly around both of Vee's, Sam Clausen was beaten unconscious; half kneeling, half lying on the floor, his head down between his knees.

Vee fought like a wild cat to tear himself free. He cursed me, kicked at my shins and despite my iron muscle I had great difficulty in holding him. In the struggle we must have struck Clausen, for his body turned, wobbled a moment, then rolled over and he lay there on his side.

"He's dead!" I gasped. "He's dead, and—"

Brown ceased to struggle in my grasp; his arms fell to his sides. His little body shook; sobs wracked his frame and I guess he half collapsed into the chair to which I had dragged him.

"I killed him. I killed him. And now he' won't—can't talk," Vee said over and over. It was the first time I had ever seen him crack up. I had always thought that was impossible.

"He's not dead, Vee. Not dead!" I said. "I just wanted—God! man, you were out of your head."

"Yes—out of my head. Thanks a lot, Dean, for—let us hope, for saving Pal's life."

He walked to the door, picked up the coil of rope he had dropped on the landing. I helped him lift the unconscious Sam Clausen onto the straight-backed chair and held the man erect while Vee systematically bound him there.

"I'm afraid," Vee said, "I was thinking of the woman in the closet and the Rierdon child. You see, I stood over her body in the morgue and swore to kill Clausen some time. I remembered that and forgot Pal. I pride myself on never losing my head; being simply a crime machine employed by the State." His shoulders moved as he tightened a knot, then held Clausen's arms and hands so tightly to his sides that he could hardly have moved his fingers. "I guess after all, Dean, I'm no better than the rest when the blood lust gets me. Yes, blood lust. For I wanted terribly to kill Clausen then."

A minute later he stood back to survey his job.

"His face is not so pretty, Dean, but I think it may help him to talk when he comes around. Go below and get the suitcase." He leaned forward, pushing up first one and then the other of Clausen's eyelids, nodded his satisfaction. "Luck there," he said. "He'll be able to see the hands of the clock moving toward the hour. Well—get the suitcase." And when I still stood by the door, "Hell! man, I won't beat him to death in your absence. I'm not thinking of him now nor the Rierdon child—nor her," he jerked a thumb toward the closed closet door. "I'm thinking only of Gertrude la Palatin—of Pal."

I LOOKED at Vee, then hurried below. In two minutes I was back in the room with the suitcase. Brown's hands were steady. He was very particular in opening that suitcase and setting it on the table so that Sam, Clausen's eyes would rest on it.

But Sam Clausen's eyes remained closed.

"Hell!" Vee impatiently knocked the battered head from one side to the other. "He's worse than I thought, and— The water tap below, Dean. I saw it earlier in the evening."

And when I shook my head, that I had not seen it, "Well, do what you can with him. I'll get the water."

Vee went below. I studied Clausen and I studied the bomb. I shook my head. I had seen a number of bombs but none as elaborate as this. Where it looked like a good job; the neatly attached wires; the well packed and carefully spaced lead pipes; the nicely shining brass caps on the storage batteries, somehow I felt it wouldn't fool me. It was too good. That was what was the matter with it. And besides, Vee Brown, detective assigned to the district attorney's office! Why, even a pickpocket would know he wouldn't use a real one. It was simply Vee's over confidence in himself; his belief that he had inspired such fear and terror in the underworld that—

I thought I heard his footsteps on the stairs.

"Vee," I said, "suppose Clausen guesses that the bomb's a fake, and—"

I stopped, turned quickly. Had I heard Clausen move in his chair? Silly, that. He couldn't move, of course. But his head might have bobbed on his chest. I looked at him. Not a movement, unless his eyelashes flickered. Well, maybe he was beginning to come around.

I had been wrong about Brown being on the stairs. I had been talking to myself, for now I heard his feet cross the cement floor below, then pound up the wood of the steps.

The second splash of water in his face brought Clausen around, then he dropped off again.

"Come on! Clausen." Brown gave him a third dose. "You're just stalling now. Where's Gertrude la Palatin?"

Clausen's head bobbed up and he looked straight at the clock; the ticking clock; which marked the time as eleven forty. He didn't seem as stunned as he might have been; but then, he was still dazed. His face was a mess.

More water! A clearer light in Clausen's eyes, and Vee sat on the edge of the table and talked to him.

"Clausen," he said, "I'm not sorry for the beating I gave you. If it wasn't for. Dean, here, I would have killed you. I will yet unless you talk. I want to know where Gertrude la Palatin is."

Clausen's tongue came out and licked at his lips. For a few seconds he looked at the open suitcase, the clock, the ominous attachments.

"What's that for?" he asked through thick swollen lips.

"That," said Vee very slowly, "is a bomb, and an extremely powerful one. The alarm on it is set for two o'clock. That should give me plenty of time to reach Gertrude la Palatin, set her free and return to save your life. You see, if you lie to me; send me into a trap, I won't be able to return by two and you'll be blown to hell. I heard you on the telephone and I know that no one will come and set you free; at least, before two. Those were your orders."

Clausen seemed to think a minute.

"You've looked in the closet?"

"Yes," said Brown, "I've looked in the closet."

"Humph!" Clausen seemed very self-possessed despite his battered condition. "You rescue this la Palatin, come back here, cut me loose and the State burns me. That's it, isn't it?"

"That," said Vee, "is it."

"Then I'll take the bomb. I can't see any advantage in roasting over blasting."

"If you don't talk," said Vee very slowly, "there will be no bomb. I'll treat you as you treated that woman in the closet, the Rierdon child; as you intend to treat Gertrude la Palatin, until you do talk."

"And if I don't talk?"

"You'll die finally, I suppose." Vee shrugged his shoulders, "But there's too much yellow inside of you. You'll talk."

"You, a copper! You wouldn't do that."

Vee's hand moved quickly; this time he reversed his gun. The sight cut deeply into that already beaten face. Blood poured into Clausen's eyes, trickled down over his swollen mouth. He cried out. So did I. It—was rather horrible. I had Vee by the arm.

"You can't, Vee. You—"

VEE WAS on his feet; his gun thrust against my chest—boring deep into it. "You never knew me to break my word, Dean. Now—" as my hand half reached for his gun. "By God! Dean, you're a powerful man. Don't you see; don't you understand? I'd have to shoot you. We can't be human tonight. We're not dealing with anything human."

I dropped back a pace, flat against the wall. I looked at Vee. No, he was not human tonight; not at that moment. Clausen broke the tension. He cried out.

"Listen, Brown. I'll make a deal with you. I'll talk. I'll tell you where the dame is; how to get her; save her. You couldn't do it without me. They'll kill her by three if I don't come. They— I don't care what happens to the others—just me. Give me a twenty-four hour start and I'll talk—talk now."

Brown hesitated. Looked at me.

"He'd talk. He'd talk in time." He half turned to Clausen, raised his hand and the gun; looked back at me. "No, I'm as weak as a woman tonight. I'd kill him. I'd kill him. I'd-" And suddenly to Clausen, "Very well—tell me. I'll save the girl, come back and cut you loose, and give you twenty-four hours start."

Clausen's dull eyes brightened.

"Your word? You've never broken that."

"My word, yes. I've never broken that."

"Good!" Clausen wet his lips, spoke rapidly. He named a street well back in town; a number of a house. "She's there, but the house is well guarded." And getting Brown to swear again to free him and give him twenty-four hours start, "There's a cellar window in the unoccupied house next door—Number 34. Enter that window; go to the coal bin. There's a door in the back of it, behind a packing case. It's a passage to the next house. That's the only way you can get in."

"The doors are locked?"

"Yes. The keys are in my vest pocket. You should be able to handle things from then on. There are only two men in that house now. The girl's in the room directly at the end of that passage, so if things go wrong a quick shift can be made from one house to the other. The door to that room has a tiny peep-hole. It's hard to find if you don't know it." And Clausen explained exactly how to locate it. "You can look into the room and see if the girl's alone there before you use the key and go in." And perhaps in fear, "Cripes! be careful."

"Fine!" Vee took the keys from Clausen's vest pocket. "I have never broken my word, Clausen. If I save the girl, and I see no reason why I shouldn't after what you've told me, two hours should be plenty of time; much more than plenty of time to set you free. I'll keep my word and do it." Vee looked at the bomb. "You should know bombs, Clausen. This one is most carefully made. At two o'clock the alarm will ring. After that, no more Sam Clausen. You'd be a fool to lie and die because of the others."

"To hell with the others!" Clausen cursed, looked at the clock. "I'm just thinking of myself. Your word, Brown?"

"My word!" said Vee. Then, "We won't waste time. Oh! Clausen, I don't imagine you think I'm bluffing about that bomb. Since I gave you my word that I'll return and set you free, I'll give you my word also that the bomb will explode at two o'clock exactly, if you've lied. Anything to add to your story? Remember—I'm pretty fond of Gertrude la Palatin. If I die; if she dies, you must of necessity die too."

CLAUSEN LOOKED at Vee, looked at the bomb, looked at me. "If you're half the man they claim you are and if your word is good, you'll come back and release me."

"O.K.!" Brown leaned forward and tied a handkerchief over Clausen's mouth. "There's a possibility someone might hear him cry out, Dean. We can't chance it."

"You'll let him go free then, even with the Rierdon child and the—the girl in the closet?"

"God!" Vee swung on me viciously. "A moment ago you were threatening me for abusing him. Now you criticize and reproach me because I let a criminal go. You say it's wrong, eh? Well, it is wrong. It's breaking faith with the department; with the people; with myself. But, Pal! God! Dean, yes—I'll let him go free. I never break my word." And stopping as we reached the head of the stairs, he returned and flung open the closet door. Just one glance at the hideous mask that had been a woman's face and Vee joined me on the stairs again.

"We'll give him a couple of hours to look at the woman he murdered anyway." This as we reached the front doors and crossed the lots to our car.

"It'll drive him mad."

"You think so?" Vee climbed in behind the wheel. "I doubt it, Dean. Still, as he watches her and the ticking clock and wonders if I'll make it or if hell blast his way suddenly into hell, it won't give him any too pleasant thoughts."

"You think he believed the bomb was real?"

Vee looked at me.

"Why not? I gave him my word on that. He'd have no reason to doubt it. I never broke my word."

"No, you never have." And when Vee just looked at me, "Why did you give him your word that the bomb is real?"

"Because I wanted to be sure he didn't lie to me. He agreed to talk very quickly." Vee shook his head. "But he'd think of himself first, and only of himself. Maybe I gave him my word because—well, because just at this moment Pal seems very close to me."

For several minutes Vee held my arm when we stood close to the wooden fence beyond which was the cellar window we were to enter. He was thinking, of course. Finally he whispered, half to me and half to himself, I thought.

"Imagine it! On the phone Clausen said the boss planned to add Gertrude la Palatin and my name to the list. Certainly it would have made a sensation; certainly; it would have been worth, maybe, millions to them. But what a nerve! What conceit! What—"

"Hadn't we better get going? We're to be back in the Bronx by two, Vee. You wouldn't want Clausen to know that you broke your word about the bomb. You don't want him to find out that it isn't real."

"No, no." I doubt that Vee heard me. "It couldn't be a trap, Dean. He couldn't have planned it in the few minutes he talked to me there. He couldn't prepare the others for our entrance, and certainly it would be without point sending us on a wild-goose chase. Hell! come on. Clausen feared death in a horrible manner, and told me the truth! Come on!"

WE CLIMBED the fence and dropped easily to the other side. It was simple to find the window Clausen had described and as simple to open it and drop to the cement floor inside. Vee was careful enough. He insisted on going first, and I stood by the window, gun in my hand; every sense alert. Nothing happened, and thirty seconds later we crossed to the coal bin, found the packing case, swung it easily aside and located the heavy door.

"So far everything is on the up and up," I told Vee.

"Sure! Why not?" Brown was eager now. "All murderers are yellow inside. What does Clausen care about the others now? He knows they won't dive into hell and put the pieces of him together again. Come on! Dean. We waste time, and Pal must be dragged out of this place."

The key in the lock; a single twist; the dull click, and the door swung noiselessly back on well oiled hinges. A pencil of light from Vee's flash; a narrow passage with cement walls damp and musty, and another door at the end of it.

Only a minute, perhaps less, and Vee was at that door, running his fingers along the heavy wood. I heard his breath draw in quickly, and I too bent and looked through the tiny hole as he raised his head. She was there, bound in a chair, per hands behind her back. The ropes were around her body but her legs were free. Nervously she was drumming them against the rungs of the chair. She was looking straight at the door, eyes wide with fear—terror.

Certainly she seemed alone in that room. No sound but the drumming of her feet upon the legs of that chair. There was a gash on her head and dried blood upon her forehead.

"The dirty rats!" Vee breathed, turned the key in the lock, and just as silently he was pushing open that door.

We entered the room together. Vee, quick; eager, for now he could see plainly the whole room; both sides, close to the door, as it was pushed back.

"Pal!" Vee said.

"Vee. God! Look!" Her words were a cry of fear deep down in her throat and her eyes raised in panic, just above our heads.

That was all of that. It came from above. Wavering shadows; falling arms; a deadening nauseating pain in my head. In a dazed way I saw the light figure of Brown crash to the floor, half his body on the cement, half on the thickness of a rug.

As for me! I staggered. My gun fell from my hand, my knees gave, and I was struggling wildly with men. Two men—three—perhaps four. I didn't know. It just seemed—many men.

I'm strong, and I guess I was giving a fairly good account of myself.

Someone shouted:

"Give him the lead!"

Then my staggering feet hit the silent form of Vee. I stumbled forward. An arm went up, and down. I sank to my knees, tried to get to my feet again. A single dull thud, followed by blackness; a deep penetrating blackness.

Sam Clausen had trapped us to our death. But how? HOW?

CHAPTER NINE
MAKE YOUR OWN CORPSE

THE CLOCK ticked on. Plainly I heard it knocking off the seconds. I opened my eyes and saw it—and the bomb. There it was in front of me, and the hand of the clock moving slowly past the half hour after one; creeping up the face toward two o'clock. Two o'clock! The zero hour when the bomb was to go off and—and—

I shook my head. No, it was not I who was watching the clock and the bomb. It was Clausen. Funny, that. I tried to clear my head; tried to think what had happened; tried— But there was no bomb for me; no clock for me. I opened my eyes wide, became fully conscious, with a clear; too clear a recollection of what had happened. There was a clock. It was on the wall directly opposite me and directly above the head of Gertrude la Palatin, still tied there in the chair. And the hour hand was creeping toward two o'clock.

I had been unconscious then for over an hour; at least, half unconscious. And Vee Brown! Where was Vee Brown? And I saw him. He was lying there on the floor, his left hand folded beneath his body, his right stretched out before him as if it gripped for something when he fell. Was he dead? Was he unconscious all this time? Was— And I saw the man who sat in the chair close to Vee's body. He was twirling a black-jack in his right hand.

As I watched him Vee moved; his head turned and misty eyes settled on me. But I don't think they saw me. Then his left hand, under him, bent; his right braced upon the floor; and slowly, painfully he raised his slim body. He tried to talk; bubbles of saliva formed on his lips.

"Boys," he whispered hoarsely. "I'll make a deal with you for Clausen's life if—"

The man in the chair swung his arm up and down. Plainly I heard the crack as the leather-covered black-jack struck Brown's head. I closed my eyes. A dull thump! I opened my eyes again. Vee planted a stool-pigeon on him; a stool-hand was again under him, his right reaching far out.

A man laughed. I turned my head. A thick-set, evil-faced man leaned against the door we had entered. A cigarette hung from his mouth. But I wasn't looking at him; I was looking above his head. Set far back into the wall was a deep alcove; a wooden platform. I knew then. It was from above; from that hidden platform—at least, hidden from us, that the attack had come. I gulped. A planned attack!

"Brown's a glutton for punishment, Smitty," the man by the door said. "That's the fourth smack since he was first flattened. I didn't know he had such a thick skull."

"Hell!" said the man with the blackjack, "it ain't that. I've only been giving him love taps. I don't want him out cold, like the big bozo was for the past hour."

Smitty nodded his head at me.

"Condon, awake—eh?" And his eyes followed mine to the platform above. "So that surprises you! You came a little early, but we were expecting you and were ready."

"You expected us?" I didn't understand; or rather, I understood one thing too clearly. Clausen had trapped us.

"Well, not both of you, maybe," Smitty said. "The instructions were that Vee Brown would come alone. What did he pay the stool-pigeon to lead him to his death?"

"I don't understand."

"Hell! You mean to say that Vee Brown brought you here without telling you how he knew the girl was here. Hear that, Lefty." He spoke to the man who sat above Vee. "Brown let Condon think he figured it out like a regular detective. Well—he didn't, Condon. The boss pigeon that Brown always trusted. Yep, was stretched upon the floor. His left and Brown never suspected a trap, listened to the stoolie, paid him—I guess, and trotted right along."

"And brought you—which we didn't expect." Lefty glared at me. "That's why there's no rope to tie him—"

BUT I wasn't listening now. I was figuring things out. Not clear at first, then too clear. Clausen had known, of course; perhaps planned sending the stool-pigeon to Brown in the hope that he would be trapped just as he was trapped. That the stool-pigeon never came to Vee didn't make any difference. These men waiting here thought that he had; were waiting for Vee's entrance. And Clausen! Why, he just gave Vee the same message; the same instructions the stoolie would have given him.

But the bomb! Clausen guessed the bomb wasn't real. But how could he be sure it wasn't? Vee did strange things, and— I gulped. I remembered suddenly my calling to Brown—yes, saying that the bomb was a fake!

I looked at the clock again, purposely avoiding Gertrude la Palatin's eyes. Five minutes of two! Five minutes more and Clausen would be certain that—

I jarred erect. A bell rang. I thought at first it was an alarm clock. Then I turned my head and saw the phone in the corner. The man who sat above Brown spoke.

"Take the call, Smitty. This Brown isn't dangerous once you've taken his hardware, but I'd better sit over him anyway." And with a grin and brutal kick at Vee, "He might creep up and bite me on the leg."

Smitty took the phone. His conversation wasn't hard to follow.

"Yeah. Hell! Boss, they're all here. Sure! The big guy too. Clausen said he'd be late. I don't know. Maybe the stoolie got to Brown ahead of time. They came just as Clausen planned it." A moment's pause as Smitty turned from the phone and put his lifeless eyes on each one of us in turn, then his lips smacked. "You couldn't make it an extra grand apiece? You will! O.K., boss. They get the works right away."

Smitty hung up the receiver. He was rubbing his hands as he nodded at his friend.

"Lucky the other two lads have gone, Lefty. There's an extra grand apiece in it for you and me for wiping them out." He jerked a gun into his hand, looked at me—at the girl. "In a way, you people are getting a break. Clausen kills mean. Give it to Brown, Lefty. I'll take the girl first."

God! The thing was impossible! There was no excitement; no struggle to live. These men were going to shoot the three of us just as you might wipe out some insects. It didn't seem real—just a dream. Not even a nightmare of horror. Maybe I was stunned; stupefied, but it was as if I were watching a play; as if I were not in the picture. And Vee Brown lay silently, perhaps mercifully unconscious on the floor, his left hand still beneath his small body, his right still stretched out before him.

Lefty came to his feet; the blackjack went to his pocket. Fascinated, my head turned and I watched Smitty; watched Gertrude la Palatin. No wasted time now. It was simply going to be seconds.

Smitty didn't hesitate. He held his gun close to his body, gripped it tightly in his right hand as he walked straight to the girl. Just a step or two from her body and his gun shot up.

I DIDN'T turn my head then. I couldn't. A second now; a split second. Gertrude la Palatin suddenly kicked up with both her feet. I saw the whiteness of Smitty's hand as it jumped into the air, heard the roar of the gun and saw the plaster just above the girl's head fall to the floor. Then I saw the black object—Smitty's gun, in the air. It was curving back over his shoulder; turning easily in the air, toward Lefty.

A moment's respite; nothing more. Just the natural, perhaps involuntary actions of a woman who saw death and did everything to delay it. I looked at Lefty. He was standing there with a gun in his hand, looking down at Vee. He hadn't seen the kicking feet, the flying gun; the gun that was coming toward him.

Smitty cursed and Lefty looked up. He jarred erect, jerked his gun from covering Vee so that it wavered between me and the girl. There was doubt in his eyes; uncertainty of just what had happened.

And Smitty's gun struck the floor with a dull thud, almost at Lefty's feet, not over a foot from that outstretched hand of the unconscious Brown. My mouth hung open. I gasped, threw myself forward in the chair, to attract Lefty's attention. For Vee was no longer unconscious. His right hand had moved with lightning-like speed. Just the single lurch of his body, and he had that gun.

Smitty cried out a warning as Vee swung suddenly on his back. I think they fired together; at least, I saw the two spurts of orange flame, as Lefty's body bent directly over Brown.

Lefty's head went up and back as if a heavy-weight champion had punched him straight on the chin. I saw the torn hole in his face just before his body followed that head. Lefty, blasted clean off his feet by the flying lead, crashed to the floor.

I looked at Vee. He was turning over on his side; actually turning to face the stunned Smitty—yes, turning after being drilled straight through the forehead. But, no; he couldn't have been. Yet, across the top of his head was the crease of a bullet.

"Good work, Vee!" I cried out. There was elation in my voice. There was— My God! there was blood in Vee's eyes, running down from his forehead. I saw him rise to his elbow; try to brush the blood away. Then I saw the gun waver in his hand, saw it search sort of blindly about the room and finally rest on an empty chair in a far corner.

"Don't move!" Vee Brown spoke to the blank wall, "or I'll plug you."

Smitty turned his head and looked in the direction Brown's gun was pointing. Surprise was written quite plainly on his face, but he didn't realize—at least, as soon as I did, that Vee couldn't see him.

Then Smitty knew. It showed in his face. He moved cautiously, carefully a few inches to one side. Then his hand crept under his coat. Nervous fingers were searching for another gun.

Yes—nervous fingers. For his whole arm trembled. His face was very white. I didn't blame him for that. For now Vee was braced on both elbows; his left hand was close to his left eye. The fingers were pushing at the eyelids, holding them apart. His right hand held the gun, and that right hand was very steady though the gun was not pointed at Smitty.

Then the gun was. It swung suddenly, pointing to the left of Smitty, then directly at him, and finally to the right.

"I see three of you, Smitty—three of you." Vee's voice was hardly more than a whisper. "Three of you, and three right hands reaching for—getting—getting— Drop that gun, Smitty!"

And Smitty's hand came out; his gun flashed up, and Vee fired.

Smitty clicked his heels together like a drill sergeant, stood perfectly straight as he spun around. Then he fell forward on his face. Vee Brown laughed.

"Not bad, Dean," he said. "Not bad at all. One bullet, and three Smitty's fall." And more seriously, "Thank God I had sense enough to fire at the middle Smitty. Yes, that's real business. The elimination of the middle-man."

And the clock on the wall struck. Once—twice. Two o'clock!

"Clausen will know you broke your word now," I said. "He'll know you didn't return to him."

"Yes." Vee was trying to drag himself to his feet. "Clausen will know."

After we had seen—or rather, I had seen—Gertrude la Palatin home, for Vee waited in the car, we visited Vee's doctor.

"Vee," I said, after he had telephoned headquarters to pick up the dead men in that house and never mentioned Clausen in the Bronx garage, "I know you're all in, though the doctor says a day or two will fix you up. Suppose I go up to the Bronx with a couple of cops—"

"No, no. We both go home to bed."

"But," I insisted, thinking of the raps on his head, "we've got Clausen for the murder of Ida Trent anyway. He lied to you. You don't have to keep your word to him now, and—"

"Dean," Vee looked at me as the car drew up before our apartment house, "Clausen is not the real leader of this Murder Syndicate. If I had not listened to you tonight I'd have gotten more information from Clausen. But you were right. I'd have killed him. Our trouble with the Murder Syndicate is probably just beginning; our trouble with Sam Clausen is over."

"You're going to let him get clean away; let someone come and free him—"

"Don't tell me how to run my business. God in Heaven!" He stopped. Then, as we entered our apartment, "Some things bother a man, Dean." And in a low voice as he laid a hand upon my arm, "There's a good fellow. Don't mention Clausen's name to me again." He snapped his fingers. "I've got a swell entrance for la Palatin in that Review. It goes—"

He started to hum, stopped, lighted a cigarette, went into the music room.

FOR TWENTY minutes, perhaps, notes strummed out upon the piano. Then he came from the room. His face was very white; drained clean of blood. I didn't help him; I didn't even question him further, but I did follow him as he swayed to his bedroom and I did wake Wong to help him undress.

As for me! I paced that large living room. Clausen, the foulest murderer in the city today! What strange complex had hit Brown that he let him live? Brown, who had sworn to get Clausen; even to kill Clausen! Now he went to bed, when he had only to lift the phone, to send Clausen to the electric chair.

The thing was still on my mind when I went to bed. The Rierdon child brutally tortured to death! Ida Trent, her poor mangled body with her face torn beyond recognition! And Gertrude la Palatin; Vee, myself! The thing was beyond understanding.

Vee Brown was still sleeping when Wong served me breakfast. I lifted my coffee, opened the late edition of the morning paper—and the steaming coffee slopped over the cup upon my hand. But I did not feel it; my eyes were bulging.

It was there all right. I read it again.

BOMB IN BRONX GARAGE.
RACKETEER IDENTIFIED BY—

Paper in hand, I rushed from the room, flung open Vee's bedroom door.

"Vee. Vee!" I cried as I shook him. "Clausen is dead. The bomb was real."

Vee Brown sat up, rubbed his eyes, grinned crookedly and said: "You're telling me!"